Nick Lake lives near Oxford with  in
…ing by day and writes boo   n
His powerful and moving   …e
…n earthquake, won the 20   …d
…shortlisted for the Carnegie Medal. *Hostage Three* has also
received huge acclaim. *There Will Be Lies* is Nick's third book
…loomsbury.

@nicholaslake

PRAISE FOR *THERE WILL BE LIES* BY NICK LAKE

'This novel is such a series of revelations that it would
spoil it to talk about the plot. Lake's writing is clear and
skilful: he creates Shelby's down-to-earth voice with
humour and credibility, brings home to us the value of all
our senses, juggles shifting notions of reality, describes
…aces and emotions vividly and resonantly, and keeps us
curious throughout this gripping novel'
Nicolette Jones, The Sunday Times

'This ambitious and sharply written story explores the
…mplex emotional area of family and identity with
originality and warmth'
Sally Morris, Daily Mail

'Experience the rollercoaster of plot twists and turns'
Mary Arrigan, Irish Examiner

PRAISE FOR *HOSTAGE THREE* BY NICK LAKE

'Well researched and nuanced, *Hostage Three* goes beyond the tropes of genre fiction, and does something rather more humane and interesting'
Guardian

'Lake handles these difficult themes with great skill, making political points while never losing the balance between emotion and action. He captures Amy's sense of abandonment with moving sensitivity and maintains the plot tension throughout'
Daily Mail

'Nick Lake's portrait of *Hostage Three* is so skilfully rendered'
Telegraph

'An achievement to admire'
Five star review, Books For Keeps

'Lake is adept at unusual tales inspired by real events'
The Times

'This is a complex and thought-provoking thriller'
Marilyn Brocklehurst, The Bookseller

THERE WILL BE LIES

NICK LAKE

BLOOMSBURY

LONDON NEW DELHI NEW YORK SYDNEY

Bloomsbury Publishing, London, New Delhi, New York and Sydney

First published in Great Britain in January 2015 by Bloomsbury Publishing Plc
50 Bedford Square, London WC1B 3DP

This paperback edition published in June 2015

www.bloomsbury.com

Bloomsbury is a registered trademark of Bloomsbury Publishing Plc

A CIP catalogue record for this book is available from the British Library

ISBN 978 1 4088 5383 2

Typeset by Hewer Text UK Ltd, Edinburgh
Printed and bound in Great Britain by CPI Group (UK) Ltd, Croydon CR0 4YY

1 3 5 7 9 10 8 6 4 2

To Hannah, for always.
To Brooms, for now.

My left hand will live longer than my right. The rivers
of my palms tell me so.
Never argue with rivers. Never expect your lives to finish
at the same time.

– BOB HICOK, from
Other Lives and Dimensions and Finally a Love Poem

I'M GOING TO BE hit by a car in about four hours, but I don't know that yet.

The weird thing is, it's not the car that's going to kill me, that's going to erase me from the world.

It's something totally different. Something that happens eight days from now and threatens to end everything.

My name is Shelby Jane Cooper – is, was, whatever.

I'm seventeen years old when the car crash happens.

This is my story.

8 . . .

CHAPTER
1

WHEN I COME INTO the living room, Mom is not even slightly ready, which doesn't surprise me. She's got the TV on full blast; it's so loud, the ground is vibrating. At the same time she's got the closed captions on: Mom is a believer in total communication. She's on the couch, in her pyjama jeans, working on one of her cross-stitches. On the screen, it's news: something about a plane crashing somewhere cold looking; torn metal gleaming in snow. I glance at the closed captions.

> *... with all 336 passengers lost, the black rocks – black box is yet to be discovered ...*

This is how they do it, see: there's an actual person typing this stuff, and when they make a mistake, like saying black rocks instead of black box, they do that line, I don't know what it's called, like a long hyphen, and then they correct it.

It's actually kind of hypnotic, because you start to picture this person, this totally ordinary person, not a presenter or anything, just sitting there and trying to write down what the anchor is saying and sometimes screwing up. It makes the TV feel human, I guess: I can see why Mom likes it.

Black rocks? says Mom, and I didn't even realise she was watching. *I mean, the context alone.*

Oh yeah: this is the other reason she keeps the closed captions on. She loves to see how other people do it. Mom's a stenographer at the courthouse. She spends her whole working life transcribing the words of lawyers and witnesses, so for her, the people who do it on the TV are like unseen competitors.

You coming? I ask.

Where?

I mime the swing, the slight pause when the bat strikes the ball, then the follow-through.

Mom checks her watch, ties off her thread, and wipes her hands on her pyjama jeans. *Sorry*, she says. *Got caught up. You finish your essay?*

Yes, I say. I have just been typing a three-thousand-word essay on decolonisation for her, with a special emphasis on French Indochina. That's when I haven't been talking to my online friends on the forums, anyway. I love it: I love how I can talk so quickly, I mean, I can talk at the speed I type, which is super fast. Mom doesn't know I even HAVE online friends, she wouldn't let me have Facebook, that's for sure, but she doesn't know that you can open a private browser window either, and then no one can see your history.

OK, clarification: friends might be a stretch. But, you know, I have people I can talk to about TV shows and books that I love. And they know who I am, they welcome me when I log on. I know they could be anyone, they could be fifty-year-old creeps in their underpants, but I like talking to them. So sue me.

And anyway, it's good for my typing skills, which helps when it comes to the tasks Mom sets me.

Mom is big on homework but she's also big on typing and writing in general – it's that total communication thing again, plus I guess she is a stenographer so it's 110 per cent obvious why typing would be important to her. So I don't just have to do the essays, I have to do them in a set time. This decolonisation essay she assigned me yesterday.

Good, she says, about the homework. *I'll read it tomorrow.*

She puts aside the picture she's been stitching. It's the same as all the others – a Scottish Highlands scene, purple mountains in the distance, a loch in the foreground. This time, a thistle growing up in the very front, just so you really know it's Scotland. Not that I believe Scotland really looks like that – I mean, there's no way any real place has colours like that.

Don't ask me why Scotland, either. It's just what she does. Always landscape, never with a person in the frame. She covers the walls, and then when she runs out of space, she starts to throw them out and begins all over again. She orders the patterns from the internet – for some reason, Scottish landscapes are popular enough that she pretty much never repeats herself.

One day, she often says, *we'll go there. See the mountains for ourselves. The stags.*

No we won't, I always think. We might see mountains, but not these ones. Not these crazy fairy-tale peaks with their bright cotton colours. Still, I would like to go. I'd like to get out of this city in the desert, which is the only place I've ever known. To stand in the mountains, smelling the heather and the gorse. Seeing the mist rise off the ground, wreathing the horns of a stag. Hell, seeing mist. The closest we get is that heat shimmer off the roads; off the sand of the desert.

But of course we'll never go. We'll never leave the Phoenix area. I have asked a thousand times for a vacation; to go to some other place. Mom always says no when it comes right down to it. We've never even been to the Grand Canyon, and you can fly there in like an hour. There's a little air strip in Scottsdale – it costs a thousand dollars per person, they fly you up there and all around the canyon, looking at it from above. A day trip. There was a time, when I was younger and brattier, I used to talk about it all the time, ask to go, mention it when my birthday was coming up. Now I know better. Now I know we can't afford it – and even if we could, the scared look my mom gets on her face when it comes up, I think she's scared of the plane.

So, SCOTLAND? Scotland is just a silly dream – hers more than mine, but mine too, I have to admit. If only to see what it really looks like.

Mom hauls her ass out of the easy chair, goes to the hall and pulls on a light jacket over her T-shirt and PYJAMA JEANS, and I'm putting that in all caps now in case you didn't pick up on my subliminal referencing of her disgusting PYJAMA JEANS earlier. Also, in case it wasn't obvious when I talked about her hauling her ass, she is not the slimmest, whereas I am naturally athletic, and this makes the pyjama jeans look even worse. I mean, I love her anyway, she's got meat on her bones, whatever, but she doesn't have to wear that ridiculous garment.

Do you have to wear those? I say.

Yes, says Mom.

It's two in the afternoon, I say. *You can't go out in pyjamas.*

That's why they're made to look like jeans.

They do not look like –

8

But she's turned around, so she doesn't catch that. She just grabs her bag and motions for me to follow. I sigh and shake my head, giving up. I have told her about those horrible pants so many times now, and she just doesn't listen. It's almost like she WANTS to look like a loser, so you know, shrug.

No, I take back the shrug. It does bother me.

Because it's just . . . it's just, she looks like a loser RIGHT NEXT TO ME.

So anyway, I pick up my own bag and go out with her on to the warm street.

Keep up, says Mom. *And stay close. Sometimes cars come up on the kerb and hit people.*

I know, I say. *I know.*

I don't know – not then, not for sure; I just believe her, like I believe her on everything.

Later, though, I do know for real.

9

CHAPTER
2

WE LIVE IN A three-storey apartment building in Scottsdale, Arizona, which is about as high as Scottsdale gets. We're on Via Linda. That means 'pretty road' in Spanish, inaccurately. On the plus side we have a shared pool, which gets cleaned, oh, ABOUT EVERY THREE YEARS, and if you continue walking on Via Linda you get to the desert in about a half-hour, which is awesome.

That last bit isn't meant to be sarcastic, by the way: I love the desert. Whenever I can, I go out there and just climb a hill or something. When I say 'when I can' what I mean is, when I can persuade Mom to come with me. From my description of her ass in the pyjama jeans you can guess that this is not a frequent occurrence. But sometimes, once every couple of months maybe, she'll give in and haul herself, sweating, up a hill with me, and then at the top through panting breaths she'll admit that, yes, it is beautiful.

Anyway, the mountains. There are loads of them. Then you can see to about infinity in every direction, all sandy flatness covered in scrub and cacti, and pale little hills sticking up under the endless wispy-clouded sky.

It's possible to imagine, then, that you're standing in five hundred years ago, before the settlers came, when the Apache and the

Navajo and the Yavapai wandered the desert. Now they don't wander so much – they stick to the Yavapai Nation reservation up in the hills near Flagstaff. Not that I've seen it – that would mean an actual honest-to-goodness trip, and Mom is never going to sign on for that. I don't think there's much there apart from a casino anyway.

Mom and I lived in Alaska till I was four – not that I remember it. South Alaska, not the full-on North Pole. Then we were in Albuquerque for like a year, I only vaguely remember it, and ever since then we've been in Scottsdale. Here. Once, I asked Mom why she came south to the desert, and she said, *Alaska has fingers of rain and its eyes are always half closed.*

It is maybe relevant that Mom had a cooler of wine on board at this point, but she does say strange things even when she's sober. For instance, she talks a lot about rain – she says I'm her daughter, and she loves me, and if she wants to keep the rain from falling on me, then what's wrong with that?

Uh, nothing, I say when she comes out with crap like that, because the important thing is to agree with her.

Although, I kind of know what she means. That is, I only remember Arizona and New Mexico, so I don't have anything to compare them to, but it's true that it never rains here and there are no shadows, and you couldn't call it sleepy or half awake. It's light all day, then the land closes its eyes and BOOM, it's night. It gets cold at night – it's because of the lack of moisture in the desert. Apart from that it's almost always warm. Right now it's spring and it's like mid-seventies all the time. That's another thing that Mom likes about it. She says, *The cold in Alaska gets into your skeleton, and you can never shake it.*

Right now, Mom is mainly trying to shake it by walking surprisingly fast down the street, her ass rippling in her, ahem, pyjama jeans. That's not subliminal any more, by the way. It's just description. No one walks in this part of Arizona – no one besides us anyway, because we don't have a car. I mean, it's just houses and strip malls.

And even though she's overweight, she's twenty feet ahead of me now, passing the Apache Dreams restaurant, a low block of a building with floor-to-ceiling windows. As far as I know it serves mainly waffles, which is a weird thing for an Apache to dream about.

I hurry to catch up. I've got jeans on – NOT pyjama jeans – and there's sweat trickling down my back, but it's either that or show my scars, and I'm not doing that. My hair is pulled back in a ponytail, like always. I am wearing a T-shirt with a band name on it; it's kind of a joke between me and my mom.

I read a load of books – *Harry Potter, Twilight*, but also George Eliot, Dickens, Faulkner – whatever. My mom taught me to read when I was, like, four. She's pretty proud of it, and you know, I don't really blame her. I'm glad, anyway – reading is awesome. Just escaping into someone else's life, into another world. In books, everything is possible.

And . . . it seems that in girl books there's always some description of the girl so you know what she looks like, but here's the thing, I don't KNOW what I look like. I mean, I have seen myself in mirrors, obviously. But OK, you tell me what you look like.

Not so easy, is it?

But, fine, to get it out of the way: I have brown hair. I have eyes. I have a nose, and a mouth. My mom says I'm beautiful, the most beautiful girl in the world, but she would say that, wouldn't she? I guess it's possible I'm pretty. I'm five-five. One hundred and fifteen pounds. Athletic, you could say.

OK?

Moving on.

Ice cream for dinner after, honey? Mom asks when I'm walking beside her.

I nod. That's what we do every Friday, of course, but she likes to ask, and what does it hurt? Anyway I love Ice Cream for Dinner Night. I always have. Me, I'd happily have Ice Cream for Dinner Night every night, like forever. I think Mom would too, but even though she shops in the plus-size section herself, it's important to her that I stay healthy.

I like that – even more than I would like ice cream for dinner every night.

I step out into the street to cross over, and there's a Chevy station wagon I didn't see and –

– AND I TOLD YOU four hours, didn't I? That's only been, like, a half-hour, don't get ahead of yourself.

So Mom reaches out and gets a hold of my T-shirt and pulls me back on to the sidewalk, where I teeter for a moment.

No, Shelby, says Mom, shouts it, actually, which shows that she's had a shock because she hardly ever uses her voice with me. Shelby is my name – I said that already, I think. Mom named me after a Ford Mustang Shelby GT, because she says it's beautiful and powerful at the same time, and that's what she wants for me. Mom's weird like that – she doesn't even seem that interested in cars, but you never know what little thing she's going to turn out to randomly know a load about.

You can never quite get a handle on her, is what it means. And you can never cheat on a test. Or make something up in an essay.

Sorry, I say.

It's not . . . it's not an apology that I need, says Mom. *I need to know you're safe when I'm not there. You're just always dreaming. You KNOW, Shelby. You KNOW you look both ways before you –*

Yes. I know. Then I get pissed, suddenly, like when a house light goes off on a timer. *But you're ALWAYS there*, I say. *You never leave me alone.*

This is true – I mean, I'm homeschooled, so we spend a lot of time together. And no one could deny that Mom is über-protective and kind of scared of everything. When I was a kid she never let me out of her sight; she covered me in SPF-50 if we even stepped outside; she wouldn't let me ride a bike.

But it's cruel of me to say it that way, to tell her she never leaves me alone, because it's not like I mind it – I mean, she loves me and she doesn't want anything bad to happen to me; I get it. Right at that moment though I just want to hurt her.

Mom takes a deep breath . . . and says nothing. She just takes my hand and leads me across the road, as if I'm a little girl again. *It's Ice Cream for Dinner Night*, she says just to herself, like a calming mantra, but I see it. I see the fear on her face.

CHAPTER
3

AT THE BATTING CAGES we check in and book a lane. Well, Mom does. And even though it's the same zit-covered kid who greets us every Friday, she doesn't look him in the eye – the whole time she's talking to him, she's directing her words and her slight smile to the worn carpet on the ground, as if it could answer. The kid hands over a token with a grin.

Lane eight, he says. *Have a great time.* He's looking at Mom as he says it, but it's the counter she nods to as she walks away. The word 'shy' doesn't even begin to cover it with Mom. The way she acts, it's like everyone could have a knife hidden somewhere, ready to slice her up. I mean, yeah, she's pretty strict with me, she keeps me safe, but put her in front of any kind of stranger and she just snaps shut, like an oyster.

Me, I can feel energy crackling down my arms already, the excitement of being here. Because this is my treat, you see. My special day of the week. Every other day is the same: I get up, I watch TV, I chat online, I work with Mom when she finishes her shift. Then we eat in, trays on our laps: Mom's idea of a kitchen is a fridge and a microwave.

And at the end of it, I go to bed and while I'm sleeping the stage hands of my life rebuild the set exactly the same, the layout of my room, the apartment, so that when I wake up everything is the same, repeating seamlessly.

Except for today, because today is baseball, ice cream and library day.

Every Friday, without fail.

I frown. So actually today is part of the sameness, because it's always baseball, ice cream and library on a Friday, always the same routine. But I don't really care. I like it. At least it's not homework.

Today, I head to lane eight while Mom goes to the cafe, then I unzip my bag and take out my bat. It's a DeMarini CF4 ST with a composite handle and barrel, and it's approximately 3,904 times more awesome than your average baseball bat, mostly because it flexes to reduce recoil and hand-shiver when you hit the ball.

Hand-shiver is not a technical term, BTW. I made it up. But you know what I mean.

If you are familiar with bats, then you know that the CF4 ST runs pretty expensive and so maybe you're thinking that we're rich, but let me tell you, court stenographers do not take home mad money, do not build up fat stacks. Here's how you buy a bat like that if you're me:

You get five dollars allowance a week.

You wait for a hundred weeks and you don't buy shit.

That's it.

There are a few kids waiting in the concessions area, because they know when I come, and they can see my lane from there – the eighty mph lane, which is the whole reason we come here, as it's a full ten mph faster than anything else in the state. I don't nod to them or anything; that would be weird. But they nod to me.

There's a guy in there, but I check the sheet and see he's only got another couple of minutes. He's showing off in front of his friends – gym-rat type, muscles stretching his sleeveless tee. But his strength doesn't give him speed, it seems like, because as I watch, the ball sails past his bat and smacks the back wire behind him. He curses.

Lame, says one of his friends from outside the cage.

Yeah? Watch –

BANG.

This time he swings just right, and the bat connects with the ball and it skitters along the ground past the throwing machine.

Sweet, says the friend.

The kids have walked over now. They're, like, ten but they're wearing low-slung jeans and chains, as if they're gangsters.

One of them says, *You think that was sweet? You have no idea.*

What's that, loser? says gym rat's friend. He's got a tattoo of a chilli on his bicep and a diamond in his front tooth.

Wait till she gets in there, says the kid. *Then you'll see.*

That right? says diamond tooth, turning to me. *You good?*

I shrug. My DeMarini is light in my hand. Mom looks over at me from the cafeteria, where she's drinking some kind of coffee or something from a paper cup. Her whole body is a question, but I shake my head a little.

She don't speak, says the kid.

What, never?

Never has, says another kid.

In the cage, gym rat misses another ball, then he steps out. His time is up. I go past him and shut the wire door behind me.

The cage is long, like seventy feet. At the opposite end to me is the throwing machine, a squat thing the size of a clothes dryer with the end of a pipe at the top of it, a circular hole: O.

18

A light goes from green to red above it, and I settle into the stance.

The trick is:

You don't swing when the ball comes out of the cannon. Reaction time from your brain to your hand is, what, one-sixteenth of a second? You wait to see the ball and you're swinging at empty air, while the ball barrels into the chain-link fence behind you.

What you do:

You swing before you see anything, and half the skill of it is knowing when to start. It's also the beauty of it, for me. The thing that made me save for two fricking years to buy this bat. Mom gave me this book once, about Zen archers – how monks would train by firing an empty bow at a target for years, before being allowed to use an actual arrow. Because the point isn't to fire the arrow into the target, it's to imagine that the arrow is already in the target. To make the act of shooting more like meditation than action.

Yeah – my education is kind of eclectic. Two days a week, Mom goes to her job, and I do homework, mostly. Cook myself lunch – Mom is big on Learning Self-Sufficiency. Sometimes I cook dinner for Mom too when she gets back, if she texts me to remind me. The weekend I have off, and the other three days, Mom teaches me. She gets books from the library, on all kinds of topics, and we go through them together. She gives me math problems, essays to write – you name it. You'd think it would be boring, but it isn't. I don't have friends to hang out with, but I get to learn about Zen archery.

Anyway, the eighty lane is like that. Like a kind of Zen thing. You're swinging at NOTHING. Your bat describes this curve in the air, swatting at emptiness . . .

. . . the ball gets from the cannon to you in, literally, half a second . . .

19

. . . and your bat connects . . .

. . . and something magic happens.

The ball, which has been moving at eighty mph towards you, that's about one hundred and twenty feet a second, contracts in on itself:

$$(\qquad)$$
$$(\quad)$$
$$( )$$

And then it pretty much explodes off the bat, as you continue your arc, and it flies like a bullet to the other end of the batting cage.

Except that all this happens like:

that.

As I shift my head, getting in the stance again, I catch gym rat's eyes. He mouths, *holy crap.* He has this look that I recognise: it means he's going to ask me out when I leave the cage. He'll say something like, *you feel like hooking up?* This is how guys are: half of them hate it when I hit the ball. The other half want to do me.

I ignore him and concentrate on sending the next ball straight down the cage. I mean straight: like a beautiful flat line. Whoosh. I can feel gym rat's gaze on me. I don't think anyone knows whether they're hot or not, I mean, not really. Not unless you're some kind of model. But guys do look at me sometimes, I guess, so I'm not repulsive evidently.

Of course, the guys who check me out, they don't see my scars to begin with, because of the jeans. They don't see my scars ever, actually, because I've never gone out with any of them. My mom would freak out. And anyway I'd be too scared.

Another ball flies back; this one hits the machine and *pock*, it flicks up into the top of the cage, ricochets.

I get them all: I never miss. A couple of times, scouts have been at the batting cages, and they've asked me to play for teams. One guy talked to Mom and offered me a full scholarship to Arizona State, as long as I passed my SATs. Mom said no. She says I wouldn't be safe at college, that people would take advantage of me. I don't mind, too much, that she says no. I mean, I would like to go to college. To study and make friends. But I know my mom is looking out for me – she always has.

Anyway: I'm not interested in playing baseball. I'm just interested in the fast batting cage, the feeling of connecting the motion of the bat with the motion of the ball, of reversing something fast and inevitable. This is the lesson of the baseball cage: everything can be vanquished; everything can be beaten; everything can be turned around.

The ball's going like that, quick as snapped fingers:

⟶

And I make it go like that:

⟵

It's like, in that cage, I can beat anything.
Even time.
Even death.

CHAPTER
4

GYM RAT DOESN'T SAY, *You feel like hooking up?* but he does say, *You feel like hanging out?* so I was close.

I shake my head as I walk past, and I see his mouth say, *Bitch*, silently.

So yeah, sad face. I really missed out there.

I make a gesture that leaves him standing with his mouth open, and I go over to Mom. She's, it turns out, got one of those patterns in her bag, because she's doing the antlers of a stag standing in a glen when I get up to her.

I roll my eyes when I see it. I mean, she's obsessed. But then, I think, there are worse things to be obsessed with. And it's not like she drinks any more, I mean, hardly ever. And I guess it's kind of cute, the stitching thing. Also crazy! But a little bit cute.

Those antlers are huge, I say, because I can't think of anything else.

Beautiful, isn't he? says Mom. She looks up. *I ever tell you my dad's family came from Scotland?*

No, Mom, I say. *I don't think you ever mentioned it.*

Oh, well, they were from –

She catches my eyes. Then she shakes her head. *Very smart, Shelby Jane Cooper,* she says.

I was wondering, I say. *I was wondering if you could tell me about how cold it is in Alaska. I don't think I've heard –*

Ha-ha, she says. She gets up. *Coming?*

I nod and we leave the batting cages and go to the ice-cream place. It isn't hard: it's right next door, within this parking lot square, which is about as close as Scottsdale gets to a downtown. There's a family restaurant too (ten kinds of burgers!) and a bookstore that's surprisingly good. Sometimes we go in there, but Mom can't afford to buy too many books, and unlike the library they get pissed when you read stuff and don't buy anything.

We pull up stools at the counter, and Mom orders the usual, talking to the barstool of course instead of the girl with the pink hair and piercings who nods blandly as she scoops the ice cream. A mint choc chip cone for Mom, and a cup for me, with one scoop of butterscotch and one scoop of cookie dough. I reach over to the toppings rail and hit mine with chocolate sprinkles, popping candy, chocolate sauce, edible glitter, M&Ms, the works.

Mom says, *You'll give yourself a stomach ache,* as she does every time, but it's like a ritual, or an actor saying lines in a play, because I always have the same, and I never get a stomach ache. Mom told me once that I got my sweet tooth from my dad – it's one of the only things she ever said about him. I mean, I know that he died when I was very young, and I have this dim memory of him hugging me in a room somewhere, wood panelling on the walls, so I guess maybe this was some cabin in Alaska or something; the way he smelled of pine trees. But that's it. His face isn't there in my memory. Mom doesn't even have any photos of him.

Sometimes I think: I'd like him to come back, not because I miss him, but just to see what he looks like. Mom hates talking about him so much, it's almost like he never existed, and I'd like to undo his death

23

just so I can know that he really did exist, once. It's hard to explain. Anyway, the problem: in the baseball cage, you feel like you can turn back time. But you can't. Not really.

Mom's smiling as she watches me destroy my ice cream, so I figure it's a good time to mention my birthday again.

Mom, I say. *You know I'm going to be eighteen soon.*

Mom flinches, like I've just pulled out a knife. *Yes?*

I was thinking, you know, about what we talked about before. Me taking my SATs, maybe. So I can study.

She sighs. *It's not safe, Shelby. College! Think of all the young men. Think what they'd do to you.*

I nod. I've seen the news. I've seen the films, with Mom. I know what young men do. Even if there's a tiny bit of me that would like to find out for myself. With Mark from the library, for example. Sometimes I think about him, late at night. I mean, he doesn't seem like a serial killer or a rapist. Of course Mom would say that you can never tell.

What about, like, training to be a librarian? I say. *That would be mostly girls and you can't get safer than a library.*

We'll discuss it later, says Mom.

Later when? I'm eighteen in a couple of months.

Just later, Shelby, she says, and I know the conversation is over. Her face has gone all weird, like a shadow has come across it. Now I feel bad for making her worry so much.

When we're done Mom calls a cab. We go out on to the street and she walks on the outside of me, like always, as if a car is just going to jump up on to the sidewalk and hit me. I don't know if she even knows she's doing it – the habit of protection is so deep inside her, like oil rubbed into wood.

At the corner, our cab pulls up. Then she reaches out and turns my face towards her as the car idles by the sidewalk. *OK, honey, I'll see you at eight, sharp*, she says. *The judge will want to wrap it up. It's Ricardo: he likes to get to his cabin at weekends.*

OK, I say.

And you'll go straight to the library?

Yes, Mom.

She kisses my forehead. *My little princess*, she says. *I love you . . .*

. . . all the way to Cape Cod and back, I finish.

She smiles, and more or less shoves me into the cab. She tells the cab driver to take me to the library, then starts to walk towards the courthouse. I love you too, I think. I don't know why it gets harder to say that as you get older, but it does.

I do love my mom, though, even if we're really different. I mean, everything: our personalities, our hair colour – she's a redhead – our physique, our eyes. It's like we're not even related at all. Plus she is officially the most nervous person in the world and I'm, as she puts it, reckless. So when I was younger, I thought for sure, because of all the fairy tales and kids' stories she used to tell me, that I was really a princess, put here with my mom by accident, that my real mother was a queen who lived far away in a beautiful castle.

Now I figure that every kid thinks this kind of thing. Me and my mom, we may be different, but she looks out for me. She keeps me safe. She teaches me. And yeah, sometimes I feel stifled, but that's life, isn't it?

The driver pulls away. After two blocks he stops.

He turns to me. *Here you are*, he says.

I can tell from his expression that he thinks it's weird, me using a cab to go, like, half a mile. I mean, people don't walk here, but people dressed in Walmart clothes like Mom don't blow ten dollars on a pointless cab ride either. I shrug at him, like, what do you want me to say? It's like he's never had a mother. I count out the money Mom gave me and hand it to him, then get out.

The library is just in front of me. If you're imagining something with columns, like on TV, then stop. Pretty much everything in Scottsdale and most all of Phoenix is just flat, single-storey: bungalows, malls, offices. Every building, including the library, just looks like an unbranded Rite Aid, for real. The only variation, I guess, comes from a few fake adobe things, made to look like old Mexican houses.

Fake, because Scottsdale is new. Really new – since the silicon boom in the Eighties, mostly. A whole patch of desert just turned into city, in a decade. Mom says, the thing about the silicon boom is that before that, there were all these kids in Phoenix with no future and a meth habit.

Now there are still kids with no future and a meth habit, but because of the companies making computer chips, now they have people to steal from.

Then, she will wink and say, *hey, it keeps me gainfully employed.*

CHAPTER
5

I GO IN AND the AC settles around me like a cocoon of coolness. I have a tingly feeling that I get when there are books all around me. The library! I know it's geeky but I love it. Just sitting between the shelves of books, reading – it's the safest feeling.

Ever since I can remember, I've loved the place. Mom used to bring me here, ever since we moved to Scottsdale, would read me stories from the kids' section, mostly fairy tales. I'd sit on her knee – she'd be cross-legged on the floor – and she'd tell me about princesses and curses and old crones making magic spells, and little girls who could outwit wolves.

It was like a doorway into another world. Just, you know, a doorway that smelled a bit like old ladies. Now, still, I love coming here to read, while Mom's working. I'm safe here, inside, with the books – she knows where I am, and so neither of us has to worry. And anyway, I can just pick up a book and be anywhere I want, even if we don't ever physically leave Phoenix.

Although . . .

Although, there is another reason I love the library.

There is the Boy too.

I don't see him at the desk as I come in, and my stomach clenches with disappointment. I walk further into the library, not really aiming for anything in particular. At the rear, there's a Native American section. It has a colourful rug on the floor, photos on the walls of people dancing, wearing masks. A drum sits on a shelf.

I've never been in this part of the library, fiction is more my thing, but on the table in the middle, there's an open book. I stroll over, meaning to pick it up and put it back on the shelf. When I get close, I glance down at the page. I see a line that says:

If Coyote crosses your path, turn back and do not continue your journey. Something terrible will happen –

But just then I sense movement behind me and I turn. It's the boy, Mark, and he reaches past me to snare the book, flips it shut with one hand – and smiles at me as he puts it back on the shelf. It says *Navajo Ceremonial Tales* on the cover.

Hi, Shelby, he says.

Hey, I told you don't do that, I say, my heart racing. *Don't sneak up on me like that.*

Sorry, he says. *My bad.*

He's from somewhere in South America, I think. He has an accent, a different cadence to the way he moves, a different rhythm to his hands. Not that I care: he's pretty much the only person I've spoken to properly, apart from my mom, since I used to play with a girl in our old house in Albuquerque – the one other place I remember living – when I was five years old, giving tea parties to our dolls in the dust of the backyard. So he could speak entirely in curse words, and I wouldn't mind.

I mean, I love my mom. But she is pretty literally the only person I ever speak to. It's nice to have a change.

His name is Mark, but I suspect it isn't, really. He looks like a cross between Tyler the werewolf from *The Vampire Diaries* and Bradley Cooper – he has this whole hot Latino thing going on, but with easy-going charm laid on top of it like smooth turf over bare earth.

Mark leans against the shelves.

Cue angelic music. Cue the end of Shelby Jane Cooper.

Not literally, though. That comes later.

Mark has this tattoo, I think it's a dog, just above his collarbone, and when his top shirt button is undone as it is now, you can see it. It's meant to make him look badass, obviously, but it's kind of cute. And his neck muscles, I can't even.

I can't. Even.

I notice then that one of his hands is behind his back. He takes it out, and there's a book in it.

For you, he says.

I take the book. *Thanks*, I say. *You think I should read this one next?*

He looks uncomfortable. *It's not the library's. It's a gift*, he says.

I look at it. *Grimm's Fairy Tales*, in hardcover. It looks old.

They'll blow your mind, says Mark.

Wow, I say. *Thank you. No one's ever given me a book before. Apart from, like, my mom.* As soon as I say this, I think, Wow, super lame thing to say to a boy. At the same time, I'm thinking, Where am I going to hide this from Mom so she doesn't know I've been talking to a boy? *I'm a bit old for fairy tales*, I say. *Don't you think?*

No one is too old for fairy tales, says Mark.

Yeah, that's what my mom says. She loves them. She'd still read them to me now if she could.

Mark smiles. *These are not like the fairy tales your mother told you*, he says. *They're the originals. They're dark.*

DARK? I ask. *What, like, Cinderella is a serial killer?*

No. Like her stepsisters cut off their heels and their toes, to try to make the slipper fit.

I raise my eyebrows. That was NOT in the version Mom told me. *Oh, OK, then*, I say.

After that we talk for a bit about what I've been learning with Mom, and he tells me some books he thinks I should look at that relate to some of the topics. Says again that I should start thinking about college, about what I could major in. I ignore him. My mom doesn't even like me to walk on the street on my own. She isn't going to let me go to college.

But, you know.

I do think about majoring in English lit.

Sometimes.

As I'm thinking, Mark gets called away by someone who's looking for something.

Thanks for the book, I say as he heads away to hunt.

He turns and says something that I don't understand, in another language, maybe.

I read a bit longer, but it's nearly eight and Mom has a cab booked for me, so I head outside and nod at Mark as I leave – he's talking to a different patron now, and he smiles back at me. Something twisty happens inside me when he does that. I mean, sure, he's a year or two older than me. But the guys at the batting cages never made my stomach lift like he does.

As I'm approaching the door, he's suddenly beside me. I don't know how he did that; it's like he teleported. I stop abruptly.

Listen . . . he says. *Things are . . . starting to happen. Do you think you could meet me, later? My shift ends in a half-hour.*

30

My heart stutters. *I can't*, I say. *Sorry*.

I really am sorry – I mean, there's a part of me that wants to. A big part. But I'm not stupid: he's a man and much stronger than me, and if I meet him somewhere alone, somewhere that isn't a library, he could overpower me, he could do anything he wanted to me. He's hot and he's kind and I like him, but he's still a man.

He's still dangerous.

So I lower my eyes like my mom does and I turn away from him, just catching his frown out of the corner of my vision. But I don't turn back.

Outside, the automatic door closes behind me and my cocoon vanishes, and the heat rushes into the vacuum, like air into lungs, and in fact the heat is in my lungs, so it's outside me and inside me all at once.

Ugh. Sometimes I feel like I'd like to have some cold in my bones, like Mom, to carry around with me in Arizona.

I go out on to the sidewalk, and walk to the spot where the cab will pick me up. I glance at my watch – it's about four minutes before she's due to arrive, and she always arrives when she's due.

I stand there for a moment, holding the book. I don't know how I'm going to explain it to Mom. I guess I'll just say it's from the library and hope she doesn't look inside and see that it doesn't have a stamp.

I look at my watch again. Three more minutes, and then Mom will be there to take me home.

But no.

That doesn't happen.

What happens instead is:

A car, which is actually a Humvee, and as it will turn out is being driven by a driver considerably under the influence, bounces

31

up on to the sidewalk, takes out a trash can, slows just enough not to kill me instantly, then collides with my body hard enough to throw me ten feet through the air.

Lying there, on the concrete, I don't feel any pain at first. I am on my side and there is a warm trickling feeling all over my leg which doesn't seem to forebode anything good, though I can't just now remember how I got to this position.

I am facing the library, or at least the gap between the library and the next building, which I think is a software company. In the cool dark shadow between the buildings, I see two eyes, gleaming.

A coyote steps out and towards me, right there in the dusk. I've never seen one before – I know people do at night, especially in North Scottsdale, but he's my first. I sense that it's a he.

He, the coyote, comes closer and sniffs at me. He's beautiful – this wild thing, here in low-rise suburbia. Like walking into a bedroom and seeing a tree growing in there. His fur is red like sunset, his eyes are shining and telling me something that I don't know how to read, but there's a kind of light of intelligence in them.

I think: Of course, it's not a dog, Mark's tattoo. It's a coyote. I don't know why I thought it was a dog.

I stare at the coyote. There's a crackle about him, almost a halo, like his life is running at a voltage different from other living creatures. Like he's magic. I could really believe that. Then I believe it even more, because the coyote speaks directly into my head, or that's what it feels like.

There will be two lies, it says. Then there will be the truth. And that will be the hardest of all.

There's something weird about the way the coyote says this, like

32

the words are somehow inside my head, echoing, but I can't put my finger on it. It's like grasping a slick frog – it squirts out of my hands.

Then something startles him and he backs away, turns skittishly, almost falling over, and runs back into the shadow where he disappears.

And it's like he was never there, and I feel bummed about that. This is all wrong, anyway, I think, remembering the book in the library, the open one. You're meant to see the coyote BEFORE the horrible thing happens to you. Not after.

I roll a bit and look up and see the moon, pale in the still-light sky, looking down on me like a parent looking down at a sick child.

This is – I think.

And then blackness.

7 . . .

CHAPTER
6

WHEN I OPEN MY eyes again I'm lying in a bed next to a flashing machine with a wave on it that I realise is my heartbeat. I think how it's weird to suddenly see something that before I've only felt or heard.

Then I think that the fact I'm thinking means I'm not dead.

I look around and see that, as far as I can tell, I'm not in the ER, or on ventilation or anything. There's a drip in my hand connected to a tube on a stand, and that thing monitoring my heart, but that's it for machines. I check my arms – fine. I'm in a blank white-walled room, old-fashioned flowery curtains on the windows. A granular light seeps in, the kind that has been filtered through a thin white blind or netting.

Then a memory tweaks at me. My leg.

I sit up a bit and see this ENORMOUS BOX THING covering the lower half of my right leg, with the bed covers sort of drawn over it so I can't see what's under there. I mean, I hope it's my fricking FOOT under there but who knows? They might have had to amputate it.

Oh my God, they amputated my foot.

I jerk forward, to try to move the box, and there must be

something stuck to my chest because instantly the heart machine starts flashing in a way more full-on way, the wave flatlines, and the door opens.

A doctor comes in, followed by Mom. The doctor's eyes do this quick flicker from the line on the screen to me, then back to the screen, and I can practically hear his thoughts as he realises that it's just me accidentally pulling off the sticky things. He has a moustache and his name tag says Dr Maklowitz.

Shelby, honey! says Mom. *I'm so glad to see you!*

She comes close and holds me and when Dr Maklowitz is leaning forward to adjust the monitor, she says just to me, *What the hell were you doing out on the street?*

I don't answer any of this.

What's the deal with my foot? I ask.

Shelby, says Dr Maklowitz, speaking slowly like I'm special or something. *We'll come to your foot. But you sustained a pretty bad head injury – we need to make sure that . . .*

He walks over to my bedside and takes a small flashlight from his shirt pocket. Then he flicks it on and shines it in my eyes. *Look left*, he says. *Right. Up.*

I do.

OK, he says. *Who is the current president of the United States?*

Barack Obama, I say out loud. The sounds feel strange in my mouth – my tongue is dry and feels too large for the cavity it is in; I don't seem to have full control over my lips. Painkillers, I guess.

Good, says Dr Maklowitz. *Good. We need to do more tests, run the whole inventory of the Belfast [   ], but I think with the scans too we can probably rule out major brain damage or [   ].*

He's speaking fast and my brain is slow, affected by the drugs, so I don't catch everything he says.

You also had some wounds that we have stitched up, he says. *To your leg, mostly – we think you fell on some glass. And your ankle is –*

You could have died, says Mom.

Dr Maklowitz gives her a look, like, shut up. *We stopped the bleeding*, he says. *You're going to be OK. Some scarring, but of course you already have . . .* He tails off. *Anyway, we'll have you out of here soon. For now, you just need to rest.*

I look at him. *Will I . . . walk again?* I ask hesitantly, looking down at the box over my lower leg.

He stares at me for a moment and then laughs. *Of course! Yes, of course you will. Sorry, I didn't mean to worry you. We think you must have damaged your foot and ankle when you fell – you must have [   ] and twisted it. Actually most of your injuries – and they're fairly minor ones – come from falling, not the car itself. We should be able to discharge you soon, once we've –*

What about her foot? says Mom. She seems weirdly impatient.

Two things, says the doctor. *On the ankle, a stable oblique fracture of the lateral m[   ], and on the foot, a displaced extra-[   ] fracture, requiring –*

Oh God, says Mom.

He smiles again. *No, no, those are OK. I mean, the best kinds of fractures. We need to give you a small operation, reduce the displacement of the [   ], but it's easy. We can do it under local.*

I nod.

You were really very lucky, he says. *An SUV like that . . . It's actually remarkable what little damage you have suffered.*

Will she need a wheelchair? asks Mom. *Crutches?*

He shakes his head. *Should be fine with a . . .* and then he says something like *camera*.

A what? says Mom.

Dr Maklowitz goes over to a corner of the room and brings back a sheet of paper, which he hands to Mom. *They cost a couple hundred dollars, I'm afraid, but they're amazing things.*

Show me, I say.

Mom tilts the paper and I see CAM Walker. Oh, so that was what he said. There's a picture of a massive boot on someone's leg – like the bottom part of a storm trooper's armour or something. It's plastic, robotic.

I have to wear THAT? I ask.

You'd prefer a wheelchair? says Dr Maklowitz.

I shake my head.

He smiles. I like his smile. *It's only for four weeks,* he says. *And you can take it off at night. Of course. Like I say, you were lucky. If the car had been going a bit faster . . .*

I lie back. I don't feel very fricking lucky. But I do feel about 159 times more relaxed now I know they didn't saw off my leg.

Mom and Dr Maklowitz take a step away from me and lower their heads to have a conversation, so I don't catch all of it. But I follow some. To start, Mom is timid, facing the ground, as usual. And the doctor is tough, assertive. His words fly flat at her, like projectiles, like baseballs; hers fall at his feet, like a mouse being offered in tribute by a cat.

But as they keep talking, Mom's head slowly comes up, as if there's a string attached to it and someone is pulling on it. She's still hunched, still nervous, but she's pissed and she's not backing down.

Interesting, I think.

Mom: *[   ]*

Dr Maklowitz: *We can't discharge her immediately after the operation.*

Mom: *But they said at the desk that [   ]*

Dr Maklowitz: *Yes, that's right. The law requires [   ]*

Mom: *[   ] So we're paying for everything at this point? I mean, for tonight, and the next operation?*

Dr Maklowitz: *We stabilise patients in the ER, regardless of insurance status. Everything after that has to be paid for. If the patient is uninsured, then they or their legal guardian must pay.*

Mom (head fully up now and pulling severe angry face): *She's hardly stable, she's got furniture on her –*

Dr Maklowitz: *She's stable in the sense that she's no longer dying. That's what it means. Even after the operation, even after she has her CAM Walker, we're going to need to –*

Then Mom makes another face at him and pulls him to the other end of the room, which is totally out of character, and they turn away from me, which makes the rest of the conversation just [   ]. I can tell from Dr Maklowitz's body language though that he is uncomfortable dealing with someone like Mom, who has to push two hundred pounds and can be a real badass when she wants to be.

But from what has already been said, I gather that:

I am not insured, which is news to me, because I figured I was on Mom's work insurance.

Mom is going to have to pay for the rest of my treatment, however long that takes.

Mom is behaving really weirdly, facing up to people and dragging them around rooms and stuff, being all amped up and unlike herself.

Dr Maklowitz leaves the room, looking stressed, and Mom comes back to the head of the bed.

How can I not be insured? I ask.

It's complicated, says Mom. She seems tense, and I guess she must be worrying about the money.

But this will be thousands of dollars, I say.

Mom smiles, only I can tell she's doing it just for me. Then a nurse comes in, with a tray. *Dinner*, she says. *It's mac and cheese.*

Oh good. I hate mac and cheese. It's like eating barf. I leave it on the nightstand. Mom starts trying to talk about the food but I'm not letting her off the hook.

The money, Mom, I say. *What are we going to do?*

Don't worry, she says, *you know we have something saved away for a rainy day.*

It never rains in Arizona, I say.

Exactly, Mom replies.

42

CHAPTER
7

THE REST OF THE day is boring as hell and I would be happy, actually, to never spend another hour in a hospital, ever.

Mom does figure out how to get the TV working, using her credit card, which is all forty-nine flavours of awesome, though. Then she opens the blind and because we're in Phoenix General we're actually up in the air and you can see the city, and the mountains beyond. It's almost like when I climb up in the desert, and look at the land all around. When I can make Mom drag herself up a hill with me anyway. It's not like she would let me go hiking on my own.

They also bring me some food, and even though it's gross it's welcome, because I realise suddenly that I'm starving.

I eat mechanically, not thinking about anything.

Then I go cold all over.

Mom, I say. *My bat. What happened to* –

She smiles and reaches under the bed and pulls out the DeMarini and I'm so happy I totally die right then and there. So this is my ghost writing now – hey, how are you? Me, I'm good, thanks, because I've got my five-hundred-dollar bat back and nobody cut off any of my limbs, even if I am a ghost and –

They had to dispose of your bag, Mom says, in a tone that makes me stop stroking my bat like some kind of freak. *It had blood on it.*

I should be more careful with that stuff, I say. *Shouldn't go spilling it everywhere.*

Mom laughs but then a tear is all of a sudden in her eye and she brushes it away, and I feel ashamed. She reaches down and picks something up – something flat and oblong.

Oh no – *Grimm's Fairy Tales.*

You know anything about this? she says.

I stare at it, keeping my expression flat. *No,* I say. *Why?*

It was lying near you, on the sidewalk.

I was outside the library, I say. *I guess someone dropped it.*

Hmm, she says.

There's a moment of very UNcomfortable silence. Mom stares at me icily. She is really bringing her A-game to this chilly make-your-daughter-feel-bad thing. I need to get her off this topic.

Mom . . . I say. *Is it really expensive?*

The hospital?

Yes, the hospital.

I don't know . . . ten thousand dollars.

Oh, I think. I mean, I knew it would be thousands, but ten thousand? That, as junkies would say, is mad bank. I don't even really know what to say. Oops, I cost you ten grand?

We watch TV for a while – *America's Next Top Model.* Mom puts the closed captions on, of course, so we can fully appreciate the inane comments of the models.

All this time, I've been waiting for her to ask again, about what I was doing out of the library, and eventually she does.

Why did you go outside early? she says. *I TOLD you eight o'clock, like always.*

I stare at her. *I was there, like, four minutes early. I was just –*

You should just do what I told you. You're still a child. You do what your mother says. And I say you wait for me at eight o'clock EXACTLY. Do you think I say these things for fun? No. I say them because –

I'm not a child.

What?

You said I was a child. I'm not. I'm seventeen.

You're a child under the law, she says.

I glower at her.

She closes her eyes for a long moment. *I'm sorry. I know the car came up on the sidewalk. But . . . that's why you have to be careful, Shelby.*

I didn't want the car to hit me!

No, she says. *No, of course not. But someone else might have seen it in time, or heard it, you know. You're special, Shelby. You're in your own world. That's why you need to be careful. That's why you need me.*

I know, I say.

A pause.

Is it a boy? she says, suddenly.

What? I say, wrongfooted.

The book. It's not a library book. I'm still wondering where you got it.

No! I say, all horrified. And I'm not totally lying. I mean, there is a boy, of course. But he works for the library. So in a way, it kind of is a library book.

She looks at me, hard, like: Spill.

OK, there's a boy, I say.

She raises her eyebrows, like: Spill more.

45

He works at the library, I say. *His name is Mark. He's nice.*

Now Mom is almost shaking with fear and anger. Boys and men – those are the things you have to watch out for the most. In her version of the world, they're like wolves and we're like sheep; they're circling us all the time, looking for weakness.

He's NICE? Everything I've ever taught you and you tell me he's – Wait.

Mom is fixing me with this very odd look, her brow furrowed, like she doesn't understand something.

What? I ask. *What is it?*

When you came out of the ER . . . she says. *I . . . I wanted to understand what had happened. I went down to the library. The police were asking questions.*

Oh, right, I say. *So you met him. What is it, the tattoo?*

Now she's looking at me as if she's sorry for me, or as if she thinks I'm crazy, which I guess amounts to the same thing.

What? I say, more insistently now.

Shelby, honey, she says. *There was no man at the library when I went down there.*

CHAPTER
8

I DON'T KNOW IF you've ever tried to sleep in a hospital bed, but it's pretty much impossible. There's always someone coming in to check on you, or people walking up and down in the corridor – or running, sometimes, which is more worrying. You get those shadows of moving feet in the crack of light under the door, flickering, like a movie projector, except the pattern draws your eye without meaning anything.

There's a meditation trick Mom taught me where you focus on your breathing, try to subtract everything else from your consciousness, and I try that for a while until I realise I'm thinking about Mark, and how Mom says he doesn't exist. Which is, to say the least, a disquieting development.

A nurse comes and takes my blood pressure.

I press the button to feed more painkillers into my IV but I guess I must have already done it recently, because nothing happens. I don't remember though.

The moon shines into the room. I told them not to close the curtains – I like seeing the world out there. It makes me feel less like the next flood has come, and this hospital room is the only thing saved; just floating on its own through dark water.

I try to think about the crash, and the coyote, but the images slip away from me, fish in a pond, flitting under cover when your shadow creeps over them.

Instead, the picture that keeps coming to me is of a park, one dusty summer when I'm, I guess, ten, maybe just turned eleven. Mom and I are walking to a clear patch in the middle, the grass brown and dying. There aren't many people – it's a weekday, presumably, and Mom isn't working right then. I can see a couple of men ambling around, one of them with a dog on a lead. I don't look at them – I know these men will bundle me into a van if I'm not careful, chop me up into dog meat, or worse. Mom is never specific about what actually happens in the van, which only makes it more scary.

So: I keep my head down, and I don't meet those men's eyes. Ever. Mom is holding my hand but you can never be too safe, that's a thing I know; a thing I have been told, over and over.

Just once, I see something that makes me feel sad, instead of scared. It's a family, all out together; I think they're going to have a picnic. The dad has the younger child, a girl, on his shoulders, and she's laughing. The other kid, a boy, is walking along kicking a soccer ball, chatting to the mom, who is smiling like there's a light inside her and she has to let it out. In fact, all of them are smiling, and this is what gets me, squeezes my heart –

I think, I would like that – a brother, a dad.

But instead I'm on the outside, and even though it's so hot, the feeling is a cold one, the feeling of looking into a brightly lit room that you're locked out of.

I shiver, and I look away from the family.

There's a shimmering haze at the edge of the park and the sun is white above us, in a cloudless sky. Mom is sweating in the heat – her hand is clammy around mine, slippery but strong, like being held by a squid. I know she doesn't want to be doing this and I feel guilty and warm inside, at the same time.

When we get to the empty part, Mom puts down the bag she's carrying and takes out the ball and the bat. I don't know if this is the first time I play – it's my first memory of it, anyway. But I must have got the idea of batting from somewhere, so maybe it isn't the first time.

Anyway.

So Mom hands me the bat and then she walks a couple of dozen paces away. It's a softball and Mom is overweight, not athletic at all, so when she throws it, the ball falls short and she shrugs her shoulders at me, moves closer. Seeing her try to pitch to me, the effort she's putting into it, makes me feel again that strange mixture of pleasure and shame.

Closer up, she does better – the ball comes at me flat and I swat at it, miss. The next one I hit – it lofts into the gauzy summer air, arcs over Mom's head, and bounces on the dried-out grass; twice, three times.

Mom shuffles off to get it. She's not quick, but she doesn't complain, and when she comes back she just throws again, and I swing.

That all you got? she says with a smile when she brings the ball back.

I smile too, and the next one, I hit harder, almost to the edge of the park, where the low suburban homes start. The air is so dry that it's like breathing in sand. Mom's hair is dark with sweat when she brings the ball back, yet again.

But she keeps going: the ball flying, a slow parabola in the shining summer sky; and Mom going to get it, as fast as she can manage, despite her size.

And my heart? My heart swells till it feels like it's going to burst out of my chest. Because there's my mom, my unfit, sports-hating mom, chasing after the balls I'm hitting, throwing to me over and over, the perspiration running down her in rivulets.

I'm only a kid, and I guess when you're a kid you just think about yourself most of the time, you don't think about your parents or how much they love you, but on that day, in that memory, I know it – I see it blazing out of my mom's every moment, this fierce love.

I don't know how long we kept that up, the batting. I know that in my memory, it doesn't end, and that makes me think we were there for hours, but it could have been a half-hour. I don't know – I don't remember leaving the park, I just remember the joy of the bat meeting the ball, the perfect, mathematically precise track of the ball through the sky, and my mom bringing it back, again and again.

And thinking about it is good, because it makes me feel less mad about Mom fussing over me, and Mark, and the horrible fear that I saw in her eyes when we spoke earlier in the hospital room. I picture the park that day, and it makes my anger and my guilt abate, slowly.

And then my breathing slows, and I'm conscious of it, but in a dim and distant way.

And I look out of the window and I see that the sun is coming up, a glow on the horizon. The contrail of a jet plane above catches the low light and is set on fire, a perfectly straight streak of electricity, and I'm aware that I haven't properly slept all night.

I press the painkiller button:

Click, and a warm rush.

6 . . .

CHAPTER
9

THERE ISN'T MUCH TIME for worrying about Mark the next day, because I go into the OR early for my operation. I don't get general anesthesia this time – they just knock my leg out and go to town. There's a kind of screen to stop me seeing what they're doing; not that I'd mind, I'm not squeamish.

I don't exactly know what they're doing. Something to do with the bones in my foot. One of them needs to be moved, I think, back to its proper position.

Whatever it is, it takes a long time. I figure the architecture of the body must be pretty complicated down there; lots of ligaments and tendons, twisting and stretching without me knowing, to accomplish the simple task of walking.

That's the main thing I worry about: what if they screw something up? What if I don't walk again, with or without a CAM Walker?

But I try not to let it get to me. And anyway there's another thought swirling around in there, in me. Where did Mark go?

When I'm wheeled back to my room, I've got stitches down from my ankle to nearly my toes. There's going to be an impressive scar.

But I don't mind about that. A scar is nothing to me. I mean, I already have a whole lot of them. They stretch from my waist right down to my knees – pockmarks, streaks, like a meteor storm, like the surface of the moon. I was two when it happened: I didn't hear my mom shouting to me to stop, and I pulled a pan of hot oil from the stove, spilled it on myself. I was wearing a shirt that protected my stomach, but my legs were bare.

My dad was already dead – he passed away when I was tiny. So it was all on her, and she's never let go of the guilt of it. Sometimes, when she looks at my legs, I see the tears in her eyes. Not even just when she sees the scars.

At the same time, she hates it when I feel embarrassed by them. She wishes I would go swimming with her. Mom says the scars are part of the story of me.

I say, in that case, the story of me is a freaking horror story.

I'd recommend at least a week's bed rest, says Dr Maklowitz.

But she could leave, right? says Mom.

Of course. If necessary. We'll have to train her in using the CAM Walker before we can discharge her, though. And of course we'll need a follow-up appointment to make sure everything is healing OK. Say two months?

So, a couple of hours later, the hospital pharmacy brings me my CAM Walker. A nurse shows me how to put it on – it's exactly like an enormous, ugly boot. My one is white, just to add to the storm trooper vibe. There's a sticker on the back of it that says PROPERTY OF PHOENIX GENERAL.

The nurse makes me practise walking on it, up and down the hospital room, until she's satisfied that I have mastered the art of WALKING. Then she shows us how to take care of the stitches, tells us about covering them up with a plastic bag if I'm in the shower or something.

Then she sends us to the hospital pharmacy with a prescription for some hardcore painkillers – high-dose codeine, which Mom explains is a derivative of morphine, only not as strong. We walk down a blank corridor, its walls marked here and there with suspicious stains. It reminds me of a recurring dream I have, which freaks me out a bit. The child crying, the need to get to it, to save it.

Finally we arrive at the pharmacy. There are two counters, with what looks like bulletproof glass protecting the people walking behind it. Actually, it probably is bulletproof glass. Phoenix is like the meth capital of America after all.

We go to the first counter and hand over the prescription sheet. The woman behind the counter – she has a faint moustache – hands a ticket with a number on it through the little slot that's open at the bottom of the glass. It says 496 on it. I look up at a screen where the number 451 is displayed.

It'll be a half-hour, says the woman.

A full hour and a half later, our number comes up on the screen and we go to the second counter, where a tall young man in glasses hands us two bottles of pills.

Taken these before? he says.

I shake my head.

There's sixty milligrams in each tab, he says. *No more than* six *in one day. You may find they constipate you a little.*

Ugh, I think. Super gross.

You find the pain is getting too much, try elevating the foot, he says. Then he nods at us and goes to grab some drugs for another patient.

Mom holds my hand to steady me and we walk back down the corridor, then take an elevator to the main reception hall. There are doctors going back and forth, having fast conversations, nurses

55

running. A couple of receptionists are working on the phones and also trying to deal with walk-ins.

Mom leads me to the coffee-table area with the magazines, then, weirdly, seems to wait till the place is especially busy before walking us up to the counter. There's a Mexican girl there, and she holds up a hand to us as she finishes a conversation on the phone. She says something in Spanish, then turns to us.

Yes?

We'd, ah, we'd like to pay, says Mom. She hands over some paperwork. She's all nervous again, folded in on herself, as if holding something important under her chin, which she has to protect.

Credit card?

Actually . . . uh . . . Dr Maklowitz and me, we agreed a cash discount. Ten per cent.

The girl nods. She shuffles the papers and keys something into the computer beside her. Paramedics rush in, a guy on a gurney hooked up to tubes, and run down the corridor, and she doesn't even look up. She's pretty – long black eyelashes that flick up from the screen.

ID, she says flatly.

Whose? says Mom, her hands fluttering, fidgeting. *My daughter's? Both of you.*

But . . . Mom kind of stammers. *But we're paying cash. She's uninsured, you guys know that already.*

I can't take a cash payment without ID. And we need ID for . . . Shelby, for our records.

Mom is flustered. I'm not surprised, if she's got ten thousand dollars in her purse. She roots around in there for a second, then looks back at the girl. *I don't exactly carry around her birth certificate,* she says.

56

The girl shrugs. *You can bring Shelby's when you come for the follow-up. But I need to take yours now.*

Mom does this apologetic hand-opening thing. *I just don't –*

I lean into her field of vision. *Your driver's licence,* I say. *You keep it in your purse.*

Mom smiles, though it almost seems like she grimaces first. *Oh yes.*

She takes out her licence and hands it over, and the receptionist enters her details, then holds out her hand and Mom takes a surprisingly small wad of cash from her purse and gives her that too. But I guess if it's hundred-dollar bills, you don't need that many.

The receptionist prints Mom a receipt using one of those really old-fashioned printers that spit out thin pink paper, with holes down each side. It's long – I guess it lists all the stuff that was done to me.

Uh, thanks, says Mom, but she's already turning around, holding my hand, manoeuvring me out of there in my slow hobbling way.

The girl gives a brisk nod and answers the phone.

In the parking lot, Mom takes a small black unit from her purse that I slowly recognise as a car key. She presses a button and the lights of a grey sedan flash.

Since when do we have a car? I ask.

Since I rented one, says Mom. The weird thing is – that whole looking-down shtick of hers, the nervousness, she's doing it with ME now, as if I'm making her anxious by asking questions.

It's enough to freak me out pretty seriously. *Um, where are we going?* I ask. *What's the deal? Why are you acting so weird?*

We're going on a trip, says Mom. *A vacation.*

A vacation? We never go on vacation.

Well, we are now.

Fine, I say.

She won't meet my eye. *It's going to be a long vacation.*

I put my hands on my hips – or try to, because I'm a little unbalanced by the CAM Walker, so as a manoeuvre it is pretty doomed to failure, and instead I do an ungraceful little jerky dance. *Mom,* I say. *I'm not going anywhere with you until you tell me what's going on.*

She says nothing but helps me into the front seat, adjusts it so that I have enough room to stretch out my leg, then takes my hospital bag and puts it in the back seat of the car. I turn and see that there's a load of other stuff in there too – bulging suitcases, piles of Scottish landscapes.

Mom? I ask again. *Why have you got, like, all our stuff in the car?*

Mom takes a deep breath. *OK,* she finally says, looking up at me. *There's something I haven't told you. See . . . ah . . .*

Yes? I say, impatient.

It's your father. He's not really dead.

CHAPTER

10

MOM IS DRIVING PRETTY FAST, north out of Phoenix, on three-lane blacktop.

Sitting beside her, looking at her flapping mouth as she tries to explain, I am silent. Inside, though, I am thinking, WHAT THE HELL? We pass a Motel 8 and I barely see it, it's as if all objects and things have gone transparent, and there is only this insane new fact in the world, disguised by glassy fake motels and gas stations and streetlights, a thin watery covering over insanity.

I can imagine what you must be thinking, she says.

Oh yeah? I think.

I know this must come as a shock, she continues. *I know it's a lot to take in.*

Uh, yes, I think. You told me my dad was DEAD.

I glance out of the window – scrub and sand as we join I-17, leaving the city behind. Mountains in the distance. Blue sky forever; no clouds. It's weird: we're actually, finally leaving the city, which is what I've dreamed about forever. But now I don't even care.

Shelby, say something, she says. She has to kind of turn in the seat to talk to me, which is super dangerous at this speed, but she doesn't seem to care.

My dad has been dead my whole life – it's pretty much the only thing I actually know about him. It's a defining feature of my life. It's like being told that the moon actually IS made of cheese after all. I just can't even. I can't. Even.

I look out the window instead, so she can't talk to me. I curl up into my seat, like a wounded animal.

It's scary how quick, when you drive out of Phoenix, you're in just pure desert. I mean, this landscape hasn't changed since the Native Americans rode their horses across it. It's not like dunes – it's more like Wile E. Coyote, you know? Rocks and bits of grass in the sand, and these reddish outcrops sticking up, though not massive ones like in Utah.

It's partly why I didn't like you leaving the house, continues Mom. *Why I've always been so protective. He's . . . a dangerous man. I don't know what he's capable of. Remember when we left Albuquerque? That was because he found us. He spoke to a woman I worked with in the court. A judge's secretary.*

Now, I literally don't know what to say to this. So my dad isn't dead, he's just some kind of homicidal lunatic chasing us down. Way to spring some serious shit on your daughter, Mom.

At least I can be grateful you're not wearing your pyjama jeans, I say eventually.

Shelby! This isn't the time for your jokes.

Then what is it the time for? What the hell do you want me to say, Mom? That it's no big deal?

Don't curse, Shelby.

Oh, no, you're right, THAT'S the take-home message here. Cursing is bad.

Mom sighs and turns back to the road, which I'm kind of happy about because she was swerving a little bit.

For the longest time, neither of us says anything. We just eat up road, Mom sticking to the express lane, putting Phoenix behind us at eighty miles an hour, going as fast as the baseballs I like to hit.

Where are we going? I ask.

Flagstaff, says Mom.

Flagstaff? Why?

I don't know. It's not Phoenix. And it's big, and surrounded by forest. It's a good place to hide. She pauses. *Hey! We could even go to the Grand Canyon. Like you always wanted, right?*

It's dumb, because I'm still freaking out about my dad and everything Mom has just dumped on me, but I still get this spike of excitement. *Yeah?* I say. I don't know why I want to go so much – I guess it's the idea of this big crack in the world, like it's a place where you can see under the world's skin, to what's beneath. To the truth below the earth. I don't know. That sounds crazy, when I say it like that.

Yeah, says Mom. *We'll be close enough to drive. No plane.*

Cool, I say.

We're climbing out of flat desert, following I-17 into the mountains. I've never been this far from the city before. It's almost like I can feel the air getting colder.

For miles and miles, it's desert plateau – not just sand like around Phoenix, but a kind of scrubby desert, saguaro cacti like buried hands. And in the distance, high blue mountains, far away across the brush. It's a vast landscape, incredibly beautiful, and I find myself, despite everything, kind of just gazing at it raptly as we drive. We pass a sign that says AGUA FRIA NATIONAL MONUMENT. There is hardly anyone else on the I-17 – it feels like a road movie, the ribbon of highway stretching out in front of us, across the desert. The mountains dreaming in the distance.

Then, like an hour later, we start to pull out of desert and into forest. I start to see pine trees – at first just a thin covering, red rock outcrops behind them. Then the world shifts slowly from reds and yellows to greens and greys. Big things jut out of the trees that make me think of the word 'stone', not 'rock'.

Mom pulls over at a gas station with a 7-Eleven. She gets out of the car and goes in – and when she comes back she's got a disposable barbecue, and a bag that looks like it contains burgers and buns.

After another half-hour, there's a sign that says we're entering the Ores National Forest, and Mom swings off the highway on to a smaller road that very obviously does not lead to Flagstaff. Forest swallows us immediately, a throat of shadow around us. The sun is going down too, slanting low through the leaves and the needles.

We drive another ten minutes, then turn on to an even smaller road, with a sign saying PUBLIC CAMPING AREA, NO BARBECUES, PICK UP YOUR OWN TRASH, THIS AIN'T COMMUNIST RUSSIA. Next to it there's a mailbox and a smaller sign hanging from it: $10 A NITE. HONESTY IS A VIRTUE.

Someone has shot the sign with a shotgun, it looks like, which I take to be promising.

We pull into a gravelled area scooped out of the woods – there's one other car there, a newish Honda Civic, and near it, under the trees, a little one-person tent. Mom helps me out of the car. She shoots a glance at the tent and frowns. I look around. I've never been in a forest before. It's weird – like being in a building but one made of wood and leaves. But I like the way it's cool and smells like air freshener.

What's the plan here? I say. *We don't have a tent.*

We'll sleep in the car, Mom says. *It's not cold. We'll just have to snuggle is all.*

I hobble around a bit but there isn't much to see and pretty soon I sit down.

So, this thing with Dad . . . I say.

Mom runs her hand through her hair. *He's a violent man, Shelby*, she says. *That's why I left him.*

OK, I say. *But why would he want to kill us?*

She hesitates. I consider the coyote, how it said, there will be two lies, and then there will be the truth. I think: Is this the first lie? Is Mom lying to me right now, spinning me a story about this violent father? But I can't figure the angle, if it's the case. I mean, what would she gain?

Anyway Mom at this point stops frowning, and her face settles, like water after the ripples have passed. *He started hurting you*, she says very softly. *I threatened to leave. He said if I did he would hunt us down.*

Oh, I say.

She puts her hands on mine. *You are my little Shelby*, she says. *I would die before I let anyone hurt you.* There are tears in her eyes, and I put my arms around her, which is awkward because the CAM Walker unbalances me, but she holds me up.

When she straightens, I say, *I just don't understand how he –*

But that's as far as I get, because this pasty overweight guy pops up from among the trees, swinging what looks like a can of water. He shields his eyes from the horizontal light of the nearly gone sun, and walks over to us.

There is a knife in his hands – a hunting knife, with a long serrated blade.

CHAPTER
11

MOM BACKS AWAY, PULLING me with her.

The man raises his hands in the air. *Easy*, he says.

I am looking at his pale skin, the lines around his mouth. He has two chins and only one working eye, or only one that moves anyway. It's weird – like he's looking at an invisible person beside you. He's maybe fifty, his hair grey around his ears. I know I should be scared, but I'm mainly thinking – is this my dad? Is this what he looks like?

Then the guy, my dad, whoever he is, must see that our eyes are on his knife, because he looks up at it, and his mouth drops open. *Oh*, he says. He pulls a sheath from his pocket, slides the knife into it, puts it away in his jacket. *Kindling*, he says.

He points with his foot to a little pile of sticks on the ground.

You have to peel off the bark, if it's green wood. If it's damp.

Mom has stopped retreating. She nods very slightly. This isn't my dad, I realise. It's some random guy.

Let's start again, says the man. *Howdy*. He walks over to us, but slowly, like we're small animals – mice, lizards – that might shy from an approaching figure.

Howdy, says Mom. She's on edge, I can see it.

You folks vacationing? Or travelling? asks the man.

Both, I guess, says Mom hesitantly. *We're headed to the Grand Canyon, but we're taking it slow.*

Me too, he says. Then he sticks out his hand to shake Mom's. She flinches instinctively, but then takes it. *Luke. My wife died on me there a year back, and I've kinda been wandering ever since.*

I'm, ah, sorry to hear that, says Mom.

Don't be, she was a hard-ass, says Luke, without much emotion. *Made my life hell for twenty years.*

Mom laughs and tucks her hair behind her ear, as if this was a really funny joke. I tilt my head, registering that she's looking him in the eye too. Is she FLIRTING?

Opening the car door, Mom pulls out the barbecue grill and the plastic bag. *Join us for dinner?* she says.

OK, I think. The weird behaviour just hit the next level. Where is the shyness? What happened to addressing the ground?

Luke hesitates, looking at the bag. *If it's pork, I can't,* he says.

Mom acts surprised. *You Jewish?* she says.

No, says Luke. *I was a paramedic. First response.*

Mom looks at him, like, what?

I don't wanna spell it out, says Luke. *But it's the smell. After . . . after a house fire.*

I look at him. Joy! The man is talking about burning human flesh! This day just keeps getting better.

Mom has blanched too, like this is too much even for Strange New Confident Mom. But she gets a grip on herself quickly, steps closer to him, and touches his arm. *You poor man,* she says. *And no, it's burgers. Beef burgers.*

Well, all right, then, says Luke.

This is officially now by about a factor of 5,000 the worst evening of my life. I mean, Mom touching Luke's arm as he tells us that pork on a barbecue smells like people burning.

I sit there, eating charred burger, while Luke and Mom continue to revoltingly flirt, like something on the Discovery Channel – Two People Doing a Mating Dance. Mom asks him about being a paramedic, and he tells some stories. They are not entertaining or fun stories. One of them is about a boy who swung too hard at a piñata and smashed in a girl's face with his stick – she had to have three reconstructive surgeries.

What happened to your leg there? he says to me, after this. *Car crash?*

No, says Mom. *She's a climber. Fell off a rock.*

You don't climb with a rope? he says to me.

I shrug.

You should be careful, he says. *You only get one life.*

What I keep telling her, says Mom.

I roll my eyes at her. In real life, when she's not, oh, suddenly acting like a totally different person, she would as soon see me climb up a rock as she'd give me a loaded pistol and tell me to play some Russian roulette. When I was a kid, she wouldn't even let me have a bike. Said I could kill myself just by hitting a kerb too hard.

So, what? I think. I fell off a ROCK? This means I'm 100 per cent, for real, now living in some kind of thriller film where people start lying and suddenly there are violent people chasing you. It would be scary if it wasn't so totally random.

Your daughter's not a talker, huh? he says.

Mom laughs. *Teenage blues*, she replies.

Luke laughs too. *Never had kids – wife didn't want 'em. But I got me a TV. I've seen* My Super Sweet 16.

Well, she's not that bad, says Mom. *But we have our differences. Climbing without safety ropes is one of them.*

Dangerous sport at the best of times, climbing, says Luke to me. *You should give it a rest. I've seen –*

And he launches into this charming story about cutting down a climber who hanged himself with his own rope, by accident. I see Mom go slightly white again, but she has a core of steel, it seems like, because she keeps the smile painted on her face.

I stand up and go and sit further away from the fire, just watching the shadows shifting in the forest. I see something fly past, maybe a bat, maybe an owl. It's fast; it swoops, and then it's gone.

Out of the corner of my eye, I see Mom beckon me over. I lever myself up and go inelegantly on my CAM Walker to her. She nods to Luke.

Luke here is driving south, she says. *To Phoenix, then Mexico.*

I look at her, like, so what?

He's been telling me about these . . . what were they?

Ancient ruins. Pre-Columbus. They're at the Agua Fria National Monument, like an hour south of here.

I know, I think. We passed it on the way up here.

I told Luke how fascinated I am by prehistory, says Mom.

I think: Oh yeah?

He's offered us a lift tomorrow, she goes on. *To see them. And then he'll bring us back here to our car. Does that sound fun, honey? We're on vacation, a day off our schedule can't hurt.*

It sounds WEIRD, is what it sounds like, since we'd be going back the way we've just come, and we're supposedly running away.

Also:

He's a man, I say. *Men are bad.*

Not all men are bad, says Mom.

67

I throw my hands up, like, what?

Teenagers, says Luke, and Mom laughs.

You're going to Flagstaff, right? asks Luke.

Mom nods. *To see Route 66.*

This is news to me but I don't say anything.

Shame, says Luke. *If you were going south too, we could travel together.*

Shame, says Mom. *Still, we've got the ruins, tomorrow.*

Yep, says Luke. *We've got tomorrow.* The way he says this is nauseatingly romantic.

They stay by the fire for a while, chatting, laughing. They talk Apache culture, which I'm surprised to find Mom knows something about. The Navajo Star Chant, whatever that is. Luke gets very excited about something to do with the four sacred colours, or something.

At several points, Mom touches Luke's arm and I nearly puke.

Finally, she says we've got to go to sleep. Luke offers his tent, but, thank God, Mom says no, that we'll be fine in our car.

We climb into the back seat, and kind of spoon together. Mom has brought sleeping bags, and we zip them together to make a duvet.

When we see Luke go into his tent, I tap Mom's shoulder.

What's the deal? I say. *With this Monument place. It's back the way we came.*

Exactly, says Mom.

What do you mean exactly? I thought we were running away.

We are. But now we're acting unexpected. I mean, your father wouldn't expect to find us at a tourist destination, with some guy. And if he tracks the rental car . . . well, we won't be in it. We'll be in Luke's car.

I have to admit there is some kind of logic to this.

This is all freaking me out, Mom, I say.

I know, honey, she says. *I know. But we'll get through it.*

OK, I say. I know we will, because she has said so.

I close my eyes and try to sleep. But there are constellations bursting behind my eyelids, and thoughts racing around like cats, and I can't settle. I open my eyes again and stare out at the darkness outside the window, the faint glow of the stars.

Clouds pass, and the moon is revealed, an eye opening.

And there, under the trees, is a coyote standing in the light of the moon outside the car.

I think: If a coyote crosses your path, turn back, or terrible things will –

But then I think: Screw that. This coyote has turned up like two times now, and it said that weird thing to me about how I would be given two lies and then the truth, and I've had just about enough of people messing with my head. People, coyotes, whatever.

I close my eyes for a long moment.

I open them.

And the coyote is gone, like it was never there.

I'M IN THE HOSPITAL.

Not the hospital I was taken to after the car hit me. THE hospital. The one I end up in, again and again, when I'm sleeping. So there's a part of me that knows it's a dream, but it doesn't FEEL like a dream.

It feels real.

The walls are painted a yellow that is meant to be cheerful but just looks jaundiced. There are double doors in front of me, with round windows in them, the glass frosted. Behind the doors there is a child crying. I don't precisely HEAR the crying – I feel it, deep inside my bones. A resonance.

How can I describe it? The crying of that child? It's . . . it's beyond distress. It's beyond pain. It's NEED. This child needs me; this child has been hurt or abandoned and it needs to be held, to be comforted.

I feel the pull of the child – I have to find it, I have to stop it crying, even though at the same time I know this is just a dream. I look around, I feel like doctors should be running, nurses, to this child – I mean, the walls are shaking with its crying – but there is no one.

I push open the doors.

I always do this.

The crying is worse now. Not louder, but more insistent. I am 100 per cent freaked out, and now I only 50 per cent know this is a dream. The room I have stepped into is too solid, too detailed, to be imaginary. I'm in a square waiting room open at the other end, where there is a corridor that leads – I know – to another waiting room, and branching off that are the examination rooms.

There are plastic chairs set out in the first waiting room, but they're empty. To my right is a wooden kitchen, for young kids to play with. I walk past it. There's a low table with Legos on it. Another with magazines for the parents, jumbled up, all of them tattered and old. I pass a poster that says

IF YOUR CHILD HAS CHICKEN POX
OR HAS BEEN EXPOSED TO CHICKEN POX,
TELL RECEPTION IMMEDIATELY

I'm at the reception desk now. There are two computers behind it, papers, phones. A bell you can ring. But I don't ring it; no one would come. I know that because I have done it before.

Opposite the reception desk, on the other wall of the corridor, is an old rocking horse, its paint faded and peeled. It's enormous – like a horse from a fairground ride. It must be a hundred years old. The mane looks like it's made from real horsehair. Next to it is a plaque.

DONATED BY ROCKING RESTORATIONS, JUNEAU

All this time the child is crying, I can feel it in my bones. I am drawn towards it, irresistibly. I want to touch the horse, touch its hair, the worn smoothness of its saddle, but I can't.

I have to follow the crying. It's filling me now, it's not so much in my ears as in my head. The terror, the need. The loneliness.

The corridor is short, and there's no door at the end – it just opens into the second waiting room, with the doors along its walls, where the doctors see people. I don't know how I know what's behind the doors, but I do. I move quickly – the child is in the second waiting room, waiting for me, crying for me.

The child is always in the second waiting room.

I reach the open doorway. There are the doctors' doors. And to my right, another corridor, leading deeper into the hospital. An arrow is on the wall, and next to it, in green, restroom signs – a man and a woman in simple silhouette, the woman known by her triangle dress. Below it is a low shelf with picture books on it.

More plastic chairs.

And sitting in the middle of the floor, next to a play mat with grey roads and green fields, is the child.

It's a little girl, she's a little girl, maybe two years old. She is cross-legged on the floor, wearing a dress with birds on it, and her head is tilted up and she's crying, crying, crying. Her chubby arms are wrapped around herself, her hair is tied back in a tiny ponytail. In one of her hands is a stuffed grey bunny, at least I think it's a bunny, I'm not exactly sure because it's pressed into her body, but I see the long ears. Her whole body is shaking with her fear and her need.

I move quickly to the centre of the room, and she looks up and sees me, and just for one moment her big brown eyes look into mine and she stops crying – breath hitching in her chest, as if catching on something – and then she starts again, even louder than before, reaching her hands out for me to pick her up. I can see now that it definitely is a bunny she's holding. Soft, plush fur, worn and shiny as if it's been washed lots of times.

I bend down, put my hands under her arms, I'm about to feel the weight of her, to hoist her into the air and hold her tight against me, to stroke her hair and tells her it's going to be OK, it's going to be OK, to –

And then I wake up, with a start; I'm all twisted up in my sleeping bag, drenched in sweat.

Mom sits up next to me. She turns on a flashlight. *What's wrong, honey?* she says.

Nothing.

You're crying, Shelby.

Just a bad dream, I say.

The little girl? she says.

Yes.

She puts her arm around me. *Tomorrow is a new day*, she says.

I lean into her. *I'm scared, Mom*, I say.

I know.

Is Dad . . . I mean . . . He really wants to kill us?

She sighs. *He's a very bad man*, she says. *But I'll keep us safe. I promise you, I'll keep us safe.*

I close my eyes and we stay like that for a moment, in the flickering light of the flashlight, in the back of the rental car. I feel OK, the amped-up emotion of the dream is fading, the painful urge to comfort that child, to stop her crying, and I'm in the car with Mom, I can feel the warmth of her – it's hard to imagine some guy, some father I never knew, turning up and breaking into this picture.

Still.

Still, it's a promise she can't keep, her promise to protect me, and part of me already knows it.

5 . . .

CHAPTER
12

THE NEXT MORNING, LUKE cooks eggs. Then we get into his car. He actually watches me fastening my seat belt, making sure. He starts talking to Mom about side impact or something but I'm not really paying attention.

We pull out from the little campsite, leaving our rental car behind, and follow the road down from the forest to the desert plateau. I take shotgun, and Mom rides in the back.

I coulda worked around here, says Luke as we drive, sort of to himself. He's looking around at the trees, the rocks. *Nice and cold. Hell, where I was in El Paso, every other day in summer we were breaking down a door to find an old lady who'd cooked herself, 'cause she was scared to go outside, with all the dealers on the corners.* He turns to me. *They can't afford air-conditioning*, he adds, as if this needs explaining.

I say nothing. I can see sweat beading on Luke's forehead, and it's got to be only forty degrees. His dead eye is focused on the sky, or a squashed bug on the windshield. I love being in Luke's car. I love how my life has got so weird lately and now I'm riding shotgun in a weird old half-blind guy's car. It's THE BOMB.

I can tell Mom isn't too happy either, no matter how good an actress she turns out to be – the dead old women stuff has freaked her out too, and she's fidgeting, I can feel her feet rubbing against the back of my seat.

Here they've got the hikers, I guess, he says. *Mountain bikers. But what's that? Broken legs? And no smell. Really, the smell, with those old women . . . Yeah. A couple of skiers and climbers, just extreme-sport dumbasses stupid enough to break their own limbs? I could have dealt with that.*

Then he swallows.

I . . . ah . . . I mean, present company excepted, he says. *From the whole dumbass thing, you know.*

I look down at my leg and remember I was supposed to have broken it climbing. Crap, I'm going to have to speak. This is going to be the first time I've spoken to him. I can feel Mom's nerves behind me, like there's an electrical storm suddenly brewing in the car; clouds gathering, sparking.

I lick my lips.

That's fine, I say.

She speaks! says Luke, and it's totally cool, he's laughing, and then Mom's laughing. The storm breaks, and in the car the sun bursts through clouds. The relief is enormous, like someone was standing on my chest that whole time, and I only half knew it, and now they have stepped off.

Luke turns off when we get to the sign that says AGUA FRIA NATIONAL MONUMENT. We follow something called Bloody Basin Road, which seems like a bad omen to me, until we get to a parking lot.

Luke pulls up and stretches when he gets out of the car. There is literally no one else here. It's not exactly Disneyland, of course. Grassland, with little shrubs, stretches out to the end of the world, where mountains rise, purple against the pale blue sky. A couple of cacti prod the air with their fingers, reaching for the torn clouds. The words that come to mind are:

Vast.

Epic.

Enormity.

I've never been beyond the desert just outside Phoenix, I've never seen anything like this before in my life. It's like standing in the landscape from a story, the way it stretches to the horizon, the dreamlike quality of it. It is just unbelievably beautiful.

As I'm standing there, probably with my mouth open, a couple of deer appear on a rise just in front of us, silhouetted for a moment against the sky. Deer! For a second a bad thought goes through my head, like a twinge of neuralgia – the coyote, standing outside the car last night.

But no. I imagined that, or something.

The deer see us and spook; they spring into the air like a weapon being fired, and ghost away down the other side of the low hill. An after-image of their bodies, elegantly in flight, burns against my retinas.

Sacred animal, says Luke.

He reaches in the back of the car and takes out a couple of bottles of water – big ones, like gallon ones. He also puts a compass in his pocket, along with his knife.

You think we're gonna get lost? says Mom. I'm still watching the beautiful scenery in front of me so I'm only half concentrating on their conversation.

I've treated people for sunstroke and [   ] who only went for a walk in the woods behind their [   ]. I don't take chances.

79

Mom: [   ], giggling.

Me: barf.

Luke gestures to the path and we follow, me going slowly on my CAM Walker.

Luke stops when he sees me walking gingerly on it. *You sure you shouldn't wait in the car?* he says.

Yeah, Shelby, says Mom. *Maybe you –*

I'm fine, I say, as loud and clearly as I can.

We're on a little plateau within the larger plateau, next to a miniature canyon that opens on a tiny creek that runs silvery below us. We come to some ruins – little low stone walls, all fallen down.

Is this Apache? says Mom.

No, says Luke. *It's P–*

I don't get what he says after that but it doesn't matter because there's a sign, telling us not to leave the path or touch the ruins, and it says that these ruins belong to the Perry Mesa culture and date from around 1,000 CE. They predate the Apache, Yavapai or Navajo, and not much is understood about their culture.

Luke is gesturing at everything, beaming, like it's all really exciting and not some stones.

I roll my eyes at the crappy ruins and Luke sees me.

Ah, he says. *But it's the [   ] that we're really here for.*

I frown at him.

Pe-tro-glyphs, he says. *Rock paintings. Over a thousand years old.*

I shrug.

He takes out a little guidebook and leafs through it. Then he points to the canyon over to the right. *Down there,* he says.

Down there? says Mom. It's pretty steep – we can see the little ribbon of the creek, all green with algae, a long way below.

There should be a path, says Luke.

Suitable for a girl with a cast thing on her foot?

He frowns at me. *I don't know. Let's see.*

It turns out, though, that the path is quite smooth, and zigzags around the steepest section of cliff, taking us down into cooler and cooler shadow. It takes a while, especially with me hobbling, but then it's not like we have anything better to do.

Down there, when we step out from the shadow of the cliff, the creek is surprisingly wide, and when I look up I see why: the cliff towers above us, the plateau gone now, and we're locked away down here in a rocky ravine. Spiny trees grow on both sides of the lichen-green water, which runs sluggishly past us.

Luke consults the book again and then leads us along the creek, towards some other cliffs, lower, overhanging. He offers me his hand to help me over a couple of rocks, but I shake my head, and sit on them and then swing my heavy storm trooper leg around, using my butt as the fulcrum of a lever, and then limp past the fleshy leaves of a cactus. We come to the cliff face and Luke points up.

I look.

There, on the reddish wall of the rock, are little drawings scratched into the stone: deer, some kind of stag, geometric patterns.

Despite myself, I feel something resonate inside me, a plucked string. More than a thousand years ago, someone scraped these pictures into being. A man with a spear. A sun.

Luke turns to me and Mom. *This one is thought to be some kind of star map,* he reads from the book, while pointing to a circle, in which have been carved shapes like starbursts.

See how many elks there are? he says. He gestures, and shapes I hadn't quite discerned pop into being as I look at them, become antlered creatures, large deer.

Ah, I think. Not stags. Elks.

Elks were sacred to the Perry Mesa people, it seems like, he goes on. *The modern-day peoples here – the Yavapai, the Apache – don't particularly revere them. But there are so many of them on the rocks all around this area that they just have to be significant.*

He's no longer reading from the book, and I realise suddenly that this is his thing: prehistory, or Native Americans, or whatever.

Not that I'm complaining. I mean, rock paintings are 789 times better than stories about people being cooked alive and stuff.

We spend like an hour down there, in the creek. Not in the creek, you know what I mean. The ravine. A couple of times, Mom and Luke climb up somewhere I can't get to, looking at some pictures, but after a while they all look the same to me so I don't mind that I can't follow.

Finally, Luke seems to have had enough. *You want to get some lunch before we head back to camp?* he says. *I figure I'll stay there tonight again if you are. Mexico can wait another day.*

Sure, says Mom.

Luke turns and starts making his way up the path, back to the plateau. Mom glances at me. Then she picks up a heavy, smooth rock. She hefts it in her hand.

What are you doing? I say.

She looks down at the rock as if she doesn't know how it got into her hands, as if it materialised there. *Nothing,* she says. *But we need to switch cars.*

Luke is still walking, facing away from us, and Mom speeds up, still holding the rock.

I don't think: I just snap my foot out, putting my weight on the CAM Walker, and trip her. She goes down on one knee, the rock clatters off and comes to a rest by the stream. She stares at me.

What the hell, Shelby?

82

What the hell, MOM? What were you . . . were you going to knock him out? Was that your plan?

No.

Bullshit. I'm furious, all the pent-up confusion and frustration of the last twenty-four hours boiling over inside me, brimming past the point where I can contain it.

Mom is pissed too, she stands up and puffs her chest out, primal, facing up to me. Then she seems to catch herself, and I see something departing her eyes, like a sparrow taking flight, leaving her behind, and all the anger is suddenly gone from her and she kind of slumps.

But it's not like that's going to stop me – I mean, after everything that's happened, this last day, I feel like someone's pulled a rug out from under me. I hate it, and I've had enough of it.

For God's sake, Mom, I say. *Have you thought about this AT ALL? That rock could have killed him.*

She shakes her head.

Yes. And how do I know you're not going to try to, I don't know, tie him up tonight or something? That's your plan, right? Steal his car and then we can –

But Mom isn't paying attention, she's staring at something behind me, and there's a cold crawling thing on my spine, and I realise I got turned around on the path, and what's behind me is –

Luke, says Mom.

I turn.

He's been watching me, watching me speak; his mouth is open.

But mine is not.

Because I don't speak with my mouth, I have not been speaking with my mouth to Mom.

Wait, says Luke, looking at my hands. *You're deaf?*

CHAPTER
13

So yes, BTW, I'm deaf.

And Luke knowing that I'm deaf is SUPER AWESOME. Because now he's got a whole load of stories about deaf people getting hit by cars and stuff like that, and he tells them all as we have lunch at this little truck-stop diner. There's a particularly sweet tale about a cyclist who got dragged under a semi-truck because she didn't hear it coming – Luke uses the word 'hamburger' when he describes her body.

Worse still, Mom is on his side – she's all, like, *yes I worry about her so much on the street.*

She doesn't add that I don't go anywhere without her, maybe even she thinks she might be a tiny bit overprotective sometimes.

I have ten per cent hearing, I say. Of course I do: I wouldn't be able to lip-read so well otherwise.

Luke looks blank.

She says she can hear a bit, my mom translates, interpreting my hand gestures. *But not much. Sorry, she doesn't like speaking. Because she can't really hear herself, you know, her voice sounds weird.*

Yeah, thanks, Mom, I think. Way to build up my confidence.

I get that, says Luke. *But you could have told me, you know. I mean, it's no big deal, but just for safety, you know? It's nothing to be ashamed of.*

No, I think. No, it's not. Actually, I'm not sure why we didn't tell him; we both just kind of fell into it, or maybe my mom led me into it. Looking back, yes, I realise, she was the one who said something about me not speaking much. Cover, I guess, because my father is looking for someone with a deaf daughter? I make a mental note to ask Mom later.

Anyway, we've blown that cover now, and with all of Luke's gross stories, I'm kind of wishing by the time the cheque comes that I had let Mom brain him with this rock, which is totally what she was planning even though she denies it now.

The sun is already setting when we go back to the car – it was a late lunch, and Mom and Luke talked and laughed for a long time in the diner, like teenagers. It was, like everything to do with over-weight glassy-eyed Luke, THE BOMB. Especially when she touched his arm when he was speaking. I have made a particularly high-lighted mental note to myself to NEVER DO THIS when I'm speaking to a guy.

If I ever speak to a guy. Which if my mom gets her way is unlikely.

We get in the car and this time I go in the back so the two of them can talk in front – I can't see their lips so I don't know what they're saying.

Back at the campsite, Luke parks the car and then busies himself making dinner on the stove, to repay us for the burgers. I think it's some kind of chicken. He has cans of sauce and little plastic plates.

My foot is killing me, after the walk in the reserve, so I snag my backpack from the car. Mom packed me a make-up bag when we left the hospital and I put my two bottles of codeine in it – now I take two pills out and wash them down with a bottle of water from the front seat. Then I go back to the fire.

The whole time, I'm wanting to talk to Mom, grill her about, oh, the whole bashing-in-Luke's-head-with-a-rock thing, but I never get the chance because there's no way to get her on her own. Instead, we all sit together by the light of a fire that Luke has built and eat, and I wonder how soon I can say I'm tired and go to bed.

I say bed.

I mean car.

Because I totally sleep in a car now, with a woman who thinks nothing of picking up a rock to smash someone's head in. That is my life. And it is super!

To be clear, I'm being sarcastic here. It is not super AT ALL. It is so not super that I feel like I'm going to cry, only the tears won't come, and anyway you don't want to hear about that. It's depressing.

After a while, it's obvious that neither of them is paying much attention to me, so I get into the car and close my eyes.

When I open them, there's a blanket over me, and it's full night. I sit up – Mom isn't in the front seat, but I see the glow of a flash-light or something from Luke's tent. And I see two shadows in there, kind of intertwined. Oh, no.

Oh, no, no, no, no, no.

Not only is Mom no longer Shy Mom, but she's being un-shy over there in LUKE'S TENT. WITH LUKE. UGH, I think. And then an image flashes in my mind of Luke's double chin and I think, UGH, again, UGH X 10,000.

I die inside a little, that very moment. This is my mom, who has lectured me my whole entire life about being careful of men, about what they want, and how they get it, and here she is in Luke's tent.

At the same time, I'm worried about her. I mean, I know how it is. I know how much more Luke weighs than her, even though she's big. I know he could do anything he liked to her, hurt her, kill her.

Men are dangerous – I know that. Mom told me, but I watch a lot of TV, I could have worked it out for myself. I mean, the serial killer is never a woman, right?

So what is Mom doing putting herself in danger?

What is happening to her?

What is happening to me?

I think about those fairy tales Mom used to tell me, the ones about the changelings, where fairies would take a human child because they found it beautiful, and replace it with a fairy baby. Right now, though, it feels like Mom is the changeling, like she's been taken away and replaced with some other mother, some simulacrum, some clockwork woman.

I lie there, and I think how screwed up my life is, and I wish I could just be back in our apartment in Scottsdale, doing the same thing every day, living the old routine. I promise, I tell myself, closing my eyes. I promise, I'll never complain about going to the Grand Canyon again, or college, or whatever, if I can just go back to my old life.

Then I open my eyes again and I look out of the other window of the car and I see Mark standing there. Right out there, his feet on the pine needles. His eyes are kind of glowing. He is wearing the black jeans and white shirt he always wears, and he is smiling at me. I think about Mom, telling me how no one named Mark worked at the library. How no *man* worked there at all.

Blink.

Still there.

Of course, I say to myself – I'm dreaming. Mom isn't really in

Luke's tent, doing whatever it is she's doing with him. Mark isn't really standing on the forest floor outside the car. Everything is totally fine! Apart from the little fact that the father I always thought was dead is after us, and evidently has the power to check hospital records. Which is totally not fine!

But since this is a dream, just like the hospital, and so it makes zero difference what I do, I open the car door gently and get out, banging my storm trooper CAM Walker on the door as I do, only when I walk my leg doesn't hurt at all, which tells me it really is definitely a dream, to the MAX, because when Luke was driving it felt like someone was hammering nails into me.

Mark does not move, just keeps gazing at me with those glowing eyes as I approach. I'm on the other side of the car from Luke's tent, so they couldn't see me even if they weren't, ugh, busy.

There are pine needles on the ground and it feels like floating, as I walk over to Mark. I move smoothly, despite the CAM Walker. I still have my sweatpants on, with a slit down the side to accommodate the enormous boot. Mark stays very still. I can see his breath, turning to vapor in the night air, as if something inside him is smoking.

I'm really close now – I could reach out and touch him, but I don't really believe he's there. I think this is a dream again, like the child in the hospital. Maybe every time I've seen Mark it's been a dream, and I'm actually deeply mentally ill, maybe –

Mark reaches out and takes my hand.

Hello, Shelby, he says with his mouth.

CHAPTER
14

I touch Mark's cheek, still convinced that this isn't real.

He lets go of my hand.

How are you, Shelby? he says, in sign.

What?

How are –

I heard you, I say. *But I mean . . . what? What the hell? What are you doing here? Mom said there was no one at the library with your name. Who ARE you?*

Mark blinks his beautiful eyes and I see that they weren't glowing, before, they were just reflecting the moon. *You shouldn't trust everything your mother says*, he says.

I think of the coyote, saying *there will be two lies and then there will be the truth*. Was that the first lie then? Or was it . . . was it Mom telling me about Dad chasing us?

I hold Mark's gaze. *You're saying she was lying?*

I'm not saying that. I'm saying you shouldn't trust everything she says.

I shake my head. *I can't deal with this.*

I tried to save you, he says. *Outside the library. I tried to pull you back from the car. But I wasn't quick enough.*

It's OK, I say. *It's just my leg. Don't worry about me.*

But I do worry about you, he says.

Well, stop.

No, he says. *It's my job to worry about you. That's why I came.*

I close my eyes. I kind of hope when I open them he will be gone and I can go back to normalcy, but he's still there, still VERY there, I can smell the warm scent of him, weirdly comforting. *I don't understand*, I say. *Why are you here exactly?*

He smiles, but it's a sad smile. *I'm here to take you to the Dreaming*, he says.

I'm not dreaming now?

No.

No?

This scares me somehow, though I don't really know why. I mean, him saying it's not a dream doesn't mean anything; even if it were a dream, he'd probably say that. But there's something disturbingly real about the pine needles and moss below my feet – my foot, I should say, because only one of my feet is bare, the other is encased in a massive white exoskeleton – about the breeze on my face, Mark's cheek when I touched it, faintly raspy with stubble.

What the hell is going on?

Calm down, says Mark. *It's all right. I'm here to help you.*

Why?

Because you need help.

I hold his gaze without looking away. His eyes are like tunnels into forever.

Take my hand, he says.

He holds out a hand to me, like it's obvious to him that I'm going to do whatever he says, and maybe he's right, because I take it.

We're stepping sideways, he says. *Through the air.*

I don't know how to –

We step sideways, through the air.

For a moment, I'm still a girl.

Then I disappear, slowly, a Polaroid picture in reverse, washing out of existence. I look down to see my hands fade away, then my arms, then my body.

I am nothing but electrons and empty space between them, eons of space. In my eyes are pinwheels, blazing against the skylike darkness that is everywhere and everything, and at the same time is just my mind, spooling out to erase the world.

STARS.
EVERYTHING IS STARS.

CHAPTER
15

WHEN I OPEN MY eyes again, the world has come back. Or some world has come back, because I sense instantly that we're not in the same place.

We're in a forest, still, but it's *more* forest. I don't know how to explain it. It's like . . . like seeing a movie in 3-D. It's just . . . *more*.

Or, OK, like when the first day of summer comes, and you forgot that the light could do that, flood everything, submerge it in brightness; except that here it's night, and the stars are doing the illuminating, a trillion stars, glowing brightly like dust in the sky. The colours are more vivid than the forest I left behind, the leaves are more finely traced, more detailed. It's crazy.

The cars have gone, and the gravel, and we're in a tiny clearing and it's just trees in every direction, and thorny undergrowth, and the light of the stars is very dim because of all the leaves above us, making a lace brocade of glow on the forest floor. I notice that the trees are kind of brown and sick looking.

Also, both my feet are on the ground. I mean, obviously. But in the sense that I am not wearing the CAM Walker any more. I am barefoot, the cold forest floor beneath my skin.

Where are we? I ask. At least I think I do – but speaking is suddenly strange, and it comes from the world outside me but also inside my head.

We're in the Dreaming, says Mark. His voice is happening in my mind, not outside it; he's no longer speaking with those graceful gestures of his. His voice is entering through my ears and into my head; it's an experience I've never had before, not really.

I touch my ears. I . . . your voice is in my head, I say.

Yes, he says. It is called hearing.

I can . . . I can hear?

Yes, he says. In the Dreaming, yes.

I stare at him. It's so beautiful, his voice, I can't express it at all; it's the most beautiful thing I have ever experienced. I can hear it, loud and clear, rippling in the air, vibrating in my eardrums. Till now, all I've heard is static and faint sounds; now I'm standing in this weird forest and I realise that there are multiple strange sensations coming through my ears, that's the only way I can describe it. Faint, scratching *resonances*, from the outside world, from the forest. I realise that as well as Mark's voice I can hear some kind of bird calling, and insects crawling in the undergrowth, and the rustle of leaves in the moving air.

And then . . .

Suddenly . . .

I am crying.

Oh crap, I am crying, tears running down my cheeks like something has melted at the front of my mind and is leaking out.

Then I love the Dreaming, I say, and I don't need to move my hands to say it, I just open my mouth and speak, and I hear my own voice in my ears, the voice of a stranger.

Good, isn't it? says Mark. It's a place of magic.

I know this already. I don't just hear the forest, I *feel* it. Or maybe it's better to say that it feels me and I just know it; I sense it, all around us; it coils; it can see in the dark.

Yes, I say. But, I mean, what is it? Where are we, really?

There was a time before time existed and that is called the Dreaming, and that is where we are, he says.

Oh, that clears it up, I say. Basically it's a dream, right?

No, he says. It's not a dream. It's the Dreaming.

What I mean is . . . I say. What I mean is, it's not real. You're not real. This place isn't real. I'm imagining it all. Obviously.

The things you imagine are not real? he says.

Well, no, I say.

How do you know?

What?

A dream, he says, is real to *you*. While it is happening, you are not aware you're dreaming, correct?

I guess. Sometimes.

So it's a kind of reality. Just a reality personal to you.

I laugh. An illusion, in other words, I say. I mean, if my mom woke up, would I be gone from the car?

Mark shrugs. I don't know.

Because surely that's the test of whether something is real, I say. Whether more than one person experiences it. And according to Mom, you don't even *exist*, so you don't count.

I exist, he says.

Who says?

Me, he says, and smiles.

I roll my eyes, exasperated. OK, I say. So we're in some sort of dream that you insist is real, but what am I –

95

The Dreaming, he says. Not a dream.

Whatever, I say. The point is –

Then suddenly, the sound of the forest, the rustle and hiss and crackle all around me, gets suddenly louder. All of this is INSIDE my head, like Mark's voice, something that has not yet ceased to amaze me. I glimpse fur, rushing towards us – foxes, badgers. And a clattering of wings as birds approach, hawks, beaks extended before them like weapons.

Mark hisses and squeezes my hand.

This is Shelby, he says in a formal but quick tone, his voice suddenly echoing slightly, as if we have entered an invisible cave of hard rock. And she enters the Dreaming on my sufferance, at my forfeit, and under my protection. I stand for her.

A tension drops out of the air.

The birds reach us, and bank steeply, and shoot up into the trees and disappear; the foxes are undergrowth again and can't be seen. The forest is back to normal, which is to say, back to dying – because the more I look around me, the more I see that the leaves are blackening and shrivelling, the undergrowth at our feet dry and thin. Everything looks diseased, or thirsty maybe, like it hasn't rained here in the Dreaming for months.

You *stand* for me? I say.

Yes.

I stare at him. Who *are* you?

I'm Mark, he says.

Yeah right, I say.

He shrugs again, this is kind of his thing at the moment and it is getting super annoying. On the other hand, he is practically the only person apart from my mom I have ever spoken to, he was the only one I knew who could sign, and now I'm in this magical place with him and I can actually hear him with my ears and I love the sound of his voice.

What am I doing here, though? I say. What is the point of this? I mean, I know dreams don't have to have a point, but still.

The Dreaming is suffering, says Mark. He reaches to his side and pulls a leaf from a tree. It is little more than a tracery skeleton – ribs, held together by a gossamer gauze of brown tissue. He blows on it and it scatters into dust.

Yeah, I can see, I say. Everything is really dry.

Dry and dying, says Mark. He indicates a flower that is bent over, most of its curled-up petals on the ground.

What does that have to do with me? I say.

Everything, says Mark.

What, why does –

But then there's a high, plaintive howl, coming from somewhere behind us in the forest.

Alarm floods Mark's eyes. We have to move, he says urgently, in a low tone. Wolves.

You can't tell them you stand for me, like you said to the foxes and whatever?

He laughs a hollow laugh. No, he says. Wolves serve the Crone.

The Crone? I say.

An owl hoots.

Owls also serve the Crone, says Mark.

Who is the Crone? I say. What does this have to do with –

Quiet, says Mark. Just go.

This really doesn't seem like the time for arguing, so I hurry behind him, and it seems like we go for hours, jumping over roots, twisting to avoid trees. Even though I haven't been wearing the CAM Walker long in the real world, it's extraordinary now to be without it, to glide through the forest, over the grass and moss and twigs, barefoot. It feels primal and free, and I would be enjoying it – the air in my lungs, the rhythm of the running – if it weren't for the howls behind us, gaining. Getting louder.

Mark stops for a moment and frowns, deeply.

Then there's another high-pitched howl, very close this time. I look where he's looking, and see eyes glinting in the depths of the forest, and hear snarls. Deep, hungry snarls.

I have only been able to hear for less than an hour but those snarls speak to something very, very deep inside me, something older than I thought I was, and I realise it's a human instinct from a million years ago, buried in my genes.

It says *RUN*.

CHAPTER
16

I START RUNNING. THE forest flashes past, leaves and tree trunks strobing, like slowed-down celluloid film.

My legs piston along, my breath rasping in my throat; I don't know when I last ran like this. I am gasping.

Then suddenly I'm not running but lying down, and I'm looking up at Mom and she is shouting, gesticulating wildly. SHELBY? SHELBY, HONEY? TIME TO WAKE UP.

Then I snap back into the Dreaming and I'm running again, flying over the forest floor, jumping to clear some roots, stumbling over a rocky section, then splashing through some sucking mud where a stream must have been – I can see its banks, though there is no water flowing.

I run and run, following Mark's fleet, agile form, duck under some ivy and then –

Tree trunk.

I swerve left, miss the tree by inches, but there's a root elevated above the mossy ground and I don't notice it till my foot hooks under it and I go right over, smash my chin into the ground and do a clumsy roll, then lie there winded on my back.

Mark appears above me, looking down at me with concern in his grey eyes. *Shelby, rise and shine!* he says.

Huh? I say.

Get up, he says.

Then again:

Get up.

What are you talking about? I say. Just then he disappears, as does the lacework of leaves above him, the tracer-fire of the brown vegetation, and instead in its place is the grey fabric of a car ceiling – is it called a ceiling in a car? – and the little light you can turn on, or set just to illuminate when the doors are open, and Mom is there leaning over me and –

Mark frowns as a wolf howls, close behind us.

You are flickering in and out of this world, he says.

What does that mean? I say.

Mark closes his eyes, then opens them again. It means you have to go, he says. I will be back for you. But you must get up and step through the air now.

On my own?

Yes.

But I don't know how.

You do. You just don't know that you do.

Oh, that's helpful, I say.

He grabs my arm and levers me up into a standing position. Then he presses a knife into my hand.

Hold this, he says. Close your eyes. The knife knows who you are and knows its way back to the Dreaming, and so do you, deep down. Then take a step sideways. If you need to get back here, to me, you do the same thing – but from your side of the air.

I don't know –

Yes, you do. But be fast. And remember, I will be back for you.

We must rescue the Child within a matter of days, or your world ends.

Days? I say.

Yes, he says. Days. Now move. Step through the air. Do it.

And I do.

4 . . .

CHAPTER
17

I'M IN THE CAR, under a blanket, where I started off. Mom is leaning over me, frowning. I look down and see that I'm shaking.

What? What? I say.

It's morning, honey, she says.

Oh.

Did you have a nightmare?

I look at her. *Uh, yes, I guess*, I say.

Sorry, honey.

When I realise that her voice isn't in my head, that she's speaking to me with her hands, I nearly cry. For a moment, I wish so powerfully that I was back in the Dreaming again, that it's like a pain in my chest.

Luke made eggs, she says. *He has a kerosene stove.*

Mom helps me to lever myself out of the car, swinging the heavy CAM Walker out and down. I stand slowly – the pain is back in my leg, a constant throbbing, like there's another heart down there, a big one. Mom goes over to Luke.

That's when I feel something hard pressing against my other leg, and I check my sweatpants pocket. My hand closes around a handle of bone, and I gingerly touch the blade below it, and yes, it's the knife that Mark gave me.

In the Dreaming.

What the hell?

I try to calm my breathing, because now Luke and Mom are looking over at me. I smile and point to my right leg, as if to say, I got a twinge of pain, you know?

Mom clasps her hands over her chest like, poor sweetheart, and Luke gives me a sympathetic look. Then they beckon me over.

I leave the cocoon of the car; step out into the forest. It is silent. After the Dreaming it is so silent. The birds have swallowed their song, the wind has closed its mouth, the leaves are still and their rustling is gone. I feel like I am going to cry all the tears. All of them.

But no. I need to reserve some tears for the whole Luke and Mom situation.

Because I look at them and I see the way Luke's and Mom's hands touch as he hands her a plastic plate of eggs, and a pang of – what? Hurt? Jealousy? Both? – shoots through me. But I sit down anyway and accept my own plate, and also some muddy, bitter coffee that Luke has brewed who knows how.

I can still feel the knife pressing into my leg. Its bone handle, its blade. I try to mentally will it into disappearing, into not being there.

Only . . .

Only . . .

I can't get one feeling out of my head: it's the feeling of sound, glorious sound, trickling into my ears, buzzing in my head. I know already that I would go back to the Dreaming again in a second, if I could, that I would embrace madness like an old friend – if madness is what it is – just to hear those leaves in the breeze again, just to hear my own voice.

After breakfast, Luke walks into the forest, I guess to use the bathroom. Mom comes quickly over to me.

Are you OK? she says.

Yes. Why?

You look pale, honey.

Oh, I say. *I'm just worried, I guess. About what's going to hap-pen to us.* This is at least partly true. OK, 100 per cent true. I mean, what IS going to happen if my dad, who I always thought was dead and gone, catches up with us? Is he seriously going to kill us? What kind of lunatic does something like that?

I understand, Mom says, her hands moving quickly. *I'm sorry about that. But right now I have to do something. We'll discuss it later.* She looks over to the forest, checking that Luke isn't coming back, then steps to the front of the car and pops the hood, then bends over it. I see her disconnect some stuff, and pull on some other stuff.

Mom, I say. *What are you doing?*

But she doesn't answer me. She sits in the front seat, and turns the ignition. Then she nods, satisfied.

Mom.

She comes over to me. She touches my hair, brushing a strand of it behind my ear. Her hand is trembling a little. *We can't keep the car*, she says. *It could be traced.*

I blink. *Traced?*

Yes. It's not safe. This way we can hitch a ride with Luke.

This is insane, I say.

She gets like a pained expression. *I know*, she says. *I'm sorry. But it's better than hitting him with a rock, huh?*

Uh, yeah, but that doesn't –

107

She shakes her head. *I wish it were –*

She turns, suddenly, because Luke is waving to her, smiling broadly, as he returns from the forest.

A short while later, after everything is cleared away, Mom says we have to get going – we want to be in Flagstaff this morning.

Special plans? says Luke.

Oh no, says Mom. *But we do want to see Route 66, don't we, honey? Before we go on to the Canyon.*

I look at her and she shoots me daggers, and I nod.

She makes a big show then of getting me into the front seat, which is super annoying because I know that she has sabotaged the engine and I'm going to have to get back out again, but I don't say anything. I watch while she puts on a dumb show of trying to start the engine, throwing up her hands, the whole works.

Then she gets out and pops the hood again.

Luke comes over and I know Mom so well that I can read just in the movement of her face that she's really, really hoping he doesn't know mechanics. But from the way he looks at the engine I can tell he doesn't.

Damn rental car, says Mom.

You have a cell? asks Luke.

Mom reaches into the car and snags her cell from her purse. She checks it. *No coverage,* she says.

Luke starts for his car. *You can use mine,* he says. *Call the rental company.*

Well . . . says Mom.

Luke stops. His face is hope and suspicion, mixed. I don't know who this person is who's stepped into my mom's skin, but she freaks me out.

108

I'm thinking ... says Mom. *We don't have that long for our vacation. If we have to wait for the tow truck ... I mean, say you gave us a ride to Flagstaff. Then we could rent another car, to get to the Canyon, and we could call Hertz and tell them to come pick up this one. And no one ...*

... wastes their time, says Luke, considering.

What do you say? asks Mom. *You have space for two more?*

Watching Luke's face, it's fascinating. You can see that he doesn't buy it, that he has figured by now something weird is going on, but that he really, really wants to. *Sure,* he says eventually, *I mean it was fun yesterday, right? We may as well stick together for another day.* He has walked all the way back now and he kicks the tyre of the rental.

You don't want to travel in this anyway, he says. *I don't even know how many people I've seen cut out of these. The crumple zone is a piece of crap.*

CHAPTER
18

FLAGSTAFF IS COLD, WHEN we get there like an hour later. If Alaska has fingers of rain, then Flagstaff has teeth of ice.

It's high up, that's why, like thousands of feet, and it couldn't be more different from Phoenix. It's got history, for one thing. There's a bit of the old Route 66 that runs through it, and you can still see the Fifties motels that people used to stay in. There's also a full-on downtown, with stores and buildings of more than three storeys pretty much everywhere.

Phoenix is surrounded by desert; Flagstaff is surrounded by forest, mostly pine, and mountains. It's almost alpine, a palette of blues and greys and greens, where Phoenix is just all shades of red.

That's the historic Weatherford Hotel, says Luke as the car noses down the main street, like he's some kind of fricking tour guide. *It's been there since, like, pioneer days.*

I look – it's OK, I guess. Like the saloon in *Deadwood*, with a wooden balcony running around the outside of it.

Amazing, says Mom, and I make a barfing motion that she doesn't see, or chooses not to.

We're cruising the streets, looking for somewhere to park for lunch. It's cute, I have to admit. Old-style buildings, wooden beams, that kind of stuff. We pass a store called Gene's Western Wear, with cowboy hats in the window, and boots, and then a climbing store called the Flagstaff Climbing Store, which must have taken a full second to think up, and the window is all ropes and crampons or whatever they're called.

It's mostly a tourist economy now, says Luke, who has obviously read some kind of book. *The Grand Canyon, obviously. But also skiing in winter. 'Course, if you want to ski and end up in a coma, you're welcome, far as I'm concerned.*

It seems affluent, says Mom, who is leaning forward into the space between me and Luke from the back, in her stupid fake-friendly chatting way. I'm in the front – more space for my leg to stretch out. *Like there's a lot of [   ],* she continues, but I don't catch that last bit because she sits back in her seat.

Oh yeah, well, there's big companies here too, says Luke. *Walmart has a distribution centre. And there's the astronomical telescope.*

Who'd a thunk it? I want to say.

We circle, looking for a parking spot.

We pull up by a meter, and Luke gets out. Mom shouts after him; hands him some coins from her purse. He pays and we walk a short distance down the street to the Downtown Diner. I'll say something for Luke: he stuck it out for a space close to the restaurant, so I wouldn't have to walk far.

Mom helps me out of the car and I stand up. It's rained, sometime recently – I'm not used to this, from living in Phoenix, but I can see it glistening on the sidewalk and the road, and smell it as it evaporates into the air; it smells like the earth is opening its secret heart to me. I feel it seeping into my pores, the moisture in the air.

I almost want to close my eyes and breathe it in, but I don't.

Ugh, feel that? says Mom.

What?

The rain, in the air.

Yeah, I say. *It's cool. I like it.*

She shakes her head in disgust. *It's wrong,* she says. *It's not natural, the air all wet like that. Sooner we get back to the desert the better.*

Luke turns. *You two coming?* he says.

We grab pizza at an Italian place and as we're eating it, Luke gives Mom a little complicit smile that makes me want to puke. *So,* he says. *You going to call the rental-car company?*

I don't know, says Mom. *What's your plan?*

He shrugs. *Check out some of the [   ]. Head to the Grand Canyon.*

Today? asks Mom.

No. It's like a three hours' drive from here. I thought I'd check into one of the motels. Flagstaff is kind of famous for them. Old art [   ] motels from like the glory days of Route 66, you know? Kitsch, but in a good way.

Route 66 goes through here? asks Mom, faux-naive like she has not known this forever.

Yep. And a couple of the old motels are still open.

Mom nods and smiles and I know what she's going to say before she says it, I can read it in her face.

Well, she says, *maybe we'll stay one night here too. I mean, before we get our car. How could we miss out on [   ]?*

Luke grins. *Great,* he says.

I look at him. Is that a friendly grin or a wolf grin? Mom says all men can be dangerous, but how can you tell when they are?

After lunch we head to the car but Mom makes Luke stop as

we pass Gene's Western Wear – she puts her hand on his arm; the touch looks very deliberate and he smiles at her quizzically.

What? he says.

I want a hat, says Mom.

The store is on a corner. The sign says that it's not just Gene's Western Wear but also a SHOE HOSPITAL. We walk in and it's like stepping back in time. There's a guy in chaps and a leather apron, with a grey moustache and nearly bald head, who smiles at us and welcomes us to Gene's.

One whole wall is just rows of cowboy boots. There are bull-horns on the walls and rodeo posters.

Mom finds a rack with cowboy hats on it – I'm surprised by how expensive they are. Like, hundreds of dollars, some of them. She picks a pink one and puts it on her head, at a tilt. She winks at Luke and he laughs.

That one, he says. *Definitely.*

She leaves the hat on, picks up another, a grey one with a red band around it. *Here, Shelby*, she says.

I shuffle up, glaring at her. She kind of spins the hat on her finger and lands it on my head. *Perfect*, she says.

I look in the mirror. I look like a different person. A different, weirder person.

[   ], says the guy with the moustache who greeted us. I feel him behind us though so I turn and he nods at me. *Nice choice*, he says. *You need any help?*

I think we're good, says Mom. *I think we'll take these.*

On me, says Luke.

Oh no – starts Mom.

No, I insist, says Luke.

Well, hey, says moustache. *What are husbands for?*

113

And Mom . . . Mom DOES NOT CORRECT HIM. She just laughs, and Luke doesn't correct him either; he takes the two hats to the counter and pays for them with his credit card.

We leave the store and Mom puts on her hat and tells me to do the same. It's only then that I realise – because apparently I'm an idiot – that she's *disguising* us. She's dressing us in hats and making us go around with Luke and she's happy that people think he's her husband because we look like a family, we don't look like a mother and a daughter on the run.

But won't my dad recognise her? I mean, if he sees under the hat?

But then I think:

1. Maybe not. It's been years, hasn't it? I mean, I always thought he was dead, and I'm seventeen, so he's been gone for like fifteen years at least.

2. Who even knows if my dad really is chasing us? The coyote said there would be two lies and then the truth, and of course I probably didn't see the coyote anyway and it was just a hallucination, from the shock of being, oh, HIT BY A CAR, but there's still something seriously weird up with Mom, and I don't know that I believe anything she's saying at the moment.

So.

Sigh.

I put on the hat anyway and we all wander around Flagstaff for a bit, checking out the different stores, looking in the window of the bookstore, the climbing place, and so on. Luke jokes about how I must have been put off climbing now, surely, with my injury, and I try to fake a smile.

114

If you think an injury's going to put her off, says Mom, *then you don't know the teenage mentality.*

I don't know, he says, *I feel kinda like a teenager right now*, and he gives her this significant look.

And I spray vomit from my mouth and nose all over him, a great geyser of sick and –

No, not really.

Like an hour later, we go back to the car.

Oh wait, says Mom.

Yeah?

I need to go back and grab something. You two don't go any-where.

Oh yeah, sure, I think. Like with my CAM Walker and Luke's massive boner for my mom we're going to be rushing off somewhere. We stand by the car for like ten minutes before Mom comes back carrying a bag that says FLAGSTAFF WINE AND LIQUOR on it.

We get in the car and Luke drives us out of town and back to the highway. I grab my make-up bag from my backpack and take two codeine pills from it – my leg is aching after all the walking around town.

I dry-swallow the codeine and it's probably my imagination but it's like the throbbing eases almost immediately.

We turn on to Route 66 and as the sun lowers in the sky, we take the off-ramp to the Wagon Wheel Motel.

There's an old neon sign at the entrance to the parking lot. WAGON WHEEL is lit up in bright blue, and underneath it is MOTEL in those yellow-bulb letters, like a Broadway show. Riding above the whole sign is a train of horses pulling a wagon, the horses made of various neon tracks so that as the light cycles, they seem to gallop.

115

Underneath is one of those signboards churches have, where the letters can be rearranged. At the moment they are saying:

VACANCIES
EUROPEAN HOSTESS
WKLY SPECIALS
HBO COFFEE
BIG RANCH

I find it strange that they have to specify they have coffee – wouldn't any motel have coffee? And what's the deal with the European hostess? But as we park up in the parking lot in front of the low building, Mom is all clasping-hands-cutely.

It's historic, says Luke.

I can see that, says Mom.

We get out of the car and go into the reception, where a girl who must be no older than me checks us in, looking like she might die of boredom at any moment. Her fingernails are painted all in different colours and she's chewing gum and smells of cigarette smoke. Her skin is sallow.

How many rooms? she says.

Three? says Luke. *Or do you and Shelby want to share?*

How about two? says Mom. *Shelby can sleep on her own, she's old enough.*

It takes a while for this to sink in, for Luke, but then he flushes and smiles. *OK*, he says.

OH GOD KILL ME NOW.

116

CHAPTER
19

IN THE END WE get a suite, which the receptionist tells us has a main bedroom, with a little seating area and TV and stuff, and then another bedroom adjoining it.

You two head up, says Mom, when we go back to the car with the key from the bored reception girl. *I'll be right behind you. Shelby, I'll bring our bags.*

Sure, says Luke.

He snags his own bag and we go up the stairs – our room is 213, on the second floor. He wants to help me up the steps, but I shake my head and hold on to the rail instead, half lifting myself up with my CAM Walker. It takes ages – by the time we get to the top Mom is pretty much right behind us anyway.

I turn, as we walk along the walkway to the room. You can see mountains in the distance, forest, across the blurred brightness of the highway. The parking lot is only half full and as I look, a cop car turns in, headlights on but blues off. For a moment I have that feeling, you know the one? Where you're convinced they're here for you, though there's no rational reason to think so.

Or here for Mom? I mean . . .

But then they pull a little closer and are under a light and I see that the two cops inside are just eating something – burgers, maybe – from cardboard boxes, chatting as they have their meal. Something they bought from a drive-through, I guess. One of them lights a cigarette and rolls down his window, blows smoke out of it.

Not here for us, then.

I turn away and follow Mom and Luke, who are gesticulating at me impatiently from the doorway with 213 on it in peeling white paint.

We go in and it's fine – I mean, it's not charming, because what motel is? But it's clean and serviceable. There's a smell of some kind of pine-based air freshener, tingly and fresh and ever-so-slightly reminiscent of the Dreaming, but too chemical in its undertones to be more than a hint.

Mom takes my bag into this annexe bedroom and her own stuff to the main bedroom she's going to . . . share . . . with . . . Luke.

Ugh. Even *saying* that disgusts me.

What do you want to do? says Luke afterwards.

How about we order room service and watch a movie? says Mom. *They have HBO.*

Sounds good, says Luke. *Shelby?*

I just shrug at him and go to turn on the TV. But Mom gets up from where she's been sitting on the bed and stops me. *Why don't you take a bath, Shelby?* she says, with her hands. *We could all use a freshen-up.*

I look at her. *Uh, OK*, I say.

I left some stuff in the car, says Luke. *I'll go grab it, get some takeout menus from reception. You two girls do your thing.*

He leaves and I bring my make-up bag into the bathroom and Mom runs me a bath. *Don't look at me*, I say.

It's nothing I haven't seen before, she says.

It's not the same, I say.

Oh come on, I changed your diaper ten times a day when you were a baby.

I just glare at her until she sighs and closes her eyes as I undress. Then I take off the CAM Walker, and she kind of awkwardly helps me to cover my stitched-up foot in plastic bags while averting her eyes; I notice that one of them is the Flagstaff Wines and Spirits bag. She wraps elastic bands around them to make them watertight and then eases me into the water, her hands under my armpits.

I feel pissed off with her for making my entire life so weird and for bossing me around so much but I kind of forget that as I sink into the warm water because it's kind of amazing.

I soak in the tub for the longest time, before my foot starts to twinge again and I shout for Mom to come and help me out.

–*Don't look*, I say.

She crosses her heart and then mimes shooting herself, before closing her eyes and supporting my arm as I get out. I put on a nearly white robe hanging on the back of the door and hobble over to the sink, where my make-up bag is. I look inside and reach for –

Huh.

I could have sworn both bottles of codeine were still in there when I took some pills in the car. I try to picture the scene – the sun setting, the lights of the highway, the panel in front of me saying AIRBAG as I reached into the bag, leaning into the seat belt and –

And I can't fix the image in my mind. Maybe there was only one bottle then, and the other fell out somewhere. Fell out in the forest maybe? I hope I have enough left in this one bottle.

I count the pills in the bottle. Thirty-six – six days' worth if I follow the pharmacist's instructions. OK, fine. I toss back two of the pills and bend over to wash them down with cold water from the tap.

Then I go into the room, cinching my robe tight around me – I don't want it slipping off in front of Luke. He isn't there though; just Mom sitting on the bed reading some kind of tourist pamphlet.

I think the water's still pretty hot.

Thanks, she says.

I pick up the remote from the bedside table and point it at the TV; press the on button.

It's not working, says Mom, redundantly, as the TV fails to come on. There isn't even a red light on it, you know the standby light thing? The set is completely dead and again I could swear I saw that little red light before, blinking.

I shake my head. I'm losing it.

I glance at the table in the seating area – there's an open bottle of red wine and two coffee cups taken from the sidebar where the kettle is. The bottle is half empty – the rest of the wine is in the cups. So that's what Mom got in Flagstaff – wine for her and Luke.

I point the remote at the TV again and try to turn it on, even though I'm not expecting it to work.

Just then Mom turns to the door and I figure there's been a knock because then Luke comes in. He sees me holding the remote.

TV not working? he says.

I shake my head.

I'll call down, get someone to fix it, he says.

Oh no, says Mom. *We can just talk, don't you think? Get to know each other a little better.*

Ugh.

120

'Course, says Luke. *Shelby might want to watch –*

But Mom does this eyebrow thing at me and I sigh inside and shake my head, putting down the remote. Mom doesn't want the TV on, that's for sure. I am like 99 per cent sure she has unplugged it or cut the cable or something, and for the 156th time I reflect on how screwed up my life has become, so quickly.

As soon as we get some proper time alone me and Mom are having a SERIOUS talk. If I can think of how to ask the questions, anyway.

You get menus? says Mom.

Yep, says Luke. He holds up two folded sheets of glossy paper. *Mexican or Chinese.*

Mexican sounds good. Shelby?

I shrug. This is basically my signature move at the moment.

Mexican it is, says Luke.

Mom swings herself up from the bed and walks over to the little table. *I got us a little surprise*, she says. *Grand cru Bordeaux from Chateau [   ]. I thought once Shelby had gone to bed we could share it. It needs to breathe anyway, to ox[   ] the [   ].*

Luke looks pained; embarrassed. *I'm . . . I'm sorry*, he says. *I don't drink.*

Something flashes across Mom's face. Embarrassment too? No. It looks more like . . . anger? Or frustration? It's weird, anyway. But it's gone quickly and she smoothes her sweater and smiles. *Oh well*, she says. *More for me.*

Luke passes around the menu and we each choose what we want, then he calls up and orders the food.

When it comes, we eat our burritos and chips in silence, and then

Mom does this really theatrical yawn. *I'm so tired*, she says. *Shelby, you must be exhausted too.*

I look at her, and Luke is not in my sightline so I raise my eyebrows sardonically.

She narrows her eyes back at me.

Fine, I think. Fine, I'll leave the two of you to whatever sick game you're playing.

Sighing, I get up and CAM Walk over to the door to my little annexe room. I wave goodnight to Luke and go in and shut the door behind me, drop another couple of codeine tabs, then lie down on my bed, knowing that I will NEVER be able to sleep with the knowledge of what is going down in the room next to me.

There is only one source of solace.

This is an AMAZING time to be deaf.

I lie there and I can't hear a thing, can't hear Mom and Luke making out which I'm 1,000,000 per cent certain they're doing, and I'm so grateful for it I have no words. I'm also surprised to find that I AM tired, even though I have so many questions, have so much to ask my mom, so much to try to understand.

Like: why would my dad even want us dead?

What kind of psycho is he?

And what the hell is the Dreaming? Am I just going crazy?

I am thinking about that, my eyes closed, random fragments of the day spooling behind my eyelids – the streetlights, the cowboy hats, the rows of boots, the pizza from lunch, the way Mom smiles at Luke, when all these images fall away and there are only –

STARS, BEHIND MY EYELIDS

CHAPTER
20

– AND I'M STANDING IN the forest, Mark beside me.

Keep running, he says. Then takes off, the howling of the wolves loud behind us. Even though it's a scary sound, I'm glad to hear it, I'm glad to hear, period.

The leaves and twigs crunch beneath my feet, every rustle an explosion of pleasure in me. My feet free and swift without the CAM Walker. And if the wolves chew on my flesh at least I will hear them do it.

Another howl, even closer.

Hmm.

Maybe hearing them eating me wouldn't be such fun after all. I start running faster, my breath heaving in my chest. The smell of sap and decaying vegetation is in my nostrils.

Eventually the forest runs out, just like that, suddenly. In front of us is a vast prairie, spreading to the horizon. Mark holds his hand up for us to stop and we stand for a moment, still in the shadow of the forest. The prairie is dry, I see now – all the grass is dead.

Mark isn't even breathing hard, and I'm gasping for breath. Then he steps out on to the prairie, leaving the forest behind.

Come, he says. The wolves don't like to leave the trees.

I follow him, out on to the brown, dry grass. The landscape reminds me of the place we went to with Luke, the reserve – a vast landscape of grassland, stretching out to the horizon, creased with thin gullies and canyons. Above us, a dark mirror to the lightness of the grass, is an enormous bowl of night, studded with millions and millions of stars.

I look up, stunned, forgetting about the wolves behind us. I have never seen a night sky like this. The scale of it is just . . . I can't describe it. It's like it's the first time I have ever seen stars, really seen them, I mean. There are so many of them, it seems impossible.

I start to walk further out on to the prairie, wanting to look at the stars, and to get away from those hungry, hungry wolves I can still hear behind us, wanting to put as much space as –

but Mark reaches out a hand and closes it over my arm and I stop, stunned by his strength; it's like being held by a concrete pillar.

No, says Mark. They don't like to leave the forest, but they will if they have to. And we should not be on open ground when they come.

He turns and nods towards the forest. I look where he wants me to and see the glinting eyes again, the hard eyes of the wolves lurking there at the edge of the forest.

We stand here or not at all, he says.

Then he adopts a stance somewhat like the one I use in the batting cage. Hawks, he says, and his voice has gone strange again, has that echo in it. Foxes. Badgers. Will you stand?

His voice is urgent too. The words coming out fast, but with a strange kind of authority and shimmer. Like a tuning fork after the first bright shine of the note.

Nothing happens, but there's another feeling around us, like

125

when Mark spoke those words when I first entered the Dreaming, like the whole air is asking a question.

Mark nods.

And . . . and, well, movement happens.

It's not dramatic – it's more like there's a sense of feathers in the air, in there among the leaves, and the undergrowth is suddenly alive, and suddenly those gleaming eyes of the wolves are flicking around in panic, and it's as if the forest is eating them alive.

Then everything is still.

The wolf eyes are gone.

Mark waits for a moment, tilts his head, and nods again. Your sacrifice will not be forgotten, he says, but who he's saying it to, I don't know. I don't see anything moving any more.

What the hell? I say. Who *are* you? How come you can talk to badgers and hawks and foxes and whatever?

This is the Dreaming, he says.

I can only shrug in response to that. I mean, yeah. OK. It's the Dreaming. It figures. And anyway I'm weirdly glad to be here with him, with Mark – to be talking to someone who isn't my mother, even if it's someone who might not actually totally technically 100 per cent exist.

At least tell me what I'm doing here, I say.

I was trying to, he says. When the wolves came. You see the grass? The trees?

I look at the brown grass, desperate for water. At the trees, with their shrivelled leaves. I crouch down and touch the grass. It's dry as straw, colourless. There's a drought? I ask Mark.

It never rains, he says. Not any more.

Really, never?

Not any more. It used to be said, the Dreaming has a face of sunshine and fingers of rain, and it holds us all in its arms, and we will never want, for everything will grow. But now –

Wait, I say. What did you say?

But now –

No, about the rain.

He blinks. A face of sunshine and fingers of rain . . .

That, yes. Where did you hear that?

It is said.

Yes, but when?

Forever. Since the beginning of time. Since the Dreaming began.

I turn away from him. Whatever, I think. But I'm feeling pretty majorly unsettled by this whole fingers of rain thing. By the fact that this is almost exactly what my mom said about leaving Alaska.

Why doesn't it rain? I say.

Because of the Crone, he says. And it's getting worse. She will not allow it to rain. This is why we need you, in the Dreaming. She has stopped the rain and she has also captured –

Just then Mark whirls around, and I'm about to say, oh come on, you have to be kidding me, but then I follow his acute gaze, and I see a movement in the forest. Then there's a rustle of sound, the sound of leaves being parted by bodies, of twigs cracking underfoot.

Get behind me, says Mark.

We watch the leaves, trembling. We see branches pushing out towards us, a section of the forest seeming to bulge, as something begins to emerge. I begin to edge around behind Mark, my eyes always on the trees, and the wolves that are about to come out.

Then . . .

A spiked stick appears, I think for a moment it's a weapon, and then I realise that it's an antler. The branches part, and an elk moves out of the shelter of the trees. I recognise it from the rock paintings Luke took us to see.

Mark breathes out a sigh of relief and his body relaxes, a fist unclosing. Oh, he says.

The elk approaches us, big gentle eyes full of fear, its step trembling. It's afraid, but curious too. It stays a safe distance from us, but keeps its eyes on us.

People, it says, its words echoing within the walls of my head. In the Dreaming.

Yes, says Mark. Greetings, elk.

Greetings, man. Greetings, woman.

Uh, greetings, I say. To an elk. In a dream world. While my mom is screwing Luke in the real world. Then the elk comes a little closer and I look into its huge brown eyes and I am back in the moment again.

We are well met, says Mark to the elk, in that weird formal voice he used with the foxes.

Yes, we are well met, says the elk.

But where are your kin? says Mark.

The elk turns back to the forest. There's a loud sound of hooves passing over twigs and through leaves, and then a whole herd of them step out on to the dry brown grass of the prairie, some small and some large, their antlers twisting up into the night sky.

The wolves were chasing you, says the first elk, who seems to be the leader. Then they were gone.

Yes, says Mark.

You used some kind of human magic? says the elk.

Something like that, says Mark.

We are grateful, says the elk. The wolves were preying on our young.

Mark frowns. But why were you in the forest, where the wolves have their home? he says. Why do you not run on the prairie, as elks should?

No grass, says the first elk. We entered the forest because we thought we could reach the leaves of the trees . . . But elks do not climb.

The elks look up at the brown leaves of the trees, and their eyes are big with sadness. I notice then that their ribs are showing through their flesh, striations of bone, so each elk is like a punctuation elk, like this:

:")))?

They are terribly, terribly thin. I didn't see it so much with the first one, because he was close to us, and facing us, but when they turn to look at the forest and I see them from the side it is unmistakable. These elks are starving.

See? says Mark to me. It is because there is no rain. They have nothing to eat.

I look up and see green leaves in the trees above us. Leaves the elks cannot reach. Can they eat those? I ask.

Mark nods.

Well, I can climb, I say, surprising myself.

Your leg –

We're in the Dreaming, though, right? I ask.

Mark sighs. You have more important things to do. It's dangerous to –

As dangerous as bringing me to some world where there are wolves that want to kill me?

His shoulders slump. Be fast, he says. Be careful. Use your knife. I reach into my pocket and it's there, with its bone handle, the shape of an antler still imprinted in it. I test the edge with my thumb, and the knife slicks with blood. It's so sharp it's like it's greasy.

Ouch, I say.

It's a knife, says Mark in a withering tone.

I walk over to the nearest tree. I lean back, looking up – there are leaves right at the top, in the, what do you call it, the canopy. It's a long way up. I put my hands on the raspy trunk. There are easy holds, thick branches at even intervals. It doesn't look like any tree I know; an oak would be closest, maybe. I've never climbed a tree before, but how hard can it be?

Hard.

It can be hard.

I slip, about twenty feet up, and fall –

Crunch

Crash

And . . . catch.

I swing from a branch, my hands and arms burning. Muscles tense, I pull myself up until I can get my left knee over the branch, then I straddle it, panting. I can hear Mark calling from below but I ignore him. I keep going, hand over hand, trying to use my right foot as little as possible – it isn't hurting, but even in the Dreaming, it must still be broken.

Finally, I look up, and I'm in green, starlight filtering through; the feeling it gives me is something like the word 'sacrosanct', made into a picture. I slow my breathing, and start cutting the branches above me, choosing ones that will fall without striking me. The knife goes through them like a steak knife through meat.

The green leaves fall softly down, turning and bouncing, and some get caught but most reach the ground, I think. I cut and cut until my hand is aching and there's another wolf howl, from far away in the woods, and Mark shouts in my head, *Enough*.

There's a tone I haven't heard before in his voice, and I choose to obey.

Climbing down is even worse, but finally I step down on to the ground. There are leaves all around me, green on the ground like emeralds in the starlight, and the elks are already noses down, eating.

About time, says Mark. We're no longer safe. There are more wolves coming. We must go.

Go where? I say.

To the Crone's castle.

What for?

Mark glances at the knife still in my hand. To rescue the Child, and to kill the Crone. He says this like it's a perfectly normal thing to say.

Who's the Child?

Mark is watching the elk eating the leaves I cut for them. He turns his head when there's another howl from deep in the forest. But he must figure it's far enough away, because he nods to himself. All right, he says. We have a little time. Sit. He motions for me to sit down on a tuft of grass.

I sit.

He sits too, on a rock. In the Dreaming, as in all things, there is balance, he says. He is speaking quietly so that the elks can't hear. There is First Woman and First Man, says Mark. There is the Crone, who is the energy of destruction. And there is Coyote, who is the energy of chaos.

Coyote? I say, thinking of the coyote I saw after the car hit me, and again by the car, in the forest.

Yes. Also, there is the End, and there is the Child. That is balanced, as it should be. But the Crone has captured the Child, and this is what has given her the power to stop the rain. But by taking the Child she is hastening the End.

Which means what? I say. I don't understand. It's not real. This world isn't real.

It is real, it's just different. We must rescue the Child, and kill the Crone, to break the spell of no rain.

Or what?

Without rain everything dies, he says. The Child is very young. Defenceless. She will not survive long in the Crone's care.

Suddenly I flash back to my recurring dream – the child in the hospital, crying for someone to come, crying for help. What if . . . what if the dream has been trying to tell me something? Warn me about something?

You mean the Dreaming will end? I say. If the Child dies?

He shakes his head sadly. No. The Dreaming. Your world. Your everything.

I stare at him. Are you serious?

I am very serious, he says.

I am thinking that this is all crazy – the Dreaming, talking elks, wolves baying for blood. I don't understand him at all. But I do believe him.

What do I have to do with all of this? I say.

You're the only one who can save the Child, says Mark.

Why?

But he doesn't answer, because –

132

3 . . .

CHAPTER
21

I SNAP INTO THE room in the motel, cold liquid dripping from my face, my hair.

What the –

Then I see Mom standing over me, an empty water glass in her hand.

Sorry, honey, she says. *You wouldn't wake up.*

Mom! I'm soaking. What the hell?

She pulls a face. *Sorry. Sorry. Hey, when I was a Girl Guide, in Alaska, this was how they woke us up every morning at camp.*

You were a Girl Guide?

Yep.

Wow. I can't imagine this AT ALL. I mean, 0 per cent. My mom is the least Girl-Guide person in the world. She'd get the cross-stitch badge no problem, but before this week, the closest she's ever come to the outdoors is those pictures of Scotland she makes. She would never even come climb the little mountains next to Phoenix with me.

I was a terrible Guide, she says.

Yeah, no shit, I say.

OK, OK, my bad, she says. She tosses me a towel. *Get dry and get dressed. It's eleven a.m., sleepyhead. They've stopped serving breakfast here.*

I put on my CAM Walker and then pull my slit jeans over it, and grab my T-shirt and sweater. It's so much colder here than in Phoenix; I can feel the air creeping through my clothes, wanting to chill the life out of me.

OK, overdramatic, but it's what I feel. Like the cold is leaching something from me. Some force. For the first time I get what Mom means about the rain.

Anyway, I walk into the main room and Mom and Luke are standing there with their bags by their feet.

Finally, Sleeping Beauty appears, says Luke.

I mime gut-busting laughter and Mom rolls her eyes. *We thought we'd go to a diner*, she says. *In town.*

OK, I say.

Then I see her glance over at the still-full coffee cups of wine on the table. *Luke, you want to take the bags to the car?* she says. *We'll follow.*

He nods with that kind of oh-yes-girl-stuff nod and picks up the bags, leaves the room.

Mom goes over to the cups and takes them to the bathroom – I see her tip them into the sink, then rinse them out. Weird. She comes back into the room and claps her hands together, like, let's go.

I'm sure the maid would have got those, I say.

Yes, yes, she says. *I don't like to leave a mess. I was a Guide, remember?*

She smiles but I don't. I'm looking at the bottle of wine, the still half-full bottle of wine that she has left on the table, like she doesn't consider that to be mess. What gives?

There's something obvious here, but I can't quite put my finger on it. Then Mom puts HER fingers on my arm and steers me out of the room, and then down to the car.

Luke drives us back into town and we find a parking spot on the main drag opposite the Western Frontier diner, close to the corner with Gene's Western Wear on it. He gets out and inserts coins into an old-fashioned parking meter and we walk to the diner – or rather Mom and Luke walk, and I do my elegant CAM Walker shuffle.

We go in and get a booth close to the entrance. Luke tosses the car keys on to the table, and they slide to a stop by the ketchup, which comes in a bottle shaped like a tomato. Mom orders me a strawberry milkshake and burger, and a hot dog for herself. Luke goes for home fries and a steak.

Our server's name is Candy, and she has a smiley-face button on her uniform. She doesn't have a smiley face on her FACE, though. She looks like we just ran over her cat. Who knows, maybe we did. Or maybe she's met Luke before, and she thinks he's going to tell her a story about attending a scene in a diner where someone chopped off their hand.

I almost want to show him the scars all over my legs, and say, You ever see anything like that?

Anyway, my shake comes, and it's good.

Leaves blow past, outside.

Candy brings us our food, and just about holds herself back from spitting in it in front of us. She hands Luke a steak knife and takes away his normal knife.

And then Luke's mouth drops open, and doesn't close.

He's facing the other way to me and Mom – we turn in our seats and see the TV mounted on a bracket on the wall. It's on mute, you can see from the little red symbol in the corner of the screen, a speaker with a line through it. But that's not really what I'm look-ing at.

No, what I'm looking at is footage from the hospital CCTV

137

cameras, of me and Mom leaving Phoenix General, me in my wheel-chair. Closed captions flash up.

You're not going to believe this, Veronica, says the male anchor, *but police think these images may just show An –*

I turn around as I feel Mom moving very quickly. She has Luke's steak knife in her hand, like it just jumped there from the table, all of its own accord.

I'm so sorry, Luke, she says.

Then she brings the knife down like a hammer, and it goes through Luke's hand like, well, like you know what. It sticks in the table too, because when she takes her own hand away it's standing up like a flag in a burger bun.

Luke stares down at it, and his mouth goes, O-O-O-O-O-O.

I'm guessing his scream is loud. But I'm deaf. I only hear like 10 per cent of it. That 10 per cent is bad enough for me, though. I feel like my stomach is falling out through a hole in my pelvis. I guess that's shock.

Mom grabs the car keys and my arm, and pushes me out of the booth and then out of the door. Candy is rushing to Luke, behind us, who is still just staring at the blood gushing out of his hand like a whale's blowhole spraying red, and all this is happening but only like half a second has gone by.

If anyone chased us, we'd be screwed, because I'm going as fast as I can on my CAM Walker, using the weird rocking gait that you have to use with it, not knowing why Mom did that and why we're running, and Mom is not an athlete. But we get to the Honda with-out anyone stopping us, and I guess that's because they're freaking out about Luke's hand and trying to help him, and then a little scary voice at the back of my mind says, Yeah, she knew that would happen, that's probably why she did it.

And then I'm in the car, and Mom shuts my door and gets in the driver's seat and pretty much floors it, and the tyres smoke as we gun it out of there.

CHAPTER
22

YOU'RE ANYA MAXWELL? I say as we drive out of Flagstaff and on to I-17 again.

Mom says she heard sirens behind us, but we figure they won't know what car we're in – no one even stepped out of the diner when we ran. So they're not going to be able to follow us. That's Mom's thinking, anyway. I don't know if she's right.

Yes, says Mom.

Wow, I say. Anya Maxwell is kind of a legendary figure – she smashed her husband's head in like fifteen years ago with a kitchen TV. He bled out and got electrocuted too – the Double Death, they called it. Later it turned out, because all her friends came forward, that he'd been beating her and raping her for years, and she'd just snapped. So she became a sort of heroine to some feminists, and then got even more famous when she skipped bail and disappeared, totally.

It's a bit like that whole Elvis-being-alive thing – people say, if someone's a bit mysterious, *maybe she's Anya Maxwell.* That kind of thing. Now, the idea that this woman is my mother is just disorienting. All my life, she's been Shaylene Cooper, and now she's Anya Maxwell, and it's like someone just took a big tug on the earth beneath me and pulled it a thousand miles along, like a rug, so I'm living on some totally other part of the world.

You cut off the TV in the motel room, didn't you? I say.

Yes. I couldn't afford for the news to come on.

Wow, I say again.

We pass a sign that says APACHE/YAVAPAI NATION 3 MILES: it is pointing down a side road. I think of the Dreaming, the elks and the Crone and the Child, and whether if we went down that road I could find some wise elder or something, ask them some questions.

But we continue past it, and the forest keeps flickering past.

Eventually Mom pulls over at a rest stop. There's a short section of desert south of Flagstaff, similar to the scrubland where we saw the petroglyphs, then you get up on to the forest plateau again, where the pines start to crowd in. There's a sign that says PRESCOTT NATIONAL FOREST 5 MILES. It doesn't occur to me to ask why we're heading back in the direction of Phoenix.

I just . . . she says. *I couldn't go to prison. Not with you. You were so young – losing you like that, it would have broken my heart. So I took you, and I ran. I changed my name. I changed my job.*

So . . . Alaska . . .

A lie. I'm sorry. I had to keep you safe. Her hands when she gesticulates don't look human any more; they look like starfish flapping. And it's a cliché, but my head is spinning. I mean really spinning, like vertigo. I feel like I'm going to throw up.

Then Mom saying 'lie', like that, makes me think of something – of the coyote, before my accident, saying there will be two lies and then there will be the truth. My dad wanting to kill us, that was the first lie, right? So what if this is the second?

I feel as if my body is dropping through thin air, my stomach rising.

Anya Maxwell didn't have a daughter, I say slowly.

They kept you secret, says Mom. *To protect you.*

141

Right, I say.

She frowns at me. *From my reputation, you know. And from knowing that I killed your dad, I guess. Then when I took you they never changed the story, I don't know why. Maybe it would have looked weird.*

Uh-huh, I say. *Mom, are you lying to me right now?*

She looks so shocked I instantly feel bad. *What? Why would I lie to you about this? You're my only girl. My little princess.*

And you're Anya Maxwell.

Yes. Anya Maxwell, who had a daughter the authorities kept quiet about, and who knew that people would be looking for her. For her and her teenage girl.

Oh, I say, realising something. *So when we were with Luke, you didn't break our engine just to change cars, you did it because . . .*

. . . Because I knew they'd be looking for a woman and a girl. Not a family. Or what seemed like a family.

Suddenly, everything is clear. That line on the closed caption:

Police think these images may just show An–

Police think this may be Anya fricking Maxwell.

Though I guess the person typing out the closed captions probably wouldn't have included the fricking. This, though – this is why Mom stabbed Luke through the hand, nailing him to the table. So that he wouldn't pick up on the news story.

But . . . I say. *Can't you turn yourself in? I mean, I'm older now. I could come visit you, we could –*

No way, says Mom. *The DA was pushing for the electric chair. It was California, remember?*

California? I say. *I thought we lived in Alaska.*

Well . . . says Mom. *I had to protect you.*

God, I say. *But your husband . . . my dad . . . he was hurting you.*

There's no material evidence. Only witness testimony.

She starts to cry, suddenly, and something clicks inside me, some cog, and I lean over and put my hands around her. Then my stomach flips and I pull away.

Luke! I say.

Yeah, says Mom, still crying. *That was unfortunate.*

His hand . . . In my head, it runs again, like a rewound video – the blade, sticking out of his flesh, the blood spurting. The memory of it is jagged in my head, uncomfortable, sharp-edged. It hurts me; I can't imagine how much it hurt him.

It'll be fine, says Mom. *No arteries.*

It'll be FINE?

She closes her eyes, for a moment. *Sorry,* she says. *Sorry. It was the only thing I could think of. You know I wouldn't normally do that, right? You know it was wrong?*

Uh, yes, Mom, I know it was wrong. You impaled his hand. And what do you mean you wouldn't normally do that? You were all ready to smash his head in with a rock.

She blinks. *But I didn't.*

Because I tripped you!

Sorry, she says. *Sorry. I did stab him. I did, and I'm sorry for it. I wish I hadn't had to. But he would have seen, or heard. You understand that, don't you? He would have realised. Who I was. Who you were.*

Yes, I say.

143

And then . . . I would have lost you. I can't lose you.

She's crying hard now, and I touch the tears on her cheek. *It's OK, Mom*, I say, *I get it.*

Thank you, she says.

We sit there for a while in silence.

Then Mom takes a long deep breath, scrubs her face with her hands. She turns to me. A glint in her eye. *Anyway*, she says slowly, *now he'll have a story to tell about himself, for once.*

I can't help it – I laugh. It's awful, it's terrible, but I laugh. And then Mom is laughing too, and we sort of have to hold on to each other, because we get all hysterical. It's funny! And also tragic and disgusting and appalling. But funny too!

When we come back to our senses, Mom starts the car and pulls out, indicating carefully. We follow I-17 another few miles. Forest flickers past the window of the car, the trees different and the same. It's like someone is shuffling a deck of cards, with pictures of trees on them. Then Mom sees a sign for the Prescott National Forest again, and she turns off. We pass a gas station, fluorescent lit, and Mom pulls up.

Wait here, she says.

She goes into the store and I wait. The engine is still running. I watch a wasp crawl across the windshield. I start to feel nervous – we're the only car parked here – but then Mom reappears, shielding her eyes from the low late-afternoon sun. She walks back to the car at what I think she imagines is an inconspicuous pace, only it looks suspicious to me.

But, you know, I saw what she did with the steak knife, so it's not like I'm an unbiased observer.

I watch her pull something from her pocket, something dark like a Taser. Her face is all cold and hard determination.

Two lies, and then the truth.

I pull back into the seat, as if I could push myself through it, as if I was made of ectoplasm, thinking about how this was a person who would make a knife stand out of someone's hand just to stop them from watching TV, and that this is a person, too, who knows that when I'm with her I slow her down.

A person who killed my dad.

A person who was willing to smash Luke's brains in with a rock, and leave him to die in the middle of nowhere.

A person, I suddenly realise, who just might hit me with ten thousand volts and leave me behind, leave me to wake up on a kerb as policemen ask me questions and I just blink at them, like, what the hell?

I keep my eyes on her hand, raising the black object, and I brace myself.

CHAPTER
23

WHAT'S WRONG WITH YOU?

Mom gets in and hands the black something to me – it's a basic cell phone – keys big enough for a giant to operate. Then she gives me another one, identical.

I am shaking. *Nothing*, I say. *Nothing.*

One for you, one for me, she says. *Your job is: programme my number into yours, and vice versa.*

What? Why?

They're prepaid. No contract. The cops don't know we have them.

The COPS? What is this, TV?

OK, the police, whatever. Just keep yours on you.

We're together, I say.

We may get separated, she says.

I roll my eyes. *I can't believe you got us burners, like on* The Wire, I say.

Mom shrugs. *What can I say. I love that show. Charge the cell tonight and keep it safe.*

So we're on the run. And we have burner cells. It would be bitching if it wasn't so totally weird and awful. In my mind's eye, a flash, like firework-afterburn: Luke's hand again, the knife sticking out of it like a flag.

Mom checks a big fold-out map she also got in the 7-Eleven, then opens her purse, takes out her old cell phone, and tosses it out of the window. Then she pushes the lever from *P* to *D* and we pull out, pine needles crunching under the tyres. At a fork, Mom takes another turn on to a smaller highway.

It's not the same road we were on before, and we follow it for maybe an hour – I don't know; I programme the numbers into the cells, but then I think I fall asleep for a while.

Next I know, we're turning on to another road, and then another. We're in deep forest now, and I gasp.

There's a canyon, I say.

What?

A canyon. I point – it's not as big as the Grand Canyon, but it's impressive, running alongside the road, a big gouge in the land, red rock descending to a ribbon of blue water. Pine trees hug the sides, and encompass us all around. We're on little more than a dirt track, I realise.

A rabbit runs on to the track in front of us, startles, and dashes back into the bushes.

A little later, I see a deer flit through the trees beside us, on the forest side. It gives me a strange feeling to see them there. It's getting harder and harder to remember what happened with Mark and the elks. And there were wolves, I think? But the dream has stuck with me, unsettling me, and now it's as if it's bleeding into reality, like newspaper print left behind on damp clothes.

Where are we going? I ask.

Judge Ricardo's cabin, says Mom. *He's not there at all this week – his mom had a stroke. He had to fly back east. He got the call at the end of the day on Friday.*

You know where Judge Ricardo's cabin is?

I know everything. I'm the stenographer.

And sure enough, there's another couple of turns, and then I see a log cabin in front of us, a little semicircle of gravel drive in front of it, all neat and tidy. It's set into the side of a hill that rises up beside the canyon, and it looks down over it, over the river below and the trees and the rock.

And this river: it's not like the creek we saw before, with Luke, slowly flowing, brown and green. This is swift, and foamy, and racing past – it is a true river.

I don't think I've ever seen a river before. I am entranced by it – by the way that it is always shifting, always moving, the ripple and the currents and the eddies, but at the same time it is one indivisible still thing. The effect is of something crumpled, but shining; tinfoil.

It's beautiful. It feels like . . . like my dream, I realise, woozily. That same sense of no civilisation, of just primal nature, like there would have been a million years ago, when people hadn't messed everything up. Though of course here, there's obviously rain, because it isn't all dry and broken.

It's lush, and green, and there is luxuriant undergrowth everywhere and many colours of leaves.

We'll be safe here, says Mom as she gets out of the car.

She is wrong, but I don't know that yet.

CHAPTER
24

THE CABIN IS INCREDIBLE, when we finally get into it. We don't have a key, of course, but we find one under a stone frog near the door. I guess if we hadn't, Mom was going to bust out some previously unsuspected lock-picking skills, since she is all about surprising me these days.

The interior is all wooden floors with patterned rugs on them, and open fires, with big stone fireplaces. It's bigger than it looked from outside, like a cottage in a fairy tale, and there are two big rooms for me and Mom, with king-size beds.

We both know, of course, that we can't exactly stay here forever, but we deliberately don't talk about what we're going to do next.

There are cans in the kitchen – we make beans for dinner, and sausages. Then we share a can of peaches. In a cupboard we find enough bottled water to survive a nuclear holocaust.

We can't figure out the closed captions on the TV, and anyway both of us are exhausted, so as soon as the sun sets, we both yawn.

Sleepy? says Mom.

Yeah.

I love you . . . she says.

. . . all the way to Cape Cod and back, I finish. I give her a weak smile. My head is a mess, but I do love her, I do. I've wondered,

sometimes – can you still love someone if you find out they did something bad? Turns out, you don't have much choice. You love them whatever. You love them forever.

Mom takes out a cross-stitch kit from her purse and settles down on the couch. Fake Scottish trees in the middle of amazing real forest.

You're kidding? I say.

She puts down the needle for a second. *It'll help me sleep*, she says. *You mind?*

Knock yourself out, I say.

I go to my room. There are soft blankets on the bed, a deep rug next to it, so when you get out with bare feet, you don't get the shock of the cold wooden floor. It's chilly – we decided not to light the fires, because of the smoke. I go over to a socket in the wall and plug in my cell – I gave the other one to Mom.

I don't undress; I just get into the bed and pull the blankets over me. I close my eyes.

And I see the knife plunge into Luke's hand; see the blood spurt up.

I try again.

And I see the same thing.

I lie there, very still, trying to force my mind into the low gear that allows sleep, but hey, if I knew that trick I would be a millionaire.

I close my eyes, focus on the shapes swirling against my eyelids. I wait for a long time, watching them, trying to tune out the world around me, to still my thoughts.

Hospital doors.

A child, crying. The whole hospital trembling with it, my body vibrating with the pain of it.

I have to get to the child, I have to rescue the –

NO.

I snap myself back into the room. I'm drenched in sweat, my heart pistoning in my chest.

Not that again, I think. I get up. I ease my CAM Walker on to the wooden floor and walk as softly as possible through the cabin. I feel like the sound of the CAM Walker on the wood is sure to wake Mom, but I don't see her come out of her room. I go to the front door and very quietly open it.

Outside, the forest is breathing, low and slow. It's dark, but a sliver of moon paints a glow on the leaves. There's a sense of something sleeping, but very alert, at the same time. I see a flash of white – an owl swooping overhead. Insects dance around my head. Something black and fast rushes past me in a flurry of wings – a bat.

Wow, I think. This place is awesome.

I step out on to the gravel, balancing as best I can, and before I know it I'm in the woods. My hand knows what I'm doing before I do, because it takes the knife from my pocket and holds it.

I look down at it.

I can't seriously think this is going to work, can I?

But at the same time, I'm thinking of Mark's biceps, of the dimples in his cheeks when his mouth quirks into a smile. And I'm thinking of sound, the richness of it, how in my dream I could hear even the smallest creatures, the wind itself.

How Mark's voice enters through my ears and is in my mind, shimmering, like something that blends sight and touch. The utter beauty of it. The simplicity too, the ease of just opening my mouth and letting noise jump out, shaped by my tongue and teeth, rolling in waves through the air.

And the Child. The Child Mark wants us to rescue, and the idea that the world might end in days if we don't, which of course I rationally don't believe, but it's night-time and reason is less strong at night-time.

Yeah, screw it, I think.

I hold the knife very tightly in my hand, and close my eyes.

Then I step

through –

the air.

AND INTO A MILLION STARS.

CHAPTER
25

– THEN MARK IS WAITING for me where we left each other, on the border of the forest and the prairie. He nods when I appear, totally cool, even though he can't have known when I would show up.

God, he's hot.

But he doesn't let my gaze linger on him because he grabs my hand. It's good that you returned, he says. After tonight there will be only two days left in your world.

Fireworks of joy go off in me when I hear his voice inside my head again – it's like being closer to someone than you can imagine; it's like in my dreams where I can hear, but more.

More.

Then I think about what he said. Wait, I say. My world ends in two days?

Yes, he says. I told you that.

Oh.

But we have an advantage, says Mark. Because when you are in the Dreaming, time in your world passes slower. As long as you are here, you are safe.

So why don't I just stay here? I ask.

You can't, says Mark. It doesn't work like that.

Oh, I think. Well, that's clear.

I hear hooves rustling on the ground, so I look around and see that the elks are still there, standing in a group on the dry grass, looking at me with their big eyes.

Will you reach us more leaves? one of them says.

No, says Mark. We must use this time in the Dreaming. We must go to the castle.

But the Crone is there, says the elk.

Yes, says Mark.

She will kill you.

No, says Mark. We will kill her. And rescue the Child. And when we do, there will be rain again, and you will have all the grass you can eat.

The elk opens its big brown eyes even wider. But it is not he who speaks, it is another, its hide dappled, sleek. Who are you to do such a thing?

Me? says Mark. I am no one. But this is the Maiden. He is pointing to me. The elks all turn to look at me.

What? I say.

They approach us, cautiously. This is a great honour, says the first one. To think that you climbed a tree for us! He turns to Mark. Can we help you? he says. We would . . . we would accompany you if you wished.

But he is trembling as he says it, and I can see that he is afraid. Afraid of the Crone, I guess.

Mark shakes his head. The quest is for the Maiden, he says. I am only a guide. You should stay here and wait for our return. He turns to me. We need to go.

Where? I say.

There, he says, pointing.

Very, very far in the distance, there's a thin point sticking into the sky, which could just be a spire, if you squinted.

That's the Crone's castle, says Mark.

That? That thing *five million miles* away?

No, the other castle, the one right in front of us. He indicates the openness of the prairie, the emptiness of it.

I stare at him for a moment. Was that a joke? I ask.

He smiles. Not a good one. The Crone's castle is not easy to reach, he says. Otherwise it would be easy to kill her, and crones are not easy to kill. Come, he says. We need to hurry.

Why do you think I would say yes to this? I say.

He holds my eyes. Because you need to save the Child, he says. You have always known this. Haven't you dreamed about it?

I blink at him, a little shaken. Yes, I say. But it was just a dream.

The Child needs you, he says. Are you coming with me?

I think for a moment. Filling my mind is the child in the hospital, the one I can't pick up, the one I can't ever pick up and comfort.

I'm coming with you, I say. But I still don't see what this has to do with me. Why you want me to come.

It's your destiny, says Mark.

You believe in that? I ask. Destiny?

He just stares at me, like I have asked him if he believes in mud. Yes, he says, at last. Yes, I believe in it.

Mark stretches. Farewell, elks, he says, and nods to the elks.

They bend their front legs and bow again, and I flush with embarrassment. Farewell, human and Maiden, they say.

Mark takes my hand and begins to walk over the prairie. I stumble along beside him through the dead brown grass, and we walk.

My CAM Walker isn't here, it's back in the other world, and I don't miss it.

And we walk.

And we walk.

I don't know how long we continue on for, under the bright starlight of the Dreaming, but my guess is eons. Mark isn't in a talkative mood, that much is pretty obvious. When I tried to ask him some question, some little casual thing, he just said, the Crone isn't going to kill herself.

After another while, my feet start to ache, and my legs too. My broken one doesn't hurt here like it does in my world, but we've been walking for approximately 4,300 years and that takes it out of anyone.

Please, I say, can't we –

I break off, because we can't walk any more. There's a canyon in front of us. It's not like the one beside the cabin Mom and I are staying in – I mean, it has some similarities, but the big difference is that this one is *massive*. I haven't been to the Grand Canyon, but I think it would fit inside this one, easily.

The ground just stops

(

)

and starts again, maybe a mile away. And below, very far below, is not a ribbon of blue but a fast-flowing river, and I can tell it's fast because I see the white of the foam.

The canyon wasn't visible from the edge of the forest, I guess because it's more of an absence than a presence – it's just a big gap in the world, and when you're looking horizontally along a plane you don't see a crack like that. But there's no way we can cross it, is there . . . ?

How the hell do we get across that? I say.

There's a path, says Mark.

Where?

He pulls me forward and shows me – and yes, there's a little track down the side of the canyon, that makes several U-turns on its way down. It looks very steep, very narrow, and very precarious.

OK, I say. And what about the river?

We have to cross it, he says, like I'm a moron.

Easy as that?

Well, no, he says, totally missing my sarcasm. There are also snakes.

In the water?

Yes.

Poisonous ones?

Yes.

He starts down the path and I follow, feeling sick. There are several times when I think I'm going to have to stop, I'm so dizzy, but I just keep telling myself that the further down I go, the less distance I have to fall if I slip, and that turns out to be a pretty awesome motivator.

Finally, I take the last bend and I get to the bottom, where Mark is waiting for me, grinning. You made it at last, he says. Now for the snakes.

I close my eyes and try not to cry.

He approaches the river, which really is moving very fast, I can see now, and frowns.

What is it?

The current. I don't like it.

Is this you screwing with me still?

He gives me a serious look. No. I swear it. I don't understand –
there's been no rain. The Crone must have put a spell on it.

OK, that really is you screwing with me, right?

No.

Oh.

He stands there, looking out over the fast-flowing water, and as I
stand next to him, I see something move from the shallows near my
feet, out into the rushing middle – something that swims in a shape
similar to the wave of my heartbeat, on the monitor in the hospital.
Like:

~

A snake.

It's possible, says Mark, that this is going to be very dangerous
indeed. Snakes serve the Crone.

Great, I say. Is there anything that doesn't serve the Crone?

He frowns. Yes. Me. Elk. Badger. Fox. Ra –

He's interrupted by a clattering noise above us. He turns, and I
turn too, and we see a stone bouncing down the slope towards us. It
stops in the dust at our feet.

Something is coming, says Mark.

He whirls to face what is clattering down the path, and are his fingers now claws? And are his teeth now pointed, and does his jaw –

CHAPTER
26

THEN AN ELK COMES into view, taking one of the bends, carefully planting its feet as it descends the path.

I stare at Mark, whose whole body has shrunk a little, like a balloon left a long time. But I could swear . . . I could swear for a moment there he had seemed to *ripple*, to shift, and I had seen sharpness, and fur.

What the – I start to say to him, but he holds up his hand to shush me.

Then another elk appears.

And another.

Mark and I watch in amazement as the elks come slowly down to the bottom of the canyon, then stand before us.

There are wolves following you, says the one that first spoke before – it has a white blaze on its forehead. You gave us food. We will take you across the river.

But the water, says Mark.

It is fast, says the elk. It is not deep.

There are snakes, says Mark. You could be killed.

If one of us falls, the herd remains. We are Elk.

As he says this, more of the beautiful creatures join him, lining up, flank to flank. Their bodies steam in the night air; they breathe like dragons. Their flanks are molten moon. Their antlers pierce the sky and rock. They are magnificent.

I will take the Maiden, says the leader. He tips his antlers towards another large elk. And she will take you, human, he says to Mark.

The leader steps shyly towards me, stepping high. He lowers his head, then bends his foreleg, bringing his back down, his great antlers, so that I can climb up on to him.

You're sure? I ask.

Yes, says the elk. Our backs are strong. We oppose the Crone. We cleave to our task. We are Elk.

I lift my leg and straddle his back. He is warm, and his . . . fur? hair? . . . I don't know what it's called on an elk, but it's soft, so soft, and I grip his neck and it smells like something ancient, something gracious, something that says love and companionship and destiny and . . . rightness.

You see? says the elk. We were made for this.

For the very first time, I understand, truly understand, what we lost when we made trains and cars and planes, and even when we began to grow things. But I'm not able to think about it for long because the elk steps forward, without hesitating, and into the river. Beside me, Mark rides too, on the high dappled female, his face grim-set.

And on either side of us, the herd moves as one.

The snakes come at us fast, angry. They slip between the legs of the elks, and I see their fangs, and the elks stamp their feet, snorting, mouths foaming, eyes rolling. But they keep going, as scared and as thrashing as they are. The moon is behind clouds. Above us are only stars, sharp and shining as teeth.

I see an elk to my left go down, suddenly, like its legs just aren't there any more – it rolls, once, then disappears under the water, and I just catch a glimpse of its hooves as it tumbles down the rocky rapids.

Then another falls to my right, and another.

I hold my breath, terrified, and I see that Mark has blanched, his face drained of all blood. I can see the other shore, only ten feet away now . . .

Five . . .

My elk, the leader, stumbles, and I'm thrown forward towards the water –

but then his head comes up again and I cling on, as he pushes on. Three . . .

And then we're through, and on the bank, and the elk walks me up and away from the river, before dropping his forelegs so I can scoot down and off. Mark alights too, and many of the elks shake water from their tails and flanks beside us. At least five, though, are gone.

I'm sorry, I say.

The leader looks up at me. We are many, he says. We are Elk. The herd survives.

But his voice is sad.

One of the other elks snorts, in alarm, and I turn. Mark is tense, poised, looking at the river. I see it. A pair of eyes above the water, a snout. Sharp teeth. A wolf.

And another.

And another.

CHAPTER
27

THERE IS A PACK of wolves, swimming across the river towards us. They see that we have spotted them and begin to swim faster, their eyes shining. The snakes are leaving them alone: in fact I can't see the snakes at all.

Wolves serve the Crone, I think. And snakes serve the Crone.

The elks turn, panicked breath misting the air, looking for somewhere to run, but there is nowhere, only a narrow path, all curves and switchbacks, that runs up the other side of the canyon, and will only fit them single file.

Mark looks to the river, at the onrushing forms of the wolf heads. They are getting close now; I can see the sharpness of their teeth. The mineral hardness of their eyes, glinting in the starlight. I can hear them snarling madly as they swim, their mouths foaming, mingling with the foam of the river.

Very well, says Mark, as if to himself.

Then he closes his arms around his chest and –

and *collapses into himself*, his body folding like paper, his skin shifting, blurring into fur, bristling, his jeans and T-shirt melting away, his jaw extending, his fingernails pushing out into claws until . . .

. . . until there is a coyote standing there, beside the river, a huge coyote the size of a man – a coyote that a second ago *was* a man.

Behind me, the lead elk lets out a kind of bellow, but I can't tell if it's one of rage or surprise or triumph, because at that moment the wolves hesitate, I see them slow in the water, and they sniff at the air in confusion.

But then the biggest of them snarls and their eyes flash again, and they come forward, reaching the shallows now, scrabbling for purchase with their paws on the riverbed. They rush up on to the sand then, bursting out of the river, spraying droplets of water as they charge at us, mouth open wide and slathering, eyes full of murder.

The coyote twists and, in Mark's voice, says, Stay back. Stay behind me.

Then it catches the first wolf with a blow of its red paw, just as the wolf leaps, smashing it down in a cloud of sand. Immediately the coyote – Mark – whirs around and jumps into the air, closes its jaw on the throat of the biggest wolf, and in less time than it takes to tell it, tears out a great hunk of flesh in an explosion of red, and the wolf falls twitching to the ground, missing half of its neck.

There are three more wolves, and they hang back now, whimpering, their snouts downturned. They glance at one another, seem to draw some strength from each other, some resolve, and then all three of them hurl themselves at the giant coyote together.

But the coyote is ready.

It dives under one wolf, twisting its body as it does so, and its claws rake up, eviscerate the wolf as it moves through the air, its guts falling steaming to the sand. Another wolf jumps over it, and it snaps at the air and misses, the wolf hitting the ground hard and careering towards me, towards the elk, jaws wide open –

But the coyote has spun around, too fast to be possible, and sunk its teeth into the wolf's back leg – the wolf stops as if anchored by a steel cable, its head crashing into a rock that is lying in the sand, and it is instantly still.

The last wolf doesn't even make for me, it turns its tail and flees – or it would, if the coyote didn't chase it to the water's edge, and end it in a swirl of water and blood.

The elks behind me are whickering and wheezing, distressed by the smell of blood, which is ringingly metallic in the air around us, the whole atmosphere turned to iron. I half turn to them and their eyes are rolling and staring. Some of them have tried to escape up the narrow path but have got stuck, feet drumming at the ground, antlers locked with hooves.

The coyote leaves the water's edge and begins to walk towards me.

But no.

That wasn't the last wolf. The last wolf surges out of the water upstream of me, a grey wave, and it is huge. It bounds, snarling, past the coyote and towards the elks that are jumbled together at the foot of the path up the canyon wall. It is fast, this wolf, and it is snarling, eyes gleaming, getting closer and closer.

The coyote reacts, but maybe not fast enough, turning from me and throwing itself in the wolf's direction –

Shelby Cooper, come back in here, says the elk closest to me, its eyes bulging.

What? I say.

Another elk takes my shoulder with its hand; I feel the fingers digging into my flesh.

What the – ?

Then the rocky ravine drops away like a curtain falling, and there is forest behind it, dark forest, and my mom swings me around to face her. I stumble, but she catches me.

It's two a.m., she says. *Come inside.*

I stare at her. I'm thinking about the trapped elks, the wolf closing in on them, wanting to lock its teeth on their flesh, and I want to go back and see if they're all right, I want to know why Mark is SUDDENLY A COYOTE. But I can't very well try to step back over there into the Dreaming, not with Mom right here beside me.

OK, Mom, I say.

2 . . .

CHAPTER
28

THE NEXT MORNING, THE smell of bacon wakes me. I get up and CAM Walk into the kitchen, a kind of rolling walk that I'm sure looks really cool, where Mom is bent over the pan. A thought goes through my head: This woman is a murderer. But I grab it and push it down, burying it. I raise my eyebrows into a question.

Vacuum packed, says Mom. *There are croissants too. Frozen.* She indicates the oven where they are cooking. Outside the window there is a pale moon in the blue morning sky, and it makes me feel like I don't know what is real any more and what is a dream.

I sit down and soon she brings me over a plate, a mug of coffee. *Thanks*, I say. I stare at her. *What do I call you? Anya? Shaylene?*

She frowns. *Call me Mom*, she says.

My fork stops on the way to my mouth. I nod slowly. *So, what's the plan?* I ask.

We'll hold tight here a while, says Mom. *There's a ton of food. And the judge won't be here for a long time.*

And then what? I say. *It's not sustainable long term.*

Mom hits the table with her knife; it makes me jump. *I know, Shelby*, she says. *I know. I'm working on it, OK?*

OK, I say. *Fine.*

Have I ever let you down? she asks. *Have I ever not looked after you?*

No, Mom, I say.

Well, then.

We sit in silence for a while, finishing our bacon and croissants.

I'm going to get some firewood, says Mom. *Read a book or something.*

OK.

She clears away the plates and mugs. She washes them in the sink and I pick up a towel, and when she has finished washing she silently hands me each item and I dry it – we make a good team.

After that she leaves the room and I go to the bathroom to brush my teeth – Mom bought toothbrushes and deodorant and stuff from the gas station. When I hit the living room, Mom isn't there, and I guess she's outside, chopping firewood. The image is so incongruous, so *Little House on the Prairie*, that it makes me laugh.

It's weird – I don't know what my laugh sounds like.

I look at the bookshelves but it's all *Stories of the Hopi* and *Navajo Firelight* and *The Mythology of the Major Native American Tribes*. Nothing that appeals to me. I look around for a moment, sweeping the room, and that's when I see an Apple computer on an old nineteenth-century desk in the corner, inlaid with green leather tooled with gold.

I go over to the computer and, without even really thinking about it, turn it on. I'm kind of surprised when the Apple logo on the button glows blue, and then the screen flickers on. Soon the home screen appears – no password, which seems foolish for a judge.

I look to see if there's a modem, but if anything the computer is probably just plugged right into the phone line, for broadband. I click on Safari and after a moment a window pops up. Google. Wow.

First I search for 'Anya Maxwell'. There are a ton of pages. Wikipedia, obviously, but also news articles, blogs, discussions.

Images.

I click on the Images tab and the screen is filled with tessellated little photos – a dark-haired woman, shown in old family photographs, thin and nervous looking. She looks like a beaten wife, that's for sure.

But does she look like Mom?

Yeah, kind of. Same limp hair, same snub nose. The eyes look different – bigger, wider, but that could just be because she's younger here. Yes, there's a definite resemblance.

Wow.

I navigate away from the images. I search for 'vivid dreams' and 'dream symbolism', but I just get a load of new age crap.

And anyway, am I sure it's a dream? I touch the knife in my pocket, the very real-feeling knife that Mark gave me. No, not sure at all. Only, Mark just turned into a coyote. What was that all about? The whole thing was already weird and now it was twelve thousand times weirder.

I key in 'coyote' and hit Enter.

The coyote is a member of the genus –
Coyote: the trickster archetype in Navajo blah blah blah.

Prince of mischief, the coyote is seen as a clever . . .

If you cross a coyote it is bad luck, you should turn around
or –

I shiver and close the tab; open a new one. But an after-image floats in my inner vision, like the silhouette of something outlined by the sun – the image is the word 'trickster'. Trickster. Liar. Someone who plays tricks.

Mark.

I shake my head to rid myself of the idea.

Then I type in the address of one of the forums I like to hang out on – a subforum of one of the big discussion sites for home-schooled teenagers. There are a few messages from other users wondering where I have gone – usually I post a few times every night.

Deafgirl97 where you at girl?

Hey **Deafgirl97** you on vacation or something?

I smile. Someone has missed me. But as I scroll down the page I realise there's nothing here I can identify with. It's all about Jared Leto and *Pretty Little Liars* and there's nothing at all on the topic of what to do if you find out that your mother is a notorious murderer on the run from the police.

I'm about to type a reply to one of the messages, to say that I'm fine but may be offline for a while, when Mom walks in. She sees me sitting at the computer and shouts – at least I assume she shouts; she opens her mouth and I hear a faint sound.

She rushes over and holds down the power button till the computer switches off. Then she goes straight into the kitchen, and comes back with a pair of scissors – she leans behind the desk and cuts something, then folds her arms and looks at me.

What did you do? I say. *What the hell, Mom?*

Cut the Ethernet cable, she says. *What are you thinking?*

I was just –

You were on the internet. You were posting something. They can trace that.

What? How?

Are you serious? Have you heard of IP addresses?

Huh.

Sorry, Mom, I say.

And what was that, anyway? A forum?

Yes, I say.

We need to talk about this, she says.

Me being on a forum? You're a murderer! The words are formed by my hands before I can take them back.

She stares at me, like she's been slapped. *You cannot believe the things your father did, the things he –*

But even as she is speaking something is clicking into place in my mind, slotting into the right grooves. The coffee cups of wine, the bottle of codeine missing from my make-up bag.

I hold up my hand to cut her off. *You were going to drug Luke*, I say.

What?

The wine. It is oh so clear in my mind now, crystal fricking clear. *You put my codeine in his wine and that was why you looked all pissed when he said he didn't drink.*

I didn't –

Mom, don't lie!

OK, fine, she says. *I put a little bit of codeine in his drink. Just to make him sleep, so we could get out of there, I mean, he was*

173

*becoming a problem. He knew us, he knew what we looked like,
and he was useful for a while but –*

2,700 milligrams, I say. I don't know the sign for milligrams so I
say it with my mouth.

What?

The amount. Of codeine.

She looks at me blankly.

He would have died, I say. *From that much.*

How do you know I put all of them in the –

*Oh, so you didn't? Where are they then? Because they're not in
my make-up bag. I'm going to run out in like five days because I
only have my first bottle.*

I didn't think, she says.

*Yeah. You just thought about killing Luke so he couldn't rat
on us.*

As I say this, I'm sure I'm right. I mean why bother knocking
him out and then leaving? It would be the same as just saying see-
you-later and getting on a bus or getting a taxi to take us back to our
car. No, the only way to be sure he wouldn't tell anyone about us
would be to . . .

. . . to kill him.

Shut up, says Mom.

*Why? You don't like hearing what you did? What you are?
Once a murderer, always a murderer, Mom.*

Even as I say it, I'm aware that it's something I can't take back,
and so I'm not surprised when Mom slaps me. I don't hear it, it's
almost totally silent, but I feel the shock of it, the sudden blossom-
ing of red-hot pain.

Go to your room, she says. *I'll come for you when it's time
for lunch.*

I want to ask her, did you lie to me again? This story about you being Anya Maxwell, is it another lie, like when you said that Dad was alive and wanted to kill us? But I don't know how to ask that question. I know how to argue with her about codeine but not how to challenge the whole *story* we're living in.

And anyway my blood is boiling too much to allow me to speak to her.

Instead:

Fine, I say.

I go into the room that has been assigned to me and stand by the bed. I don't mind being alone, because (*a*) Mom is freaking me the hell out, and (*b*) I want to get back into the Dreaming, to find out what is going on. First a coyote appears on the street when I get hit by a car, then I see one from the window of *our* car, then Mark turns into one?

There is something seriously messed up happening and I want to know what it is.

And Mark has some explaining to do. I mean, I trusted him. I liked talking to him. I liked having someone other than my mother to talk to, and he was that someone. Now I don't know what to think any more and continue to be glad that I'm apart from Mom for a bit, giving me the time to sort through some thoughts in my head.

Thoughts like, (*c*) Mark doesn't exist in any meaningful way, apart from in the Dreaming, and (*d*) Mark is a fricking coyote. Or Coyote, I should say, with a capital *C*. Whatever.

I'm sure there's an *e* too, and *f* and *g* and *h*, in terms of good reasons to be in this wood-panelled room on my own, but I don't follow that train of thought because there's a quick way to get answers.

Holding the knife, I close my eyes and focus on finding the gap between worlds, between here and the Dreaming. It is getting easier and easier, and part of it is thinking about sound, thinking about those vibrations coming into my ears, the rushing of the river water, the breathing of the elks, the hooting of owls, far off in the distance, the canyon and above it the long strip of black sky, dusted with –

———

STARS.

CHAPTER
29

THE SCENE TAKES A second to resolve itself in front of me, and then the wolf is flying through the air towards the first of the trapped elks.

Huh, I think. Mark was right. Time doesn't pass the same in the Dreaming, when I'm in my world.

I move forward, thinking in some vague way that I have to try to protect the elks, though who knows what I'm going to do. At the same time, the coyote that used to be Mark is flowing, there is no other word for it, flowing liquidly towards the same place –

and the elk leader is moving too, all of us converging –

but it's the leader who gets there first, the big elk who carried me over the river, and he lowers his head as he charges, folds his forelegs so he skids across the sand – he must weigh close to a ton, and when his antlers hit the leaping wolf, they spear it right through.

The elk stands, then violently shakes its head, and the wolf is dashed on to a rock, lying limp and unnatural over it, blood haloing the elk's antlers. The elk bellows, stamping its foot.

The coyote slides to a halt, panting.

For what feels like a long time, there is silence. The elks are all watching the coyote, fear in their eyes. All apart from the leader, who is looking at it – looking at Mark, I keep having to remind myself – with an expression of prideful resistance, and something like anger. But mixed up with . . . what? What would you call it?

Submission, I think. A kind of reluctant, angry submission.

Coyote, says the big elk. Then the resistance fades from his eyes, and he lowers his head.

Coyote, say the others. Tension pulses in the brightness of their eyes, and they bend their front legs and bow, half in trepidation, half in tribute – the posture says fear, very clearly. But unless I'm imagining it, it also says reverence.

Tension hangs in the air, like mist.

Coyote, says the first elk, when finally he looks up. Would you change your skin? You are scaring our young.

As the elk says it, I see it's true – the smaller elk are cowering behind the larger ones.

Mark, Coyote, whatever, nods and then jumps up into the air again, shifting as he does, fur becoming skin, and clothes, until it's a man standing there; Mark.

Thank you, says the elk.

You are welcome, says Mark. I did not mean to frighten you.

The elk kind of snorts air through its nostrils, like it's laughing. You are Coyote, it says. Who knows what you mean?

I frown.

Maiden, says the elk. I look around, and then realise it's addressing me. Why do you walk with First Angry?

First Angry? I say.

Yes. The One Who Caused the Flood, the One Who Created Death, the One Who Scattered the Stars. Coyote. He has many names.

I glance at him. I don't –

I am helping her to rescue the Child, says Mark. To kill the Crone.

Why? says the lead elk.

Mark gestures to the dead wolves, to the parched ground beyond the thin strip of beach. Because of all this. The drought. The wolves.

The lead elk snorts. Was it not given to Coyote and to Coyote alone to call the rain? he says. It is one of your gifts. Why can you not simply make it rain?

I look at Mark. You can make it *rain*? I say.

Yes, he says. I mean no. Usually I can. Usually, I am the only one who can. But not now.

Why not?

Because the balance has been upset, he says. The Crone has the Child. Now her power is greater than mine. I have no more say over the rain. When she is dead, then . . . then I can call a downpour and soak the land. But not before.

Truly? says the elk.

Would I lie? says Mark.

Yes, says the elk. You are Coyote. The Liar. The Player of Tricks.

I am not lying now, says Mark.

Listen, I say loudly. Mark and the elks turn to look at me. Can someone tell me what the *hell* is going on here? I am *not* the Maiden, I am Shelby Jane Cooper. You are Mark. But you're . . . you're a coyote, suddenly?

No, says Mark. I am Coyote.

And the difference is . . .

The difference is that between a lightbulb and the sun.

Oh, yeah, I say, fake unfazed. Totally. Sure. That's normal.

Coyotes are born and die every day, he says. I am older than this

180

world. I am the son of the sky and the earth. Some say that I made man and woman.

And did you? I say.

He just shrugs.

And outside the library . . . when the car hit me . . . that was you?

Yes, he says. I wanted to warn you.

About the lies. 'There will be two lies and then there will be the truth,' right?

Yes, he says.

So you being Coyote, and keeping it secret, was that one of the lies?

No, he says.

What about my mother saying that Dad was coming to kill us?

He nods his head.

And this stuff about being Anya Maxwell?

I can't tell you that. Some things you have to learn for yourself.

If you want me to kill this crone, or whatever she is, and rescue this child, you need to answer my –

I don't want you to rescue the Child, says Coyote. *You* want to rescue the Child.

I stare at him. What? I say.

Listen, he says. Close your eyes, and listen to the wind.

What? Why would –

Just do it, he says.

I close my eyes and I hear Mark mutter some words. I concentrate on the wind. It is not loud – it is a low breeze, humming through the canyon, a quiet hushing sound difficult to separate from the running of the water, but very slightly higher pitched, almost like a voice, almost like someone . . .

someone crying . . .

and then I hear it, under the wind, so faint, but there. The sound of a child crying, and then it seems to get louder and louder, until it's vibrating in every cell of my body, resonating in me, like it does in my dreams.

And of course that's what it is, I realise.

It is the crying from my dreams. The very same crying. The little child, sitting on the floor of the hospital, reaching its arms up to me, wanting to be comforted, wanting to be held . . .

I feel wetness welling up in my eyes. I open them and take a breath. Stop it, I say to Mark.

He nods, and the crying is gone.

That was the Child, he says. It is dying. We must save it. Yes?

Yes, I say. Yes.

We all look at one another for a moment.

I hid my true face from you, says Mark to the elks. And I am sorry for that. But will you still stand with me? Will you stand with the Maiden?

Yes, say the elks, together.

But I don't understand, I say. The Child, who is it? I mean, did I have a sister once, or . . . or what? Why do I know that crying?

It is the Child, says Mark, as if that's a simple answer that makes any kind of sense. The Dreaming bleeds into your world.

I don't know what that means, I say.

No, he says. But you will.

The Crone's castle is still unimaginably far away but the elks offer to carry us. They take a step forward, and begin to bend their backs, for us to mount them. The big leader steps delicately around the corpse of the wolf at his feet, skirting the rock on which its back broke by splashing through the shallows of the river. And at that moment, I see a movement out of the corner of my eye. A liquid movement, a sine wave slipping through the water, fast.

I grab my knife and shout. Look out –

But it's too late. The snake's head flicks up out of the river, and its fangs glisten for a moment in the starlight, and then it clamps down on the majestic elk's leg, mouth snapping shut with a click that I can hear.

No, I say.

Knock.

Mark whips into motion, his hand seizing the snake as he bends, and then he flings it far out into the river, where it hits the water with a splash.

He pushes the elk out of the shallows, towards the rock wall, the path. He is patting its side, whispering to it, eyes narrow with concern. The other elks are doing that panicked bellowing again.

Knock.

I look down at the leader's leg.

Two drops of crimson welling from the fur. The hide. Whatever it's called. Suddenly I wish I knew what it was called.

No, I say.

It is all right, says the elk.

No, I say. No, it's not all –

But his legs are already crumpling. We are many, he says as his eyes begin to dim out of the world. We are Elk.

No, I say. I'm still clutching the knife like a talisman, like something that can keep me safe. Keep us all safe.

Knock.

Save the Child, says the elk. Don't let us all die. Don't let –

But he doesn't say anything else because then his legs buckle and he falls to the ground, foam beginning to fleck the corners of his mouth.

Shelby? Shelby, what are you doing in there? Shelby, I'm coming in.

It's Mom's voice, breaking into the Dreaming.

No, I scream. No, not now; but then there is a hand on my shoulder and it's not a hand in this world and I am –

CHAPTER
30

— STANDING IN THE MIDDLE of the room in the judge's cabin, and Mom is shaking my shoulder.

I HEARD her, I think. I heard her, when I was in the Dreaming. Calling through the door. How is that possible?

But then I suppose if she was shouting loud enough, I WOULD hear. I mean, I have 10 per cent hearing.

She must have been shouting loud. She must have been worried.

Mom takes a step back and signs at me. *What the hell, Shelby? Are you OK?*

I . . . My hands are shaking. A physical stammer. *I'm . . . fine.*

Then I realise that the knife is still in my hand. I look down at it, the sharp blade reflecting liquid light.

Mom looks too.

It's not mine, I say. *I found it in –*

What's not yours?

I stare at her. *What?*

What are you talking about? she says.

This, I say. I show her the knife.

Your hand?

I shake the knife. *This. This knife.*

I don't see a knife, she says. *I just see your hands.*

Shocked, I look down, but yes, the knife is in my hand, the solid antler handle of it, the wicked gleam of the blade.

Are you kidding? I say.

She touches my face. *I'm really worried about you, Shelby,* she says. *I think you need to have something to eat. Then you need to rest this afternoon.*

What the hell?

Am I losing my mind? Am I going crazy? I guess it wouldn't be surprising, what with everything that has happened. Maybe something has snapped inside me, like an elastic band stretched too far. Or maybe it IS just a dream, and now the dream is lingering somehow in the real world, and that's how come the knife.

But . . . who dreams standing up? Who FALLS ASLEEP standing up?

I look up and see that Mom has an expression of really major concern on her face. I don't want to see that.

I'm all right, I say. *Just a daydream, I think.*

She frowns, unconvinced.

Really. I'm fine. Did you say lunch?

Yes, she says. *Baked potatoes. Tuna.*

Great, I say.

But nothing feels very great. My mom's a murderer, I'm apparently going insane, and the big elk is dying, the one who carried me on his back, and I'm stuck here in this place where I can't help and I can't even HEAR anything, this half-world that I live in with my psycho mother.

I didn't even know his name – but then maybe elks don't have names, they are a herd, they are many, they are Elk –

Shelby? says Mom. *Earth to Shelby? It's like you're living in another world.*

Yes, I think. Yes it is.

CHAPTER
31

Mom and I have lunch – baked potatoes with canned tuna – and then she insists that I rest in the living room for the afternoon. She finds a pack of cards and we play a few games, then Scrabble – Mom is good at Scrabble, from all the courtroom touch-typing, and I'm not bad either. But she always beats me.

Though this time, she lets me win a couple of games. I think it's because she's feeling weird about her being a secret murderer, though she doesn't mention it, which in itself is weird.

It's like neither of us knows how to bring it up.

The moon is gone from the sky now, at least, so when I look out of the window the world seems normal and bright, though colder than Phoenix. Wisps of cloud scud across the sun and the air is crystal clear. Some kind of hawk flies past the window.

Can we go outside? I say when we finish our game of Scrabble.

She frowns. *I wanted you to rest.*

I've rested. I'm fine. Honestly. But it looks nice out there.

OK, honey. We can take a look at that canyon, she says. *It's no Grand Canyon, but still.*

I smile because she's making an effort. *Yeah, thanks*, I say.

We go through the cabin and out of the front door. The sun is low in the sky. We're so cut off from everything here – deep in the forest, at the end of this little dirt track, the green leaves all around us, the canyon scarring the earth in front of us. It's like a gingerbread cottage in a fairy tale, lost in the woods. Like no one could ever find us.

We don't walk far from the cabin, because of my CAM Walker – just to the edge of the canyon. From here, you can see the river stretching away, turning and twisting, as it cuts through the forest. The red of the rock below shines in the sun; the river is precious metal now, gleaming.

Look, says Mom. *A deer.*

I see it – a flash of antler, of haunch, and it is gone, blinking away into the woods.

Soon after that a hawk begins to circle lazily overhead. I can almost see the blue of its feathers. The air here seems thin, pure. Like you could see for miles if you climbed one of these trees, like the very atmosphere is cleaner and lighter than anything I have ever known before.

We sit down on smooth rocks, furred with moss. The forest breathes around us. I see a rabbit, breaking cover and running fast for the undergrowth. I see a squirrel run up a tree.

It's like a fairy tale, says Mom.

What I was thinking, I say.

Other than that we stay silent. We sit there for like 499 hours, it feels like. But I never get bored – I love watching the river, how it's never quite the same, the foam breaking, leaves rushing past, caught in its swell, the eddies and currents like someone doodling, endlessly.

At some point, we go inside and eat a snack. Beans – from a can again. Then we go outside again and sit, without speaking to each other. It's like we've been wounded, and we're slowly healing without saying anything about it. Getting used to a new idea of what we are.

I wonder if there are coyotes here, I think as we sit in the gradually darkening forest.

Then I push the thought down with the other one

(the Mom being a murderer one)

and I bury them in the same shallow grave, and I don't let them out again. There are no coyotes. I mean, there are coyotes. Of course there are coyotes. I'm not mental. But there is no Coyote, no Player of Tricks with capital letters in his name. I shiver: a memory flashes through me, like a glinting fish, of the wolf impaled on the antlers of the elk.

The elk who is dying, bitten by the –

Ugh.

I bury that thought too. My weird dreams should stay in the dark, where they belong. Under the stars.

Another minnow flashes through my mind: Mark's skin melting, prickling into fur –

No.

I close my eyes, let the sun make red patterns against my eyelids. I must doze off because when I open them again the sun is setting, a burning ball of dark red, like blood through the trees. The clouds above it are on fire, streaked with pink against the pale blue of the sky.

Beautiful, Mom murmurs.

Yes, I say.

After that we go inside. There's a fireplace, and next to it a great pile of split wood in like an alcove thing. It's an enormous, open fire-place. *Light that, would you, honey?* says Mom. *I'll make dinner.*

What about the smoke? I say. *What if someone sees?*

We're ten miles from anything, says Mom. *And I'm cold.*

I stare at the grate.

How do I light it?

Mom rolls her eyes. *What have I been teaching you?* she says. *Your curriculum. Typing.*

She smiles. *OK, well I'm adding fire-building to the curriculum. Honestly, Shelby,* she says, *the things you don't know, it's –*

She stops, stricken, her hands falling to her sides.

Sorry, she says. *I didn't think how that was going to come out. I mean, I know I lied to you and –*

It's OK, I say. *You were scared, right? That I would judge you for what you did?*

She nods.

I get it, I say. But I don't say: I get it and I don't judge you. I don't know if that would be true, and I don't want to say something that's a lie.

(He is the First Liar. He is not to be trusted.)

I just give her a wan smile and she stands there for a long moment looking at me, waiting, and I feel like a bitch to the power of fricking ten, and then she looks away, breaks it first, and I feel so grateful to her.

We can talk about it later, I say a little desperately.

Sure, she says. The movements of her hands are flat.

But she kneels in front of the fireplace. She shows me a little basket with wood shavings in it; sawdust. *Tinder,* she says. She builds a little pile of it in the middle of the grate, she finds a piece of paper for it to sit on, from a message pad next to the phone, so the dust doesn't fall down through the bars.

Kindling, she says, taking some small pieces of wood from the basket. She arranges these cross-wise over the pile of tinder.

Then logs, right? I say.

Quick study, my daughter, she says. She takes three logs and places them in a kind of teepee over the other stuff.

What now? I say.

Now you light the tinder.

That's it?

That's it.

Oh, OK, I say. I snag the matches and strike one – it flares bright orange and then settles into a wavering flame. I touch it to the tinder, and soon the whole thing is flickering flame.

Mom stands there nodding.

What does it sound like? I say.

She gives me a sad look. *It crackles,* she says. *And fizzes . . . and pops . . . There aren't any words. It sounds like a fire.*

I nod.

I'm sorry, she says.

I shrug.

Dinner, she says, and goes to the kitchen. I sit by the fire in a low-slung leather armchair. I feel very warm and comfortable. I feel like a lamp that's switched on; like to someone else looking at me my skin might be alight.

I want to turn on the TV but I figure Mom might be pissed; I remember her cutting the cable of the computer.

Then I think of the books on the shelf – the folk tales and Native American stuff that I dismissed before. Only now the elks have

191

been talking about Coyote, and I picture the Google results when I typed in 'coyote', the stuff about him being a trickster god in Native American mythology. I get up and hobble over to the books, then glance down the spines. I see one on Apache folk tales so I take it down and go and sit again, curling up, the book in my lap. The fire glows, expands and contracts, filling the room with throbbing light. It's beautiful – I can't quite take my eyes off it, though I try to leaf through the book.

Words leap out at me.

Coyote.

Trickster.

The moon. The stars.

Coyote kills the Giant.

The Man who became a sheep.

When Coyote stole fire from the Fire God. I scan the page. There was a time when only the Fire God possessed fire, and all others were cold on this earth.

The Fire God lived in a hogan with high walls. Coyote went to the geese and asked them to help him fly; they made him wings of their feathers, and he was able to join them in the skies.

Then Coyote flew over the walls of the Fire God's house. He tied a small branch to his tail, dipped it into the fire to light it. The Fire God saw him and chased him, murder in his eyes, but Coyote used his goose wings and leapt into the air, flying over the wall.

Everywhere he went, the burning brand on his tail set fire to things – to bushes, to grass, to trees. The first forest fire began, destroying many acres and lives.

But after that, fire was out in the world, was loose, and people were able to use it.

I blink, trying to wash the tiredness out of my eyes. There is an idea buzzing around my consciousness, like a fly. A thought, about chaos and order, and what they mean. About stealing. I can't quite catch it, though.

I sit there trying to empty my mind for a long time, empty it into a wide net to seize that flashing fish of a thought, its scales gleaming as it disappears into the blackness of deep water, and then I must fall asleep because when I open my eyes I'm surrounded by

THE BRIGHT, BRIGHT MULTITUDE OF THE STARS

CHAPTER
32

AND THEN I'M IN the Dreaming, kneeling by the fallen elk.

My hand is on his chest, feeling his slow breathing. Flecks of foam are starting to form at the edges of his mouth. Mark is standing next to me – I can feel him, the heat of him. He is a human-shaped furnace, and I wonder why I didn't notice that, that he's too hot to be a real person.

The other elks are crowded around, in a circle, looking down at their leader, their eyes brimming with sadness. Their heads low. Forming a kind of honour guard, a phalanx – is that right? – all around us. A barrier no wolves or snakes can get through.

Except that it's too late now.

Come on, says Mark. We need to go. We need to continue on to the castle. To the Child.

But I will not leave the elk, not while he is alive.

No, I say. No, I'm not going anywhere.

Mark puts his hands on his hips. We must hurry, he says. The Crone –

Can wait, I say. I'm not leaving him on his own.

Mark sighs.

All right, he says. I will scout this side of the river. Make sure it's safe. Then I will build a fire.

He turns and walks off, away upstream, looking all around. Once he is out of earshot, I am surprised to see the eye of the dying elk roll towards me – I thought he was nearly gone, and this movement startles me.

Be careful of him, says the elk in a quiet voice. As if using the last of its strength.

What? I say. Why?

He is Coyote, says the elk softly. He is the Player of Tricks. He is the First Liar.

I sit cross-legged next to him, still with my hand on his warm body. The breathing is getting even slower now, I can almost feel the life force leave him. He doesn't seem like a liar, I say. He seems . . . nice.

It is easier to trick with charm than with aggression, says the elk. Just remain vigilant.

The dying elk's great soft eyes, fringed with long lashes, flutter up to the sky. The spirits and First Man and First Woman made the stars in patterns. They laid them out on a rug, to plan them. Then Coyote said it was taking too long, and he picked up the rug and scattered the stars across the heavens, a great mess of fire in the firmament.

I look up, at the vast glittering chaos of space.

Then I look down at the elk again, and see that his eyes are beginning to shut. Something sharp drives itself into my heart. But only he can bring rain, I say. He said that.

The elk breathes out, slowly. Yes, that is true, he says. It is given to Coyote to control the rain.

The rain is disruptive, says one elk.

The rain is disorder, says another.

The rain is chaos, they all say.

But you need it, I say. For the grass. To eat.

196

Reluctantly, the elks nod. We do.

Coyote is not evil, says my elk. He simply plays tricks. But he is not to be trusted.

Before Coyote, says another elk, a female, there was no death. Then Coyote threw a stone in a lake, and he said to First Man and First Woman, if the stone sinks, then there will be death. And the stone sank, so there was death.

But stones always sink, I say.

Yes, says the leader. That is the nature of Coyote.

So you're saying I shouldn't kill the Crone? I shouldn't rescue the Child.

No, says the elk. You must do these things. Otherwise all will be lost. I am only saying you must be careful of Coyote.

I lean against him, feeling the departing warmth of him. I don't understand any of this, I say. I don't even understand what this place is. The Dreaming.

It is the First World, says the elk. It is the place before time, before Coyote stole the sun and moon and –

Ah, says Mark, coming between two of the honour guard of elks, breaking into the circle. You are telling my tales?

First Angry, says the elk.

Elk, says Mark.

Look after the Maiden, says the elk. Keep her safe.

I promise it, says Mark.

Your promises are nothing, says the elk. You are Coyote.

Then, quite abruptly, it closes its eyes, takes one last deep breath, and dies. I sense it, I almost see it, like when a bright light goes off and a person's shadow jumps back into them; there is an energy that is pulled back in, and disappears.

The body is still beneath my palm.

Mark closes his eyes. Let his spirit be reborn, he says.

Let his spirit be reborn, say the other elks.

I touch my eyes – they are wet, and my breath is hitching. I have never seen anything die before, and the elk was so beautiful.

And now, of course, I don't know what to think. Who to trust. The elk said not to believe Mark, to be careful of him. But at the same time it said the same thing as him – that I need to kill the Crone, and rescue the Child. So why would I not trust Coyote?

I mean Mark. I mean Mark.

I can hear the crying of the Child now, faintly, even without Mark doing that magic spell – a kind of constant, low soundtrack, like the moaning of the wind. It is calling me, a dull ache inside me, I feel the urge now that the elk is dead to follow it and make it stop.

To pick up the Child, and hold it in my arms, and make the crying cease.

Ah, says Mark. You hear it.

The Child? I say. Yes.

It is calling you. There is not much time left.

I take his hand and he pulls me to my feet. The castle is still a long way away, he says. We have no time to lose.

What about them? I say, looking at the elks that are still standing in a circle around us.

What about them?

I turn to the elks. But they have been listening to our conversation.

We are coming with you, Maiden, they say. To the Crone. To the Child.

And with me? says Mark. You will suffer the presence of Coyote?

198

We do not know your goals, says the elk. But you are Coyote. You lived before the world. We will do as you ask.

I think to myself – as soon as he and I are alone Mark and I are having a *serious* talk about all this Coyote stuff. But now is not the time. I nod at the elks. Thank you, I say.

They begin to walk up the narrow, winding path leading out of the canyon. Mark and I follow.

We keep climbing, higher and higher, and I try not to look down.

Then, out of the corner of my eye, as I round a bend, I see a swift shape behind us. It's shadow, grey, and it's following us fast, gaining on us.

Then another.

And another.

Mark whirls around too, stops. More wolves, he says.

I see their muzzles now, their legs and tails, the sleek projectile speed of them. They are running flat out, trying to catch us. It looks like they're going to succeed. The first one appears from behind a stone, races fluidly upwards – a grey needle, stitching the yellow slope of stone. Of course! I think. Why worry about the drop when there are wolves to kill you?

Mark's eyes skitter over the ground. The path is rocky, and the slope is mostly scree – bits of small stone and like, gravelly stuff, from when the river was much higher, I guess.

I'm going to make a landslide, he says. You get out of here. Ride.

Ride?

Elks run faster than people.

I can't leave you, I say. I can't leave you to –

I'll be fine. Go.

He begins to kick rocks, sending them down the slope. Nothing

199

much happens, and the wolves are gaining. I can see their teeth now, their slobbering tongues. Mark curses, keeps kicking. He picks up a really big rock and throws it, towards a large patch of loose-looking scree.

There's a pause.

Then a slow movement, like molasses running down the side of a bottle.

Go, says Mark.

I run up the last section of slope with the elks. When we reach the top I see the prairie stretching out before us again, under the vastness of the stars. In the distance is the dark spire of the Crone's castle, where we're headed.

Maiden, says the big female elk. Mount. She bends her forelegs so that I can climb on to her back. Quickly, she says.

I grab the fur where her neck and back meet, and pull myself up. Barely are my legs around her before she rises, and begins to run. The sensation is completely different to that of crossing the river – it's fast, and shakes my bones. I hold on for dear life as the elk flings itself along the ground away from the wolves.

The other elks are running too, their hooves flickering over the dry grass of the prairie. I look back, clinging to my elk's neck, and see the side of the canyon give way behind us, or that's what it seems like, rocks roaring downhill like a wave away from us, dust puffing up in clouds.

Holy – I start to think, but I don't finish the thought, because then the whole world goes out. I mean, it just goes black, everything, the stars disappearing, the river, the gnarled trees clinging to the cliff face, the huddled elks – *all* of it just switches off.

Click.

Like a light going off.

What the hell? I say to myself, in the darkness. The elk keeps running, but I can sense its fear, I can feel its head turning from side to side, and it slows, as it tries to work out what is happening.

Everything is gone – no sky, no prairie, no castle spire in the far distance. I freeze, because if I took a wrong step I would fall to my death.

And the crying of the Child is loud now, so loud, not just a sighing like the breeze, underneath everything, but an all-encompassing noise I can't block out, exactly as if someone turned out the light in a baby's room, and the baby is screaming –

Something is wrong, says Mark's voice, loud and breathless in my ear. I look to the side where his voice came from, searching for him in the utter darkness, and –

suddenly there is a burst of light, like a bolt of lightning except that there is no lightning, just that instant the stars are blazing again and there he is, but he is Coyote, streaming along beside my elk, muscles flowing, fur shadowy in the starlight. His mouth is open, long sharp teeth visible, pink tongue lolling, panting as he runs – more like some enormous grey bird flying just over the ground, than an animal.

Something is wrong in your world, he says. Shouts, more like.

Is it Mom? I say, is it –

And at that moment the world disappears again, I mean the Dreaming disappears, everything turning off, the stars gone, and I hear my elk snort and whinny in panic, it is weaving from side to side now, terrified.

I don't know, says Mark's voice from the blackness.

Then hands are touching my head, stroking my hair.

Shelby? Shelby, honey, there's been –

201

CHAPTER
33

– A POWER OUTAGE, SAYS MOM.

Huh? I say.

I'm on the other side of the air, in the armchair by the fire. I look around. The fire in the fireplace is little more than embers now, gently smouldering, but giving enough reddish light to see by. There's a blanket over me; I guess Mom must have put it there.

The lights are all off – the lamps and the overhead lights. Outside the windows is pure blackness.

I'm going to see if there's a generator, she says. *I think I saw one in the woodshed.*

What time is it? I say.

Five a.m., says Mom. *Early. I didn't want to wake you, but you should probably go to bed. Get some more sleep.*

Yeah, I say. My eyes are still sandy with exhaustion. *Yeah, OK.*

She leaves the room, opens the door to the outside. There's a little blast of cold night air and then she's gone.

I slowly sit up, and that's when I see a sandwich on a little tray on the table next to me. A glass of milk. I smile. I fell asleep before dinner and Mom didn't want me to go hungry. I take a bite of the sandwich – it's good. Corned beef, I think, mayo, tomatoes.

Where the hell she got the tomatoes I don't know. I find myself suddenly hungry and finish the sandwich quickly. Then I drink the milk.

I should go to bed, I guess, like Mom said. But I have just been asleep – I know I would lie there in the darkness, eyes open, mind refusing to switch off. I glance at the book that got lodged between the cushion and arm of the chair, the Apache folk tales. I shiver, and don't touch it. These dreams have been getting way too weird, too real, for my liking. I can still feel the knife in my hand – the one Mom doesn't seem able to see.

I slip it into my pocket, and out of my mind.

I get up and stretch, and nearly fall over because I've forgotten about the bulk of the CAM Walker on my foot. I grab on to the fireplace and steady myself.

I remember going outside the night before last, the moths flying, the moon bright in the sky above the trees. Fireflies leaving vapour trails in the air. I decide to go out again, to drink in the stillness, the peace.

Opening the door quietly, I ease myself out into the inky night. I wonder where this woodshed is that Mom mentioned – I can't see her and of course I can't hear her either.

It's very dark – the moon hidden behind some clouds. I can feel living things around me – bats flitting, insects careering. For a moment I remember the sounds of the elks in the Dreaming, and I am filled with grief.

No.

I get a grip on myself.

I'm here, in the real world, and I can't hear the insects, and it's a real shame but just fricking deal with it, Shelby.

I look back at the cabin and it's weird seeing no lights on in there, just the dim glow of the fire, red through the windows. It's actually kind of creepy – a lonely cold feeling.

Should I be worried that the power went out?

Could someone have MADE the power go out?

I wonder if Mom thought about that too. I cast my mind back, to try to remember if she was looking anxious when she woke me up. In the meantime I turn away from the cabin, from its dead dark eyes.

Over there in the woods, I see something gleam. I blink. What was that? I make my way over to the tree line. I'm barefoot apart from my CAM Walker; I can feel the gravel under one foot, then the grass and moss, the bark, and it's a little piece of the Dreaming in this world. I peer into the deeper darkness between the trees. Nothing. I make my way further into the forest, avoiding fallen logs and stones as I get deeper into the trees.

Another flash – I turn and it's gone. I head in its direction but I can't hear anything. A creepy thought crosses my mind: If something weird was going on, I would have one less sense to detect it. What if there's a sound that anyone else, anyone who could hear, would identify immediately as a hunting mountain lion?

Then I think:

No, a hunting mountain lion would be silent. Even someone who could hear would be screwed.

This thought cheers me up by a factor of approximately 6,700, except that it totally doesn't. I take the knife from my pocket and hold it out in front of me, a feeble defence, especially because the knife probably isn't real.

Enough of this crap, I'm going back in, I think.

I turn, and there's a guy in front of me in a black uniform and with night-vision goggles on his face and an assault rifle in his hands.

CHAPTER
34

MY BODY GOES STILL as deep water. The guy hasn't seen me – he makes some signal, some Call of Duty stuff, and I see another shadow moving beside him, both of them heading towards the house. I whirl. More of them, tiny red lights glowing on their night-vision goggles like –

like the eyes of wolves, shining in the forest of the Dreaming –

and they are getting closer and closer to the cabin, moving lithe and dangerous through the trees like a wolf pack, closing in.

Armed police, I think.

For a second, I just stand there, not knowing what to do. I mean, these guys have SERIOUS guns, and they can see in the dark. I'm a teenage girl wearing a CAM Walker that seriously impedes my movement, I'm not going to be outrunning anyone anytime soon. I feel my hands shaking, my empty hand and my other hand that's holding the kn–

Knife.

The police are after Mom, I know that, but I also know it isn't going to look good if they find me with this big blade in my hand. Mom couldn't see it, but I don't know what that means yet. For all I know I'm going totally crazy and it doesn't exist at all. Or she pretended not to see it, for some reason I still don't understand, and it IS real.

Whatever: I throw the knife into the undergrowth; instantly, I can no longer see where it landed.

How the hell did they find us?

I could try to run away, or hobble away, anyway – I won't be doing any running. But . . . Mom's here somewhere, probably back in the cabin in bed. The police – I don't know how they found us – are going to find her and arrest her, and do I want her to be alone for that? She killed someone, but it was self-defence and –

Without even really thinking about it, I'm moving back towards the cabin, following the SWAT team, or whatever they are. At the edge of the clearing, I stop. One of the men, the leader, I guess, holds up three fingers, then makes like a turning motion with his hand – three men peel off and head around the back of the cabin. Then he points to his eyes, and arrows his finger at the windows.

Two guys creep forward, crouching, and look inside. They shake their heads.

Leader makes another gesture, and now the two by the window stand on either side of the door. Another man steps forward – he's got like a personal battering ram in his hands. He approaches the door.

I lean my weight on my CAM Walker, brace myself, and take a step for –

A hand closes over my mouth, jerking me back. The other hand kind of snakes behind both my arms and does something complicated, and I can't move. I'm propelled forward to the driveway, my feet not even touching the earth.

I'm brought to the leader, and he nods when he sees me. He

holds up a finger to his lips, which seems pretty redundant, when I've still got a gloved hand holding my mouth shut. I struggle a bit, at first, but it seems kind of pointless and I stop. The ground is bitter with sharp shards of gravel.

Now I wish I hadn't thrown away the knife.

MOM, I call in my head. MOM.

And if this was the Dreaming, she would hear me. If this was the Dreaming, she would know.

But it's not the Dreaming.

The battering ram hits the door and it shakes on its hinges, warping, like someone just put a spell on it and it's changing into something else. Then again. And then, on the third time, the door just disappears into the house, just like that, like, as quick as reading:

door

[no door]

I mean, it's not, like, hanging on its hinges, it's just not there. And everywhere around me there's rapid-fire movement as the SWAT team ready their weapons.

The men pour in, and that's the right word for it, like liquid.

I wait – I have zero point zero choice about it. I almost want to close my eyes but I don't.

Forty-seven seconds later the men come out again. The first one moves his hands in a way that obviously means, she's not in there.

Mom?

The SWAT guys huddle, all apart from the one holding me. Then the leader comes up to me.

Where is she? he asks.

The guy behind me takes his hand away so I can speak but he's still holding my arms. I shake my head.

208

Where is she? he asks again.

I shake my head again too, and I must look as scared as I feel because he sighs and points to the woods. *Do a sweep,* he says. *Gomez, McCarthy, Rhodes. Get the chopper on it too. Tell them to use the thermal.*

Then the leader says something into the radio attached to his shoulder and a car is suddenly there, a big black Cadillac, and it glides to a stop near us.

One of the team opens the door and the one behind me presses his hand on my head to help me down into the car. And that's it – I'm in custody, and Mom is gone.

CHAPTER
35

THEY DON'T CUFF ME or anything.

They close the door of the Cadillac and leave me in there. I don't know if there's a driver in the car – there's a dark pane of glass between the back seats and the front. Anyway we don't go anywhere, we just sit there.

No one comes to speak to me. I'm on my own for, oh, I don't know, 113 hours. Or maybe twenty minutes.

Finally the opposite door opens and a guy in a dark pinstriped suit gets in. He sits in the other back seat and looks at me. There's an odd expression on his face. Like he doesn't want me to be afraid of him, but at the same time very serious, and concerned. Concerned FOR ME, I think. I figure him for some kind of Fed – FBI maybe. He's youngish, with pale green eyes and short-cropped brown hair.

Where is Shaylene Cooper? he says eventually.

I don't say anything.

We need to find her, he says. *Your mother. Do you know where she is?*

Interesting, I think. So they don't have Mom. But how would she have got away? I think of her going to look for the generator, going to the woodshed, she had said.

Maybe she knew they were coming, the moment the power cut, and she ran for the canyon? Or something?

What the hell, Mom?

He is still looking at me, the Fed, waiting for me to answer. But I don't. This guy won't know sign, and I don't want to talk to him with my mouth – I'm feeling pretty fricking vulnerable already in this situation and don't want to be even weaker.

At length he sighs; at least I assume he sighs, his shoulders kind of hunch up and then fall, slowly. *Do you need anything?* he says. *Water?*

I shake my head.

So you understand me? he says. *Where is Shaylene Cooper? Where did she go?*

I shake my head again.

You don't know or you won't tell me?

I shrug.

He sits very still for a long time, then he raps on the darkened glass divider with his knuckles and says something, but he's facing forward as he says it so I don't catch it.

The car starts up – I feel the engine rumbling through the floor, the vibrations. Then we roll, and I feel the gravel of the drive give way to smooth asphalt road, and then we carry on driving for what feels like eons. When we leave the canopy of the forest, and join the main road, I begin to see a little more through the window – the trees flashing by as we go.

I get the impression we're going north, back to Flagstaff. Back to where Mom stabbed that knife through Luke's hand . . .

Yeah, I think, that was the gas station where we stopped. We drive through forest for maybe an hour before gradually descending into high desert plateau again, the black silhouettes of mountains in the distance. The whole time, the guy in the suit just looks ahead, not meeting my eye. As we drive the sun rises, flooding the world with red light, setting the shreds of cloud on the western horizon on fire.

The headrest is soft as I lean back against it, the fur of the elk beneath my legs warm.

I look out of the window and see the forest, tree trunks shuttering in and out of existence. The agent sitting beside me suddenly seems a long way away, and I'm so tired, so, so tired. The radio is on loud – I assume so anyway, since I can just hear crackles of updates from other agents, but it sounds like they don't know where Mom is, so that's good at least.

Well, I *think* it's good.

I look up at the star-filled sky above, take a deep lungful of clear, pure air. I grip on to the elk's mane and –

the car's engine drones and –

the wind is in my hair and –

I'm flying along beneath

THE INFINITE STARS

CHAPTER
36

– MY ELK GALLOPING ACROSS the prairie, Coyote running beside me, flowing over the ground.

Then I see that he's slowing, and my elk begins to slow too – the whole herd comes to a stop, on the dark grassland beneath the million billion stars of the Dreaming.

Coyote turns and my elk wheels around too and I hear the susurration of the grass beneath the hooves and I'm glad; my heart fills with it. We look back and the chasm is just a dark scar in the distance.

There are no wolves pursuing us, not a single one. It's just us, and our long shadows, on the prairie.

We should go back, says Coyote/Mark.

Why? says the elk. There is a nervous whinnying from the others.

To make sure, says Coyote. If you are afraid I will go alone.

The elk snorts. We are not afraid, it says. We are Elk. We are many.

Good, says Coyote/Mark.

OK, it's not going to work, me writing Coyote/Mark. When he's in Coyote form I'm just going to call him Coyote, OK? But remember that he is Mark too.

We all canter back until we reach the lip of the canyon. I slide down from the elk and walk over beside Coyote, then we peer down the devastated slope. I can't see anything at first, but then I just make out the tail of a wolf, poking out from beneath a grave of stones.

They are gone, says Coyote. Crushed.

The closest elk nods its head. This is good, it says.

Then Coyote ripples and shifts, twisting, until Mark is standing there beside us. We must keep moving, he says. To the castle. You can remain here if you wish. It may be safer. The wolves will keep coming, even if these are dead.

An elk stamps its feet beside me. No, we will continue to carry you, it says.

I look across the prairie and see the distant spire of the castle, small on the horizon, beyond a smudge that may be woods.

The elk nearest me, a male with huge antlers, bends down to allow me to mount.

The elk closest to Mark bows down too, and Mark doesn't waste time with polite protesting, he just swings himself up, and after a second I do the same. We take off at a quick canter across the plain.

We ride for what feels like several days, though it's always night; I sleep on the back of my elk, lulled by its motion, my face pressed into its fur, smelling its deep and ancient scent; musky, comforting. Above me the stars wheel, impossibly slowly, the whole night sky shining, like mother of pearl.

It's hard to tell, but it seems like the elks aren't just canter-ing, actually, though the movement is smooth. We're eating up the miles, the ground moving past at what is actually kind of a scary –

Whoa, OK, note to self: Don't look too closely at the ground. The elks' hooves are barely touching the forest floor; it's as if they could take off into the air and fly if they wanted to, but are holding back out of self-sacrifice, or maybe to spare me fear.

Yet, when the ache in my ass subsides, the speed gets gradually less scary and I come to love the riding – the constant motion of the elk, the warmth of it beneath me, the sense that we are one organism, moving together. The hypnotising rhythm of it. I feel like, if I die right now, my ghost will keep on riding, forever, happy.

I wake and the landscape has shifted – we're starting to enter thin woods, not a forest like before, with pines, but a deciduous one, like something you'd expect to see in Europe or something. Starlight filters down through the leaves and branches, dappling everything. Here, too, the trees are dry and dying.

But they're not like the trees from before, I realise. They're sharp and gnarled, angry looking. They have spikes growing from them.

The Forest of Thorns, says Mark, from the elk beside me. We're getting closer to the castle.

It's creepy, I say, looking at the twisting branches, the knifelike thorns.

Yes, says Mark. Soon we'll stop, for the elks to rest. And to light a fire. The creatures that serve the witch do not like fire.

We're on a broad path that leads through the forest but it is getting narrower and narrower, and the elks are having to slow more and more. As we ride, I listen to the whistling of the wind in the thorns, in the leaves. It sounds like crying.

We carry on, for maybe another hour, the path getting trickier all the time, thorns starting to push in towards us from the trees, to catch on the fur of the elks, on my sleeve.

And the wind . . .

It *is* crying, I realise. It's the crying of the child, from my dream. And as we ride, it's getting louder, like a vibration that lies under everything, like I imagine the sea must be, if you live near it.

Can you hear it? I say to Mark. I have to turn because we are riding single file now, and he is behind me.

The Child? he says.

Yes, I say.

He nods. We must save it, he says.

I don't say anything. But the sound feels like it's crowding everything else out of my mind, taking me over. I would do anything to make it stop. Anything. I just want to get to that child and help it, to protect it from the Crone, or whatever it is that is hurting it.

I didn't care about the Crone or the Child or any of that stuff before, it was all abstract, but then the snake bit the elk and now . . . now the crying in my ears, exactly the same as in my dream . . .

Hell, doing what Mark said – killing the Crone and saving the Child – it would be worth it even if it just stopped me having that dream again. And then there is the anger too. Now that I have had my hand on an elk as its flame went out, as it went dark, I would be happy to kill the Crone.

I am looking forward to killing her.

Maybe a half-hour later, Mark calls for the elks to stop. It's getting too hard for them to press on through the forest. We come to a halt just before a small clearing in the thorny, nasty woods. Mark dismounts and I swing myself down too – the ground is sharp with stones underfoot, little flinty stones.

I don't think you can go any further, he says to the elks. We will go from here on foot.

The elks nod. We will wait here. For your return journey.

217

We will not be returning, says Mark. Whatever happens.

I stare at him.

Don't worry about it, he says. You will see.

Good luck, say the elks.

Thank you, says Mark. He turns and waves them back. Go, he says. You have served. You have stood.

We have stood, says the elk that Mark was riding, not proud, just like a statement of fact. We are Elk. Make the rain return, Coyote.

I will, says Mark. I will, with the Maiden's help.

Then the elks turn and in a blur of hooves, they're gone. I feel almost like crying, they were so beautiful, and so gentle.

Mark doesn't look at me, he just pushes through the branches – I see the thorns raise red welts on his arms, raking him as he passes. I follow him, cursing as the thorns scratch me too.

We emerge into the little clearing. All around us, the forest presses in, sharp and many-sided, busy with thorns. But this is a small, round haven, roofed with stars.

There are still good places, within the Crone's territory, says Mark. This is one of them. The last, I think.

Places can be good and bad? I ask.

Oh yes, says Mark. You haven't noticed?

CHAPTER
37

MARK BEGINS GATHERING TWIGS and small branches, dry leaves, and then sets about building a fire. He makes a small pile of moss and leaves, then a wigwam of twigs above it. He takes two stones from his pocket and strikes them together until sparks fly – they catch a leaf and erase it from the world, turning it to a brightly glowing tracery of veins that is there, deep orange, for a second, and then gone into dust.

The other leaves catch too, and the tinder flares, setting fire to the twigs. Mark leans larger branches over them, until the fire is blazing. Flames begin to lick up into the cold night air; smoke spirals up into the starlit blackness. The trees around the clearing flicker horribly, twisting and contorting in the firelight, as if they have come alive, as if they're reaching for us, wanting to wrap their limbs around us, drag us in.

This is probably true, I realise, with a shiver. And all the time the Child is crying, filling the air with its unhappiness, wanting me. Needing me.

Despite my terror of the trees, the thorns, it is all I can do not to get up and run into the forest, towards the castle, towards that voice, to find the Child and comfort it . . .

No.

No, I am here in the clearing, with Mark, and there is the warmth of the fire, its shifting light. Keeping the darkness at bay, the creatures of the Crone at bay. I close my eyes and let the fire wash over me.

Huh.

There is something else too, something that for the first time in maybe an hour distracts me from the constant background of the Child's crying.

This thing is:

I hear it. I hear the fire.

Mom was right, when she said in the cabin that it was indescribable. There are no words. The fire is like a living thing, and the noise of it is the noise of its living; it crackles, pops, fizzes, crunches, cracks. The sound is constant, comforting.

Mark is gazing into the flames, an unreadable, pensive expression on his face.

The elk that died, he said I shouldn't trust you, I say.

Mark makes a noise in his throat.

He said you played tricks, I continue.

Do I look like I'm playing tricks? says Mark. He is still looking at the fire and his face stays deadly serious.

No, I say.

Well, he says.

But it wouldn't be a trick if you seemed untrustworthy, would it? I say.

He laughs. No, I suppose not.

So, I say again, can I trust you?

Mark sighs. Trust is the wrong word, he says.

What does that mean?

I am Coyote, he says. I gave knowledge to people. I stole fire and gave it to them. I made death, so that their lives would matter. Twice I killed the Crone, when she was an owl and when she was a giant. I taught Man and Woman how to write. You can trust me to help you. It's just . . . you might not like it.

Oh, I say quietly.

We sit there in silence for a moment – or not silence, I realise. The constant noise of the crackling, spitting, creaking fire. The wind in the trees. The crying of the Child, in the background, pulling at me like an enormous magnet. The fire curls and ripples and rolls, as if its true nature is liquid. Above its flaring heat, the icy stars gleam. There are so many of them, a messy multitude, the constellations subtly different from the ones I'm used to. The light is bright – a bluish glow that illuminates everything.

He shakes his head. The problem, he says, is that in your world the days continue to follow one another. To run out. This is in the Crone's favour.

Because?

Because if we do not save the Child, and soon, your world will end. I told you this.

So what are we doing sitting here by a fire? I say.

He smiles. Conserving our energy, he says. Preparing.

And when does the sun come up? I say.

It doesn't, he says. Here there is no time.

What? I say. But we're moving and talking and –

Yes, he says. Time flows. But there is no sun, no moon. Only stars. So there are no days and everything is forever.

I stare at him. I'm thinking of the elk, closing its eyes. Apart from things that die, I say. Because you are Coyote and you made death.

221

Yes, he says.

Neither of us speaks for a while.

So when do we go? I ask eventually. I mean, we can't wait till dawn, if there isn't going to be a dawn.

Soon, he says, with another smile.

Then I feel something on my arm, something or someone touching me. I look at Mark, but he's sitting a foot away from me, and there's no one else there, no one I can see.

I look at the moving forms of the trees, their twisted shadows. Has one of them come forward into the clearing?

Who – I say.

Then the hand around my arm tightens and I open my eyes and –

1....

CHAPTER
38

– I'M IN THE CAR, and the Fed has his hand on my arm.

We're nearly there, he says.

I look down at his hand and he coughs, then removes it; it snaps back to his side as if on elastic.

We're in Flagstaff, I think. It's morning but early. We cruise down still-streetlit avenues, it's that time between night and day when everything is kind of grey, past anonymous office blocks and warehouses, until finally we reach some kind of public-looking building.

Pinstriped suit gets out of the car and comes around to my side. Then he opens my door and leads me into the building. I don't get a chance to see it properly – I just get a brief vignette of sidewalk and rotating doors, then I'm in a big air-conditioned atrium, a fish tank on a wall and a tired-looking receptionist sitting at a desk.

We turn right, go down a blank corridor, just flickering fluorescent lights above; a water fountain on the wall. White walls. We pass maybe three doors before suit stops at one of them and opens it. He ushers me inside.

It's a small, square room with four white walls, a single bed in the corner, a basin in the other corner, a toilet next to it.

It's basically a cell, I realise. It's basically a fricking cell.

Your cell, he says.

I stare at him for a moment, and he blinks. *I mean, your cell phone*, he says.

I shake my head. My cell is plugged into the wall in the judge's cabin.

You're refusing to give me your cell?

I give him what I hope is a look that can kill but he doesn't die so oh well. I turn out my pockets, so he can see the white insides.

Oh, he says. *OK. No cell. I need your watch though.*

Shaking my head, I take the watch from my wrist and give it to him with exaggerated servility, like I'm really eager to please him, trying to make him conscious of the monstrousness of what he's doing.

It must work because he stands there with his hand on the door handle for a moment. He's looking at me with something like . . . something like embarrassment. Like he's not quite sure whether he's doing the right thing, like there are usually protocols to be followed and right now he has no fricking idea what the protocol is.

I may be reading too much into it. But I'm pretty sure that's what I see.

Someone will come, soon, he says. *To talk to you.*

I frown at him. What does that mean? Does that mean he's just going to shut me in h–

Oh.

Yes.

It does.

After he shuts the door, I look around again. There really isn't anything in the room but the bed, the basin and the toilet. Is this some kind of cop station? I have no idea. But I know that whatever is going down is serious to the power of 100.

When guys in black Cadillacs drive you to some random building and lock you in what amounts to a cell, you know that shit just got real.

Maybe, I think, Mom really is Anya Maxwell. But in that case, what's the second lie? The Coyote – Mark, I remind myself – Mark said that there would be two lies and then the truth. But then maybe the second lie was something else. Maybe it was –

Oh God, I'm so tired.

I barely slept and some kind of SWAT team just came for Mom and I thought Mark was my friend but then he turned out to be some kind of trickster god that the elks are afraid of.

And what am I doing even THINKING about trickster gods and elks? I mean, what is the relevance? I should be thinking about how my life somehow went from comfortable routine – homeschooling, baseball cages, ice cream – to being locked in a bare room.

I don't even have the knife any more, so I can't step over into the Dreaming to escape from here.

I sit down on the bed, and I cry all the tears. All the tears inside me, all the tears in the world.

I keep doing that for two thousand years.

Finally, the tears dry up, my chest is still doing these kind of racking sobs but there's nothing coming out, and no one has come to see me, like the guy in the suit said they would.

So . . .

There are thirty-two cracks in the far wall of the room.

There are twelve pubes in the toilet – seriously, I counted them. None of them are mine, I would like to state for the record.

There are –

But then the door opens and someone comes in – a woman this

time, also in a suit, only hers is all dark navy, rather than pinstriped. She is thin and beautiful, with pale eyes. She smiles at me and asks how I am.

I don't answer.

She asks me lots of other questions. She asks me where my mother is – only, like the other Fed, she never calls her my mother, she always calls her Shaylene Cooper.

Where's Shaylene Cooper?

Where did Shaylene Cooper go?

Was Shaylene Cooper at the cabin with you?

Nine hundred ninety-nine permutations on the exact same fricking question, and I just sit there and don't say anything at all in response. As far as I'm concerned, they can tell me what's going on and maybe I'll speak to them, but I'm not answering their questions about my mom.

It's not even like I DO know where she is, and even if I did I wouldn't tell. I have my issues with her – she has lied to me repeatedly and she made Luke's hand into a kebab but I don't want her spending her whole life in prison.

Which, apparently, is what's happening to me, since when the woman in the dark suit leaves, I'm on my own again for hours and hours.

There are sixty-seven human hairs on the bed!

Seventeen of them are pubes!

Zero of them are mine because I will never lie on this thing, ever!

Hmm.

Of course, like an hour later I'm lying on the bed, having brushed it down as best I can, because, well, lock someone in a room with a bed for hours and eventually they're going to lie on it, no matter how gross and pube-y it is.

I watch the ceiling for a while – it's grey concrete and there is literally nothing, zero, nil, zilch that is interesting about it – and then I must fall asleep for a while because . . .

Well, you think I'm going to say that I wake up in the Dreaming, but I don't. I find myself in the hospital again, the one from my dream. I am in the first waiting room already, the Legos are in front of me and the crying of the lost child is in my bones. It's desperate this time, hurt – it needs so badly for someone to come cradle it and so I run . . .

I run to the second waiting room, past the rocking horse, and there's the child sitting in the middle of the floor, face screwed up, wailing, and no one around, no one responding. I rush forward. The child, I think it's a girl, I don't know why I suddenly see that but I do, looks up at me and for just a second stops crying.

I reach out my arms to scoop her up, and –

– and I snap back into the room, and look over to see that someone has come in with a tray.

Lunch, says this person, who is a woman and looks a bit like a nurse. Why would there be nurses here? At an FBI facility? But she's wearing a green papery dress and I'm pretty sure I'm right.

I ignore her as she sets the tray down, and then leaves. I'm thinking: Lunch? Seriously? That means I've been in here, what, only five hours maybe?

I'm also thinking that I'm not eating their food. I refuse. I absolutely refuse.

Yeah, OK, so I eat the food. It's lasagne.

It's actually quite good.

229

CHAPTER
39

I STILL WON'T SAY anything to them.

They try – they try over and over.

They come into the room where I'm being held – it's not a prison cell, but it's not much different – and they talk and talk and talk. They ask me about my life, about where we have been living, about what Mom has said to me, what I know.

They ask and ask but they're not TELLING me anything, so I don't answer.

I'm still in the same room – the bed, the toilet, the basin. That's it. Nothing else. Not even a TV, which might help with the, oh, what is it? oh yeah, that's it, the COLOSSAL, CRUSHING BOREDOM of sitting in here for hour after hour. It's homely! If you consider a hospital room to be homely.

You're thinking – she's bored? When her mom has just disappeared and is probably going to get the death penalty when she's caught, for killing her husband? And the answer is: yes. You try it.

Go on – shut yourself in a blank room. Your bathroom maybe. Sit there for ten hours.

Go on. Do it. I mean it. Ten hours. Look at the wall or something. Bored yet?

So, yes.

It's like suicide watch, in, like, *Girl, Interrupted* or something.

Have they caught Mom yet? I wonder. I hope not.

This is bad, I think. Really, really bad.

Then I need the toilet, and that's 7,890 times worse. After, I don't know, there's no way to tell the time because of course they took my watch, a nurse comes in. I can tell she's a nurse because she has a white uniform and one of those things for listening to your chest around her neck, but I think it's just for show because she doesn't use it. There's a guard with her, not a SWAT guy but just a hard-looking man with a gun in a holster.

Do you mind if I take some blood? asks the nurse.

I don't answer, but I'm thinking, What, why?

Do you mind if I –

I just look away, but I don't, like, resist or anything, so the nurse sticks a needle in me. She's good – she finds a vein right away. Then she takes some blood.

She says, *I'd like to check your leg too.*

Again, I don't answer.

She shrugs, then cautiously approaches. I don't move. She comes close – she has freckles, red hair. Crow's feet around her eyes, but I put her at maybe thirty. She's pretty, a diamond on her finger. I wonder if she has kids.

She leans down and opens the slit in my sweatpants. She takes off the CAM Walker and examines my leg. She has a bag with her and she takes some stuff from it and, I guess, changes the dressings or something. Then she nods, satisfied, apparently.

For a moment, I think about sticking my thumbs in her eyes and squeezing.

231

But I don't, and they leave, and that's the only interesting thing that's happened, and it's over.

A while later, someone who is obviously a therapist comes in and asks me a load of questions. The first one is, *Where is your mother?* And I want to laugh out loud because he's just told me that they haven't found her.

Then he rephrases it – *where is Shaylene Cooper?* This is weird, but maybe they think I don't know that she's Anya Maxwell?

Anyway, I don't give anything away. The therapist asks me about Phoenix, and school, which makes me think that they don't know Mom homeschooled me. They don't seem to know much, actually, but that doesn't stop him asking questions. He is bald, the therapist, with a birthmark on his head and big fleshy lips that make me think of a fish.

Maybe this is his therapist trick, I think. To gross people out with his appearance so that they get unsettled into talking.

Anyway, it doesn't work on me.

He asks whether Mom abused me, whether she ever hit me. What the hell is this? I am thinking. He asks if I have been confined, if I have been locked in a room.

Apart from now? I want to ask him, but I don't.

He says, *Does the name Angelica Watson mean anything to you?*

I blink. Angelica? But I don't say anything, I don't even shake my head.

The therapist notices the blink, though, because he keeps asking this question, and different permutations of it. But I never answer, and eventually he gets bored, or he's asked all the questions he planned to, and he leaves too.

I try the door – it's locked.

I wish I had the knife with me – I could hold it, and step through the air, and be back in the Dreaming, even if the wolves are chasing me.

Here, the wolves have caught me already. I'm trapped. I have nowhere to go.

A bit after that, the lights go off, and I figure that means they want me to sleep, so I lie down on the bed.

I mean, there's nothing else to do.

CHAPTER
40

DARKNESS.

This isn't the cabin this isn't the car what the –

Oh, I'm in the cell. Room, whatever. It's locked, so it may as well be a cell.

But something woke me. What was it?

A movement.

I whirl; there are two glowing points, low down near the floor.

Eyes.

I scoot back on the bed, heart racing, adrenalin like a bitter sharpness in me, as if my whole body was taste buds inside.

Then the eyes come closer and I see what it is – a coyote.

M-Mark? I say.

The coyote comes closer, lays a paw on my hand. Yes, it says. Yes and no.

Coyote.

Yes.

Coyote tips his head on one side, and regards me, there is no other word for it, it's not just simple looking. I feel like I caught sight of the moon, and now the moon has caught sight of me, and is LOOK-ING BACK. It creeps me out.

You have had the two lies, Coyote says. And soon you will have the truth.

What do you mean? I ask.

Coyote remains silent.

You mean that my dad was chasing us? That was the first lie, right? And, what? That whole story about being Anya Maxwell . . . is that a lie? Is there something else?

Coyote just holds my eyes and says nothing.

Whatever, I say, don't tell me.

I can't, he says. It's the truth. You don't tell it. It just is. Someone else will tell you. Or you will see. But it is not for me to do.

What do you want, then? I say. If you're not going to tell me anything.

I want you to step through. Into the Dreaming.

Now?

Yes, now. We don't have long.

I don't have the knife, I say. The one you said was for killing the Crone? I dropped it in the forest – I mean, I threw it, because I worried that –

You don't need the knife.

I stare at his doglike muzzle. Then how will I kill the Crone?

You will know how, says Coyote. When the time arrives. Now come. Time is running out.

Till what?

Till the Child dies, says Coyote.

I stare at it, thinking of my dream, the new desperate tone to the crying. It feels like something is getting closer, it's true, something that is going to change everything. But I don't know what it is and it's freaking me out to the power of ten.

235

What if I don't come? I say.

Then everything ends, says Coyote. You must face the Crone at the right time.

According to who? I say. You? The elks called you the First Liar.

Coyote is silent, and I don't know if that's because he doesn't know the answer or because he doesn't want to answer. Then I think, it doesn't make a single infinitesimal iota of difference to me, and right now I'm trapped in this cell anyway, so what am I worrying about?

OK, I say. I stand up and take a step and I've forgotten about my leg so I go pitching forward and –

EVERYWHERE IS STARS

CHAPTER
41

THEN MARK AND I are standing next to the fire, the Forest of Thorns looming around us. I can smell wood smoke and I feel the heat of the fire prickling my skin. Most of all, I can hear the sound of the flames eating the wood, the low unending crepitation of it, so beautiful in my ears.

Only . . .

Only I can hear the crying too, and just like in my dream it's more desperate now, louder, the Child sounds like it needs someone right now. Needs *me* right now.

Time to go, says Mark.

Yes, I say. The crying is like a physical pull on me; a hook in my flesh.

We push out of the clearing and further into the forest, on a path that is little more than a faint trace on the ground, branches pressing into us. Soon my arms and cheeks are covered with scratches. Mark is bleeding too, from a hundred little grazes.

Are the thorns poisonous? I say.

Yes, but not for you, says Mark.

What?

The forest will let you through, he says. You are the Maiden.

Then he turns forward again and keeps on, and I see that the conversation is over.

We battle through the woods for what must be an hour. It's painful going, the thorns constantly tearing at my skin. It's also claustrophobic – I can't see the stars any more, the night sky above. Only a canopy of intertwined trees, twisted thorns.

Panic starts to grip me, and grip is exactly the right word, it's like there's a band tightening around my chest. I can't breathe properly, I can't get enough oxygen into my lungs.

I'm about to tell Mark to stop, when the thorns begin to thin, and the path is suddenly stony underfoot, and we emerge into another, much wider clearing, dotted with flowers that are a sick, acid yellow.

There's a structure in the clearing – it looks like a batting cage at first, but as we get closer I see that it's more like a hutch, only an enormous one, towering above the trees. Walls made of some kind of woven wire. I can hear sound coming from it too – a sad voice, crying, it sounds like the Child but I can also still hear the Child's louder voice, far ahead of us somewhere, so that this voice is like a strange little echo.

I press ahead, getting closer to the structure, Mark beside me.

What is it? I ask. As I do so, I see something in the cage. It looks like a small person.

Mark walks closer to the cage – I can see that it *is* a cage, now, made of rusted iron, it looks like. Not a small person, I realise – a child.

Could it be *the* Child? The one Mark keeps talking about? It is upset, I can hear its wails, but I can still hear crying floating over the trees from the horizon, so that there is a kind of stereo effect happening.

Is that . . . ? I say.

The Child? says Mark. I don't know. It feels like it. But also it feels . . . other.

What do you mean? I ask.

He shakes his head. Some Crone magic, he says. We should be careful. I sense a trap.

I ignore him and approach the cage. It is building-sized, and it stretches as far as a building too. It's been built around the few trees in the clearing, so that there are trees inside it, like a monkey exhibit in a zoo. As I get closer, the child stops crying and looks up at me, its huge damp eyes riveting mine. The crying that's coming from far away also stops, so there is only the sighing of wind in the trees.

The child is sitting on the grass in the middle of the cage, clutching something to its chest. I can't quite see what it's holding but there is an impression of fur – grey fur. A squirrel? When I'm standing right by the cage, the child – it's a girl, I see – stands and toddles towards me, but stops short of the wire and holds out her hands, as if to be picked up, as if to be held. The grey squirrel is still –

No. Not a squirrel.

The ears are too long.

And it isn't fur, not real fur anyway. It's plush. A plush bunny.

It's like there's a heavy magnet in my stomach, and the girl is crackling with electricity, like I have to meet those hands and pull her up and into my arms.

I reach out my hand to the wire, wanting to test it, to see if I can pull it apart, but Mark grabs my arm.

What are you doing? he says.

What?

That's iron, he says. We can't touch it.

240

But it's so delicate! I say. The iron cage is like filigree, and red with rust – a soft punch would break it open.

It's iron, says Mark again. Those of the Dreaming can't touch it. Apart from the Crone. It is very harmful to us.

What about me? I ask.

You are of the Dreaming.

Yeah, I say. But I'm from my world too. Maybe I can.

He makes a gesture that isn't like crossing himself, but it has a similar effect; it conveys a similar meaning, of warding off evil. It could hurt you, he says. Very badly. The way he says this, it's like that would be bad for him too, and it sets loose wings inside me.

But I'm looking at the child reaching out her arms towards me, imploring me with her wide-open eyes and it's just like in my dream, the feeling of need, of powerless need, and I just want to help her, to comfort her.

What if it is the Child? I say. Didn't you say we had to rescue her? All this time I don't take my eyes off hers, and I can feel her willing me to rescue her, eyes boring into me.

Yes, says Mark. But . . . there is something wrong here.

He's right. I can feel it. Something subtly but all-over wrong, like when you put on a sweater back to front. But at the same time, there's the child, and her irresistible eyes.

I have to help her, I say.

Mark sighs. But the iron –

I don't care about the iron, I say.

I shake him off, he's stronger than me but he isn't expecting it, and I reach out for the cage and at the same he is shouting, No! one long syllable of no, but it's too late because I've got the wire gripped in my fingers and I pull, as hard as I can and –

It bursts outwards, bending, and I feel no pain at all as it rips. I seize the edges of the hole and pull it further open. As I'm doing it, the child is nodding her head in excitement, bobbing up and down on her toes. I bend down and start tearing open the last section of wire and then get down on my knees and lean to her, throw my arms out ready to wrap them around her.

For the longest moment, though, she doesn't move. She stands there looking through my head and into my soul, hands by her side. She opens her mouth and speaks, a sing-song voice, speaking a language I don't understand.

Mark takes a step forward, raising a hand, but then stops. His face is pale, drawn.

What is she saying? I ask.

He hesitates. She's saying thank you, he says.

But there is something in the set of his face; he is holding something back, I think.

What is it? I ask.

Nothing, he says.

She's definitely saying something else. I can see it now in her eyes as she continues to speak, her tone raw with urgency. Gratitude, but also pity.

What is she saying, Mark?

She's saying she would like to free you also, says Mark reluctantly.

The girl stops speaking and nods. Then she raises her arms again and rushes towards me, through the gap I have made in the wire, and I lift my own hands, ready to throw them around her, to pull her into my embrace, and . . .

and . . .

and she vanishes, not instantly, but more like a dissolving, like one moment she is there and physical and present and the next moment she is a soft amalgam of shimmering particles, bubbles or shining grains, and then she is gone.

My momentum tips me over, and I face-plant on the ground, grass pressing into my cheek. I push myself up on to my hands and sit back on my knees, bewildered.

A trick, says Mark. I told you.

But there's something left behind. I reach down and pick it up, feel its warmth in my hands, and I know that the girl was somehow real, or was a projection of something real, because this is the heat of her blood in the object I'm holding.

It's the bunny, its fur polished by age and touch, its eyes scratched and worn, its ears flopping. Up to this moment I haven't wanted to recognise it, but now the dams in my mind can't hold the truth back any longer.

Hold out your hand, says Mark.

I do, showing him the bunny in my left hand.

No, he says. The other one. The one you tore the cage with.

I proffer my right hand and he frowns down at it. You are not hurt? he says. By the iron?

No, I say.

He looks stunned, but he gathers himself. Meanwhile I am just staring down at the bunny in my hand, I can't believe it's here, in the real world, or in the Dreaming anyway, which is not the same as a dream.

What is that? says Mark.

It's a toy rabbit, I say. I . . . I've seen it before.

What, here? In the Dreaming?

No, I say. In a dream. A nightmare, I guess. I've had it ever since I can remember.

What kind of a dream?

There's a hospital, I say. And a child crying, and I follow the sounds until I reach it, reach her I should say, and she's holding a bunny like this one, when I find her. She holds out her arms to me and then . . . then I wake up. Every time.

Hmm, says Mark. It may be that the Crone can see into your mind. That she is using this dream of yours to disconcert you.

Yeah, well, it's working, I say. I am feeling pretty majorly –

Suddenly Mark puts his finger to his lips. Quiet, he says.

I fall silent.

There, says Mark.

But I have already heard it – it's the crying of the Child again, and it's coming from further ahead, further through the forest, carrying on the night air.

We must carry on, says Mark.

Yes, I say. I start to stuff the bunny into my pocket but Mark shakes his head.

No, he says. The Crone left it there. It's not safe.

Reluctantly, I lay it back down on the grass. It feels like abandoning something small and helpless and for some reason tears come to my eyes, which I know is ridiculous because it isn't even alive, it's a stuffed toy.

Then I stand up straight again. We're totally alone there in the clearing, the sound of the crying Child a low constant hum.

Mark takes a last look at the rabbit and the cage, shifts uncomfortably, then starts to walk off. But as he turns away, his hand brushes the cage; I don't think he realises. And . . . nothing happens. It doesn't visibly hurt him, no sparks fly. All around us, the crying of the Child, the real one far off in the distance, continues to resonate, just another part of the world, the water in which we swim.

There are two possibilities, I think: either he lied to me, about the iron. But I don't really buy it – I saw the fear in his eyes when I said what I wanted to do.

Or, other explanation: he *can* touch iron, he just believes he can't. But why would he believe that he can't? It doesn't make any sense.

Anyway, whatever: right now I just want an answer to my question about what the Child said. I follow him and grab his sleeve.

Don't walk away from me, I say. Don't you dare. Not till you've told me what she said.

You do not give orders to Coyote, he says, a little haughtily.

Oh to hell with you, I say.

His features soften. It's not important, he says.

I don't care. Tell me right now or I swear to God I will leave this place and never come back, and your Crone can go screw herself and that child will have to just keep crying.

Please, just –

No. Tell me.

Mark sighs. She said that you would soon find out what you really were. She said she was sorry.

What I really am? I ask. What's that?

I can't tell you.

I stare at him. *What?* Why not?

Because it is not for me to say, he says. It is for someone else.

Then the Dreaming is flooded with light and the clearing disappears for an instant, is replaced by my small white room, the bed,

245

the basin and a dark figure standing there, hands clasped in front of him.

Just a flash –

And then it's gone, the stars are back, the forest. Mark standing beside me, looking worried.

Who? I say.

What?

You said it's for someone else to say, I say. Who?

Mark winces as the world goes bright again, and the cell pops into being around us, glaring white, fluorescent-light illuminated, the man standing there, looking at me.

Him, says Mark.

And then he's gone and the Dreaming is gone and it's just me in the brightly lit cell and I look up at the man and –

0...

CHAPTER
42

– I HAVEN'T EVER SEEN the man standing in my cell before – he's handsome, with greying hair and a strong jaw. He's wearing a suit that looks tailored. The same guard as before is with him. I sit up in bed and look at them, without moving or saying anything.

The man looks – and this is weird – nervous. He comes a little into the room and then stands, fidgeting. I'm nervous too. Everything my mom taught me about men is that this is bad, this is dangerous.

He must have turned on the light – it's a bright fluorescent light set in the ceiling above, set in the grey board of the ceiling, and he must have turned it on and woken me and that's how the Dreaming disappeared.

This . . . ah . . . he says.

Oh, yeah, right, I think. Well, that explains it.

He clears his throat.

My name's Rick Miranda, he says. Ridiculously, he hands me a card.

I look down at it.

RICK MIRANDA
FLAGSTAFF CITY ATTORNEY

Then a bunch of phone and email information.

I'm the city attorney for Flagstaff, he says, confirming the details on the card, though I don't know what I'm supposed to do with it. I mean, I don't have a phone or a computer so I'm not going to be calling him or emailing him. I just hold it awkwardly in my hands.

There's a pause. He seems to be expecting me to say something, but I don't.

I . . . um, he continues, *I don't know if you understand what I'm saying. The psychiatrist thought you were lucid, but you didn't say anything, so . . .*

Ah, I think. Not therapist, psychiatrist.

. . . It's . . . if it were up to me, we would do this differently, continues the city attorney. *I don't know, find some kind of halfway house for you. People to talk to you. But you haven't committed a crime, and we can't just hold you forever.*

I stare at him.

OK . . . he says. He comes closer and hunches down, bending his knees, like a father squatting to bring his kids in on some game.

I'm now officially and 100 per cent freaked out. Is Mom dead or something?

The city attorney looks at me, and I see pity in his eyes.

What the –

Your mother is not your mother, he blurts out. *I don't know – we don't know – what she told you. Your name is Angelica Watson and you disappeared from Juneau Hospital in Alaska in 1999. You were being treated for burns to your legs.*

This is my mind, right now:

That's it. Just blank. Just white, like snow.

Then: Angelica, I think.

Shaylene Cooper, we know now, posed as a nurse and took you away. She moved a whole lot – Albuquerque, right? And Phoenix? And I'm guessing she homeschooled you?

Me:

He scrubs his face with his hands, as if it's dirty, as if he wants to pummel off his skin, and find something cleaner underneath.

Your parents never stopped believing, he says. They paid private detectives. They appeared on TV. They . . . ah . . . He turns away, and so I miss the next bit, I don't catch it. Then he turns back to me. *They're here now, in Flagstaff. They've rented an apartment. We . . . we have to release you into their care.*

I think: You can trust him to take order and replace it with chaos.

I think of my life with Mom, the routine, every day the same, apart from Fridays, and then every Friday was the same, anyway. Now a stick of dynamite has been put under all that and it has been blown into the sky.

I think:

THERE WILL BE TWO LIES AND THEN THERE WILL BE THE TRUTH.

251

I think:

Screw you, Coyote.

And then I don't think anything.

There's nothing in my head, just air, but air can build to a high pressure – it's Boyle's Law, I learned it with Mom, or with WHO-EVER MOM REALLY IS, it's $P_1V_1 = P_2V_2$, which means that if the volume of something contracts then the pressure goes up, and right now the volume of my mind is a tiny tiny thing because there are NO THOUGHTS IN IT, and so I guess that means the pressure is going crazy, needle pushing into red, because –

CHAPTER
43

WHEN I WAKE UP, I'm lying on the bed. Did they put me here?

There's no one else in the room, and I feel groggy. As if I've been sedated. It's possible: my memory is all fragments, like something delicate dropped on the floor.

For a second I look at the ceiling, the thin grey panels, whorled with dust. Then I think:

My mother is not my mother.

Something like goose bumps, or like the evil twin of goose bumps, goes through me. It's as if I'm a ghost, because I don't know who I am any more. It's like I've died.

I suddenly realise:

I don't even know if my name is really Shelby. I am standing now though I don't remember doing it, and I think that I'm naked on this floor, naked on the surface of the earth, with nothing to protect me or name me. Nothing to claim me. I'm insubstantial; a wraith.

The door opens and the city attorney comes in, Rick Miranda, a detail I remember, absurdly. I half expect him to walk through me, as if through droplets diffused in the light by a garden hose. But he doesn't. He walks right up to me and kneels down on the floor.

I blink at him, surprised, but it's smart of him too, because I had blades in my mind, turned towards him, and he has taken them from me with that gesture.

I'm sorry, he says. *I told you too suddenly. I'm new to this. I'm . . .* He winces, but stays down on one knee. *I'm part of a response team. We had training. But no one said . . . no one said how you . . . how you tell. Someone.*

I don't say anything.

I mean, he says, like he doesn't need me to provide the other half of the conversation, *you figure the child knows, right? That they want to go home? That's what you think when you're in training, learning how to handle these cases.*

He sighs.

I lead this city's CART, he says. *Child Abduction Response Team. There's a bunch of people on it. Fire department; obviously not needed in this case. Police. Child Protective Services. Me. But we don't . . . I mean, this is our first case.*

Another sigh.

What will happen, we'll try to manage the transition as best we can. Your parents will stay here in Flagstaff for some time, we have yet to determine how long. CPS will visit with you, to make sure you're OK. There'll be counselling, which the state will provide.

The truck that just powered through my chest is halfway through the wall behind me now; there is brick dust and plaster and debris raining all over us, turning us grey, turning us black and blue with bruises, but he doesn't see any of it.

Slowly, peeling them off my tongue because they don't want to leave it behind, I say two words with my mouth.

My parents?

He looks at me, and I can see how out of his depth he is, because his eyes are very clearly saying, Oh crap.

Ah . . . yes, um, your birth parents. Custodial parents, we call it. He's babbling now. *They're, ah, here and –*

And nothing, because at that moment something snaps inside me, some essential restraining elasticity, and I am on the other side of the room as if there were no intervening space between, banging on the door, it hurts my hands but I don't care, and the door won't open so I hit it with my head, and then there is blood on my fingers, I guess it's mine, and I fall over because I ran on my bad leg, forgot my CAM Walker was there, the bulk and unfamiliar-still weight of it, and the city attorney is shouting for help, I think, anyway, because of course I just see his mouth moving –

and then there's a gap in what I'm aware of, and there's a guard in the room, moving towards me, and I –

I must hit the guard or push him or something because then he is kind of powering at me and wrapping his arms around me, then spinning me around to drag me out of the door, but before he can I whiplash my head back and feel something crunch, and the guard staggers back and now my hands are free so I shout at the city attorney, I shout,

What are you doing to me? What gives you the right? What gives you the fricking right?

And here's the thing:

I don't think. I shout it with my hands.

The guard circles around so that he's in front of me. There is blood running down from his nose, but his eyes are wide, wide open with shock and his jaw hasn't dropped because that doesn't happen in real life, but it's pretty close.

The city attorney is also standing very still.

Then he turns to the guard, but not so much that I can't see his lips. *We didn't know she was* deaf? he says. *Seriously? This wasn't information anyone thought might be useful?*

CHAPTER
44

THE PSYCHIATRIST IS BACK – he just gave me a shot of something, and now I'm sitting on the bed all loose, all warm, all cotton-wool headed.

The city attorney is speaking to him, and I guess they don't know that I read lips, or they don't care, because they are just standing there talking about me.

It doesn't make sense, says the city attorney. *The Watsons never said she was deaf.*

Maybe they didn't know, says the psychiatrist.

She was two, for God's sake! They wouldn't have noticed she wasn't speaking?

Don't ask me, says the psychiatrist. *Maybe she developed it later. But full deafness . . . I mean, if she is fully deaf . . . that's usually congenital.*

We need to get a translator in here, a . . . you know . . .

Sign language interpreter?

Yes.

The psychiatrist nods and leaves the room. The city attorney has his head in his hands again; I figure he had other plans for this weekend. Maybe he has a cabin too, I think.

He looks so sad, so vulnerable, that I get up and walk very slowly over to him, or kind of hop, actually, because I don't want to put weight on my leg. Even moving like this, undignified, it's like my feet aren't touching the floor, like there's a layer of feathers between me and the ground.

I keep walking. He is so far away.

In my mind is moonlight and stars, sunshine and flood. I am a tree, I think. I am rooted to the earth and that is all the mother I need, I move in years not seconds.

He is still a million miles away.

I go through all the seasons in the blink of an eyelid: I am weighed down by apples; I sleep under frozen earth; I burst into green life under warm air.

Then I am there, in front of him, and he flinches away from me, and the guard, who is still there but not important to me, steps forward.

I shape my lips. I can do it – (Mom) taught me, (Mom) would say yes, that's right, or no, that's not, here's how you should tap your teeth, here on the palate is where your tongue goes.

(Mom) spent months on that.

I look at the city attorney – he has kind eyes, one blue, one green, not that this makes either more or less kind. It's called heterochromia; my (mom) taught me that.

He doesn't look scared. He still looks sorry for me.

I don't like doing it, because I know it sounds weird, no matter what (Mom) says, I know it's freaky. But I say it anyway, I say it with my mouth.

I've been having very strange dreams, I say.

I'm scared, I say.

Who am I? I say.

And then I black out.

BLACKNESS

BLACKNESS

THEN . . .

STARS.

CHAPTER
45

BEFORE MY EYES OPEN my ears register the sound of the crying Child, the background resonance of the Dreaming, impossible to ignore now that we are so close to the Crone's castle.

Then my eyes do open and I see Mark – we're in the clearing still, with the open cage.

I take a step towards Mark, furious.

Shelby . . . he says, hands out in front of him to say *calm down*.

No, screw you, I say. My name isn't even Shelby, it's Angelica.

He shakes his head. Names are unimportant. You are the Maiden.

Oh don't give me your yoga teacher philosophical bull, I say. My mother is *not my mother* and you couldn't have mentioned it? You said you were helping me.

I warned you, he says. His eyes are shiny in the starlight.

Some warning! I say. Like I was supposed to understand a coyote talking in riddles!

I can't speak directly of your world, he says.

Oh. How handy.

I sit down quite suddenly on the ground. Anger is a wild animal inside me. I think back to the elk, dying. The elk said you played tricks, I say. You didn't even deny it. I should have listened.

Shelby . . .

So why should I trust you now? How do I even know you're telling the truth about this Crone, about the Child? When you won't fricking tell me *anything*?

He splays his hands. My tricks are only to help people.

Yeah, right, I say. That's why the elks were so afraid of you.

I am Coyote, he says. I am a predator. That is why they fear me.

You're more than that, I say. You are the son of the sky and the earth, you said. You are older than the world.

Yes.

So tell me what I'm supposed to do.

You're supposed to kill the Crone. You're supposed to rescue the Child.

Seriously? I say. Do you have *any idea* what has happened to me?

Yes. That is why you must do these things. Or the world will end.

Oh please, the world is not going to end if I don't do your stupid quest.

Yes, he says sadly. It will.

I sneer at him. I'm not going any further with you, I say. The fury is tearing at my insides now – I think of his fear of the iron. If he was so powerful, if he was so old, if he made the fricking moon and the sun, or stole them or whatever, shouldn't he be able to help some helpless little child, even if it was a trick.

And the Child, the one I can hear crying – if he cares so much then why doesn't he just go and save it himself, stand up to the Crone? He's supposedly in charge of the rain or whatever so why is this place so barren, so parched? Why are the elks wasting away?

Even the thorns look wasted, dehydrated.

Suddenly I hate him, and I am dimly aware that some of this hate is not for him, that it's for the men who plucked me out of the night outside the cabin, and threw me in a cell, who told me that my (mother) stole me as a baby

(*like a changeling like a fairy child*)

but I don't care. I throw the hate at Mark, instead, Mark with his fricking infuriating fortune cookie pronouncements.

Go, I say. Leave me here.

I'm not leaving you, he says. I am here to help you in your quest.

GO, I say, not in capitals like that but in a dangerous, low, quiet tone that I can't reproduce in type.

Mark clearly registers it though because he nods, slowly. All right, he says. If you change your mind, you know which direction to walk in.

Then he sets off, out of the clearing. He doesn't look back – he moves away from me, and as he moves he melts downwards, head and arms folding in, and then he's a coyote running swiftly through the trees, large and strong, heading forward, further into the Forest of Thorns, towards the castle.

Then gone.

Oh, I think.

Oh, now I'm on my own.

In the Dreaming.

Then I hear a sound – like a sighing, on the wind. I look up and there's a huge bird circling above me, a hawk.

No, I think: an eagle.

Its wingspan is easily my body height, and it's getting lower, gyring down towards me, I can see the white of its head feathers, the brown of its wings, the detail and tracery of its feathers. It opens its beak and emits a piercing cry, *Kiiiiiiii*.

The noise of it is unbelievable, like a stabbing in my ears.

Then the eagle folds its wings, and I start to scrabble at the ground with my hands, trying to get up, trying to get my legs under me and to piston myself up into a running –

Too late.

I glance up and the eagle is nearly on me, its talons out, like chef's knives, its eyes hard and unforgiving as stones, its sharp beak wide open, and the terror must crack the glass of the trance because just like that –

CHAPTER
46

I WAKE UP, DRENCHED in sweat, in my cell.

Scenes follow, in some order or other.

I don't really know what's going on.

Someone comes and hands me some sheets of paper, an old-ish woman who looks like a librarian. I have to fill in the problems while she watches, and times with a stopwatch. It's like an IQ test. All the time, I have a feeling like I'm on a train that just stopped.

What I mean: my (mom) took me on a train once. I don't know when it was. I guess maybe when we moved from Albuquerque to Phoenix. And there's this thing that happens, when the train stops – because it's so heavy, because its momentum is so great, the body of it keeps moving forward, just slightly, before settling back on to the wheels; you feel it in your stomach.

That's what I feel, as I fill in the test, as I do anything right now – like I've stopped, in my tracks, but there's a part of me that's still moving, still lurching forward, not yet settled.

When I'm done, and she's looking through it, she frowns.

What's wrong? I say, with my mouth, because the interpreter has not arrived yet.

The woman doesn't understand – I can't hear myself, of course, but I guess it's not too clear when I speak.

What did I do wrong? I say slowly.

The woman's eyebrows unknit a little, but she is still looking at me curiously. *Nothing*, she says. *You didn't get* any *wrong. That's not . . . It means you're very, very smart.*

I want to say, I'm deaf, I'm not a fricking moron. But I don't, so instead I just glare at her. *I want a TV*, I say.

A TV? I'm not sure –

I'm not under arrest, am I? I say. *So I want a TV. Or some books. Whatever.*

She leaves, and a little while later, they bring me a little TV – an old one, three-dimensional instead of flat. Things that are old take up more space than things that are new. Things that are new are flat and thin. Like my life.

A couple of janitor-y type guys set it up and hand me the remote. I flick through the channels for a while. I'm on, like, channel 4,000 when I see Luke standing outside a building, which is all metal and glass and about four storeys. The building I'm in, I realise.

Luke is wearing a bandage on his hand, and I feel a pang of guilt. He doesn't look happy to be talking to these people – there's someone standing next to him, someone official looking, and I figure he's been made to give an interview, to at least keep the press happy for a bit.

Because of course, I think. This is big news.

I am big news.

I look at the remote, and work out how to put the closed captions on. There's a delay, then they come up on the screen, blue against the picture.

And what about your time with this woman and her daughter, did they –

Luke's face goes still. He leans in close to the mike. The woman interviewing him, she has platinum blonde hair and very full red lips, smiles, a predator's smile, because he's about to say something serious, something personal, some kind of media gold crap.

I will say this only once, Luke says in blue closed captions. *I will not speak about them. That girl deserves her piracy – privacy.*

I laugh. My . . . I stop myself. Shaylene. The woman who . . . The woman. She would have liked that one. I am a pirate now.

Then I glance back at Luke. He is holding his arm up now.

No comment, he says. *No comment.*

Then he walks away. The woman, the reporter, is a pro, but even so she can't stop herself from scowling slightly; she'd been expecting some kind of scoop.

I switch off the TV, feeling kind of surprised. I mean, I thought Luke would love talking about it. The time he got mixed up with a baby stealer and her freaky deaf daughter, and got his hand shish-kebabbed.

Oh well. You never know with people. It's not like Luke is at the forefront of my mind, anyway.

After that, some guy in a green uniform comes in – he's got a tray of food: a Coke, a banana, and . . . mac and cheese.

Mac and fricking cheese.

Worst. Day. Ever.

CHAPTER
47

WHEN YOU REMEMBER BEING a young child you don't remember anything whole – just little bits and pieces, here and there. Like a bill, something printed on thin paper, left in a jacket pocket for a year, more, and then you find it and most of the words are faded, just the odd grey mark spared.

Sunlight slanting through a window, on a day when something clicked inside you, and you knew it was fall – something about the granularity of the light. The feel of a bigger hand holding yours as you walked down the street, jumping over cracks. Splashing in the pool, the light making jewels on the surface.

People say smell is the sense most closely linked to memory, but they're full of it. Sure, a smell can trigger a memory. But when you look back on your childhood, you don't think, hey, I remember when I smelled gas for the first time, at that gas station, do you? No. There's a clue in the phrasing – you LOOK back.

When I look back at my very early childhood, I see parts, little lost moments, like Jeffrey Dahmer has hacked up the past with a saw. But there's one that's still whole; one bubble of time, glistening, unpopped.

I walk with my (mom) to a playground, somewhere. Maybe in

Albuquerque? I don't know. I know there are a couple of trees, and the grass is brown and dry, so it must be summer. The playground is pretty much empty; it's a school day. I'm three, maybe four. I feel very small, next to my (mom); I remember that. I have a feeling like I'm tiny but the whole world is inside me, this contradictory feeling; it's almost like a dizziness.

I'm not sure what we do first. I guess (Mom) pushes me on the swing, something like that. My memory has decided that the first part is not important. But it has kept the next part, hugging it close, like some sentimental object it doesn't want to let go of, to let slip into the blackness.

I walk over to the slide. It's a big one, bigger than I'm used to. It's set on like a hill, man-made, instead of having steps up to it. I look at it, and I feel like I'm looking at a building or something, it's so high up. The sun gleams on it, whitely. It's as if the metal is melting.

Too high, I say, with my hands – I guess (Mom) has already been teaching me sign.

It's OK, honey, she says. It's just like any slide, only bigger.

No, I say.

But you love slides, says (Mom).

I look at it again. I shake my head.

You want to go on it with me? says (Mom). She takes my hand. She's smiling down at me, her head blotting out the sun, like she's filling the sky.

I nod.

She picks me up and carries me to the top of the little hill of dirt – there are scrubby little clumps of grass on it, the whole thing worn away by kids climbing up it. When we get to the top, she sits down on the slide, then puts me on her lap, and we –

go –

whoosh, down to the bottom, her arms tight around me, and in my memory it's like dropping through space itself, like being a shooting star, but belonging, at the same time; a shooting star in a family of meteors maybe, drifting through nothingness together; like a safe kind of falling.

This is the lesson of the slide: it's possible to feel fear, for your stomach to come loose and float up to your throat, but with no real danger.

Anyway.

When we get to the bottom, I look up at (Mom). Again, I say.

And so she carries me up again, and we go down, I don't know how many times. Over and over. Just the two of us, me on her knees, wrapped around by her, until the sun started to set, pulling long shadows from the swing set and the seesaw. Then she walked me home, her arm holding me, and the moon was full above us and it made me feel lonely to look at it; lonely and cold, which only made the warmth of her around my shoulders even better, even more like home.

The question is:

Knowing what I know now, knowing that my mom was never my mom, is this memory real? I don't mean, did it happen. Because I'm pretty sure it did.

I mean:

How am I supposed to feel about it? What am I supposed to do with it? Before, it meant certain things in my head, and it was the image that came into my mind when those things were spoken. Things like: belonging; things like: safety.

Now it means lies.

CHAPTER
48

I WANT A LAWYER, I say. I am signing, to the interpreter, who is a mousy woman with bad hair, who I bet has a whole load of cats. She isn't deaf, she told me. But she had a deaf brother, growing up. That's how come she signs.

Her name is Melany, with a *y* like that. When you're deaf, you know how people's names are written. She made a joke about how her parents couldn't spell very well, which I guess is a big ice-breaker for her in her job, and I laughed because it seemed like that was what she wanted.

We're in a bigger room now, with a table and chairs and coffee – maybe they figured the cell was not good for me. It's, I don't know, two days later.

The reason I needed Melany is, they – the CART team, the psychologists, everyone – have like a quota of one thousand questions an hour they have to ask me, otherwise there will be untold consequences, or that's what it feels like anyway. Questions about Shaylene, did she abuse me, did she touch me inappropriately, did she ever, did she sometimes, did she –

So many questions.

But anyway, at least now we've moved from my cell to this

bigger room, which makes it feel less like an interrogation, and I'm trying to tell myself that instead, they're just concerned about me and want to make sure I'm not screwed up in some major way. Which of course I am, but not in the way they're afraid of. I mean it's not like (Mom) used to batter me with a hot iron or anything.

We walked down a corridor to get here; the whole decor in this place is very neutral, very every-office: white walls, chrome, pine. It's like having your life turned upside down at an insurance company.

You haven't committed a crime, says FBI Special Agent Deacon, through the mousy woman. I haven't seen the city attorney since forever, and I guess maybe he's in trouble for telling me too suddenly about who I really was. Whatever the reason, it's Deacon who seems to be in charge now. He has silver hair, but his skin is smooth and his eyes are sharp. Like weapons. Right now, it seems they're on my side, though, which is good.

I know I haven't committed a crime, I say to him.

You don't need a lawyer, then, he says. *You're a victim.*

This is stupid of him, but I don't say so. I mean, if a diamond is stolen from an heiress, is it the diamond that's the victim? No – the diamond is just, I don't know, the object of the crime. It's the heiress who's the victim. Here, in this situation, if there's a victim, then I guess it's my parents, my real parents, who had me stolen from them.

And me? I'm the object. I'm the diamond.

But I don't want to explain this with sign language.

I want a lawyer anyway, I say. *A woman lawyer. I can pay.* This is true. (Mom) set up a savings account for me. It has forty thousand dollars in it. (Mom) said that anything extra left over from her salary wasn't for her, it was for me. For when she was gone and couldn't look after me any more.

273

Keep me safe.

HA HA HA HA.

Special Agent Deacon looks over at some other person in a suit, who shrugs, and then Deacon sighs. *OK*, he says. He motions to someone who leaves the room. *But can I ask you some questions now?*

No, I say. *I will ask you questions.*

Deacon blinks. *Right, yes, fine.*

My . . . I mean, Shaylene Cooper. This takes a while to spell out and Deacon watches patiently as the interpreter translates. *Have you found her?*

No.

When you do . . .

He knows where I'm going with this. *She'll be tried. Kidnapping, assault, possibly child abuse charges . . . She could get life without parole.*

No, I say.

No?

No child abuse. She was . . . she was good to me.

Deacon nods, makes a note of this in a little black book in front of him on the table.

My parents are in town? My real parents?

Yes. In this building, actually. They are very eager to see you. We've been holding them back but . . . there's no legal requirement. We have no probable cause to detain you for any crime. They . . . You went missing when you were two years old. They've been waiting fifteen years. A lot of times, people told them you must be dead. They're pretty desperate.

I have been thinking about myself, only myself, but a feeling of,

274

I don't know what, sadness, compassion, pity, something, crackles through me like electricity. I can't imagine what that must be, to lose a child. I could try, but it would hurt too much, I think.

You said I was in a hospital, when she . . . took me?

Burns. From a deep fryer. That's what first alerted Dr Maklowitz when he saw the scar tissue on your legs – I mean, it was pretty big news fifteen years ago, and the burns were mentioned a lot; an identifying characteristic, you know. You don't hear about it now, which is probably why . . . why you didn't know. But he remembered.

And that's it? That's why we ran? That's why you found us?

Partly, he says. *I mean, the burn scars wouldn't have been enough. But your . . . Shaylene gave her real name at the reception desk.*

Oh, I think. Because I reminded her about her licence, in her purse. But she knew it was there – she just didn't want to show it. For a crazy second, I wish I could go back to that moment, could take all of this back, and have it just be me and (Mom), and nothing to say any different.

From there, it wasn't difficult. There was no ID for you, so they checked her records and there was no sign of Shaylene Cooper having a daughter. And there was no Shelby Jane Cooper on file anywhere, not at your address, not in local schools . . . We lost you for a while, of course, but after that spectacle in the diner . . . Well, Luke Scheinberg has a tracker in his car. We just followed it.

Of course he does, I think.

And then we had you, he says, *and you're the biggest piece of evidence. I mean, they took blood, when you were born. Just a prick test for sickle cell anemia, PKU, you know, but it was enough. DNA.*

That's why they tested my blood, I think.

I tap my fingers on the table. *She told me she was Anya Maxwell.*

She . . . what?

After the diner. I saw us, on CCTV on the news, leaving the hospital, and she said she was Anya Maxwell. Is she?

Deacon does like a cough-laugh thing; his smooth silver hair shakes. *Absolutely not,* he says. *Anya Maxwell would be in her sixties.*

I think back: the closed captions on the TV; the police believe these pictures may show An–

Angelica Watson, I think.

They were going to say Angelica Watson. But my (mom) used it, she must have thought so FAST, to come up with that story . . . She's like some kind of really smart monster, like someone I don't know at all. Who does that? Who pretends to be a famous murderer, so their daughter doesn't know she's stolen?

I want to see my parents, I say.

Of course, we'll bring them right in and –

No. You have one of those rooms, like on TV? Where the witness or whatever sits on one side of the glass and the detectives can watch without being seen? I want to see them, but I don't want them to see me.

This is a little hard to say in sign, but I think the interpreter manages it. She's like the people who type, when the anchors are talking on the TV news, doing the closed captions – you stop noticing her after a while, and so yeah, maybe her mousiness, her forgettableness, is like a total asset for her job.

Yes, says Deacon thoughtfully. *We do.*

The other guy steps forward and I realise now he's some kind of lawyer for the FBI or the police or something because he says, *This is highly irr–*

But then Special Agent Deacon busts out this badass stance, like chin raised, chest puffed out, which he has obviously practised in front of the mirror, and he says, *I don't give one goddamn what it is,* and that's the end of that.

CHAPTER
49

THERE ARE THINGS THAT, when they break, they keep on functioning, just in some other, lesser way. Like an elevator: it breaks, and it's a room. An escalator: it breaks, and it's stairs.

The heart is the same.

It breaks, and you might not even notice, because you still feel things, you still have emotions.

But there's a dimension missing, like for the elevator; it still works as a room, but it has lost its vertical axis of motion, and it's the same with a heart: it breaks, and yeah, you can still have feelings, you can still feel sorry for someone, or angry, or sad, but there's something that's lost, a motion, a dimension. It breaks, and it's just an organ, beating.

You will never really feel happy again; you will never really, deep down, care about anyone else again.

Not ever.

This is what I'm thinking as my parents step into the room on the other side of the two-way glass, because the first thing I feel with my broken heart is an emotion I don't even have a name for, something like love, I guess, for these two people who look so unbelievably sad and also so hopeful. Pity, maybe. But then, very quickly, it's gone, and I just feel cold and empty.

I don't want to be here. I want to lie in the cold clean dust of the moon and close my eyes. But I don't. I look at them.

The father is older, maybe fifty. He has a bald patch at the back of his head, and he's wearing clothes that look like they come from L.L. Bean, that whole hiking-in-the-hills look. He isn't wearing sandals over socks but he is, like, one step away from it.

The mother is 139 times more attractive than him, and maybe ten years younger. She has long hair that I guess is naturally red, from her freckles, but is also obviously dyed, the same colour. She is wearing jeans and a T-shirt, very little make-up, and if she wasn't the homecoming queen then I am a fricking walrus. She must have been beautiful, and I don't mean beautiful like people usually use it to describe any old thing, I mean beautiful like stunning.

This woman can't be my mother, I think.

Around her neck, there's a gold cross on a chain. She keeps touching it, unconsciously – a God-person, I realise. Still, I think. I guess she has had reasons for praying.

The mother is also crying like nothing I have ever seen, like she's a balloon person full of water, and someone has put pinpricks in her eyes, she's just crying and crying and crying, leaking all over her face.

Father puts his arms around her, awkwardly.

This, I think, is awful! And weird! And creepy!

But I keep watching. They turn to the glass, I guess they know I'm here, and their faces are so full of it, so full of expectation and hope that I don't know if I can bear it.

I mean, they're strangers to me.

Then the mother reaches into her jeans pocket and takes something out and she moves suddenly forward – I flinch back, even though there's glass between us – and the father tries to catch her arm, to hold her back, but he's not fast enough and she is there, pressing something against the glass.

It's a photo.

It's a photo, of her looking much younger and yes, just as beautiful as I thought, and she is holding this baby under the arms, she's lying back on a couch and the baby is above her, kind of dandling its feet on her chest, and she's laughing up at it.

This baby – me.

The expression on her face, though, man, the expression on her face.

It's not love, it's so far beyond that, it's like love is the normal engines and this, whatever it is, it's warp drive – it's something so intense that even as the father pulls her back, her face shaking, her lips trembling, I am leaning forward to keep looking at that photo, to keep seeing that thing that I see in her face fifteen years ago.

Not love. Something bigger.

But – and this is how I know my heart is broken – I step back and I close the valves that have opened, and they turn back into strangers, people I don't know.

I'm supposed to live with THEM? I say.

They've said they'll hire an interpreter. To stay in the house, until, you know, they can learn, says Deacon.

When's my lawyer coming? I say. *I want to talk with her. This is NOT happening.*

Oh, honey, says Deacon, and for the first time those ballistic eyes of his go soft. *I'm sorry, but it is happening.*

280

CHAPTER
50

I'M NOT IN LOVE with my lawyer, but, you know, she's OK.

It's just, she's one of those people who feel sorry for you because you're deaf. I want to say to her, it's not a fricking disease. I want to say all kinds of things to her.

I mean, OK, here:

I watched this show on TV once, and the characters were talking, and their whole conversation was, like, what would be worse, being blind or being deaf? So, right there – the assumption. People think it's terrible, being deaf, something to be frightened of.

But,

A) I have never known what it is like to not be deaf, except
   in the Dreaming, and that's not real. It's just a part of
   me. I don't have anything to compare it to. It's not bad.
   It's not good. It just is.

B) You want to know what would be the worst? What would
   be the worst sense to lose? Touch. That's what SHOULD
   scare people.

Touch.

See, we walk around on the earth, all the time, on two feet, which is kind of a miracle of balance, and it's only because of touch. It's the touch of feet on ground that tells us when we hit the zero moment point in the wave of our walking, and it took like forty years for scientists to teach robots to do that, to walk on two feet – I know because (Mom) taught me.

People say a bird is free.

But a bird isn't free, it just has different architecture. A bird is an open window on to thin air; and thick air; thermals, eddies, currents. A person is a ground floor, foundations driven deep in the earth.

A bird: what it can't do is throw arms around its mate. Some of them, even, they can't ever land, like swifts: they can't touch, so they can't love. Right now, I have an idea of how that might feel – it's like I'm disconnected, like a bird, just floating in empty space. No one to hold me.

I want to say to my lawyer: I don't care that I can't hear. But someone just took my (mom) away, my (mom) took me away, and I never had any friends anyway, so now I don't have anyone to touch, and the ground is gone below my feet, and I don't have anyone and so I'm like a swift, lost in the wide unanchored air, and I don't have love any more.

But I don't say any of that. It would take way too long.

I don't want to live with them, is what I do say, or what Melany with a *y* says for me. We're in a private room that my lawyer says they're not allowed to bug, unless they want the whole Supreme Court to climb up their asses, and that makes me smile at least.

It'll be OK, says my lawyer. Her name is Carla Rainer and she has a faint moustache. Plain gold band on her ring finger. *You'll have regular visits from Child Protective Services, to check up on you. And the state is providing a counsellor for you. They know it's important to manage your, ah, return to, uh, your birth parents.*

No, I say. *It's not that. It's just, I don't know them. I want to be on my own.*

She sighs, but the movement of her body tells me it's a sympathetic sigh, not an irritated one. *You don't have a choice, I'm afraid,* she says. *You're a minor. If you'd been mistreated by them, there'd be a case for protective custody, but . . . you're their daughter.*

So we go back to, what, Alaska?

You don't want to do that?

It's Alaska!

She smiles. *I think they're happy to stay here as long as you need. As you can imagine, they want very much to get to know you. You know they rented a place?*

Yes.

So, yeah, I think we could negotiate for a . . . transition period here in Arizona.

Like a diver going into a decompression tank, I say. It takes Melany some time to understand what I'm saying, and translate it. I don't know the sign for decompression tank, so I have to kind of make it up.

But Melany gets it, I guess. The lawyer, Carla, does an eyebrows-up face, like it's somehow surprising that I have watched documentaries and read books. *Yes. Probably not long, though. I mean, they have jobs.*

I had not thought of this. *What do they do?*

Your father – Michael – is a journalist. Your mother – Jennifer – is a teacher.

Wow, I think. *Other kids?*

Five, she says. *Three older than you. Two younger. They are . . .* She consults some notes. *Tyler and James are in college. Victoria is six, she's the youngest, and Richie, he's in middle school. And Anna is in the army.*

Oh, I say. I have five brothers and sisters. This information is somehow too big to fit into my head.

And in a month's time? I ask.

Huh?

When I'm eighteen. What happens then? Can I live on my own?

She sits back. *Interesting question*, she says. *I guess you would be free to live wherever you want. I mean, I need to make some phone calls, check some precedents. If there even are any. I think that's what it would mean, though. But your parents have made it clear they want to support you. Pay for any education needs that you might have, I'm told that your IQ is –*

I don't need their money, I say. *So, for now, I have to stay with them, right? For a month?*

Yes.

OK, I say. *Fine.* I am aware that I'm being a bitch, please don't think I'm not. But you have to understand – I don't KNOW these people. I might as well be going to live with total strangers. I AM going to live with total strangers.

I know they have missed me. I know this is a big party for them. But it's not a win-win situation for me, to say the fricking least.

I have one more item, says my lawyer.

Yes?

Luke Scheinberg.

It takes some time for Melany to spell this out. I am blank for a moment, a piece of paper waiting for words, then I get it.

Oh, right. I dimly remember someone, the city attorney maybe, using that surname.

He wants to see you.

Really? Why?

I don't know, she says. *He won't say. But he insists on speaking to you personally.* She puts her hands up. *You don't have to. But if you want to, I would be present. And Melany, of course.*

When? I say.

He's in the building, says the lawyer. *He's waiting. You could see him anytime. But like I say, it's your call.*

I shrug. Whatever.

So I should let him come?

Sure, I say. *How much worse can things get?*

If you are ever tempted to say these words, or sign them, or whatever, here is my advice: don't. Because here is the thing: it might not be right away, it might not be immediate, but the truth is, things can always get worse.

Much, much worse.

CHAPTER
51

LUKE IS NERVOUS, I can see it in his eyes.

Don't worry, I say as he comes into the meeting room. *I'm not going to stab you.*

Melany doesn't translate this. My lawyer is sitting in a corner, making notes, not saying anything, just showing everyone she's there. Showing Luke she's there, mainly, I guess.

It's weird seeing Luke here, under the fluorescent lights of the federal building. He looks drawn, grey, like he hasn't slept in forever. His hand hangs by his side, in its white bandage. He can't seem to meet my eye.

Hello, Luke, I say.

Melany translates this time.

Hello, he says. *How are you feeling?*

I blink. *Great,* I say. *My mom is not my real mom. I'm some other person from who I thought I was. It's fantastic.*

Melany signs quickly.

I'm sorry, says Luke.

Don't be, I say. *Look at your hand. At least I stopped you getting killed with a rock. And it's a good thing you don't drink – otherwise you'd have had a massive overdose of codeine.*

Melany lowers her eyebrows at me, like, what? I shake my head –
forget it.

How's the hand? I say, and Melany puts it on to the air as vibrations, and into Luke's ears.

Not too bad, says Luke. *Missed the artery. Some nerve damage,
but could be worse.*

I nod. I'm glad.

So . . . he says. *So, I wanted to let you know about something.*

OK, I say.

He doesn't know how to begin. He sits down, and I don't, and
that just makes him more uncomfortable. He takes a deep breath, as
if he's going to have to dive deep down inside himself to bring up his
next words; like pearls. *See, here's the thing*, he says. *The media want
the story on you. My two days in the desert with – well, you know.
But I don't want to tell. I . . . I want you to have a life again, and I
don't see how you could, after all this, if people knew who you were.
I mean . . .* He looks over at Carla. *You're her lawyer, right?*

Yes, says Carla, or at least I guess she does, I'm not looking
at her.

*So you'll want to get some kind of anonymity for her? I mean,
there's been no photos of . . . Shelby, in the news.*

We want to protect her, yes, says Carla slowly. I am looking at
her now.

*She might get a new name, a new identity? I mean, if and when
she's not living with her birth parents.*

Ye-e-e-e-es, says Carla. *She might.* Her tone is like: Where are
you going with this?

So, says Luke, and I see for the first time that he is very far from
stupid. *That's what I wanted to tell you. That I wouldn't blow it.*

287

I won't, you know, say that you're deaf or anything. I mean, that could really screw your cover.

Uh . . . thank you, I say.

You should see what they've offered me, he says. *We're talking hundreds of thousands. But you're just a girl. You deserve a new life.*

My mind is like this now, not blank, but like static, a detuned TV:

****
****
****

I don't know what to think about any of this. I hadn't even considered the idea of a new identity, I mean I knew I'd be living with my real mom and dad for a month, but wouldn't their names be public knowledge? Or maybe Luke is thinking of when I leave their house, when I'm eighteen . . . Shit, I think, he really is smart. I didn't consider ANY of this.

Carla, it seems, has though.

I see, she says. *You have been offered a lot. So how much do you want from Shelby to keep her story to yourself? To not reveal details, like her deafness?* Here's one thing I like about my lawyer: she doesn't put ellipses of hesitation before my name, like she's not sure if she should say it, because it's not my real name any more.

Luke looks appalled. He smacks the table with his bandaged hand, then curses. His face goes a little purple. *NO,* he says. *NO.* He turns to me. *I just wanted to tell you, in person, that I would not speak of you. For any money. And that I'm sorry for what has happened to you.*

Suddenly, without warning, I am crying; the tears are hot in my eyes, burning.

Thank you, I say. *Thank you*. And then I think of how I kept thinking he was a douche, how I laughed at him inside my own head, at his awful stories, his weight, his lazy half-blind eye, which even now is looking at me milkily, sadly. Guilt is a twisting kitten inside me. *I'm so sorry*, I say, and this time I say it with my mouth. *I'm so so sorry.*

It's not your fault, says Luke, totally missing my point. *You didn't know who she was.*

No, I think. No, I didn't.

Luke levers himself up from the table. *Well, that was all I wanted to say*, he says. *Thank you for your time.*

Thank you, Luke, I say, again with my mouth. He's been so kind, it is making me cry all over again, and he seems to sense it's too much for me, because he opens the door and leaves.

Well, says Carla. *That was an interesting first.*

What?

Someone who doesn't want money. I don't think I've met one before.

I smile through my tears. *You're a lawyer. You wouldn't.*

She smiles back. *OK*, she says. *I think that's it for this morning. I've asked for the meeting with your parents to be put back by a couple of hours. Give you a chance to rest.*

Thanks, I say.

Anything you want in the meantime? she asks.

I shake my head and she starts towards the door.

No, wait, I say, out loud, which is becoming a habit.

Yes? she says.

There is something I want, I say. *Something of mine.*

Right, says my lawyer. *That should be doable.*

My cell phone, I say.

Where is it?

It was in the cabin, I say. *Plugged into the wall.*

The FBI took some things into evidence that they're still analysing, she says. *Luke's car, stuff like that. But it's your cell, and you haven't committed a crime. I'll have it returned to you. Anything else?*

No, I say. I mean, my baseball bat is there too, but that doesn't seem important now.

Wait, I say. *There is something.*

Yes?

I want a pack of cigarettes. And a lighter.

What brand?

It doesn't matter.

She looks at me, a little surprised; maybe I look really clean cut or something. Straight edge. *You smoke?*

No, I say. *But I'm thinking of starting.*

CHAPTER
52

I'M READY, I SAY.

Carla opens the door and I walk in.

The mother, Jennifer, takes a step towards me, her hand going to the cross at her neck at the same time, and seems about to throw her arms around me, but the father, Michael, must have some kind of empathy, some kind of sense of the state of mind of others, because he puts a hand on her shoulder and stops her.

Still – he can't look at me. His gaze lands on mine and then ricochets off, hits a lamp; a computer on a desk.

The mother is at least not crying this time, though her eyes are red, like she just stopped. She touches her cross.

She looks at me. She touches her cross.

She sort of half smiles. She touches her cross.

And do you see how I am subliminally telling you how she KEEPS TOUCHING THAT CROSS? She seems like a person carved out of worry, like the cross is the only thing stopping her from breaking into a thousand pieces; an anchor.

Angelica, she says, and for a second, a stupid second, I don't know who she's talking to. OH YES, I realise. THAT WOULD BE ME.

She starts talking again and Melany signs beside me.

It's all right, I sign back to Melany. *I can lip-read. My mom taught –*

Oh. I keep doing that. Keep calling her mom.

Melany catches my look of horror and gives me a sympathetic, like, grimace-smile. *You're sure?*

Yes, I say.

What is she saying? says Michael.

She's saying she can lip-read, says Melany. Her eyes meet mine, and we both know she left out the part about MY MOM, who is not my mom at all. I'm grateful for that little thing.

Oh, good, says Michael. *Can she talk? I mean . . . Sorry. Can you talk?*

I can talk, I say slowly. *But I don't like to.*

Oh . . . ah . . . right, says Michael. He looks like he doesn't know where to put his hands; or even whether to stand or sit; and I know how he feels. We're in a much more comfortable room than before, with a low coffee table, and magazines, and armchairs – kind of like a doctor's waiting room.

We missed you so much, Jennifer Watson says. *We never stopped hoping. Never. Never, honey. We kept looking for you always. We –*

She turns to her husband, my dad, as she talks, and so I don't see what she's saying.

Immediately she realises her mistake. She turns back to me. *I'm sorry*, she says. *This is going to take some getting used to.*

You didn't know I was deaf? I sign this, and Melany translates.

We suspected, says Michael. *You weren't speaking; we thought . . . I don't know, we hoped you were just a slow starter.*

Your other kids?

Melany looks at me. *You mean, are any of their other kids deaf?* she signs.

Yes.

Melany translates for my parents.

No, says Jennifer. *But you were a forceps birth, so maybe . . .* She touches the cross again. *I just thank Jesus for bringing you back to me*, she says. *I went to the church every day, I prayed every day, I prayed every hour. I knew that if I was truly humble and never forgot you, if I only asked for you, if I put aside all my desires, all my sins, that Jesus would –*

Sure, sure, honey, says Michael, and I think, What am I walking into here? *The important thing is you're back*, he says. He has a red nose, veins bursting like fireworks. Alcoholic, I think. For sure. His hands are shaking too.

Jennifer Watson reaches into her purse and takes something out. It's a moment before I realise what it is – a milk carton. I'm confused, but then I see the picture of the toddler on it.

That's you, she says. *That's you, and this has been on my bedside table every day for fifteen years.*

Poor Michael, I think.

And now you're here, she says. *In front of me.*

She stares at the milk carton like she doesn't know how it got into her hands.

I look at the picture – it could be any toddler. I mean, I could kid myself there was a resemblance, sure, but who looks like they did when they were two, anyway?

Then she throws the carton in the trash – there's something about the way she does it, that makes me think it's something she's pictured many times. Fantasised about. A symbolic gesture. A ritual for her – long awaited.

Can I . . . can I hold you? she asks.

I nod slowly – sign language for dummies.

Jennifer inches forward and puts her arms around me, and I stand there with my hands at my sides, not sure what to do with them. *Oh my little princess Angelica*, she says. *Oh I love you I love you I love you.*

Then she cries and cries and cries, and she's shaking like there's an engine inside her that's come loose.

Me, I don't feel anything.

CHAPTER
53

WE DON'T JUST WALK out of there, of course. I think at first that's what's going to happen, but Carla takes me and Melany over to the tall windows on one side of the building and points down. The windows are greyish, and I realise that people outside can't see in. We're, like, three floors up and I see what she means immediately: there's a street, trees on the other side of it, and on our side of it there's a crowd of people outside the door, some with cameras. TV vans with satellite dishes on top of them. Not just local either: NBC. CBS.

We've kept your image out of the press, says Carla. *For now at least. But we're hoping to get a privacy order. A closed trial, ah, I mean, when they get your, uh, when they catch Shaylene. It's a long road.*

And now? I say.

Now we take you down to the basement and put you in an unmarked car with your parents, and we move you to their apartment without telling anyone down there.

You're kidding?

No.

Oh. OK. I look at her. *Are you coming?*

She smiles. She looks quite pretty when she smiles. *I can come if you want me to. But it might be weird.*

And Melany?

Again, if you want.

I think about this. Actually they might get in the way of what I am planning, or maybe planning, whatever. *No, it's cool*, I say. *I'll go with them. But we'll see each other, right?*

Yes. And CPS will be visiting. Every day to begin with.

I put my hand in my pocket, wanting to feel the knife that Mark gave me, Coyote gave me, feel its hard smooth bone handle. Then I remember that:

1. The knife only exists in the Dreaming, I mean my (mom) couldn't see it anyway and

2. Even if it did exist in this world, I threw it into the undergrowth by the cabin, when the SWAT guys came along.

Still, even just thinking about the Dreaming, about Coyote and the knife, has made me feel stronger, somehow. Like there is something that belongs to me and not to anyone else. Not my identity, not my name, since it seems like anyone can just come along and take those things away, change them right under me, but a whole world. A dream.

Right, I say. *Let's do this.*

CHAPTER
54

IN THE CAR, JENNIFER sits in the back with me.

First thing she does is to grip my hand in this really intense way, like she wants to convert me or something, save my soul, and then with her other hand she takes up this tote bag with WHOLE FOODS on it and starts to take stuff out to show me.

Like:

Some kind of card with scribbles on it, that she says I made for Michael for Father's Day.

A little baby hat.

Books. Books with 'moon' in the title, seems to be the theme. *Goodnight Moon; Papa, Please Get the Moon for Me.*

I look at them blankly.

You loved the moon, she says. *You always wanted those stories, you would point to them, over and over. There are photos too that I want to show you, so many photos, but we – I – didn't want to over-whelm you.*

I put my hand to my lips, palm towards me, then move it down and out, the sign for thank you. Then I mouth the words.

That means thank you? Jennifer says. Melany of course has gone back to wherever she waits between super fun jobs like this.

I nod.

Look at me! I'm learning already, she says. *Michael, I know how to sign 'thank you'!*

I don't know what Michael says to this, if anything at all.

Then Jennifer reaches into her tote bag and takes something out that stops my heart in my chest for a moment, stops it dead. It's grey and floppy in her hand and its ears hang over her fingers and its eyes are scratched and dull and –

Are you OK? says Jennifer. *Honey? You're very pale. Are you –*

With great effort, I nod. Everything is kind of crackling and sparkling and my vision is grey as fur at the edges because this is the rabbit from my dream, from the cage in the Dreaming, the exact same one.

This is Flopsy Bunny, says Jennifer. *You carried it everywhere. In the hospital . . . In the hospital, they found it on the floor. In the corridor. I kept it for you.*

She holds it out to me and I recoil, violently. Something in Jennifer's eyes flares, and they fill with tears.

Sorry, I say, with my clumsy mouth. But I stay leaning away, and Jennifer reads something in my body language, and puts the bunny away in the bag.

But I feel it there, glowing like radiation. Emitting. Pulsing.

A piece of the Dreaming here in the real world.

A piece of my dream.

Jennifer holds up her little cross and kisses it. *Thank you Lord Jesus for returning my angel to me*, she says. Then she turns to me and her eyes are bright like jewels with tears. *I'm so sorry*, she says. *I'm so sorry about your legs . . . the burns . . .*

Michael must say something in front, from the driver's seat, because she says, *No, Michael, I have to say this. If it wasn't for me . . . If I hadn't let you burn yourself, she never would have taken you.*

I look at her blankly. She speaks slowly, so I can read her mouth. Even then, I have to kind of assume some of the words she says.

That woman, who kidnapped you . . . she pretended to be a nurse. She took you away. It was all so confusing; I was so scared for you, I didn't know what was going on, and Tyler was running around, getting under my feet, Anna was crying about something, I can't remember what . . . I didn't think. And then she never came back.

Oh, I think.

The police didn't believe me for the longest time, they thought we'd done something, but I mean, the CCTV, and everything, it was obvious I brought you in, and the doctors had seen you, you know. So it wasn't like anyone could seriously believe we killed you.

It gets worse, I think. All the pity I have to feel; all the sadness. That they were suspected of killing me – it's awful. It's too much.

Anyway, it was . . . it was my fault, that's what I want to tell you. You shouldn't have been in the kitchen with that oil; it was just because, well, James was screaming from the living room and I thought Tyler must have pulled his hair, I don't know, and I was gone for a SECOND, and . . . I'm just so, so sorry.

I think of my scars, the years that I've worn pants, even on burning hot days, the way that I've never swum, not ever, and there's a part of me that wants to say *you stupid bitch*, but that wouldn't help anything, would it?

I make a sequence of gestures.

What does that mean? she asks.

I say it with my mouth, even though I can see the way she winces when I do that; I can see in her eyes how wrong my voice sounds, and it's like knives in my belly.

I forgive you, I say. It's something easy I can say, and it might make what is going to happen easier. What I'm going to do to her.

299

CHAPTER
55

THE CAR – I GUESS it's a rental, because it's very clean and new-smelling – turns on to the main downtown street and I see, down a side street, the diner where Luke got his hand skewered. I wonder how Luke is doing now.

Then we pass Gene's Western Supplies and the climbing store, and a couple of hundred yards down the road, Michael pulls over, close to a newspaper box that will sell you the *Arizona Daily Sun* for twenty-five cents.

He turns around in the seat. *This is us*, he says. *For now.*

I look up: it's a new building, big high windows, balconies on each floor. A black metal fire escape that runs down the side, accessible from each balcony.

I follow them up. It's a top-floor condo, two bedrooms, two bathrooms, they wanted me to have my own bathroom, says Jennifer, kind of babbling. Victoria and Richie are with their grandparents – MY grandparents – back in Alaska; the younger kids know about me, evidently, have been told about me all their lives.

I wonder how they think of me. What I am, in their minds. More like a symbol than a person, I guess. Like the Easter Bunny, or Santa. When I walk into their lives, when before I've just been a toddler on a milk carton, it's going to be INTENSE for them.

Luckily, there's an elevator – I don't think I'd have got up any stairs with my CAM Walker. We stand in silence as we ride up. I am used to silence, but the parents look uncomfortable in it, like it's a heat, pressing on them.

There's a bike in the hall, a full suspension mountain bike. *That's Michael's*, says Jennifer, in her slow stage voice, mouth moving like molasses.

The trails here are [   ], says Michael, who speaks much quicker. *I wasn't sure if [   ], so I thought, why not?*

What he's saying:

He didn't know if I would turn out to be real, if the police would turn out to be right. So he brought a bike, so he could hit the trails, if it turned out to be a bust, a dead end.

Michael, I am thinking, wrote me off for dead a long time ago, and so he's going to be the one to watch out for. This whole thing may turn out to be maybe ten thousand times harder for him than for Jennifer, because she KNEW I was alive, she trusted in Jesus.

She has just had her faith confirmed; he, though – he's going to have to unbury me; unpack my dead limbs from where he has stowed them away, deep inside him.

I know I'm right about this: I see it in the veins in his nose, I see it in the way he moves so jerkily, so shakily, like we're all in HD and he's been filmed on Super 8, or whatever, some old camera stock like in black-and-white movies, where people moved like marionettes.

I see it in the way he excuses himself and goes off to the kitchen, leaving me and Jennifer alone in the living room.

Drink? says Jennifer.

I nod.

OK, great, honey, great. Coke?

I nod again.

She goes to the kitchen. The apartment is furnished in black leather, with polished mahogany floors. There are no personal touches, no photos, no flowers – I guess there wouldn't be. Good views from the windows, though – the red brick and glass of Flagstaff's downtown; mountains and forest in the distance.

Jennifer comes back with a glass of Coke, and hands it to me, the awkwardness between us giving an air of ceremony to the way she does it.

I'll make lunch, soon, she says.

I nod.

Then we need to get you some clothes, you like shopping?

I shrug.

OK . . . well, whatever, we can get you some stuff quickly. Is there anything you like? Books, games, music . . . She looks up at me, startled. *Oh, God, I'm so sorry, I'm such a klutz . . .* Then she clutches her cross. *I took your name in vain,* she says, *I'm sorry for that too, I . . . forgive me.*

It's weird – she's so beautiful, so, like, movie-star and cheerleader gorgeous, but she's too nervous and sweet and, I think, a tiny bit crazy, to really BE beautiful.

I smile, and shake my head, like, don't worry about it; it's easy to forget. And it is, I know.

Do you . . . watch movies, TV?

I nod. *Closed captions,* I say, accentuating the syllables.

Oh! Of course.

She shows me around, talking endlessly, but nothing that I really need to know, just nerves I guess. I have no words to describe how I am feeling – it's like grief, maybe, but grief for myself. I was living my life, and then something came along and killed me, erased me from the world, and now I'm not Shelby Jane Cooper any more, I'm some other person.

Except I don't know this other person. Or anything about them.

It's like I don't exist. Like some magician has taken up my life like a card – SWISH – and swapped it with another, and put them in new and separate decks. We pass a mirror, full length, and I don't recognise the girl in it. She's pretty, with dark hair tied back, big brown eyes. A little skinny, maybe.

But she's a stranger to me.

I'm not really paying attention to what Jennifer is saying but suddenly I see her mouth make the words 'Grand Canyon'.

What? I say.

She slows and exaggerates her speech. *The Grand Canyon*, she says. *We thought we could go. I mean, not today. But while we're here. It's so close.*

Two hundred conversations with my (mom) go through my head, from so many years – me saying, *It's so close, we can fly there in an hour* – her saying, *We can't afford it, honey,* but really meaning, I know now, *I'm afraid because I don't want to get caught, I don't want to lose you.*

And even though she always said no, and even though I know it's stupid . . . I don't know. I guess I always thought I would go with her.

Suddenly I realise: I miss my (mom). I mean, Shaylene Cooper, whatever. I hate her, yes, I'm fricking furious with her, for ruining everything like this, but at the same time there is a part of me that would be happy to go back in time, to roll everything back to before that car hit me, so nothing would have to change, and all the secrets would remain hidden, forever.

Her face floats in my imagination, disintegrating already.

I miss her.

I wonder where she is.

The woman who raised me. Who told me she loved me, who baked me cookies, who put Band-Aids on my cuts, who taught me to sign, who taught me to read, who put aside her money for me, gave me books, gave me hugs, took me for Ice Cream for Dinner Nights, watched everything in closed captions because of me . . .

Hell, what if Jennifer and Michael don't do ice cream for dinner?

A touch on my arm. We're standing looking into the room where I'm going to sleep. Jennifer has already put the bunny on the bed; she must have brought it from the car; I didn't see.

Angelica? Or . . . A pained look crosses Jennifer's face. *Do you . . . do you prefer Shelby?* Her arms spread outwards; it's your choice, say her hands, but her face says different. Her face says my name is Angelica.

I shrug. I think this is going to be my answer to a lot of things.

Are you feeling bad, honey?

Oh you have NO idea.

I shake my head. I have a little backpack that Carla got for me. I swing it to my front; open it. There's my cigarettes inside, they're Pall Mals, whatever that means. I show them to Jennifer.

Oh! she says. A flicker of disappointment – quick, and then she tries to hide it, but I spot it. Then she puts it away totally out of sight, under brisk helpfulness. *There's a balcony just out here*, she says, walking backwards into the living room, indicating it with her hand.

I know, I think.

I nod at her and she opens the door, sliding it. I go out, awkwardly leaning on the door jamb to lever myself and my bionic-man CAM Walker up and over the lip of the sliding door. If she thinks it's weird that I don't take off my backpack, she doesn't say anything.

Outside, I lean against the railing, looking down on the cars going by. It's a beautiful day; the sun is shining even though it's cold, and crows tumble past me, black rags against the blue sky; freewheeling. There are peaked and gabled roofs in Flagstaff, reaching up to the mountains in the background; you don't see roofs like that in Phoenix, everything is just flat. I take out a cigarette and light it – the smoke hits my lungs and I cough, but fight to control it, to hold it in.

People do this by choice? It feels like some creature with dagger-fingers has reached into my chest and yanked.

After that, I don't inhale, I just take the smoke in my mouth and then puff it out. From the corner of my eye, I watch Jennifer – she watches me for a while, kind of rapt just by my presence I guess, but when I put out the cigarette and light another one, she starts to get bored.

Everyone gets bored, even of the people they love. It's a fact of life.

Michael comes in, from their bedroom, maybe, and they talk, then walk towards the kitchen.

I am about to move, when Jennifer suddenly turns her head and then heads to the door – I guess someone has knocked on it or rung a bell. She opens it wide and a woman in a suit comes in, young, blonde. Attractive. Jennifer's body is saying that this woman has some kind of authority, and also that Jennifer doesn't like it and is afraid of it.

They come into the living space of the big open-plan room and Jennifer beckons me in.

I slide the door and go back inside. The woman sticks out her hand. Her eyes are sea-blue, her hair like sand. Everything about her says summer. *Summer Andrews*, she says. *CPS. I'm going to be looking in on you. Making sure you're OK. You want to sit? Talk a bit?*

No, I say.

She blinks but then catches herself; professional. *That's all right*, she says. *Rome wasn't built in a day. Perhaps we can all just discuss living arrangements. Clothes. Food.*

I sigh inside. I'm trapped.

For now.

CHAPTER
56

BLAH BLAH BLAH BLAH *blah blah James*, says Jennifer.

Sorry?

We're sitting on the couch, after Summer has left with a threat to come back tomorrow. Michael is fidgeting, uncomfortable.

Jennifer knows I wasn't paying attention, but she stays patient. Repeats herself slowly. *Your brother, James. Three years older. He's coming this evening.*

I nod; I'm not sure what is required of me here.

He remembers you. He was very [   ]. I mean, when you were born, your grandma brought him to visit, and he ran down the hospital [   ], shouting, Where's my baba? That's what he called you. His baba. He was three.

I nod again.

The others . . . they forgot quickly. Or they didn't know you. But James never forgot. He loved you. She puts her hand to her mouth, too late to stop the past tense from slipping out. *He loves you. He jumped on the first flight he could get. He's doing a semester abroad. The [   ]. Paris.*

Right, I say.

Jennifer puts her hands on her knees in a decisive gesture. *OK, I'm going to make some dinner. You eat chicken?*

I nod. Who doesn't eat chicken? I mean, apart from vegetarians. And vegans.

You want me to put the TV on, honey?

I nod. She picks up the remote and flicks it on – Special Agent Deacon fills the screen, a ticker tape running below him, saying, ANGELICA DENIES BEING ABUSED, SHAYLENE COOPER STILL AT LARGE, ANGELICA CURRENTLY –

Turn it off, I say.

James shows up after dinner. I am helping Jennifer to clear away the dishes – I mean, what else am I going to do? – when her head does that turning thing again and she puts down the rice bowl and walks to the door. When she opens it, a tall guy comes in: sandy hair, light stubble. He got more of his mom's looks than his dad's. In any other circumstance I would think: He's hot.

He has a carryall in each hand, and there are dark circles under his eyes; the eyes themselves are bloodshot. He is wearing a University of Calgary sweatshirt and jeans. When he sees me, he drops both bags to the floor –

– instantly, like that –

and moves fast, like the quarterback I'm sure he was, crossing the ten yards between us like it's nothing, and then his arms are around me and he lifts me up into the air, and for a moment I see the ceiling, turning, and just feel his strength wrapped around me.

Then he must feel that I'm stiff, a dead weight. Because he puts me back down on the ground and steps back, awkward.

Sorry, he says. His eyes flit away from mine, but keep coming back, like nervous birds to a feeder.

I make a gesture, like, it's no big deal. But I'm kind of trembling from shock so maybe it is a big deal, and he can tell. He looks mortified.

Angelica, he says. *I came as soon as I heard. Do you remember me? I remember you. My whole childhood, I don't think I understood, it was like I had an invisible friend and suddenly they were gone, suddenly you were [   ], but I always remembered how we [   ] and playing in the sand pit with you, and it was only when I was older that [   ] and Mom and Dad could tell me what really [   ].*

I look at him blankly.

Oh, shit, he says. He turns to Jennifer, to his mom. So what he says next is just pure [   ].

Then he turns back to me. *I knew*, he says. *No. I didn't know. But it wasn't a surprise. That you were deaf.*

Jennifer is standing watching all this with a complicated expression on her face. Love, pride, happiness. But also nervousness. Michael is unreadable.

James moves a hand to his mouth. *You remember that? That meant you were hungry.* He walks his fingers. *That meant you wanted to go for a walk. Ah . . .* He thinks for a moment. Then he makes a round cage with his hands. *Ball*, he says.

And the weird thing is, when he makes these gestures, something flares in my memory. Some dim light, in the darkness. A struck match that is then gone again, into the gloom.

I guess I didn't see the connection then, he says. *It was just something we did. But now, as an adult, it's obvious. You were deaf. So that's how we must have found to [   ].*

You never said, says Jennifer. I see reproach in her eyes.

I never knew it was important, says James. *I was five.*

Michael takes a step forward. He indicates the TV with his thumb. *Red Sox*, he says.

Michael, no! says Jennifer, angry.

But I am not really looking at her. I'm watching Michael, and something is pushing electricity through my skull. *You like baseball?* I say, with my mouth, the words tortuous.

You're kidding? says James. *Dad loves baseball. Broke his heart when I tried out for the football team, made [   ]. Oh, wait, wow. You can speak?*

I roll my eyes, like, obviously. He looks embarrassed again. For all his muscle, for all his good looks. I feel sorry for him. This situation must be so weird. But right now I am more focused on Michael, who is looking at me with very slightly narrowed eyes, like he has recognised something in me too.

You like baseball? he says.

I like batting, I say slowly. *The batting cages.*

Something collapses inside the bony armature of Michael's face, then, and he starts to cry.

I stare at him, horrified. So does James. And Jennifer.

Michael rubs at his face. *I got you a bat. A small one. You were incredible, a natural. You could throw and catch at the age of two. You [   ]. I'd pitch to you and you'd hit the ball, I mean, just in the living room.*

Jennifer has a dreaming expression. *I remember that*, she says.

And now you still hit? asks Michael. His cheeks are shiny with tears.

Yes, I say.

Come on! he says excitedly. *It's Red Sox vs Mariners. I'll get –*

310

No, says Jennifer. Her hands are on her hips.

No?

No. We're doing something as a family.

James is looking from his mom to his dad and back again, like he's watching a tennis match.

Something like what? says Michael.

I don't know, says Jennifer. *Boggle?*

James smiles. *You brought Boggle?*

Sure, says Jennifer.

James smiles even wider. *Teams?*

Me and your dad, I guess. And you and . . . and Angelica. Are you up for that, honey? She's looking at me.

Uh, OK.

Maybe she'll help you to finally beat us, says Jennifer, and I remember that Michael is a journalist and she's a teacher. It makes sense that they're good at Boggle.

Fine, says Michael. *But tomorrow,* he says to me, *you and I are going to the park.*

Then his eyes go to my leg, the CAM Walker. *Oh, no, you're –*

It's OK, I say, trying to keep my sentences short. *Only fracture. Batting, you stand still. Just . . . can't run.*

You sure?

Yes.

Jennifer looks hard at him. *You take it easy on her, OK?*

Yes, my darling.

I smile, for the first time. Maybe this isn't going to be so bad after all.

That's what I think then, anyway.

Later I think: I should stop saying these sorts of things to myself.

311

CHAPTER
57

Boggle is AWFUL.

Not because I'm not good at it. Actually, it seems like maybe I'm too good at it. Jennifer, it turns out, is about 1,781 times more competitive than I realised. And she and Michael never lose, that's the family story, the kind of myth of the Watsons. They take on, like, all their kids at the same time, their neighbours, their friends, whoever, and they don't lose.

Until now.

We agree that I can write down my words instead of shouting them out, and when I bust out INCONSEQUENTIALLY for eleven points, it's all over. James high-fives me.

Unbelievable, he says.

I had that, I say. *Last round.*

He laughs, but he's the only one laughing. On the other side of the table, Jennifer has a bona fide pissed-off expression on her face, though she's trying to hide it under smiles. Michael seems shell-shocked. I think he had me down as some kind of retard because I was deaf.

Have you applied for colleges? says Jennifer. She has stood up and walked away from the table, almost like she can't bear to look at the Boggle cubes now that she has lost. I am seeing a whole new side of her – there is a hardness in her stance now, in her eyes.

I shake my head.

But your – Shaylene, she homeschooled you?

I nod.

OK. Well, the first thing we'll need to do is check out what you know, and then have you take the SATs. Summer, I mean the CPS, is going to put us in touch with some people in Alaska.

I shrug.

Let's take it one step at a time, huh? says Michael. *You want to watch some TV?* he asks me.

I look at the clock on the microwave. It's late – past eleven. I unfold my hands like pages. *Do you have any books?*

James nods. *I have some textbooks, a [   ]. A biography of Monet.* James is a fine art student, I learned that when we were playing Boggle.

Jennifer shakes her head.

Michael holds up a finger, like, wait. He goes into the bedroom and comes back with a thick book. *A History of the Arab Peoples.*

No fiction? I ask.

They wince, like they're failing a test. Maybe they are. *Sorry, honey,* says Jennifer. *We're not really novel people.*

Not really novel people, I think. I didn't know such a thing was possible. Even Shaylene usually had a mystery or a romance in her hands, when she wasn't stitching Scottish insanity-landscapes. For the first time I realise how sheltered my life has been.

Speak for yourself, says James.

Oh yeah? says Jennifer, a glint in her eye, and I see the shared history, the deep love between her and her son. *What was the last novel you read?*

Moby Dick.

You did that for school.

So? It's still a novel.

You didn't even finish it. You googled the CliffsNotes.

I start to stand up. *I'm sleepy*, I say.

Of course, of course, says Jennifer. *We'll get you a book tomorrow. What do you like? Harry Potter?*

I stare at her. Wizards. Crones. A shiver runs through me. What is with people who don't read novels? I mean, what kind of life is that? *I read them*, I say.

She waits for me to say something more, but I don't, so she just nods eventually. *OK, well, we'll go to the bookstore, you can pick something.*

We're allowed out? I say.

We're allowed to do anything we want, she says. *We're a family.*

Yeah, I think. Sure.

That night, I lie in my bed in the spare room and I can't sleep. I run through scenarios in my mind, fantasies, trying to lull myself into sleep, tell myself a story. A lullaby. This is something I have always done – when I was younger, like I said ages ago, I would fantasise that my mom was not my real mom, that my real mom was a queen, and one day I would meet her. That I was special, in some way.

Now I know this was the most stupid-ass fantasy of all time, because I know the reality now of my mom not being my mom, and it sucks.

So instead I imagine the opposite:

I imagine:

That none of this is real.

I mean, none of the stuff that has happened to me in the actual world, since I know the Dreaming isn't real, because if it is, then I have gone totally and utterly mad, and I don't like to get too close to that thought, because it's like a fire and it burns.

This is not helping me to sleep.

I imagine:

That my mom is still my mom and we still live in Scottsdale, and every weekday apart from Friday, when Mom's not working, we do school stuff, and then every Friday we go to the baseball cage and then we get ice cream for dinner and nothing ever changes and everything is always awesome.

It doesn't work. I lie there wide awake for most of the night. But at some point I must fall asleep because one moment I'm looking at the ceiling of the rented apartment and wondering if I could actually just run away to Mexico on my own and start a totally different life, and thinking about what I could possibly do there, I mean being deaf and all –

and the next moment I'm –

A DIAMOND PINPRICK IN A CONSTELLATION OF STARS

CHAPTER
58

AND THEN I'M BACK in the Dreaming and I catch a glimpse of the great eagle swooping down towards me before I close my eyes tight.

Feathers flutter against the skin of my face, there's a sensation of the air being disturbed by something fast, falling past me, and then –

Nothing.

I open my eyes and see the eagle standing on the ground in front of me. It cocks its head, regarding me with its mineral eye. It folds its wings neatly.

You are rather small, for the one who will kill the Crone, it says.

I blink.

Do you speak? Or do you communicate with your eyelids?

I, ah, speak, I say.

Good, says the eagle. It does save time.

I still haven't got my heartbeat under control. I scoot back a bit, but don't stand up. I don't know which side this eagle is on.

You are alone? asks the eagle.

No, I say. I'm with Coyote. He has gone . . . to . . . um . . . hunt. He will be back soon.

Good, says the eagle. He will be glad of my support in this, I think.

You . . . want to help us? I ask.

Of course.

You're not with the owls? The wolves? The snakes?

If it is possible for an eagle to look disgusted, then it does now. I am nothing like those low creatures, it says. I am Eagle. I am sacred. I see all. It puffs its chest, considering me coldly.

I'm sorry, I say.

For instance, says the eagle as if I have not spoken, I see that you have sent Coyote away. Why?

I blink again.

I'm sorry, says the eagle. Does that mean something?

No, I say. I . . . I did send Coyote away. But the elks told me not to trust him.

Why?

He caused the flood. He scattered the stars. He . . . I don't know, stole fire. He also, oh, I don't know, didn't mention the small fact that the woman who raised me for seventeen years was not actually my mother at all but someone who stole me from a hospital.

The eagle actually rolls its eyes. You are a fool, it says.

What? I say. Screw you.

You are facing a challenging quest and you have sent away your strongest ally, says the eagle.

My stubborn streak is riled. He plays tricks, I say. That's what the elks told me. What if all this was a trick of his? All this fricking *crap* with my so-called mother. What if it's all some screwed-up idea of a joke on me, at my expense?

The eagle takes a step towards me. I flinch, but it merely gestures with its wing to the sky. Look up, it says.

I look up – the stars glitter above us, chips of ice, diamonds.

Coyote scattered those, it says. That is why they are so beautiful.

There is no order. There is only the vastness of the heavens, the randomness of the stars. Would they be more beautiful if they were lined up in rows?

No, I say.

It lowers its head. And the flood? Did the elks tell you why Coyote stole the River God's child?

No, I say.

Because the River God had taken two human children. Coyote paid her back. And it was because of the flood that people climbed the reed to the Fourth World, and gained knowledge, and culture, and time, and all good things.

He created death, I say.

Imagine a world without death, says the eagle contemptuously. Imagine the horror.

I frown. It has a point.

Coyote is chaos, says the eagle. He is misrule. He takes order and routine and he breaks it, he scatters it. But always, when he has done so, the world that is left is a better one. Would you want a year with no seasons?

I shake my head.

Consider the rain, says the eagle. It is in Coyote's gift to control. It can wash things away, it can destroy, it can drown. But it nourishes everything. The chain of life depends on it. That is the nature of Coyote.

To . . . nourish?

Yes. While washing away. Cleansing the past. Coyote opposes the Crone, says the eagle. The Crone takes many forms: the Owl, the Giant. But always Coyote is against that which seeks to harm people.

How do you know? I say.

319

I am Eagle. I see all.

I nod, slowly. But . . . I say. But, I mean, none of this is *true*, is it? Like, one hundred per cent actually true, in the real world. I mean, Coyote didn't have anything to do with the moon and the stars and the sun, it was all the Big Bang, or whatever.

Coyote is the Big Bang, says the eagle.

Yeah, like, metaphorically, whatever, I say, but there was no First Woman and First Man, there was no –

Yes, says the owl, there was a First Woman and a First Man. One hundred per cent, actually, really, there was.

No, there was evolution, and –

The mitochondrial DNA of every person on earth can be traced back to a woman who lived 150,000 years ago in Africa. She is known to scientists in your world as Mitochondrial Eve. She existed. Everyone on earth is descended from her. Everyone.

I am blinking again. I see the eagle looking and I stop.

Your DNA, says the eagle, is a code for the creation of protein, a specific recipe, and it has been passed down, with only minor variations, since the beginning of life on this planet. This is a metaphorical and a literal truth. An unbroken line of DNA lies between a single-celled organism in the primordial soup and you. You have letters written in nucleic acid inside your bones that are a billion years old. You are older than you can possibly imagine.

I stare. I'm – How do you . . .

I am Eagle. I see all.

So, what, these stories are all true, then?

In a manner of speaking. There are different kinds of truth.

I nod. Coyote said that too, I say.

Coyote is more ancient even than you, says the eagle. You should listen when he speaks.

OK, I say. You think I should trust him, I get it.

I think you should trust him to be untrustworthy, says the eagle. You should trust him to take peace and make it war, to take order and replace it with chaos. But always, what is left will be better.

I nod. Fine, I say. So what should I do now?

Wait for Coyote. He will return. Go with him. Kill the Crone. Save the Child.

The eagle begins to stretch out its wings. Then it pauses. Quickly it stabs its beak down into its side, and when its head comes up again there is a feather in its mouth. It drops it on the ground in front of me.

Take that, it says. It will protect you.

Protect me from what?

Everything, says Mark, behind me. It is an eagle feather. It is perhaps the most powerful thing in the Dreaming.

I turn. He is standing there, I don't know how he snuck up so quietly, over the dry grass and twigs of the Forest of Thorns.

Coyote, says the eagle.

Eagle, says Coyote.

This is their whole entire conversation, then the eagle flaps its great wings and lofts into the air. It lets out a loud cry – *Kiiiiii* – and wheels upwards, quickly reducing to a speck in the dark air.

Guard that feather, says Mark. It could save you.

I nod.

Are you ready to carry on? he says. Or do you require another tantrum?

I am about to shout but then I see the glint in his eye.

Jerk, I say.

He smiles. Didn't you hear? I am misrule.

CHAPTER
59

WE PRESS ON THROUGH the Forest of Thorns. It's weird, now that I have the eagle feather, the path seems a little wider, as if the thorny branches are shrinking back from it, withdrawing their grasping, twisting arms.

After a week's walking, or it feels like it, Mark holds up a hand.

We're close, he says.

I look around. The woods don't look any different from before.

He points and I look up:

The spire of the castle looms above us, between the trees, like a cliff, like a rock formation.

We're there? I say.

Not quite, he says. There's a moat.

Mark presses on into the woods, not wasting time with talking, and I follow behind him. The undergrowth gets thicker and thicker, even worse than it was before, twisting with vines, bristling with thorns. I cry out as they scratch at me, despite the eagle feather, blood dripping from my arms that I raise in front of me to shield my face.

Not long now, says Mark.

I can't believe it – it seems like the woods want to stop us, like the thickening vegetation is trying to trip me, to hurt me.

And then, very suddenly, we break through, into darkness, the stars behind black clouds. Then – the clouds thin and part, and the castle reverse-dissolves, mists into being in front of us, bluely, like a photo in a developing bath.

It's tall, that's the first thing I notice. The spire, obviously, but also the whole structure. And it's all black, like if someone took a Disney castle and dipped it in tar. Bats wheel around the towers, and there are slits for arrows, and crenellations. In front of the castle, on the lawn, is some kind of glass structure, like a pagoda, a little crystal palace, and it might be a tomb or it might be a greenhouse, it's impossible to tell from here.

And from the castle, all the time, so that you can just assume from here on in that it is a loud, loud and everpresent backing music, comes the sound of crying, the Child, weeping and weeping for help, a ghastly sound now that we're so close, filling the air all around us, as if the castle itself is inconsolable, sobbing. The noise sends daggers of pain into me, hooks.

It is terrifying.

The castle is terrifying.

But not quite so terrifying as what lies before it.

That's the moat? I say.

Yes.

I goggle at it. It's, like, two thousand miles deep and this time I'm not exaggerating. I can't even see the bottom. And stretching over it is a thin rope bridge, like in fricking *Indiana Jones* or something – just planks roughly held together to form a surface, and two ropes to hold on to, and some of the planks are broken, and a two-thousand-mile drop, and there's like algae dripping from the rope because the whole 'moat' is all misty and creepy and *did I mention the two-thousand-mile drop*?

You have to be kidding, I say.

I don't kid, says Mark.

Yes you do, you did that whole hilarious joke about the snakes.

Oh, yes. Well, I'm not kidding now. We cross, and you kill the Crone.

Simple as that.

Yes.

Mark, that was *sarcasm*.

I know. It just wasn't funny.

I sigh. But even when he's being like this, it's so nice to *talk* to someone for once. A friend. Someone who isn't my mom.

To hear his voice.

I can't, I say. I'm scared. Suddenly all the challenge and mocking is gone from my voice, I can hear myself how it's trembling – this is new to me, because I never heard anything before coming to the Dreaming. I didn't know that your own voice could betray you.

You don't need to be afraid, says Mark.

I don't? Just look at it. I'm a teenage girl. I've never done anything. My mother or the thing that said it was my mother kept me at home all my life.

He smiles. You're not just anything, he says. Thousands of years ago, people did not think of themselves as individuals. They said that all their ancestors lived in them. I know – I was there.

So?

So you are not just a teenage girl. Remember what Eagle told you. You are a billion years of ancestors, in one person. Every living thing can trace a lineage right back to the start of life, to when the first bacteria fell to earth in stardust.

So? I say.

So? says Coyote. So now, think of all those who were never born, because a mouse was stepped on by a dinosaur, or an ape who could walk on two legs was eaten by a lion. But not you. Every one, *every single one* of your million ancestors, whether they were amoebas or mice or, finally, apes, survived long enough to have at least one child.

OK . . . I say, unsure.

So every generation that goes into your genes is a generation of fighters, of survivors. And all those millions of lives are in you, in your blood, and do you think they would have baulked at a gap in the ground, and a bridge? No. They would look at you and they would be ashamed.

Well, that's a bit much, isn't –

You are descended from warriors, says Mark. An endless parade of warriors. You have been alive for a billion years, an unbroken line of DNA. You will not be defeated by a ditch.

I feel my heart stirring despite myself. No, I say. I can hear the crying of the Child, louder than ever now, wafting over the chasm, from the castle on the other side, and I think to myself: All those times I had that dream and it always stopped before I could pick up the kid, before I could comfort her, and this time that is *not* happening.

I am going to cross that bridge and I am going to get that child if it kills me, and I am going to hold it tight and tell it that it never needs to cry again.

Tell me again, says Mark. I won't be defeated by a ditch.

I look at him, but he isn't smiling. I won't be defeated by a ditch, I say.

Good, says Mark. In that case, you first.

Oh, no way, no –

In case the wolves are still following, he says.

Oh, right. Yeah.

325

I step towards the bridge.

Wait, says Mark. I turn to him and he takes a step towards me, then puts his arms around me and hugs me. It's the first time we've touched, properly. I gasp. Not for the obvious reason. Because it's not a boy holding me, or a man, whatever, it's something else. It's Coyote.

I remember him saying, I'm older than the world. And standing here with him, like this, our bodies touching, I can feel it – it's like holding the stars in my arms; like touching the moon. Time slows down and it's crystal clear, like ice. I close my eyes, and everything becomes inside, not outside, the universe turns inside out, like a sock. All is just the interior of my mind, the body that is also a god, contained within the span of my arms.

I pull away and stare at him. You're not a person, I say, and for the first time, I really understand that it's true.

No, he says.

Thank you, I say. Thank you for that.

I mean it: I feel like I have breathed in stardust from just after the Big Bang.

How do I know all this? I say. I mean, I've barely read any Native American myths. But this is happening inside my head, right? So how do I know?

Places have a long memory, says Coyote.

But I'm not from this place, I'm from Alaska.

You are not from here. But you are here. In Arizona. And Arizona remembers.

Why Arizona?

He sighs, but not angrily. All places remember, he says. Arizona just happens to be where you are.

This is not clearing things up, I say.

He shakes his head. I am Coyote. It is not for me to clear things up. It is for me to break things, and make them into something new.

Right, I say.

You know, he says. Since you mentioned books. I've told you before, when I was Mark, but you should really go to college. Plenty of places offer interpreters. For people like you. To take notes for you, in class.

It's surreal, him saying this, when we're in the Dreaming by a, well, by a *massive ravine.*

Uh . . . OK, I say.

You need to think about the future, he says. But right now, you must go. Go. There is no more time.

And I do, because there's something in his voice that makes me. I look back at him, then I walk towards the bridge and then on to it, and it sways and oh this was not a good idea. I cling on to the ropes on either side, my hands sweaty. I inch out over the vast drop, moving super, super slowly, taking tiny little baby steps.

Slow down, says Mark. You might slip.

I turn and give him a withering look.

See? he says. *That* was sarcasm.

I ignore him and continue to make my way across, trying to ignore the pulsing black depth of the chasm below me. After a while, I find that I'm stepping a little easier, and the other side is getting closer and closer. Soon I'm halfway across.

Oh no, says Mark from behind me.

I turn, and I see what he has seen.

327

CHAPTER
60

Everything happens very fast.

Wolves pour on to the rope bridge from behind us, then just *flow* along it towards Mark, a grey flood of teeth and claws. Mark turns to me. Go, he says. This time, I will stand.

You can't –

This is not a discussion. Run.

He turns back to the wolves, and despite myself, as the first of them barrels into him, I find myself moving backwards and away from him, towards the castle. Jaws snap – and close on thin air, as Mark twists and ducks, then powers up, sending three wolves tumbling over the side. They disappear before I see them hit anything.

But more of them fall on him, then, and there are hundreds more behind . . .

Go, shouts Mark. Just remember, you're an adult. You're not –

But his voice is cut off as a wolf barrels into him, and he focuses on grappling with it.

I start to turn, as I do so I see Mark fall –

No –

He isn't falling, he's shrinking into himself, and dark red fur bursts from him, and he is Coyote, leaping at the wolf before him, teeth closing on its throat; blood sprays wildly, like a water hose turned on. More wolves press in on him then, worry at him, there is snapping at ankles and noses and more blood flies and Coyote takes the eyes from another wolf with a swipe of his claws and batters another with his head; it scrabbles at the planks and then plummets, and –

Now, says the voice in my head, as Coyote finally disappears, buried beneath a moving blanket of grey.

Tears in my eyes, I turn and run, the rope bridge swaying beneath me, no longer seeing the horrific abyss below me.

Until . . .

I am maybe twenty feet from the other side, the castle walls rising from a dead black lawn. The crying of the Child is very loud now. Very loud.

I slow down. I can see the glass structure on the grass in front of the castle more clearly now. It is maybe thirty yards from me. I can see that it is a little palace, I was right, complete with towers and flags fluttering in the breeze, only they are not flags because they are made of glass too, the fluttering is an effect of the shifting clouds over the moon, the whole thing is made of glass, shimmering in the starlight.

Glass walls, sloping glass roof, glass buttresses.

And inside . . .

Inside is a child. Sitting on the grass, facing away from me, is a tiny child, no more than two years old. It is shaking, racked with sobs, and I realise that this is the source of the crying, this is the Child, sitting in a prison of glass.

Hey, I call. Hey, I'm here.

The Child stops crying for a second, then starts again.

Hey! Kid! Hey!

Slowly, still crying, the Child shuffles around to look at me.

The breath turns to stone in my chest.

It is the child from my dream, the girl, the exact one, from the dream I have had over and over since I was a child myself, the one that sits in the hospital waiting room, crying for someone, anyone, *me*, to come and pick it up. I stare at it, at her, horrified – but at the same time, I kind of knew, I always knew, that it was going to be.

I knew the first time Mark mentioned a child.

I'm coming I'm coming I'm coming, I say, and I launch myself forward, the Child had stopped crying for a second when it saw me but now her pudgy little arms are reaching out towards me, stiff with need, and she is crying again, screaming really, the sound like an icicle in my heart.

Then I stop dead, the crying echoing in the canyon all around me, pressing in on my skull, as if it could burst my brains.

I can't go any further.

I've come so far and the child is *right there*, the child from my dreams, the Child Mark wants me to save, that Coyote wants me to save, and I can't get there.

I can't get there.

In front of me is a six-foot gap in the rope bridge, further than I could ever jump, where there are no planks.

CHAPTER
61

I LOOK AT THE HOLE, and below it the yawning vacancy of the chasm.

I could try to hold on to the rope and haul myself along it, hand by hand, but I know I don't have the arm strength.

I'm going to have to jump.

I stand there, hesitating, and then I sense the air shift behind me, and I turn and see the wolves coming, the pack streaming towards me.

Mark, I think.

In front of me, the Child's arms are still outstretched, as if straining to reach me, across the thirty yards that separate us, across the glass walls of its prison. Her cries echo against the rock walls.

There's no time to think – I give myself as much of a run-up as I dare, then I sprint to the edge and jump –

for a moment I am in free fall; weightless –

then my forearms land on the planks on the other side and my fingers find a hold and I swing there, panting.

I glance back and see the wolves stop – not quick enough; the momentum of the pack pushes two of them off the side and down.

Ha, I think. You just try to –

The ropes spanning the gap, the ropes green with algae, snap.

My part of the bridge is still attached to the other side, but now I'm the weight of a pendulum; now I'm swinging *fast* towards the rock wall of the moat. There's ten feet of bridge between me and the side, and I know the formulas to give you the speed and the force, (Mom) taught me them, but there isn't exactly time to work them out, and when I hit the rock I hit it hard, and it smacks the breath out of me.

I dangle there, for a second, then the plank I'm holding snaps, and I fall.

My hands windmill, looking for purchase; I am maybe screaming but I can't hear it past the rush of air. Little trees and weeds and patches of ivy whip at me as I plunge down and then –

Crunch. I hit a hard branch, a thick one, and I manage to get my arms around it in like a headlock kind of move, and cling to it. I see that it's a tree, jutting out into the air. It's strong; it will hold me.

But that might not help.

I look up. No – I didn't fall that far. I can see the top, maybe fifteen feet up. And there are handholds too – little crevices in the rock, and other branches and roots; things I could cling to.

It's just . . .

If I fall, and I don't snag something again, I will die.

I hang there, cursing silently. Then I try to reach up for the next handhold I can see; a root snaking out from an earthy crack in the rock, forming a loop. But my hand trembles – I can't do it. I'm too scared, and too tired.

I'm stuck.

There's a bottomless drop below me, and a hard climb above me. And I'm no climber, and if I make a mistake, it's the end.

I'm so sorry, Child, I think. I'm so sorry, I'm so sorry, I'll find a way to come back and I'll get you out of there, I promise.

Then I do the only thing I can think of.

I concentrate very hard, and I step back –

through the air –

into my other nightmare.

CHAPTER
62

THE WHOLE OF THE next morning, over breakfast and everything, Jennifer keeps touching Michael, as if he faded into nothingness once, briefly, and so she wants to check now that he is still substantial.

Me, I feel ghostlike too, only half there. One half of me is still seeing the Child in its palace of glass, reaching out to me across the chasm, wanting me to comfort it.

The thought makes me shiver. I have to save the Child from the Crone, I think. It's totally crazy but I know that I have to do it.

Then I see Jennifer look at me with concern bruising her eyes and I try to shunt back into the room, like a train changing tracks, to cancel the image of the crying Child from my mind.

I smile at Jennifer, and she smiles back, then does that touching-Michael thing again.

I think I know what's going on with the two of them. He was the one who was broken; she had her hope, her faith, her god, and he didn't. Now she thinks she can see him mending, and she is feeling him out, like prodding a cup that you have fixed with superglue, to see if it is holding.

It's true too, he seems better. There's more colour in his cheeks, he looks less like some kind of addict. He has switched, quite suddenly, into a more positive mode, like a negative number being squared.

$-1^2 = 1$

And the thing doing the squaring, the factor of multiplication, would appear to be baseball. Ever since it came up, he's been – well, not happy, but a whole different person. Me too, I have to admit. Because it always seemed odd, you know? That I loved it so much – me, with my overweight mom who never did any exercise in her life. Now I think: I got it from him. It's something concrete he gave me, even if I look at his face and I can't for the life of me see any physical resemblance. It's something in my blood, passed down.

In my DNA.

And that makes me think of the eagle, or Eagle, whatever, and him saying how there was one unbreakable line of DNA between me and . . .

Between me and my dad.

My real dad.

I think of Mark saying that there are a billion years of ancestors inside me.

James can see it too, the unbroken-line stuff though obviously not the eagle stuff or the Mark stuff and he looks pleased, but also a tiny bit jealous. He doesn't like baseball, I know, and I wonder if this is making him feel left out. Maybe. He definitely seems closer to his mom than to his dad.

Anyway, I don't want to get into the politics of it. The fault lines of the family. I'm just glad to have a plan for the day.

So when we've finished our bagels, Michael grabs his wallet and his shoes and hugs Jennifer. *We'll be back in an hour*, he says. *We'll keep it short.*

It's OK, says Jennifer. *I waited fifteen years for her. I can manage without her for an hour.* She is looking at him with such love, this man who she must have come close to losing too.

335

Well, then, says Michael. He opens the door for me, and I go through. James waves from the couch, where he's reading about French painters.

In the hallway, we bump into Summer from the CPS. She does a small double take. *You're going out?* she says.

To the park, says Michael.

I don't know if that's advisable. There's [   ] and [   ]. You don't want to be recognised.

I turn to Michael. *No one knows what she looks like,* he says.

For now, says Summer.

Well, precisely.

I would still –

What do you want? I mean, what about when we get home? You want us to keep her inside for the rest of her life?

No, we just –

Michael is fully a positive integer now; all that defeat has left him. It's as if he inhaled a ghost and it spread out to fill his whole body, puffing him up like a balloon, taut. *I'm taking my daughter to the park,* he says.

Summer sighs. *Fine. In that case, do you mind if I come with you?*

Yes, says Michael. *Yes, I mind.*

Summer does NOT know what to do in this situation and it is all kinds of awesome. It is fifty-four flavours of awesome.

Uh, right, she says. *I'll [   ] then. Jennifer and I can discuss some of the arrangements for –*

Do what you want, says Michael. Then he walks past her.

And I follow.

CHAPTER
63

AFTER WE'VE STOPPED AT a store where Michael buys a bat, a ball and a glove – I could tell him that my DeMarini was in the cabin, so the Feds must have it, but it seems a lot to say out loud – we walk to a small park a couple of blocks from the apartment. It takes a while because of my foot. Though having said that, the pain is already a lot better. Sometimes I'm even forgetting to take the codeine, which is good since (Mom) ground up half my supply and dumped it in Luke's wine.

What bat do – did you have? he asks.

DeMarini, I say.

He nods approvingly. I like that.

Then, suddenly, when we are standing waiting for a pedestrian light, it hits me that this is the first time I've been alone with a man, ever. I mean apart from Mark, and he doesn't count, he's Coyote. I stop.

Everything OK?

I nod, just. My blood is pounding a danger signal. I know what men are like. I know what they can do.

Then I think: But do I know? Or did Shaylene tell me, and I believed her? I close my eyes for a second. I think: Anyway, he's my dad. He's my dad.

He's not going to hurt me.

Slowly, I open my eyes again and give him a faint smile. He is looking at me, concerned. *Come on*, I say.

And we cross.

We walk to a wide patch of grass where no one is sitting or playing, and Michael hands me the bat. *Here you go*, he says. *I'll pitch.*

Good, I say slowly. *I can't pitch for shit.*

He stares at me for a second and then laughs, and it's like someone up above has just lassoed us both with the same ribbon.

Don't curse like that in front of your – in front of Jennifer, he says.

I snap a salute off my forehead.

Wise-ass, he says.

I do like a low bow thing, my hand giving a flourish, like a courtier in a costume drama. Then I fall, because of my leg, and wind up on my butt.

Alarm widens Michael's eyes and he helps me to my feet – his arms are strong, I notice. It's weird – it gives me what I can only describe as a DAD feeling. I mean, I never had a dad growing up. But something about him picking me up . . . it is an action, but in the action is the word 'dad'. I don't know, I can't describe it.

You OK? he asks, making sure I can see his mouth, see him mouthing the words.

Fine, I say. I smile.

You did kind of deserve that, he says.

Yep, I say.

You really want to bat? he asks.

I nod.

He shrugs, like, OK then. He walks a few paces away from me. I roll my eyes and gesture at him, my hand flapping – further, further. He backs away, raises his eyebrows.

No, say my hands. Further.

He adjusts his shoulders fractionally, but goes back. Then he tosses the ball up and catches it a couple of times before nodding to me. I nod back, and he pulls his arm back, then curls himself around the ball as he pushes it through the air towards me.

He throws fast – the ball comes flat and low, right in the sweet spot, and I swing, feel the bat connect and the ball soar over his head, bouncing behind him. I wince – you can't hit without turning, and the torsion has twisted pins against bone and flesh in my foot.

You OK? shouts Michael, or at least I assume he shouts.

I nod.

He gives me a thumbs-up, turns, and jogs for the ball. He may drink a lot but he moves easily. When he has snagged the ball he sends it at me again, a little tighter to the body this time. I hit it true, send it up and into the sky to my right.

Michael goes and gets the ball again, throws it to me.

I think of Shaylene, that time when I was young, that time I have always remembered, taking me to the park and pitching me ball after ball, despite hating exercise, despite the sweat pouring off her. I think: Was that real? I mean, was that love real? Or do her other lies make everything untrue?

But no, it must have been real – her desire to make me happy, to do the thing I wanted to do.

But if she could do that for me, could think about my feelings like that, how could she turn a blind eye to the feelings of my parents? How could she take me from them?

It makes me feel dizzy and I try to put it out of my mind, shut it out, like a muddy dog on the other side of a door.

Michael throws, and I swing with the bat.

Again.

Again.

And every time I knock it far and high, even though I can tell he's mixing it up to test me, throwing in the odd curve ball now.

It's a bright day, just a few low clouds overhead, sometimes catching on the peaks of the mountains in the distance, disintegrating, like this sentence, into suspension dots . . .

Me, I'm just standing still, keeping the weight off my bad leg as much as I can. But Michael is running to get the ball, quicker each time, and I see the sweat coming off him.

Another throw – this one I batter down at the ground so it bounces back to him.

Another, clearly meant to trick me – he hides his hands before he throws it, and it curves misleadingly in the air. But I swipe it up and into the blue sky; it's as if it flies over the mountains, before clattering down through the branches of a tree behind Michael.

He frowns.

He returns to his imaginary mound and crouches, then sends a ball in a flat line, very fast, right at my body. I watch it come – so much slower than the batting cage, and I sort of jump the weight off my bad leg so I can get myself around it, and then I send it back to him on the same trajectory, hard.

He sees it coming just in time to twist away from it, watches it bounce away over the grass.

For a second, he looks at me. And I know he meant to bodyline me like that, and he knows that I meant to return the favour. He smiles and runs for the ball.

The next one works. He hides his hands again, but this time they do something very clever, because the ball seems to be coming to one place, and at the last moment, it dives, like something living, and slams into my waist. I double up, winded, and this makes me lose my balance, so I fall and land on my hip.

I look up at the sky, furious.

Then I see Michael's face, filling my vision, that first person POV shot you always see in movies when the protagonist has been knocked out.

Are you hurt? he asks.

No, I say. Which is not precisely true. In either sense of the word.

He lifts me to my feet again. As he does so he has to kind of hold me, and when he does I breathe in and a memory shoots through me like a blazing star lighting up the night; him hugging me, as a child, the scent of pine trees, which I can still smell. I may not remember his face, my mind may not have kept any pictures of him, but before I was two I must have breathed him into my bloodstream, that northern forest smell of his.

Maybe I was wrong. Maybe memory does live more powerfully in smell, more deeply.

I'm so sorry, he says. *I don't know what happened.*

But I see the lie in his eyes. I think he knows exactly what happened. It's written there, like closed captions. He didn't like that I was getting to every ball, that he couldn't make me miss, that I had no strikes.

It's the same thing I noticed last night, with the Boggle, though there it was Jennifer. The same competitiveness. The same urge to fight. Suddenly I am starting to understand why there's some tension between Michael and James. Super! I think. I have joined a family where the dad will take out a cripple, to show that he's the man.

You want to keep going? he asks. He is expecting me to say no, but hoping I'll say yes, I can see it in his eyes. The hunger. To play, but also to beat me.

I remember Shaylene again, going to get the ball over and over. Throwing it to me. Not, oh I don't know, throwing it AT me.

No, I say.

You want to go home? To the apartment?

Yes, please.

He nods, and then his eyes get a kind of pleading quality. *Listen . . .* he says. He shakes his head. *Sorry, that's a stupid word to use. Um . . . just, if you mention to Jennifer, about the [   ], she might get worried. Maybe, you know, don't –*

Don't mention that you hit me with the ball?

He swallows. *No.*

I look up. It's still morning, but there's a thin sliver of moon in the sky, glowing pale and very, very far away.

I shrug. *Whatever,* I say.

Awesome, I think. This is the whole teenage experience in one morning. I'm lying to one of my parents, and I just said whatever to the other one. Plus I'm smoking. I mean, I've established that, with Jennifer and Michael.

So it's all good.

My plan.

I'm golden.

And after that stuff Michael just pulled with the ball? I'm pretty much decided.

CHAPTER
64

WHEN WE GET BACK to the apartment, Jennifer is making some kind of tacos for lunch.

You two have fun? she asks. I notice that, as hard as all this must be for her, she has still had time to do her make-up immaculately.

I try to smile. *Yes,* I say.

Michael? she asks, concerned.

It was fine, he says. *Just her leg – she pulled it a bit. But she's OK. Fierce hitter, actually. She could get a baseball scholarship.*

Boggle and baseball, huh? says Jennifer. *You're going to be much in demand.*

I shrug.

You ever play for a team? says Michael.

No, I say.

Of course, he says, slapping his forehead. *You were kept pretty much alone, right?*

Yes, I say. *But I wouldn't want to anyway.*

Wouldn't want to what?

Play for a team.

What? says Michael. *Why?*

I start to sign without thinking. Then I begin to say the words but it will take too long and my words feel foreign in my mouth, like stones. So I sigh. I pick up a piece of paper from the table, on which Jennifer has been writing some kind of shopping list. She is holding out the pen before I even ask for it.

I write:

I play against the ball. I'm not interested in playing against people.

Michael reads it, his brow creasing into a frown. He shows it to Jennifer. She starts to mouth something at him but then I guess she remembers that I am all about the lip-reading, because she just smiles a not very genuine smile instead.

You're so new to us, she says. *It's like we don't know you at all.*

Yes, I say. It's true. It's as if I'm a changeling, like the ones in old stories my (mom) read me, where a human child is taken away and replaced with a fairy. That's what I am in this family: something strange and foreign, dropped into it.

Then I think, No. I am a changeling, but I am more than a changeling. I am the child that is taken away, but I am also the child that is put in its place.

I mean: Angelica Watson was stolen from these people. She was one person, a person I don't even remember being.

And now I, Shelby Cooper, have been brought back to them, swapped for her. And I am nothing like these people. I may look more like them than like my – like Shaylene, but I may as well be a fairy, from another world.

But it's exciting, Jennifer says, heedless. *It's like learning a language. And it is learning a language! I mean, sign. I'll need to do a course. We'll need to do a course.*

I don't say anything.

There's so much to find out about you, she says.

I still don't say anything.

Anyway . . . um, I'll just finish fixing lunch. She starts to turn.

Where's James? I say.

He went out to look at some gallery, says Jennifer. *A modern . . . Oh, I don't know. Something to do with landscapes.*

I look at her, at her crucifix around her neck, her glossy skin, her birdlike hands, fluttering. I think about how there are, presumably, no novels in their house in Alaska. I picture Michael, flicking balls at James in the backyard, raising bruises.

I might as well be living with aliens. I mean, my – Shaylene is an alien too, I have no fricking idea who she is, other than a liar. But at least she reads. And at least I can speak to her. At least she can sign. One thing I have had enough of: communicating without my hands. It is how a seal must feel, wriggling on a rock. It is all friction, and no smoothness, no quickness of liquid motion.

Summer is coming back after lunch, says Jennifer. *To go through some options.*

What kind of options?

Oh, I don't know. Schools. Counselling.

Fine, I say. *I'm going out for a cigarette.*

Jennifer nods, though I can see that she doesn't like it.

On my way to the sliding door, I hook up the backpack from the floor where I left it. I open the door and step out on to the little balcony. I look at the rooftops of the town, and I light a cigarette, gasping again when the harshness of it hits my lungs. I watch Jennifer as she busies herself at the cooker, frying something. Michael speaks to her for a while, and I guess maybe they argue, because he throws up his hands, then walks to the bedroom and shuts the door behind him.

I turn around, back to the view of the city.

I move quick.

We're only three storeys up, and there's no one on the sidewalk below – one person further down the street, looking in a store window, but that's it.

There's like a gate between the balcony and the fire escape, and I swing myself over it; my leg screams at me, but I don't stop. I put my hands on the rails and don't even try to walk down the steps – I just let myself slide, holding my weight up with my arms. The rail burns my hands as I go down.

At the turn, I hold on to the railing, using it as a crutch, and manoeuvre myself to slide down the next flight. My hands are red raw, but I tell myself I will let them hurt later, when there's time for it.

At the bottom, there's a drop to the ground – I saw this from the car. I release the ladder, which shoots down and hits the sidewalk. Then I climb down, trying not to use my right leg, though my arms are in agony.

On the ground, that's the worst bit – the drop is like a foot from the bottom rung and I land clumsily, because of my injured foot, then hop, but lose my balance and fall. I scrape my hands even more, protecting my face, and kind of crawl or pull myself to my feet.

I glance up – no one is following me. I hobble down the street. I have no idea where I'm going, but I know I have to get off the sidewalk like YESTERDAY because I'm too slow on this CAM Walker and they'll catch up with me in no time, once they realise I'm gone.

I turn a corner and go one block, then I see a bookstore with a green and white striped awning. DOWNTOWN BOOKS says a sign in gold leaf on an old weathered wooden board. I open the door and go in – I see a bell ring above me, but it registers only as a faint ting in my mind, buried under static.

There's no one around, though I can just make out a desk over in the gloom to the left, so I make for the further stacks to the right and go behind a big bookshelf, where I can't be seen from the street. It's only when I see embroidery on the wall and the framed photo of a guy in a mask that I realise I'm in the Native American section.

I still can't see anyone else. If someone heard the bell, they haven't bothered to check me out. I like that. A place where you can just be. It reminds me of the library.

Running my fingers along the spines, I scan the shelf. I have to look like I'm browsing. My forefinger settles on a thin, old book. I don't know why. I pull it out and look at the title. *Navajo Creation Myth*, I read. *The Story of the Emergence.* By someone called Mary C. Wheelwright. It's an ancient book, leather bound.

Let the book fall open, says Mark's voice, in my head. At least, I guess it's my imagination imitating his voice, because aside from anything else I have never heard his voice in the real world.

I do what he says, though. It's the story of the flood, I realise. I skim through it, until I see:

> *Coyote is present here as the eternal trickster and trouble-causer. But his mischief has a dual effect. It brings the dangerous and negative reaction of the flood, but also, because of the flood, forces the people up into a more complex and promising world.*

I stare at it. What is this telling me? I think. That it's somehow going to change my life for the fricking BETTER to lose my mom, to lose who I am, and have to go and live with strangers? I snap the book shut, slide it back on to the shelf. I walk along a bit, take another one out.

347

It's a collection of Navajo and Apache folk tales from Arizona. I stand there and leaf through it. There's a section on Coyote fighting an evil entity, which sometimes manifests as a giant, sometimes as an owl, sometimes as a Crone.

Hmm, I think.

I shrug and put the book back. Suddenly an old guy with white hair and a beard peers around the corner, little round glasses.

Can I help you? he asks.

Just browsing, I say with my mouth, as clearly as I can manage – I think so, anyway.

Navajo tales? he says. He comes and stands next to me. I have an urge to pick up a heavy book and hit him with it. *I recommend the [   ],* he says.

I look at him blankly.

He runs his eyes along the shelf, then selects another thin volume. He hands it to me, and I swear he winks. Then he turns and walks away. He's like a caricature of a bookstore owner, leather patches on the sleeves of his cardigan. A slight smell of pipe smoke, lingering still.

I look at the book in my hands. *Sitting on the Blue-Eyed Bear: Navajo Myths and Legends*, it says. I let it fall open – it seems like the right thing to do – and peer down at the page. I read:

> *Coyote has a life principle that may be laid aside, so that any injury done to his body affects his life only temporarily and he may even recover from apparent death.*

I blink.

I look for the bookstore owner, but he has gone.

OK, I think to myself. So Coyote never really dies. He comes back to life. I guess I should have known that. Also he DOES fight the Crone, the Owl, the Giant, whatever. The first book I looked at was pretty clear on that – he DOES stand against that which seeks to destroy people.

I flick through the book, curious about something.

Yes: there it is. Eagles and eagle feathers are sacred.

My head spins. But I didn't know any of this stuff, I think. I've only just read it now. How does that work?

But I don't worry about it for long, because I have bigger things to worry about, things like getting away from my birth parents.

Things like saving the Child, stuck in its prison of glass, its little palace. I feel like, if I can just pick up that child, just once pick up that child and soothe its cries, then I will be whole.

It's stupid.

But it's what I feel.

And Coyote might have disappeared under a tide of wolves but that doesn't mean he's dead.

He's older than the sun and the moon.

He has died before, and come back.

And suddenly, I know what I want to do, what I need to do. For the first time in a long time I have some very clear, very defined goals, and they are MY goals now, not just some agenda given to me by someone else, by Mark or a lawyer or my so-called parents or my so-called mother.

I list them in my head:

1. Kill the Crone.
2. Save the Child, and end the fricking dream that has haunted me since I was a child myself.

3. Get Coyote back. I mean Mark. I mean Coyote.

4. AND MAYBE. JUST MAYBE. GET SOME FRICKING
   CONTROL OVER MY OWN LIFE.

I leave the bookstore. I don't see the old guy again.

I walk right past Gene's Western Wear, on the corner, where Luke bought us those stupid-ass hats.

I know exactly where I'm going.

CHAPTER
65

I STEP FROM COLD outside air into cold air-conditioned air; you can almost feel the difference on your skin; a dog would smell the difference, I think.

The climbing store is a friendly warren, everything in piles, shelves making little corridors. Brand names I don't recognise are everywhere; it's a place that speaks to the climbing cognoscenti, not to me. But at the same time, I know the shape of the language, I am familiar with the structure – like seeing another Indo-European language, laid out on a twenty-six letter grid; you don't understand it, but it's familiar.

I have been in this kind of store before, to buy my baseball bat. I have learned the brand names, only for another sport.

I don't see anyone, which is good.

I go deeper, half expecting a cop to put a hand on my shoulder at any moment. Soon, by accident, I find the books. One end of the shelves is all maps; towards the other end are the instruction manuals, the introductions. I pick one that looks basic, but thick. There's an index at the back and I flick through it –

E, for equipment.

I flick to page 142, scan the paragraphs. Ropes, carabiners.

Something called a passive wedge. I don't have to read it for long before I find camming devices. Yes – that's what I want.

They have two semicircular pieces, built on a logarithmic circle, which is important for some reason to do with friction.

The way they work: you pull a trigger, and the circles align, snug to each other, narrow. They have teeth, to make them bite more. You insert them into a crack in the wall, and you pull on the shaft, which your rope is tied to; they're spring-loaded, but hinged to the shaft too; the more weight you put on it the more they expand away from each other, dig into the rock on either side.

Theoretically, then – the harder you fall, the more they hold you.

There's a graph, some equations. Applied force, normal force, friction. They're good for twelve thousand newtons of falling force, the bigger ones. I check some stuff in the appendix and then do the maths in my head. Mass, acceleration, spring constant, etc. Long story short, the camming device will hold me easily.

OK, good.

I go to the back of the book again – *K* for knots.

I spend a minute or two looking at the right pages. I hate this Girl Scout kind of thing. But I figure I can do it.

So: a rope, twenty feet, to give me room to get to the top, a couple of carabiners, to attach the rope to the loop, and the other end to me, and a camming device.

I shuffle down the aisles – there's a whole wall of the cam things, and I grab the most expensive one; it's actually a belt with like five of them on it, different sizes. Fine. Rope – easy; carabiners too.

When I have, in a TOTALLY LITERAL SENSE, got all my shit together, I move to the back of the store. I pass a little checkout, a table with a chair, a white Macbook, and a credit card machine. There's a copy of *American Gods*, face down on the table, a half-full cup of coffee.

Cigarette break, maybe? Good for me, anyway.

I pass by, and find the deepest, darkest corner of the store; it's where there's snow gear and hats, and it's summer now so I figure no one's going to come near. I put on a climbing harness, which I just took from a rotating display unit, and tie the rope to one carabiner using what I think is the right knot, then clip the carabiner to the harness.

I put down my backpack.

I close my eyes and try very hard to believe that I can just step around the world and into another place.

203 seconds pass.

I open my eyes again.

I calm my breathing. The store is still empty.

I close my eyes, and I hold my equipment very tightly and –

CHAPTER
66

MY LEFT ARM IS still hooked around the tree stump, and the climbing stuff is in my right hand.

A warm wind, like breath, runs through my hair from below, tickles the back of my neck. It carries the crying of the Child to my ears.

I look down, like a moron, and my insides turn to slush.

Breathe.

I focus on the rock wall, scanning it. There – just above and to the left, there's a vertical seam, maybe two inches wide. I loop the loose end of the rope around my neck. I have wound the belt with the cams on it around my wrist, and I select one of the medium ones. My hand is trembling. I pass it to my left hand, while I clip the carabiner to it, and loop the rope through.

My hand slips, and the cam falls – but it's on the rope, and the rope spools out a bit from my neck but then stops. I haul the device back up, like a fish on a line.

Holding the trigger that keeps the half-moons together, I push the thing into the crack: then, when it's as deep as it'll go, I pull hard on the rope.

It holds, like a bolt in hardened cement.

The rope is already attached to my harness at the other end, so now I'm tied to the rock, and it would take like ten thousand newtons of force to dislodge me.

I look up. The lip of the canyon is not far above me – maybe like ten feet. My rope is twenty feet. So: I fall, worst-case scenario, I fall for thirty feet and then the rope stops me.

It would hurt. But I could climb up once more, to here, and then try again. Now, when I climb, even though I'm going to be tied to something below me, I'm going to have some insurance. Some latitude. Longitude, I guess, technically.

No. I do not have a boyfriend.

I get a grip on myself, and start to climb. I use the same crack as the camming device is lodged in, for my first handhold, and the tree branch as my first foothold. I go very slowly – I'm not a climber, and I am very soon totally out of breath. I'm scared too, which does *not* help. I have to stop almost right away.

I press myself into the rock, keeping my eyes on it, not looking up, not looking down. My sweat is cold on my face – vertigo.

It's not sheer, though, or smooth, the surface – it's all angles and fissures and bits of vegetation growing out. There's always something to hold on to, and there's a security blanket over my twitching mind, which is that if I fall I don't fall forever.

Just when I'm thinking this, I fall – a root I grabbed snaps on me, and my hands are pawing at nothing. I plummet –

But my foot catches on an outcropping of rock before I can play out my rope, and my hand swings of its own accord and my fingers hook on to a cranny; it jars me, sends shivers of pain down my hand, but I hold on.

I take a deep breath and try again. I focus on the Child, on the unending sound of its distress. You have to get up there, I say to myself. Listen to it. Listen to *her*.

She needs you.

Maybe an hour later, I pull myself up on to the other side. My arms are quivering like fever. I flop on the dry ground, exhausted. There's a voice deep inside me that wants me to crawl further from the drop but I don't, I just lie there. The feeling of relief is a physical thing; abruptly I remember an afternoon in August, temperature in the hundreds, the heat like an assailing malevolent presence, out to suck all the lifeforce from all living things. Shaylene went to the store and came back with a big bag of ice, and cream, and we made tea, then blended it with the ice and cream and drank it on the couch till the fronts of our brains rang like bells from the cold of it.

This feeling is a bit like that.

Some indefinite amount of time passes. The icy stars are bright above me.

Eventually, I unclip the carabiner from the harness and get up. I take off the harness and step away from the gorge.

The glass structure is just in front of me. It's maybe five feet tall, wide as a car. Towers and spires at the top, buttresses at the sides. The glass looks thin – almost like ice, like an ice sculpture. The Child has scooted over to the side closest to me, and is sitting there, wailing, arms outstretched.

The Child from my dreams. Right here in the Dreaming.

Of course.

Behind it is the Crone's castle – full-size, dark, looming. An enormous and terrifying thing, squat and brooding. I don't want to look at it, not yet, it's blocking out so much of the starlight, so much of the night sky. It's like a black hole, sucking brightness out of this world.

I look away from it, shivering.

I step forward, examining the little glass castle instead. There is no door. No windows. Nothing that opens or might open. I walk all around it, the Child turning as I do, following me with her eyes, crying and crying. I realise that this is the real girl, and the one that was in the iron cage was some kind of projection.

This is the Child I need to save.

But I can't find any way in.

I come back around to the side by the chasm and reach out to touch the glass.

Ow.

It isn't glass after all, it's ice, it really is an ice sculpture, and now my hand is burning and cold at the same time. I clutch my hand to my chest, swearing, wrapping my sweatshirt around it, trying to warm it. Then I kick the ice prison, lash out my foot in anger –

The pain is colossal, like I have just kicked the most unyielding substance ever made; my toes might be broken, I think.

I hop on one leg, hand and foot blazing. The Child can see that I'm hurt and is crying even harder now, and between the agony and the sobbing all my nerves are taut and electric. I almost wish I couldn't hear, here in the Dreaming, could go back to being deaf and not have to listen to the Child.

Almost.

I take a step back and look at the Child in its ice cell again. Open sesame, I say, not really expecting anything. Which is good because absolutely nothing happens. I go around it again, looking for a seam, a gap, but there's none. Just ice – smooth, solid ice.

Inside, I see the tears running down the Child's face. When they fall from her cheeks they make drops of ice that tinkle on the ground.

Fricking hell.

It's just like my dream. She's right there, but the ice is between us, and I can't break it. I don't want to touch it again.

To my surprise, I start crying too – I feel the moisture on my cheeks, and I think it's rain at first, that by some miracle Coyote has already fulfilled the quest, but then I realise it's tears.

I sit down on the grass, unable to do anything more. I close my eyes so that I don't see the Child, holding out its hands to me.

I'm sorry, I think. I can't help you. I'm not strong enough. I'm not the one. I can't save you.

But then I hear something. A distant voice, quiet, it takes me a while to notice it – I mean I'm not used to hearing at all. But then I do. It's little more than a whisper, it could be the breeze, but I know it isn't.

It's a woman, laughing. Cruel laughter, triumphant, evil laughter, from a fairy tale. I open my eyes. It's coming from the dark castle, beyond the ice.

OK, I think.

OK, screw you.

I get up and walk past the Child, who reaches out for me as I pass, but despite all my instincts screaming at me I ignore her, I keep my eyes on the castle.

I'm close but still a way away – maybe, like, the width of a football field from the door, which is big and wooden and has rivets in it, big metal studs at regular intervals.

Between me and the door, there's just dead grass – open space, apart from one thing, an object I can't quite make out. Something sticking up from the grass, closer to the door. Something square.

Behind the castle, just like in a picture book, the deep forest begins again, yawning around the castle too, like a cave, like an open mouth, draping it and festooning it with thorny vines. The air is unmoving but suspended; a sense of something about to drop, about to move; like bated breath.

I move forward, caught in a cross stream, waves of hateful mirth reaching me from in front, a tide of tears behind, from the Child.

Closer.

And.

Here's the one thing in the grass: a sign, like a for-sale sign, a wooden board on a square pole that has been planted in the earth. I step forward and read it.

WELCOME

it says, and there's a smiley after:

This is not a bad sentiment, per se, you are perhaps thinking. It's friendly!

Ah, but.

Ah, but wait!

The sign seems very, very much like it has been written in blood.

Fresh blood.

CHAPTER
67

I NEED A WEAPON, I think.

I look at the sign, tied to a thick wooden post that is set deep in the ground. I visualise a baseball bat, striking a ball. Yeah, that could work.

Seizing the post, I try to pull it out of the ground, but it doesn't budge. I kick it, and then kick it again, and again. Eventually it begins to wobble, and then rock freely. I yank it out.

I use the ground to lever off the sign, breaking it into pieces.

Then I heft the post in my hands. It's heavy, solid. A staff. A weapon. It gives me an idea, though I know already that it's not going to work. I turn and walk back the way I came, towards the ice walls and the Child.

I walk forward, treading carefully. My breathing is very fast and shallow; I feel dizzy and nauseous. But I keep going.

When I reach the icy prison I try not to look at the Child, who has scooted over and is still, always, reaching out to me, crying its endless tears. Instead I raise the heavy piece of wood and swing it, as hard as I can, as if aiming for a fast ball.

Bang.

The post jumps out of my hands, shivering, and my fingers ring like tuning forks. I curse, shaking my arms, trying to rid myself of the needles in my flesh.

There is not a mark on the ice.

I pull my arms back, put all the twist into it that I can, and swing the staff again, hard.

The impact this time shatters the wooden post, splinters flying everywhere, one of them narrowly missing my eye. I am left holding a sheared-off, thin piece, no more use as a weapon than my own bare hands.

Some sort of spell on the ice, I figure, when my shock has eased enough for clear thoughts to form.

Well.

I didn't think it was going to work. I cast aside the broken shard.

Sighing, I turn my back yet again on the Child, and start back towards the castle. It seems not to get larger in the usual sense of things you approach, objects appearing to grow as you get closer, due to the effect of perspective, but in the *actual* sense of getting bigger, rearing up into the sky, a beast about to eat me.

Focus.

But my heart is a piston in my chest and my hands are sweating, trembling. The castle seems to sense my fear, and expands even larger, filling the sky. Blackening everything.

That cruel laughter gets louder.

I take a deep breath and step up to the massive oak door. It is twice as tall as I am. I try the handle and find that it's locked. I stand there for a second, like an idiot.

What do I do now?

Then I think: No. You're the Maiden. The first Coyote, older than the world, died to protect you. You don't get stopped by a locked door.

So I lift up my foot and kick out, flat; I'm only part thinking this might do something, but the door shatters inwards off its hinges, like when the SWAT guys raided the cabin, and because I didn't totally expect it I'm off balance. I almost fall, and catch myself on the hewn-stone archway.

The corridor beyond is dark and gloomy, flagstone floored, with torches set into sconces in the walls. There are suits of armour standing to attention – not just knights, though, but samurai too, and Native American headdresses, and bows and arrows and guns and swords. As I step tentatively forward, I think it's like a museum of killing.

At the end of the corridor, there's another door, set with locks and rivets. And a voice behind it, or rather everywhere and in my head, says,

It's open. You can kick it down if you like, but carpenters are hard to come by these days and I would very much rather you didn't.

It's the voice of an old, old woman, shot through with cruelty, glittering like seams of metal in rock.

I shrug, then kick the door down.

Inside, there's a homely little room. I blink for a second, seeing it here, in this massive castle – like finding a nest of baby birds in a cannon. The ceilings are low, blackened with soot, and there's a rug on the floor, a rocking chair by an open fire, over which hangs a copper kettle. An oak kitchen table, scarred by years of knife marks, and in the centre of it a silver dome like in restaurants, keeping something beneath it warm, and a plate beside it with a silver knife and fork.

Embroidery, framed, on the walls – pictures of landscapes; alphabets. There are windows that, somehow, improbably, look out over dappled forest. I see a deer walk past, outside, nuzzling at the ground. A rabbit hops by, fur gleaming in the sun that shouldn't be there, because it's always night in the Dreaming.

It's a cottage.

A Crone's cottage, inside the castle.

The rocking chair is facing away from me but I can see there's a woman in it; I see the feet propped up on a comfortable stool, next to a purring and fast-asleep fat old cat, the woman's hands moving as they stitch. Wizened hands, the veins showing.

This is the gingerbread house, I say.

Oh yes, says the old woman by the fire, still not turning around. And Baba Yaga's too. I could have decked it in sweets, if you had preferred. Or mounted it on chicken legs. But this time, I thought, a castle. I don't know why. A Crone's whim.

Right, I say.

I am thinking: What am I supposed to do – put out my hands and strangle her?

But my thoughts are interrupted when, surprisingly sprightly, catlike, she takes her feet from the stool, stands and turns.

I'm forgetting my manners, she says. Welcome.

I don't say anything. I just stare at the Crone, whose voice is so terrible, but whose face is the face of my mother – the woman who brought me up, anyway, my fake mom, my captor.

Shaylene Cooper.

CHAPTER
68

I STAND VERY STILL and stare. There is a shawl wrapped around her shoulders, covering her chest, and she is white-haired and wrinkled, but it *is* Shaylene Cooper, the woman who took me from a hospital in Alaska. Her eyes are black, glassy, like a plush toy's.

Surprise! she says.

The thing she is stitching is hanging in her hand, and I see the scene on it – Coyote, falling down from the bridge, into nothingness. Bleeding from a thousand wounds, wolves watching him fall, sneering. Mark.

What do you want? I ask.

A better question would be, what do you want? she says. You were sent here to kill me, no? Told that it was your destiny. So, do it.

Do . . . ?

Kill me. Kill the Crone.

I swallow.

Ha! she says. Not so easy, is it? But then, you were supposed to free the Child too, and you failed at that, didn't you?

Screw you, I say.

Very mature, she says. Controlling your temper is another thing you fail at, I see.

What's wrong with you? I say. Why are you so . . . so . . . horrible?

Horrible? Whatever are you talking about?

You stopped the rain, I say. The animals are starving. You put the Child in a prison of ice. You *killed Mark*.

Mark? Who is Mark? she says.

Coyote, I reply.

She makes a dismissive gesture. I have killed him before, she says. He has an annoying way of coming back. The rain? Rain is bad for the soul. It gets into the bones. And I am barren; I cannot have children of my own.

So you took the Child? I say.

No, she says. I took the Child to stop the rain. To give myself power over Coyote.

You're crazy, I say.

And you are weaponless. Did you truly come here without a means of defence? Did Coyote not give you a blade?

Yes, but I lost it. In the woods. In . . . in my world.

Careless, says the Crone. Without it, how will you possibly ever leave? She cackles, truly and purely, as if the verb, to cackle, originated with her.

My heart loses its rhythm for a second. She thinks I can only cross the air back into my world if I'm holding the knife, I realise. This could give me an advantage. Possibly.

The Crone-mother smiles, and this makes her look 6,578 times more scary than she already did. You are thinking that you could cross back over without the knife, yes? she says.

I flinch – it's like she's read my mind.

Not so, she continues. My castle is a castle, a redoubt. And it is

365

such in every plane, in every dimension. Not just the visible. You cannot cross from here. Try it.

I sit still for a moment, but then I do – of course I do. I want to get out of there. I want it very badly. I close my eyes and try to step –

Pain like a camera flash in my mind. Colossal; unimaginable.

Ha! says the Crone when I look at her again, my breathing unsteady from the agony of it. I asked only about the blade, because I thought you might have stabbed me with it. If you had it. Which you don't.

It looks like I'm a prisoner, then, I say.

Yes, she says.

A pause.

But wait, she adds. There is a twist.

A twist?

You came here to kill me, yes?

Uh . . . yes.

Yet you have no weapon. And I am a Crone – I could turn you into a toad with a blink of my eye. You are powerless.

I nod, slowly, not knowing where this is going.

And still, she says, there is a turn of events, a scenario, that would allow you to kill me. That would allow you to accomplish your quest. Do you know what it is?

No, I say.

Pity, says the Crone. I thought I had taught you better. I thought you were *smart*. It's not a riddle. It's just logic.

I look around the cottage, as if the answer might be embroidered into one of the garish pictures lining the walls. I look back at her, at her ghastly smile.

And then, like lightning striking, I get it.

I could kill you if you let me, I say.

She claps, softly. Precisely, she says.

But why would you do that?

The Crone smiles enigmatically. There is no reason to what the Crone does, she says. But here is just one reason: I love you. I love you all the way to Cape Cod and back.

Bitch, I say in sign. Words come more easily to my hands than to my lips.

She looks wounded, or mock-wounded, I'm not sure. She rubs her hands against each other, briskly, like she's washing them without water. Now come, she says, you must be hungry.

She moves her hands in the air; a complicated sequence of gestures, like a conductor commanding the orchestra. I find myself walking into the room, turning, pulling out the single chair at the table.

I sit down, the silver dome in front of me. There is a feeling of dread expanding in my stomach, but I don't know for what. I know, in stories, you're not supposed to eat. You're not supposed to let anything pass your lips, or it could keep you there forever. Is that it? Is that her trick?

The Crone comes up beside me, standing too close, making the hairs on my arm stand up. With a flourish, she removes the dome, leaving the plate underneath.

I gasp – on the plate, which is cracked and old, porcelain, so delicate you can almost see the grain of the table through it, there is a human heart.

It is still beating, and it is fat and squat, glistening redly with blood, valves and tubes projecting from it and quivering.

What the – I start.

The Crone twitches off her shawl; it falls to the ground like a cloud of bats, in miniature. Under it, her blouse is unbuttoned, and there is a hole in her chest. Not a smooth hole – a wound, still fresh, and suddenly I know where the blood came from on the sign outside. It's a *big* hole, left and centre, a gaping cavity where a heart should be.

She smiles her ghastly smile again, and points to the dish, to the still-beating heart.

It's easy, she says. You eat that, and I die.

CHAPTER
69

MY EYES GO FROM the hole in the Crone-mother's chest to the heart on the plate, and back again. I think I'm in shock – my mind feels like one of those desk toys made using magnets, where something spins in the air, weightless. Gravity, in my head, is suspended.

Eat it, says the Crone. I could make you, you know. I made you sit down.

As I watch, the silver knife and fork stand up, magic-trick smooth, and kind of walk the short distance over the pockmarked wood to my hands. They settle there, like cold living things.

When the heart beats, blood oozes from one of the tubes, then trickles slug-like down the side of the organ. I gag.

It will kill me, she says. And you will have won.

No, I say.

Of course! She claps her hands. I have not given you anything with which to wash it down. She clicks her fingers and a teapot appears on the table, covered with a tea cozy in the form of a sleeping cat. A teacup and saucer swoop down from an old dresser set against the wall, bone china too, decorated with blue flowers. The saucer lands near the teapot, and the cup jumps on to it with a rattle. Then the teapot tips into the air, all of its own accord, and pours tea into the cup.

The cup, in its saucer, jiggles across the table to me.

Drink, then eat, she says. This is not a trick I am playing on you. I will be dead forever. You will truly have won.

I look at the heart again. If it would destroy her, get back at her for what she has done; for the elks, for Coyote . . .

(for stealing you, says a voice very far back in my mind)

. . . then perhaps I should do it?

What would Mark tell me to do?

If you don't, of course, she says, then you must remain with her, with me. You have no knife, as you admitted yourself.

I look at the knife in my hand, the silver one, but even as I do so my hand moves, and the knife darts and pricks my other hand; blood wells up wormlike.

That knife serves me, says the Crone. It is of my house. As I was saying, you have no knife. You have no choice.

I eat that, and you're dead? I say.

As a coffin nail.

I am trying to work out the angle, the trick – because of course there is a trick, no matter what she says.

Coffin nail.

Coffin.

I look up at her, fast. That's it, I think.

What? she says. What is it?

I eat this, and you die, that's what you said.

Yes and I am not lying to –

I know you're not lying, I say. But what do I become? What does that make me?

A look almost of nervousness comes to her face, like grey clouds come to an open sky. I don't – she begins.

370

It makes me your coffin, I say. It makes me your tomb. You die, but I carry you around with me always. You *own* me always. You never let me forget you, or forgive you.

That's not true, she says, but that gleaming seam of cruelty is back in her voice.

Yes, it is. You would be dead, that's true. That's one hundred per cent true. But I would not have won. *You* would have won, because if you get your heart inside me, if you get your flesh inside me, then you have stolen me forever, you have marked me forever, and made me yours.

A wide smile, now, from the Crone, and for the first time her teeth show, and I see how they have been sharpened to points.

Well, she says. You are smart. But tell me, clever girl, how are you going to leave? How are you going to defeat me? I am Crone. I am the lurker in the forest. I am death to all unwary children. I can make you eat my heart.

And my hands move, against my will, and the fork skewers the heart, and the knife in my right hand begins to cut me a slice.

CHAPTER
70

I FEEL TEARS BEGIN to form, as I sit there, powerless. But they don't come. I don't cry easily.

I feel sick, though. The Crone is going to turn me into her tomb, and I'll never be free of her. The knife has almost finished cutting me a thin slice of heart, and it glistens sickly.

She told me she was the bane of unwary children, and I believe her.

No – wait.

Two of those words snag on briars in my mind, get caught there while the rest of the thought goes on like a disappearing deer, ghosting into nothingness.

Children.

Believe.

My hand is going back and forth, cutting into the heart while my other hand holds it still with the fork, but my mind is churning.

I remember Mark saying, Remember you're an adult. At the time I didn't understand. I still don't, not totally, but . . .

I remember him touching that iron, by mistake, not even being aware of it, and nothing happening, no scorching sizzle, no burning, magical or otherwise.

The people of the Dreaming can't touch iron because they believe they can't, I think. I bet if Mark had reached out and touched it, knowingly, it would have hurt him, because of the strength of his belief.

Belief, I think.

Children.

Belief and children . . .

What are you doing, child? says the Crone, and I look down, and see that the knife and fork are not moving; they are perfectly still in my hands. There is strain and tension in her face; veins show in her forehead.

I stare at her.

And then it all clicks into place, all bolts together. She said it herself, even, didn't she? That Crones are the bane of unwary children.

Children.

Child.

She called me child.

But that's just it, I say, out loud.

That's just what? she replies.

I'm not a child, I say. I'm an adult. As I say this, I know it's true. Sure, in my world, there's like a month to go before I'm legally not a child, before I can live on my own. But here? I'm fully grown. I have gone through puberty. The Dreaming is older than the stars; in the Dreaming, the laws of the United States of America are less than nothing, and in the Dreaming, I am not a child, not any more.

Fear distorts the Crone's features, as if her whole face is clenching around something bitter.

And your magic only works on children, doesn't it? I say.

No, not just –

On children who believe, I add. It only works on children who believe.

Storm clouds burst behind her eyes, darkness falling there, cold, shot through with lightning. But she doesn't scare me any more.

I remember my (mother), sounding so impotent in the hospital, saying she *told* me to stay at home, that I knew what could happen to me out there in the world if I strayed. But that only works on kids, doesn't it? The spell of telling children what to do is this: they believe that if they don't do it, they will be hurt, they will fall prey to the monsters under the bed, they will be lost.

They believe.

Like I believed that without my (mother) to protect me, I would be nothing but another weak victim, a morsel for the men who roamed outside the circle of firelight that my (mother) created for us.

But look what I have survived.

Like Mark believed, Coyote, with that iron cage: he believed it would cause him pain, and who knows, maybe it even would have, if he had touched it knowingly.

But it didn't hurt him when he didn't know he was touching it.

The spell of telling children what to do: that is what the Crone is doing to me, I realise; she is telling me to eat the heart, telling my hands, only she is doing it in some way that doesn't involve speaking, some older way, and because I was thinking like a child, because I was believing I couldn't stop her, it worked.

I don't believe you any more, I say. I don't believe anything you say. I don't believe you can force me to do this.

The knife trembles in my hand.

Nonsense, says the Crone. I can make you do anything. I can –

No, I say. No, you can't. And it's true. The knife and fork remain motionless in my hands. I am not even having to struggle to hold them like that. Mark told me, I say, he told me I was an adult, and now I know why he told me.

She snarls. Curse him, she says. I will feast on his entrails.

He's dead, I say. You showed me, on your embroidery – him falling from the bridge.

She nods quickly. Oh, yes.

And I think: No, you idiot, you are believing again. What if he isn't dead at all? Just like in those books, in the Flagstaff store, what if he can come back? What if I manage to kill the Crone, and rescue the Child somehow, and he *can* make it rain again?

I push my chair a little back from the table.

Stay right there, says the Crone.

No, I say. And I stand up.

The Crone's face is twisted into a mask of anger. How dare you disobey me!

Shut up, I say.

Blood drains from her skin; she is white with shock. Nobody speaks to –

How do I free the Child? I say. How do I break the ice?

You can't, says the Crone, sneering.

I bet I can.

She shakes her head, but I don't believe her, so I begin to turn, to leave her behind and return to the grass outside, to the prison of ice. If I can hold firm against her spell, then who knows what magic I can work?

Maybe I can break the ice with my mind.

Oh no, says the Crone as I move. If you will not eat the heart, I must kill you. I cannot let you leave me.

Your magic doesn't work on –

But then she draws a dagger from the folds of her clothing. It is literally like something from a fairy tale – shiny, tapering to an incredibly fine point, vicious looking. It's like it was made for cutting out hearts. Then I see a streak of blood on it, and I know it *was* used for that. Recently.

You are still unarmed, she says. Unless you count that thing in your hand. But that's not a knife. Not like this. I will have slit your throat before you even raise it to defend yourself.

She moves towards me, still with that surprising grace, like her body wastes no energy at all, like her every step is precisely calibrated, economical, and she is raising the blade.

Time turns to ice; invisible, solid.

I reach for the feather and pull it out.

Please, says the Crone. Eagle has no power here. But is that a shiver of fear in the smallest muscle beside her eye?

No, it's not, because she's still coming forward. She lifts the blade up high, and it flashes through the air as she brings it down, hard, towards me, stabbing me.

For the second time in like ten minutes I am about to die.

Shit, I think.

CHAPTER
71

THE CRONE SWINGS THE BLADE, its edge flashing in the air. For a moment, the weirdest thing: she has my face, she's me, and then she's the Crone again, my (mother).

But then I remember something else: something about fairy tales. How the Crone always brings about her own downfall, inadvertently. Like in *Hansel and Gretel*, they trick her into looking in the oven, and she ends up pushed in there, broiled alive.

I don't have to eat her heart. But I can still stop it. And she has given me the way to do it.

I look down at the pulsing thing on the plate, and then, very deliberately, I stab the knife in my hand down, right into the centre of it, as hard as I can.

The heart bursts – blood rains over me, hot and sticky. The Crone stops fractions of a second from taking my head with the dagger – doesn't just stop moving, like of her own accord, but *is stopped*, like a film frozen on a single frame; her foot is up and by all logic of gravity she should fall forward on her face, but she hangs there, immobile. The knife shimmers, still, the light from the fire playing on it like waves.

I think for a moment: She's going to explode, or something.

But she doesn't. Nothing happens at all.

I don't move, for a while. Then I get up and touch her. She is cold and hard, like stone. A statue defying physics.

I have killed the Crone, I think. I have zero point zero feelings about it. It's like I might not actually have feelings again, ever. Slowly, I go to the broken door, and walk out into the corridor. I keep glancing behind me, thinking she's going to pop up, and be like, *Ha!*, I'm a Crone, or did you forget?

But she doesn't – she stays dead. Or frozen. Or whatever.

I go through the big main door, and out on to the dead grass. I feel invincible, like I'm walking on air. I am the Maiden, and I killed the Crone.

Then I realise something.

I can still hear crying.

I walk away from the castle, back towards the ravine, half hoping that with the Crone dead the box of ice will have melted, just like that.

It hasn't.

It's still sitting there, gleaming in the permanent starlight. And the Child inside it, I see as I approach, standing now, hands against the ice, crying out for me.

I walk forward. My heart is heavy in my chest. The Crone is gone but what about the Child?

What am I supposed to do about the Child?

I am at the little ice castle now, a miniature in light, in crystal, of the dark castle behind me. The Child looks up at me, banging her little fists on the wall of ice impotently. I look around me, desperately, hoping for Coyote, hoping to see him climbing up from the ravine to help me.

But he doesn't come.

Maybe this time he is really dead, and is never coming back.

The Child's cries are pins through my whole body. Twisting. I reach out again for the ice and hammer it with the side of my hand – instantly, pain explodes down my arm, impact and coldness rolled into one sharp bolt of agony.

OK, I think.

OK, change the plan. I remember the cottage in the castle, the idea of belief. I think to myself: Believe you can do this. Believe it. I look right into the Child's enormous eyes and I steel my will.

I believe that this ice is going to melt, I think.

I think that this ice is not here.

It's like when I was a kid, and I thought that if I concentrated hard enough I could make a book fall from my desk – I tense my mind, try to force the ice through sheer power of belief to break, to melt away.

It doesn't.

It doesn't and I can't take it any more.

Screw this, I think.

I kick out, start to rain blows on the thing, with my hands and feet, it hurts like you can't believe, every nerve in me taut and reson-ating like wire, transmitting pain like white noise, pain that fuzzes everything else – the sound of the Child, the darkness around me, the ravine – into nothingness.

I keep going, shouting, cursing, willing the thing to break under my barrage of blows.

My hands are bleeding.

My foot may be broken.

Eventually, my movements slow. I can't go on – I'm exhausted, and wiped out by the burning cold of the ice prison. I slump against it, still on my feet but only just, crying now too, overwhelmed. My head rests on the roof of the structure, burning my cheek, but I don't care. I have come all this way, I have killed the Crone, and now I'm here and I can see the Child there on the other side of the thin ice wall, but I can't get through to her.

Slowly, I reach out my hands, and put them on the ice, where the Child has hers, so that we are almost touching each other, palm to palm. I look into her eyes, her desperate eyes, her tear-filled eyes, and I cry even harder.

I'm so sorry, I think. I'm so sorry. I can't get to you.

I'm so –

Hands.

Hands on my shoulders, shaking me, invisible hands, gripping, shaking, and the Dreaming disappears and I am –

CHAPTER
72

IN THE CLIMBING STORE, standing in the aisle. The counter guy is obviously back from his smoke break – I can smell the tobacco almost before I register anything else, and then I process his face, his eyes looking into mine with concern; he has long dirty white hair and a cute face, maybe twenty.

He is also holding my shoulders; it was him shaking me, I realise. I blink at him and he whisks his hands away, quickly.

Can I help you? he says. *Are you OK?*

What? I say with my mouth.

You were . . . I don't know. Having a fit or something. Kicking and punching and stuff. Then you stopped.

Oh.

So . . . you need anything? Are you . . . I don't know, epileptic or something? He glances down at my CAM Walker, he's maybe figuring me for someone who was in an accident and has a head injury. Maybe.

I just want to run out of there, run as fast as the CAM Walker will let me, but I know that will only make him more suspicious, so I force myself to look right at him, and shake my head.

I'm OK, I say. *Honestly. Just . . . letting out some frustration.*

I can see that he's not convinced. My warped, deaf-person vowels are presumably not helping. At the same time, like most people, he's not going to blatantly go against what I say. *You don't want me to call anyone?* he says.

No.

He frowns. *Let me help you to a seat, at least.*

I nod. I had better let him sit me down, go through the motions of recovering from some passing fugue type thing.

He leads me to the desk, where he lowers me into a surprisingly comfortable office-style chair.

I was watching you, he says. He gestures to a CCTV screen below the desk, I hadn't noticed it. Black-and-white footage, grainy. Old-school style.

I nod, like, OK.

You stood in the aisle for, like, a half-hour, he says. With like camming wedges and stuff. I thought about calling an ambulance, like you'd had a stroke or something.

Inside I'm thinking:

WTF? I was in THE DREAMING. I wasn't standing in the store for a half-hour. Was I?

Was I?

I realise he's looking at me, waiting for me to say something.

Just . . . came in here to think, I say slowly. *Problems with my mom.*

For the first time he smiles. *Figures,* he says. *Well, it's a free country. I mean, you wanna stand in a climbing store looking at some stuff, that's cool with me.*

Good, I say.

You don't want it, though? he says. He has cute dimples, actually. Faint marks where I guess an eyebrow stud used to be.

382

I frown at him. *Sorry?*

The stuff – the rope, the cams, whatever. I mean, you just stood there holding it and then you put it all back on the shelves. So you don't want the climbing gear?

I look down at my hands. I did? I have literally no recollection of putting the stuff back on the shelves.

Oh, I say. *No.* I pause. *I don't climb*, I say, enunciating as clearly as I can.

He looks at me like I'm mental. That was a mistake, I think. A rookie mistake.

Sorry for being weird, I say. *I'll get out of here; you don't have to worry about me.*

He is still looking at me oddly and I curse the weird way my speech sounds, to someone else it probably does sound like something has gone wrong in my brain, a stroke or concussion or something. But I hold his gaze and eventually he shrugs. *Whatever*, he says. *You got your thing, I got mine.*

I nod.

You're sure you're OK, though? You don't want me to, like, call someone?

What does he figure? That it's the head injury thing? That I'm mentally ill and had a breakdown? That I'm in recovery and need to call my sponsor? I don't know, but at least he's not adding me up with the whole child abduction story that I know is playing big on the news.

No, I say.

I smile at him, a little unconvincingly, I think, and make for the door. I am conscious of the phone in my backpack, the burner my fake mom gave me, and I have an idea of what to do with it. Then I think of something. I was going to use my cell, that was why I asked Carla for it, but now it occurs to me that the FBI has probably scanned my SIM, or whatever, they'll pick up a trace if I use it, and that's no good.

I turn.

Wait, I say. *Borrow your cell?* I'm trying to use as few words as I can.

He spreads his hands. Sure. He hands me an old Motorola, a flip phone; I didn't know people still had these things.

Now.

Now.

Now I want you to think about something, before I tell you what I do next.

This is what I want you to think about: one of those women whose husbands beat them, over and over, and every time, they end up forgiving them, they take them back, because they love them, because they think, I don't know, that this time things are going to change. The ones who actually get angry if their friends try to help. We've all seen the ads on TV.

Picture her: dirty hair, a bruise on her cheek, an expression of anger, hurt, sadness, but also forgiveness, complicating her face. She is basically looking bummed but like it's her own fault she's bummed. She is a victim, but she loves the man who hurts her, she truly loves him.

Yes?

Are you holding the image in your mind, looking at her?

OK.

So I take the phone the dude in the climbing store has given me, I open the clamshell of it, and I pull up the text message menu.

I type:

@ climbing store nr the cowboy hats. Come get me.

Then I type my (mom's) number from memory (I have a very good memory for things I have seen written down), and I press Send.

You see, my love for my (mother) is as endless as the stars, as lonely and incomprehensible as the stars, as unutterably sad. And the stars? They are scattered across the sky, Coyote did that, they are in chaos, a mess of bright lights in the darkness, but it is the chaos that makes them beautiful, the disorder.

And the stars?

Yes, a lot of them are cold, a lot of them are dead – but a lot of them are not.

CHAPTER
73

I HAND THE PHONE back and nod my thanks.

'Course, he says. *Good luck.*

Yeah, I think. I'm going to need that. Though he probably thinks I'm doing the twelve steps, thinks I just texted my sponsor.

I turn and start heading out of the store. I see him frown, out of the corner of my eye. I am limping, of course – maybe there's a description out for a girl with a massive cast on her leg – a what do they call it, an APB.

Shit.

I feel his eyes on my back as I leave him behind. I have no idea if my text is going to work, if my fake-mom is even anywhere near Flagstaff now, or if she's split for Mexico.

I open the door and smell the pine on the outside air. I feel a sense of sick rightness. All the time that she, Shaylene, has been gone, she's had this pull on me anyway, a gravity that she exerts on my mind. Like the moon – you don't see it, most of the time, but it's there, and it's pulling the sea, drawing the fringed tides of the great waters towards the sand, yanking moths around like a magnet. And who can fight gravity? I've fallen off a cliff and I'm spinning down through the air, and I can't stop myself hitting the ground, eventually, but I can tense my muscles and make the impact harder, or I can relax and let the fall take me.

I hobble a little down the street till I find a deep doorway – it's a metal door, maybe to a storeroom or a back entrance to a nightclub or something; anyway it's padlocked and it doesn't look like people use it much. There's a ghost shape of dog piss against it. Peeling flyers for local bands.

I lower my head, wishing I had a cap, and wait.

Maybe a half-hour goes by.

Then I see an old Buick station wagon pull up just down the street, a green one. I watch it for a second, wondering. Then the lights flash, once, and I limp over to it. (Mom) reaches over and pops the passenger door. I notice that she has black hair now and is wearing different clothes. She looks nervous, like she's afraid that I'm angry with her.

Spoiler alert: I am.

I open the door, hold the coat hook, and swing myself into the front seat.

Oh, honey, she says with her hands. *Oh, honey, I'm so –*

Drive, I say.

Tell me about you, she says. *What's been happening –*

Drive, I say again.

She nods and pulls out, then turns right at the next intersection. At least she's not wearing pyjama jeans, I think. I look out of the window. I am expecting to see flashing blues at any moment, but the road seems quiet. There's some kind of jiggling hula girl on the dash, and the ashtray is full of butts, so I figure this car is stolen – maybe only recently, though. Or she got it from a long-term parking lot at a bus station or a train station or an airport – that's what I'd do.

(Mom) passes the tourist motels that used to put up people doing Route 66, and I realise she's heading back to the woods between Flagstaff and Phoenix, the canyons and deep pine forest off I-17. Flagstaff, as we leave it behind, looks like a theatre in the rearview, backed by mountains like tiers of seats, a stage, where something terrible happened, but something that can be forgotten, can be left there, a story.

This is my plan, if you can call it that: forget what happened. Forget what I know. And just go back to my old life. There's a part of me that wants (Mom) to drive back to Phoenix, to our old apartment on Via Linda, but I know that can't happen.

On either side of the wide black highway, pine trees stretch into darkness.

Where are we going? I ask.

She shrugs. *I don't know. Mexico? Or Scotland, maybe. We can go to the Highlands, like in the pictures, and find a little cottage, just the two of us, it'll –*

I whirl in my seat. *Are you INSANE?* I say.

Abruptly, she hits the brakes and turns the wheel, and we pull over into a dirt track leading deeper into the forest. The car behind us flashes his lights as he passes, pissed off.

She turns to me. There are tears on her face. It's cool in the shadow of the trees.

Shelby . . . she says.

That's not my name. My real name.

She sighs. *I know. I just . . . I never meant to hurt you. All I wanted was you.*

I don't want to talk about this, I say. *I want things to go back to what they used to be. I want to pretend this never happened. I want*

*to have ice cream for dinner on Fridays, and read books, and go to the
baseball cages. Can you understand that?*

Yes.

I close my eyes. Then open them again. *You STOLE me*, I shout,
the movements of my hands vicious. *You didn't mean to hurt me?
Well, guess what, you hurt my parents. I saw them. They're a mess.*

She is really crying now. She just nods.

Why? I say. *I mean, I know you. You don't seem so crazy. Why
would you take someone's child?*

I can't explain it, she says. *I have had to live with it for fifteen
years. Every night I've prayed for forgiveness. Every night I've
thought about those parents –*

The Watsons, I say.

She visibly tenses, like she's been hit. *Right.*

For a while we sit there – the normal word in English would be
silent, but we're ALWAYS silent, I can't fricking hear, so maybe a
better word would be still.

I had six miscarriages, says (Mom). I've never seen the sign for
that word before, but it's pretty clear, when she makes it. *You can't
imagine that. Carrying something dead in your body.*

An image flickers in my mind: the heart, sitting on the plate.

I was married, she continues. *We kept it up for the longest time.
Hormone treatments, so I could get pregnant in the first place.
Then the ones that didn't . . . didn't make it. But he . . . we . . . it
was too much for both of us. Like funerals, over and over again,
where you don't even have a body to bury.*

*So, what, because you couldn't have a child, you had the right
to take someone else's?*

No, of course not. But they had three already. You were the fourth.

389

I met them, you know? At the hospital. I was pretending to be a nurse. I was going to take a baby, that was the plan. I know, I know, it was crazy. I think something had broken inside me.

They didn't even know you were deaf, she says. *That's how come you burned yourself. They called, to stop you pulling the pan. But you didn't hear. You see what I'm saying? You were two years old and they didn't even realise you were deaf. Why you were in the kitchen, I don't even know. Something about one of the other kids crying.*

So now you're saying that, what, negligent parents deserve to lose their children? The anger in me has been building up, like a pot coming up to the boil, and now it's bubbling, spilling over.

No . . . But the doctors were going to call social services anyway, I heard them talking about it. THEY knew you were deaf, of course. They knew your parents had screwed up. I mean, you should have been talking in sentences by then, singing nursery rhymes. For all I know, social services would have taken you away, just like I did.

So you figured you'd take me first?

Yes. It was so easy. I had a uniform – and your burns were bad, but they weren't third degree. It was just dressings and bandages, I mean, I can do that. I actually was a nurse once. So when the doctors took you back to your room, I walked in and told your parents you were needed for tests, and I wheeled you out of there.

And drove south.

Well, not right away, but yes.

I sink back into the seat. I want to wave my hand and make all of this go away. For the first time, I want to be magic – I get why people would want spells, potions, wands. Not to fight people, like in *Harry Potter*, but to undo bad things, to make everything OK again.

You planned it, I say. *Whatever you say about me being deaf, you had the uniform. You deliberately inflicted on someone else the same thing you had suffered. You're sick.*

Yes, says (Mom). *Almost certainly. But I love you too. My little princess.*

I'm not your little princess, I say. *I'm not anyone's little princess.*

Then why did you text me? she says.

Because I'm not eighteen yet. I need someone to look after me. And I want it to be someone I know. I don't want to live with strangers. Strangers I can't talk to because I'm DEAF and they can't SIGN. Which is my only legal option. Do you understand that? Do you understand what you've done to me? You didn't just steal me from my parents. You stole me from myself. You stole my life. Everything I thought was me . . . everything I thought was real . . . it's all gone. Now I'm living in a dream instead. A nightmare.

This is the longest thing I've said in like a thousand years.

She puts her face in her hands.

Stop crying, says the new me, me 2.0, badass me. *Get a grip. And drive.*

Where to? she says.

The Grand Canyon.

The Grand Canyon? Are you kidding? There'll be a million –

I hit the dashboard. *I don't care. I want to see it. Then we can go wherever you like. Mexico. Whatever.*

She looks at me for a while in a sort of fixed, thinking way. *The Grand Canyon is in the opposite direction from Mexico,* she says.

I know, I say.

It'll be sunset by the time we get there, she says.

Fine, I say. *All the better.*

She sighs. *OK,* she says. *You're the boss.* And she drives.

CHAPTER
74

I THINK BOTH OF us are picturing *Thelma and Louise* but we don't say it because it's so obvious and doesn't really mean anything. It's not like we're going to drive the car off the side of the canyon.

Is it?

We take 180 for a couple of hours and then swing on to 68, heading north towards the canyon. We're in the desert now, houses and streetlights and trees and even gas stations falling away behind us, civilisation dwindling in our rearview. Rocks blur past, and more cacti, and little shrub-like trees. Everything is dust and stone; we are quite literally OUT OF THE WOODS. The greens and blues of Flagstaff give way to red.

And you know what? I am ecstatic about it. I am sick of fairy tales.

We pass a sign that says DO YOU HAVE ENOUGH GAS? NO PUMPS FOR 50 MILES.

Do we? I ask.

(Mom) glances at the dash. *Should*, she says.

I'm tempted to say something sarcastic, like, well as long as you're sure, or whatever, but I don't actually care. I mean, if we break down in the middle of the desert, what difference does it make to me? I don't have a future that I can imagine anyway.

The sun is low in the sky now – it's mid-afternoon. Sharp shadows angle from posts and shrubs, slashing the desert. The car brims with red light. My eyes unfocus and I just let the sand and dust blur past.

Then something moves, and my head snaps around – I catch a glimpse of fur, of swift low legs, a canine nose.

What? says (Mom). *What is it?*

Nothing, I say. *I thought I saw a coyote, that's all.*

Could be, says (Mom). *It's the desert.*

Yeah, I say.

After another hour or so we pull into Grand Canyon Village. It's a weird little place, a whole little town that just exists for tourism. There are parked cars and RVs everywhere. We meander around a bit till we find a parking spot opposite something called Yavapai Lodge. (Mom) gets out and helps me to stand.

Come on, she says. *This way.*

You've been here before? I ask, incredulous.

Yes. A long time ago.

No wonder you didn't care about coming here with me.

She stares at me. *Well, you're here now*, she says.

I shrug. It's an incontestable fact.

We buy passes and follow signs to Mather Point. At first I'm nervous, that there might be some sort of description of us out there, that APB I was worrying about before. Girl with bionic cast; older woman. But as I look around I see that we just blend in as if we were meant to be here. An overweight mother in unfashionable clothes, and her daughter, who broke her leg cheerleading or something. We're ordinary. We're everybody.

So gradually I relax as we approach the canyon.

Coming up to it, I have this sense that the land is about to drop away – like, I know the rim is coming up even before I see it. Some ancient survival instinct, from the beginning of man, I guess. Dizziness creeps up on me, stealing its way up my spine and into my head. Then I see the other side of the canyon, looming up above the rim, and suddenly we're AT the rim, and I'm looking over. The sun is low to our left, casting its deep dark shadows through the canyon, illuminating other rocks like they're stage-lit.

The whole thing is a light show, just for me.

I stand for a moment, just drinking it in.

You know how sometimes you've imagined something so many times, waited for it for so long, that it's somehow about two thousand times more incredible than you ever thought; and at the same time it's just like, oh, OK, that's what it's like?

Well, that.

Beautiful, isn't it? says (Mom).

Yes, I say, which is true.

At the same time, it isn't true. I mean, it's so much bigger and more all-encompassing than the word 'beautiful' can possibly convey. Right where we're standing, the land basically disappears, it literally takes the earth from beneath our feet, and then it doesn't rise up again until the fricking HORIZON – there's just this gap in the world, so monumentally big that it's not even comprehensible as a canyon or a valley or whatever, or even really possible to take in with the eyes, without just dwelling on little bits of it.

I look down.

Just past our feet, the rock drops away, striped and striated with red, and below is a thin ribbon of blue river. Trees are growing down there. And then for miles and miles it's these little sort of cones and towers of red rock, rippling, shaded dark and light, until you get to the sheer red walls of the other side, which is very literally as far as the eye can see. In other words: all I can see is the canyon, and the sky, and so it's filling the world, filling my vision. Everything is enormity and redness, of varying hues and shades, the whole thing like a painting by a madman with only a couple of colours in his paint set.

I mean, I've seen it before, on TV and in pictures. I knew roughly what it would be like. But I just had no idea how BIG it was, and it's real, I mean, it's not in the Dreaming or anything. When it's on TV, it's usually people talking about the forces that created it, the power of water and time to carry out such demolition, on such a colossal scale – which is kind of interesting, I guess, if it wasn't already obvious from, I don't know, the ocean that water can be intensely powerful. For me, though, looking at it – for me it's not the way that it was made that's interesting. It's how it looks now – and what it means.

The way that the land is interrupted, like this

but then starts again, as if nothing had happened, in the same shapes and the same shades of red, only now higher, and rising into the mountains of Colorado.

It's not a lesson in the force of water. It's a lesson in endurance and continuity, a break in everything, a pause in the conversation of existence, and the thing about pauses is that they don't last. That's the lesson of the Grand Canyon. And OK, yeah, I read a lot and I know the word 'caesura'. So sue me. And if you don't know what it means, look it up.

Anyway, for quite a long time I just stand there and stare.

I feel like I'm hallucinating.

Like time has stopped.

Like I'm in a crack in the world.

A crack in time.

Then, suddenly, the moment is gone, and it's just a load of red rock. I look down, and I think about the secret heart of the world, and how I always thought that by coming here, I could see what was below the surface, below the earth's skin, and somehow understand something about it.

Do I see the secret?

No. I see a few tents, pitched by the ribbon of river. A donkey making its way down a snaking path below us, some tourist swaying on its back. There's nothing. Nothing under the reality, under the rock, under the dust.

The world just ends, and then a few dozen miles away, it starts again. It's a gap. That's all. And, at the same time, that's the whole point and meaning of it.

That things stop, fall away – and then rise up again.

And I'm not stupid, I get that this relates to me. That there's been a crack in my life, of devastating force, but that doesn't mean it can't start again, miles away, in a slightly different way – mountains instead of desert, cold instead of warmth. But this isn't anything I didn't know already.

OK, I say. *We can go.*

Yeah? Mexico?

I guess.

She looks at me, then sweeps her hand, taking in the whole majesty and grandeur of this massive divide in the very earth with just one little gesture. *It isn't what you expected?*

I think for a moment. *It is*, I say. *But at the same time it isn't.*

And again, you know – I could be talking about my life.

396

CHAPTER
75

WE FILL UP WITH gas at Grand Canyon Village and then drive back down on 68 and 180, like we're coming out of some kind of ancient rite of passage ritual – forty days in the desert – and returning to the fold of mankind, of civilisation.

Coming down from the high places.

The sun is setting to our right – sunsets are amazing in the desert. Red light washes the flat horizon and the single squat mountain rising from it, pink clouds stretch forever in still-blue sky. Cacti catch fire, like torches, burning. Everything is colours that, if you painted them, would seem made up, stupid.

Looking at it, you could almost imagine that the Scotland (Mom) used to stitch was real too – those purple heathers, those emerald-green hills.

I lie back in my seat and just watch the sun go down, till there's only a glow off there in the distance, like there's a massive party, floodlit, going down just around the curve of the earth, and then the desert closes its vast eye and

BOOM

it's night, like I said right at the start.

We have to pass through Flagstaff again – or rather by it, because we don't dare go into the town. We just follow the road south in the darkness, towards Phoenix and Mexico beyond. Retracing our steps. Revisiting the scene of the crimes. At one point we pass a police cruiser sitting in a side street, a cop in the front seat, and for like five minutes I'm convinced it's going to follow us and run its siren, make us pull over, but it doesn't.

It's just gone, just dust, behind us. We're outlaws, on the run. Why not? It's not like I know who I am any more anyway.

Past Flagstaff we ease down, through greens and blues, back to the all-red palette of the desert, and then we pass through Phoenix and keep going south, on the wide highway through the low endless sand.

Pretty soon after that, (Mom) puts the heater on – it's amazing how the warmth leaches out of the land as soon as the sun goes. It's something to do with moisture in desert climates. Did I say that already?

Oh and I'm giving up on this (Mom) in parentheses thing. It looks weird. So from now on I'm going to just say Shaylene. OK?

A couple of hours past Phoenix and we're deep in the desert now, well on the way to the Mexican border. I don't know how we're going to get through it without passports, but I figure Shaylene will think of something.

We need a motel, she says as I am thinking this. *Just for tonight.*

I nod.

Watch out for a cheap one, she says. *One where they won't ask many questions.*

I don't know exactly what I'm looking for, but I scan the side of the road as we drive – a little town flies by, more like a village really, a couple of brightly lit gas stations. A chain motel, very modern, which doesn't look right.

Then, maybe fifteen minutes later, I point. There's a rundown place ahead, just off the highway, a broken blue neon sign on its roof that reads APACHE M T L, with a wooden picture of a Native American next to it, old-fashioned racist-style, with a tomahawk in his hand and a feathered headdress, for real.

Shaylene slows, signals, and swings the car off the road and into the cracked, weed-filled lot. There are lights on in some of the rooms of the two-storey, L-shaped motel, so apparently it's open for business. Another neon sign, this one green, flickers above the door, and it says ROOMS $30. I can feel the vibrations running through me, from the cars flying past on the highway.

You stay in the car, says Shaylene. *Your CAM thing . . .*

Yeah, I say. *I get it.*

Shaylene goes inside. For a moment I think about getting out of the car, just hitching a ride south. But I wouldn't even get to the side of the highway before Shaylene came out again, with my foot like this, and anyway, where would I go? There's nowhere.

Five minutes later Shaylene comes back. She's got a key in her hand – it's hanging off a piece of wood with another cartoon Indian on it. *Second floor,* she says. *Number 22.*

She helps me out of the car, then slings a long bag, like a tennis bag, out of the back, and I follow her. The stairs are difficult; she puts a hand under my arm and I shrug her off. Then we walk along the little exposed corridor, like a long balcony, past a decaying shelf with some battered paperback novels on it, which I figure have been left behind by other people staying here, and a vending machine selling candy, to Room 22. From up here, there's a clear view of the highway – it's dark now and where the cars cross in front of us, it's a bright zone of white sodium light, then on either side, trails of red dim into the night, as the cars speed away north and south.

I try to imagine what it must sound like, so much speed and light. But I can't.

While I'm looking at the cars, Shaylene has unlocked the door, and she taps my arm to tell me to go in. The room is like something out of an old movie – woodchip door; brown blanket on the bed, black hairs on it; cracked mirror; dirty curtains. A fan slowly paddling the thick, sluggish warm air. And a Gideon Bible on the nightstand. You can feel everything very slightly vibrating with the passing vehicles.

I gaze around the room. It's gross! And there are probably roaches! But still, it's better than the nice clean new condo in Flagstaff where the Watsons were staying, where I could be right now . . . I bite my lip. I've made my choice. I peer into the bathroom – there's an avocado-coloured tub, stained yellow inside. The kind of shower curtain people get stabbed through, in movies.

Shaylene turns on the TV. A couple of anchors are talking, sitting at a desk with fake scripts in front of them, and then it cuts from the studio to a picture of me, taken in the FBI office, next to a driver's licence photo of Shaylene.

She turns it off again.

CHAPTER
76

WELL, SAYS SHAYLENE.

Well, I say.

If I could make everything right I would, she says.

I have literally no idea how to reply to this. Shaylene has sat down on the edge of the bed and I am still standing in the middle of the room, in the slow wake of the fan. The thin curtains vibrate with the passing traffic.

I wanted a baby so badly, she says.

And they had several, I say.

Yes. It seemed so unfair, and I –

It seemed unfair that they had kids and you didn't, so you took one of theirs? Like it was freaking arithmetic? That's the moral attitude of a crack addict.

It was a moment of madness, she says.

But you planned for it. You were wearing a nurse's uniform.

She shrugs. She can hardly deny it.

I know what I did was wrong, she says. *To your parents –*

What about me? I say.

What do you mean?

This is a question so big it encompasses the universe, who I am, everything. I sit down on the floor. *You took away reality,* I say. *I mean, before, I knew who I was. Who you were. I knew that I read books and you stitched, and we watched TV with the closed captions on, and every Friday we would have ice cream for dinner. I knew you were my teacher. You taught me sign. You taught me to read and write, and to type faster than any secretary. You kept me safe. I knew everything about you. I knew you liked the smell of lavender but not the smell of vanilla. I knew YOU WERE MY MOM.*

I'm still –

Still my mom? Please.

She sighs. *I was going to say, I'm still the person who did those things.*

A tear begins to roll down her cheek. She looks shrunken, like a fruit that has dried up inside, making the skin collapse on itself. *I knew it was wrong,* she says. *I wanted to undo it, right away. Take you back. But I knew they'd arrest me. I hated myself. But then . . . then I was fixing you dinner and I dropped a spoon, and you smiled. And I fell in love.*

Just like that?

Just like that. And so quick, I knew you were smart. I could see it right away – the way you looked at things, the way when I mentioned a car, a tree, whatever, you would look towards it. I could just see what you could accomplish, if only you could communicate. Because of course you couldn't speak and you didn't know what I was saying. So I started to teach you sign. And if I wasn't totally in love before, I was then.

Why?

Because of you. Because of your soul. Your personality. You were just amazing. You talked about everything. Animals, bubbles, the

402

*moon – I'd take you out in your stroller, and you'd point up at the sky
and make the sign for moon, and I'd say, don't be silly, it's daytime,
but then I'd look up and I'd see it, this pale crescent. You were always
right. If you said you saw something, you saw it. You used to ask
me for hugs. Can you imagine that? You'd be watching TV, and
then you'd turn to me and say, hug, and you'd get up and run over
with your arms out. I don't know. I can't explain. And you can't imagine it. Maybe one day, when you have a kid of your own. You were
just . . . you were like an open window. With light on the other side.*

I just look at her.

I knew your birthday, she says. *And I didn't want to change it.
Maybe six months after I . . . took you, it was your third. I made a
chocolate cake – that was your favourite. You always said, I want
brown cake. So I made it, and we did the candles, and we ate cake.
Just the two of us. You had chocolate all over your face. We were
both stuffed. But then you asked for more. I said, OK, and I got the
fork and took a little piece, and said, here's a little bit. And you
looked me dead in the eyes, and you didn't even pause, and you
said, no. A big bit. And then you just smiled and smiled.*

She is smiling too, remembering – smiling and crying, at the same
time.

Once, she says, *I took you to the park. You were scared of the
slide – it was bigger than the ones you'd been on before – so I said I
would take you with me. I slid down, with you on my lap. You
wanted to do it over and over. You were so happy. And then, walking home, your little hand in mine . . . the way you reached up to
take it when we had to cross the street . . . I don't know. It was like
it brought something to life, in here.* She touches her chest. *It was
almost painful, how much I loved you. Do you know what I mean?*

403

Yes, I want to say, but I am crying now too, looking away, as if I can erase what she has just said, erase her love. I go into the bathroom and shut the door, and for the longest time I just sit on the side of the bath, my head in my hands. I count the stains on the wall – maybe blood, maybe something worse. There are fifty-four.

When I have done that I come out again. Shaylene is curled up on the bed, but sits up when I open the door.

You saw those books we passed? I ask. *You know, left by other guests?*

I see the pain on her face – the disappointment that I'm not saying, I don't know, that I forgive her, or I love her, or something. But she pushes it down, quick, like someone pressing a drowning person back down into the water. Her face smoothes out, water ripples going still, no sign of the struggle below. She smiles, half convincingly.

Guests? she says. *I think they call them victims here.*

I mime a bellyache from laughing so much. I don't think my face is looking so happy because she stops smiling.

Yes, she says. *I saw them.*

I might go and get one, I say. It's been ages since I have read anything, and there's no way I'm just sitting in this scuzzy motel and TALKING to Shaylene all fricking night. What's she going to do, tell me again how she couldn't have a child of her own, and that makes everything all right? *And some candy,* I add. *You have cash?*

Sure, she says. She reaches in her pocket, takes out some money, and hands it to me. *Don't be long, though,* she says. I can tell she'd like to come with me, to not let me out of her sight, but at the same time she knows she can't. She knows she can't demand anything of me, after what she's done. *And . . . be careful.*

It's the corridor outside, I say. *What could possibly happen?*

She shakes her head. *Sorry.*

You want candy? I ask. We haven't stopped to eat, for reasons that are 100 per cent obvious, and she must be hungry too.

OK, she says.

What do you want?

I don't mind. Whatever.

My mind flashes back to ice cream for dinner. It seems like a different world now.

Shelby, she says.

Yes?

I was scared. You were going to be eighteen. I didn't want you to leave me, to go to college. I knew the truth would come out. That's why I . . .

She pauses. And I understand something – why Coyote came along when he did. Because of my birthday. Because things were building up to an explosion anyway.

So he brought along some TNT.

But you won't ever leave me, will you? says Shaylene. There are tear tracks on her cheeks.

No, I lie.

She smiles. *Good.*

She opens the door for me and I limp on out of there, and I don't know then that it's the last time I'll ever stand in a room with her, like everything is normal.

CHAPTER
77

I SCAN THE BOOKS on the shelves and end up picking some little airport thriller, with a picture of a stack of cash on the cover, dripping blood. There's a review on it, says it's 'Pure escapist thrills'. That sounds like what I need right now.

After I choose the book, I hobble along to the vending machine. I'm shivering a little in the cold air. I can see moths flitting around the broken, flickering fluorescent lights set on the walls. Everything else, apart from the highway, has disappeared – whisked away like a magician's trick – WHOOSH – by the Arizona night.

I get a Payday for Shaylene and a Mars and a Snickers for me. I feed dollar bills in, and corkscrews of metal spiral outwards, making the candy bars drop into a trough at the bottom. Like unavoidable fate, turning, pushing you forward, till you fall.

I turn for the room. That's when I see movement – dark, quick – in the parking lot below.

I stop. I watch.

Armed police, holding assault rifles, are heading towards the motel stairs. In a circle.

A circle that's tightening, getting smaller and smaller.

CHAPTER
78

I DON'T LIKE TO use my voice. I prefer to speak with my hands, if I have to speak.

But my hands can't talk through walls so I can't warn Shaylene.

I see one of the police spot me – he points up and for a moment time stops, as they point their guns at me. A couple of them, closest to the stairs, start to run.

The phone, I think. They had my phone. I may not have USED it, but I don't know how these things work. Plus, I realise now, I DIDN'T TURN IT OFF. How hard would it be to set up a trace anyway? Use cell towers to triangulate, or whatever it's called. Yes, that has to be it. They must have watched us, driving down south, a shining dot on a map.

Easy. Like playing hide-and-seek with a little kid. I picture those circular screens in submarine movies, the cone sweeping around, making the moving dot pulse, blip, blip, blip.

Worse, I think: suddenly I am sure the cop car we saw in Flagstaff, on the way here, was watching us, marking our passage. Biding their time till we stopped. Till we were in a place where there weren't many people, unlike, say, THE GRAND CANYON.

Waiting till we were at a deadbeat motel, our guards down.

I take a very deep breath, and I focus all my strength on my diaphragm and my chest – I have to make this LOUD, like nothing I've ever said before, because usually I am all about speaking as quietly as possible, so people don't hear what I sound like.

Then I push the air out, over my vocal cords. You don't have to think about how to do this, but I do. What I do have to think about is what to say, what word to use. In the end I go with the simplest one.

I shout:

Mom!

What happens next happens very quickly, and all at the same time:

The first men hit the top of the stairs – they go down on one knee, their guns aimed at me, or at the door to our room, I don't know. They're shouting something, but there's too much going on – *get down*, I think?

Then more guys rappel down from the fricking ROOF, and land on the walkway on the other side of me. There are also guns pointing up from below, in the parking lot. I'm, like, in the centre of a spider's web of sightlines, bullets ready to come crashing into the middle of the circle.

The door of Room 22 opens, I was going to say, with a bang, but I don't hear that – but it opens very suddenly, OK?

Shaylene steps out, and she's got a shotgun in her hands.

A *shotgun*?

A fricking *shotgun*?

Then I think: Oh yeah, the tennis bag. I have no idea where she got the gun from, but she had it all along. She's been planning for this moment.

She swings the shotgun towards the nearest cop, and since she

408

isn't already dead, shot a hundred times by those assault rifles, I know in that instant that the only thing making it tough for the cops is me – I'm standing right here, maybe three feet from Shaylene, collateral damage. Because I know, for a fact, they wouldn't hesitate to shoot a woman with a shotgun. A criminal.

I decide to make it harder for them.

I lean closer to her, then hold my hands up, telling them not to shoot, please don't shoot. There's a pause of one millionth of a second where I think bullets are going to fly, anyway, but they don't.

All of this has happened this quickly:

Cops door shotgun move.

Shaylene snakes her left arm around my neck from behind, pulls me back. The shotgun comes up, under my chin. Holy crap she's using me as a hostage. A shield. I only have time to think that and then she's pulling me back inside the room, kicking the door shut once we're in.

CHAPTER
79

SHAYLENE LETS ME GO and backs away into the room. She stands by the bed, looks at me for the longest time, or maybe just a fraction of a second, and then says, *I'm sorry, Shelby. I'm sorry for everything I did to you.*

Then she lifts the shotgun and puts it under her own chin, ready to blow her face off.

Through the dirty curtains, reddish highway glow comes weakly shining.

The Gideon Bible sits there, doing nothing. I wonder how many screwed-up things like this it has seen. I wonder how objects cope, when something terrible happens in front of them. How they get past it. How they can ever be the same again.

If she pulls the trigger, I think, this bed and this Bible and this nightstand are going to have to witness it.

Maybe that's what haunting really is: the way violence affects the things around it, the world in which it happens, the objects that can't look away.

Objects like me.

I can't look away.

Shaylene's finger is white on the trigger. She's looking right at me and there are tears on her cheeks.

Then I realise something: I'm back in the Crone's cottage, and this is the same moment, come again, only this time I didn't kick the door down to get here; this time I was dragged. But the heart is there on the plate again for me to eat.

As soon as I see this, anger surges in me; it feels like the colour of lightning. She is not the moon, I realise, yanking at the tides, yanking at me. She is a broken window on the plane, pulling me towards the cold outside. I take a step forward. There are probably people shouting things from the other side of the door, cops, but of course I can't hear so I don't know for sure.

No, I say. *You don't get out of it that easily.*

What? she says. She has to speak with her mouth; her hands are full of gun.

You told me you would die before you let anyone hurt me. When we were at the campsite.

She looks confused. *Yes*, she says. *That's why. I hurt you. I have to pay.*

This is going to hurt me more, I say.

She shakes her head, whole body shivering, a metal bar struck against stone, humming with fear and adrenalin.

You did something terrible, I say. *To the Watsons. To me.*

I know, she says. *That's why –*

I ignore her. As long as I keep talking, I keep her from splattering her nose and eyes and brain all over the ceiling. *You stole me*, I say. *It's like you killed me. The real me – Angelica Watson. You killed me and you put someone else in my place. Shelby Cooper. Like in those stories where the fairies take a baby away and put a different one in the crib.*

Changelings, she says. She is looking at me with something like fear, and something like wonder.

411

I know what they're called, I say. *That's what you did to me. And I will never ever forget that.*

The tears are really flowing from her eyes now. She's one trillionth of a second away from pulling that trigger.

But you don't get to just leave, I say. *You don't get to make it all go away.*

I take another step. One foot away from her now.

Don't come any closer, she says.

No. You're not pulling that trigger, I say. I am thinking of my body, closing around that dead heart like a tomb, making me a coffin. *You kill yourself and I have to carry you around forever. No way.*

Back off, she mouths. *I'm going to shoot.*

No, I say. *Drop the gun.*

I can't go to jail, she says. *I can't lose you.*

Suddenly she reverses the gun, and points it at me. I stare down the barrel. I can SEE what she's thinking, on her face, like reading a book. She's thinking: Two cartridges. Take us both out. And then all of this goes away, and she doesn't have to pay for her crime, and she doesn't have to be alone.

No, I say, shaking my head. *You won't lose me. That's too easy.*

She blinks. *What?*

I'll visit, I say. *In prison. I'll come see you.*

She is like a cartoon of shock. *Why?*

Because that's the only way to move on, I say. *If I don't, then you'll always be there, with me, in my mind, wherever I go. What you did will always be there. Unchanging. But if we visit . . . then what you DID will only be one thing, and the other thing will be what you DO.*

I don't get it, she says, as much with her shoulders and her eyebrows as with her mouth.

You made a mistake, I say. *But you have to LIVE with that mistake. No one forgives a dead person. I'd never forgive you if you died.*

Then both of us –

No. You don't really want to kill me. Do you?

I can tell because of the way she's shaking. I can tell because of the way she's crying. But I am worried that the gun might go off, accidentally, so I don't get any closer.

For a moment, there's stillness, which is like silence, but my version. Light is blazing through the gauze over the window, a spotlight, maybe? But then I notice that it's shifting and moving, raking the walls, filling the room, making it a vessel of light. A helicopter, then.

Her eyes twitch to the door.

What is it? I say. *What did they say?*

They say to surrender. To come out. Or they have been authorised to [   ].

I don't catch what she says there, but I guess it means: kill.

I see a reptilian flicker in her eyes.

They gave an ultimatum, didn't they? To see if I was alive.

She nods. *They said they wanted to hear your voice, or they would come in. You didn't hear.*

Of course I didn't hear, I think. And you were willing for them to assault the room, to maybe get us both killed. Because you were scared. Scared of being alone. I would pity her, if I didn't hate her more. I don't say any of this with my hands though.

But there's hating someone, and then there's wanting them to die, or allowing them to die so they get off the hook, and I'm a long way from either of those things.

413

We still have time, I say. *Put down the gun. Let's open the door. Hands in the air. You're descended from warriors. You can't let prison defeat you.*

What?

It's something someone said to me, when I was afraid.

Another moment of stillness.

I love you, Shaylene says eventually. *I love you all –*

– the way to Cape Cod and back, I say with my hands. *So drop the gun. Drop the gun.*

She lowers the shotgun, then throws it down on the bed.

CHAPTER
80

SHAYLENE LOOKS WILDLY TOWARDS the door and I see it shake on its hinges – the battering ram. I take that final step towards her.

Lie down on the ground, I say. *Put your hands behind your head.*

She doesn't say anything, just does it, and I lie on top of her, my hands on my head too, so they can't shoot her, so they can't kill her and then say that they thought she was holding the gun.

I can feel her saying something, feel her ribs expanding, her diaphragm lifting; I don't know, a prayer or something, a mantra; I don't hear the words, obviously. I remember when I was about five years old. Shaylene put some music on and turned it up way loud. Then she took my hands and put them on the speakers, so I could feel the beat – the whole room throbbing with it, as if filled with energy; Shaylene too, the pulse of the music moving her limbs, her head.

And then we danced together, me holding on to the speaker, and time spiralled out forever.

For the longest time after that, and this is the bit I don't remember, Shaylene says I went around touching things, thinking I'd be able to hear them. Like, I put my hands on a horse, at the petting zoo, so that I could know what it was saying. On stones; on trees – feeling for that vibration from within.

Not that it seemed so stupid, when she and I read through a high school physics book years later and learned about electrons, spinning around their neutrons like the earth around the sun, vast subatomic distances between them. Which means that inside a stone, inside a tree, is a whole galaxy, a universe, of spinning things, dancing things, all moving, all making music.

You could hear it if you wanted, only not with your hands; they're not sensitive enough.

From the corner of my eye, I see the door come off its hinges.

So the door does come down, I think. Just afterwards. In the Dreaming, it was all backwards.

Something hard and metal and round rolls into the room, spewing white gas. The gas pokes sharp little fingers into my eyes and my nose and my mouth; I cough and maybe I scream, I can't know.

Then black-clad men burst in, their guns raised, one of them crouching down, another behind him, covering him, then they move quickly when they see us on the ground, surrounding us. One of them secures the shotgun; cracks it and drops the shells on the ground. Rough hands pull me up, hold my arms behind my back.

I see one of the cop's mouths moving, as he stands over Shaylene. *You are under arrest for kidnapping, aggravated assault and [   ], you have the right to remain silent, you have the right to an attorney, if you cannot . . .*

Then whoever is holding me turns and walks me out of there, as if I were nothing more heavy than a grocery bag. I twist my head as I'm carried out and see them kneeling by Shaylene, grabbing her hands. My eyes are streaming; it feels as if chilli peppers have been rubbed in there.

Out on the walkway, I am pushed along, and then towards a black Cadillac with tinted windows.

I say, *Wait*, with my mouth.

I say, *Please*.

The guy carrying me pauses. He turns me around and looks at me.

I just want to see her, I say.

A long moment passes.

Then he nods. He lets me stand there and wait for her to come out.

I watch from the parking lot below as they hustle Shaylene out through the door of Room 22. Her hands are cuffed behind her and she's stumbling, crying, some of it the gas, some of it for real. She doesn't see me until she's nearly at the bottom of the stairs. She turns to me, as they start hauling her off towards another vehicle. All around us, men are talking into radios and to one another, but it's like time doesn't really exist any more, there's just the two of us, looking at each other, standing on tarmac as cars streak by at sixty miles an hour, surrounded by armed men.

Then I see her say something to one of the men escorting her. He shakes his head. But she keeps insisting. There's a pause. Another guy comes over, someone more in charge, I guess. Shaylene talks to him and he does a sort of slump that involves the shoulders, and which has a very precise meaning, it means *I really don't want to deal with this, but it turns out I'm the one who has to decide right now, and whatever I decide is going to come back on me.*

Then he nods.

The first guy, the one who shook his head, takes something from his pocket and sort of presses it to Shaylene's wrists, which are locked behind her back. I realise he's releasing her handcuffs.

Then, like it's in slow motion, she turns to me and lifts her hands. Very deliberately, she tells me something in sign, a sequence of

417

gestures so obvious it would be understandable even without an interpreter to turn it into spoken words that vibrate through the air; hell, a child could tell you what she says; probably there is a dog walking past that knows.

She points to herself.

She puts her hand over her heart.

Then she points to me.

For a moment, the world hangs in suspension, a ball at the top of its arc. Everything is still – the cars are no longer passing; their trails of red and yellow light are static threads, stretched, caramel drawn out to a taut length, about to snap.

Then I raise my own hands. One of the guys near me flinches but another puts a hand on his shoulder, and he stops.

I say . . .

No.

I'm not going to tell you what I say. It's not important. I mean, it's not important to you. But it's important to me, and it's the only thing that is mine in this world and can't be taken from me, by anyone.

She nods, sodium light making the tears on her face shine, and then they lock her cuffs again and march her away, still nodding, and put a hand on the top of her head, and she disappears into the big black car.

What was that? says the cop beside me, who apparently does need an interpreter, who apparently understands less than a dog. *What did you say?*

Nothing, I say. *Nothing.*

418

CHAPTER
81

THE INSIDE OF THE Cadillac is washed with brightness, flooded with the glare of the parking lot's arc lights. We sit there for I don't know how long, while the cop in front talks on his radio; I don't know what he's saying, of course.

No one sits in the back with me, this time.

Finally we pull out on to the highway. I wonder which city we're going to. Phoenix? Flagstaff?

It doesn't matter, I guess.

We drive past generic urban sprawl, the desert on the horizon. We pass one of those huge Chick-fil-A billboards, the ones with full-size 3-D cows telling you to go to eat chicken at Chick-fil-A – which is meant to be funny, but always seems like a big mistake to me, because all it does is remind you, chicken or cow, that you're eating an animal.

I get a flashback: Shaylene standing there with the shotgun under her chin.

I press my head back into the fabric of the seat and close my eyes.

The vibration of the road runs through me, like electricity.

Streetlights strobe over my eyelids.

My breathing slows and –

I'M SCATTERED LIKE THE STARS

– AND THEN I'M SLUMPED again on the ice prison outside the Crone's castle, the crying of the Child loud in my ears, and I know that the Dreaming is not quite done with me, not yet.

My hands and feet are throbbing, and I gasp, wondering how they got –

Oh, yeah.

I was punching and kicking the ice, trying to break it. And it didn't work. I look down, through the clear, cold roof, and there's the Child looking up at me, imploring.

Still crying, still with arms outstretched – the word that comes into my head is 'beseeching'.

Emotion sweeps through me; tidal. Frustration pricks at the corners of my eyes. Why can't I just break the ice? The Crone is dead. Why can't I do it? Why can't I get to her?

Why hasn't Coyote come back?

And all the time, the sound of sobbing is filling my ears.

Please, I think. Please, I need to pick her up. Coyote, if you're still there, help me, give me power, help me get her out. I will do anything, sacrifice anything, to save her. I don't care about me any more. I don't care about my (mother), I don't care about revenge, I don't care about what has been done to me.

I am my own person, I think, and it doesn't matter who my mother is, I am enough for myself. I am my own family.

The ice burns my hands, but I don't care. The skin sizzling, I am half expecting to smell it soon, charring and –

Ice?

Sizzling?

Then I hear more sizzling.

And then I feel something drip on to my foot.

I look down.

My tears are falling from my cheeks and landing on the ice, and when they do they bore through it, straight through it, making holes in the crystal, which are expanding, the roof dissolving like that leaf in Coyote's fire, what was there a moment ago disappearing; a magic trick.

I watch in amazement as the walls of the ice castle slowly, slowly, melt down, water running in rivulets on to the grass, soaking it. I don't know if it was my tears, or if Coyote heard me and came to my aid, I don't suppose I'll ever know, but it doesn't seem to matter. The thin wall between our hands fades – no, the right word is 'effaces'; it effaces away, something rubbed out.

Until our hands are touching. Her tiny hands, in my big ones. I grip them tightly; they are so hot and so small it makes me feel like my heart might burst in my chest.

For the first time, the Child stops crying. I think it's the shock.

Then the last of the ice drips away, and I am standing there, bending down to the Child, who is looking up at me, clinging to my hands.

I go down on one knee, and she's right in front of me, her face right there, her big brown eyes, her curly hair, and my hands are holding hers like they never could in my dream – it's the end, the end I never got to, where I'm able to pick her up.

422

And that's exactly what I do.

I put my arms around her, somehow I know exactly how to do it, like it's written into my body, how to hold a child. I cradle her with one arm, under her legs, and hoist her until she sits on my hip and throws her hands around my neck and holds on tight.

She is crying again, but lightly, in a slowing rhythm, the sound of someone who has been hysterical but is calming now, calming.

I squeeze her tight.

It's OK, I say, over and over. It's OK, it's OK, I'm here. I'm here. I've got you now. You're safe. You're safe.

Her sobs become a snuffle.

Become long, deep breaths.

Go quiet.

And then . . .

And then something very strange happens.

CHAPTER
82

I SEE IT BEFORE I feel it.

The Child's leg begins to – there is no way to say this that isn't going to sound crazy – it begins to sink into me, into my stomach, and then her face, which is pressed into my chest, is really pressing into my chest, I mean as if my body has gone soft, has turned to something almost liquid, and the Child is being absorbed into it, into me . . .

I recoil, staggering back, breath catching in my lungs.

Then I start to feel it.

It doesn't feel painful.

It feels like the most beautiful feeling in the world, like a long time ago I was split in two and now I am being sewn back together, merged back into one.

I blink, and the Child is gone.

Disappeared into me.

I stand there and I stare at the stars above me, reeling. Coyote told me to kill the Crone. To save the Child. As if it was some quest outside myself, some duty I had to face.

But.

But PLOT TWIST:

The Child was me. It was me, all along. Me, crying in a hospital for someone who was never going to come, who could never come, because I had been taken away.

But now I had come back, for myself.

I can't move. My head is spinning, obviously not my *actual* head, but my thoughts, going round and round in circles, so fast, *whoosh whoosh whoosh*, full-on vertigo.

Then I sense something shift, something change. At first I think it's a sound, but then I realise it isn't. It's . . . something I can smell on the air. A tang of ozone, of moisture in the atmosphere.

It's like . . .

Like water is gathering, all around me. Reaching out, the molecules, to other molecules, reaching out to merge into one another.

Gathering strength.

I wait, and I watch.

Grey clouds amass overhead; lightning flickers over the woods on the horizon. And then the water comes down – hard, pouring rain. I don't think I have ever seen rain like this before – showers, yeah, in Phoenix. But never anything like this.

I stand and stare.

It's amazing.

And then I realise something, or rather I remember something.

I remember:

It is given to Coyote to control the rain.

I gaze at the fat drops of moisture falling all around me, and the message that is written inside each one is that Coyote is still alive, or alive again, Mark is alive. I read it, I didn't know if it was really true, if he could come back from falling down a ravine that high, but the hissing of the rain on the ground, the wetness of it on my skin, the

425

shimmering, almost continuous haze of it in the air all tell me that he did.

I smile.

And as I smile, I hear a howl, the beautiful sound ringing in my ears, resonating there, as sounds do in the Dreaming, and I turn to where it came from, and I look out over the ravine and there's the form of a coyote, standing on the other side, looking right at me. Eyes glinting, lit by lightning.

The coyote seems to nod at me.

Coyote seems to nod at me.

Hey, I shout, but it's way too far to hear. And anyway he doesn't stay; he turns and leaps, and flows into the forest, and disappears.

I laugh, and as I laugh, I step further over the grass and I just stand there and let the rain bless me.

People talk about rain falling through the air, like air is the default state, even in places where it rains more often than not, like the water is just passing through. But that doesn't seem correct to me right now – right now, there's more water than air around me, touching me, blessing me; it reveals water as the aspect of the atmosphere it always has been, liquid replacing space. The water seems to hang in suspension rather than falling: there's so much of it, like gold flakes in tequila.

People shouldn't talk about rain in the air, I think. Better to say: sometimes we live in air, and sometimes we live in water. It is just that it's falling water, and we can breathe in it.

I raise my face, feeling the drops on my skin, in my hair. It's cold, and feels as if it is entering me, changing the molecules of my body, melting something inside me, not just landing on me. Soon my T-shirt and sweatpants are soaked through.

I listen to it too, of course. Because somehow I know this is the end for me, in the Dreaming, and I want to hold this sound in my ears for as long as I can. I listen to the rain, fizzing and pattering, a glorious percussion all around me, knowing that when I leave here, I will never hear again. I savour the sound: the million little taps and splashes.

Then there is a louder noise from behind me, a crash, as of falling masonry. I turn around and see a wall of the castle collapse, tumbling in on itself, dust puffing up like an old cushion, punched. A tower curls over for a moment, seems to hover, and then falls like bombardment, divided now into separate bricks, pouring down on the mass, as more walls and roofs fall in.

In a moment, the castle is reduced to a pile of rubble, shivering with the energy of its destruction, motes and particles of it hanging in the air above the broken pieces, like the structure's own ghost, haunting it for a moment.

At first I'm scared, I think it's the Dreaming collapsing, coming to an end, that something has gone wrong. But then I hear Coyote howl again, and it's a happy howl, full of freedom, full of the feel of running over open prairie, in the rain, and I realise that I was wrong.

It's just *my* Dreaming that is ending.

Because I don't need it any more.

Then I start to see the very grass beneath my feet dissolving into nothingness, patches of darkness, like the night sky, begin to appear in the ground and the canyon and the forest over on the other side, like threadbare holes in tapestry but coming into being very quickly and spreading, dismantling the whole fabric of the Dreaming – the whole world that I've been living in just melting away like thin snow in sunlight.

I shrug. I feel like I've been slashed, all over, but it's a slashing that makes me stronger, like pruning.

I close my eyes, and concentrate.

And the Dreaming dissolves entirely, and I'm back in the Cadillac, eating up highway, surrounded by the deep blackness of the rolling desert.

CHAPTER
83

IT'S FLAGSTAFF.

They take me to Flagstaff, to a halfway house. I'm not from Flagstaff, but it's because the Flagstaff CART team was running the case, that's what they told me.

I don't need to say anything about the halfway house. It was an in-between time, an outside-myself time.

A margin, in the story of my life.

A blank page.

LIKE THIS.

CHAPTER
84

BUT, YOU KNOW, LIFE goes on. The blank page is turned, and there is writing on the other side. And so I kept on breathing and eating and stuff, and things happened to me. I learned things.

For example:

This is the lesson of the batting cage. I thought I knew it, before, but I didn't.

Here it is.

Something can be moving in one direction, smoothly, swiftly, something like a ball, or, oh, say, A LIFE, and then a bat swings, at the perfect moment, swings true, and hits that something, and it constricts.

Like this:

$$(\qquad)$$
$$(\quad)$$
$$(\,)$$

And its energy is reversed, and it fires off in the opposite direction, completely the other way to what has been, to what seems meant to be. It's like something is doing this:

→

and then there's a great shock, an explosion, an impact, and it goes like this instead:

←

But here's the lesson:

The ball – the life, whatever – is STILL THERE. The energy hasn't destroyed it, the impact, the explosion, hasn't erased it from the world. It still exists, it's just in a different place altogether.

A place it didn't expect to end up in.

Or, you know, there is a different way to put this. You could say:

There was an order, a routine, a way in which things were arranged. Then along came something. Coyote, fate, whatever. And it takes the order and the routine, on every day the same, apart from Fridays, which are always the same as each other anyway, and it blows that routine into tiny pieces, scatters it across the skies like the chaos of the stars, and makes it into something totally new.

But here's the thing:

The something new, it isn't necessarily bad. In fact, in some ways, maybe it's better.

All the time, when I batted, I felt like it was meditation, like it was control. Like, swinging the bat at the perfect time, before you even see the ball – like that was a metaphor for something, for some kind of Zen peacefulness.

What I didn't realise was:

I got the metaphor wrong.

I was not the bat.

I was the ball.

THAT – that is the lesson of the batting cage.

1. . . .

I GET OUT OF the cab and walk towards FCI Phoenix, then get ready to cross the street for the low-security women's prison that is one half of the facility. The sun is low in the sky – Phoenix is about to close its eye. But that's OK, because somewhere over the rim of the world, it's dawn – somewhere, the sun is always rising.

We're north of the city, not in the city at all any more; the suburbs are way behind us, just a few houses left a couple of miles back that I guess go for peanuts what with, oh, the PRISON just down the road. The desert is closing in now, around the multi-storey federal concrete buildings, and the guard towers and the barbed-wire fences. When you see a group of white buildings like this, black windows, even just the architecture would be enough to tell you it was institutional – even without the towers and the wire.

They've made an effort, I have to admit, with the entrance – there are palm trees planted at the front, and there's a glass lobby, like some kind of a hotel; all low brown walls. The incongruity only makes it more sinister; I guess they just do it for press photos.

As I cross towards it, I see movement.

A shadow flows along a wall, then lowers itself inkily, on to graceful paws.

It's a coyote, standing there right by the prison, looking at me. I can't see its eyes.

Then there's a voice in my head, or maybe it's just my imagination.

Nothing dies in the Dreaming, it says. Not even Crones.

I smile, because this is something I know. I nod at the coyote. At Coyote. It begins to turn; he begins to turn, to leave me behind.

Wait, I say.

He pauses.

I think I understand some things now, I say. I think I understand why you came. That whole thing, in the Dreaming, the Crone in her cottage . . . it was the same as the motel, and the gun. It was like . . . preparation. You made me live it, before, in the Dreaming. Otherwise Shaylene might have killed herself. Might have killed me.

Yes, he says.

So you did help me, like you said.

Yes.

I take a breath. But there's something I still don't get, I say.

He just looks at me, eyes shining.

You said, at the beginning . . . You said why I had to kill the Crone and save the Child. You said that otherwise the world would end.

Yes, he says again. It seems to be all he says now.

But that wasn't true, was it? I persist. I mean, you said you played tricks but you didn't lie . . . Only, it wasn't the world that was ever going to end. If Shaylene had killed herself, if she had killed me . . . It would have destroyed *me*. But it wouldn't have ended the world.

The coyote holds my eyes for a long, long moment.

Then:

Doesn't it amount to the same thing? he says.

436

And that's it.

He turns.

For a second I sense something, on the other side of the air, like a word on the tip of the tongue. Then it's gone. And the coyote is suddenly just a coyote again, or it always was, and it panics and runs skittishly back into the shadows, and down a culvert or a gap between buildings, and is gone.

The first security booth is by a barrier for cars – no one walks or takes cabs in Phoenix. No one apart from me. And now I have to check the traffic myself when I cross the road, double-check it, because I'm on my own. Shaylene's case probably won't make it to court – her attorney's offering a plea bargain and I think the prosecutors are going to take it. But she's pretty much never getting out of here.

I go up to the glass and it slides open.

Name? says the woman behind the desk.

I slide over my ID. The name on it is not my real name, but no name is my real name, until I choose one. And I can take my time with that, I have realised; it is another of the things I have learned. Because my name doesn't matter so much, any more. The thing that matters is:

I feel . . . I feel . . . *whole*, for the first time in I don't know how long. Maybe in forever. I feel like a full person.

Visiting? says the security woman.

Shaylene Cooper, I say with my mouth. Still feels weird but I'm getting used to it.

Check your bag? says the woman lazily. She has short white hair, fat earrings, and she's wearing sunglasses. She looks like she's been processing visitors for 4,845 years and it's starting to get her down.

I hand my bag over and she flicks through the book I'm reading, a hat, my make-up. She pulls out the cross-stitch pattern in its shiny plastic wallet.

Ben Nevis by Moonlight, she reads, and she kind of makes it a question. There's a garish picture of it on the packet, to illustrate her words.

Cross-stitch, I say. *She asked for it. It's a hobby.*

She does it in there? With needles?

I shrug. *In the rec room, I think,* I say. *With supervision.*

Right, says the woman. *But this is just the pattern?* She takes it out to check.

And the thread, I say.

She is still looking at me.

Oh, I mean, yeah, no needles, I add when I realise what she means.

Fine, she says. *Go ahead. You've been here before, yes?*

Yes, I say. *Yes, I've been here before.*

2 . . .

I PUT THE CHICKEN in the oven. I haven't cooked for people before, and I'm nervous. I haven't spent time with kids before either – I have bought some toys, and put them in the living room, but they are probably the wrong things. The kids will probably ask for guns. Or meth! Or something.

I don't know.

I look around, checking for dirt, trying to see the place with a critical eye, like someone would see it who had never been here before. I spot one of my sweaters on a chair, and move it to the bedroom.

There's a textbook on the table – I pick that up too, and put it on a shelf. It's *The Golden Bough*, for my module on folk tales. I'm at Arizona State now – full scholarship, majoring in English lit. Mark was right – they gave me someone to take notes for me in class. Cindy. She's sweet, not much older than me. Has a deaf brother. Sometimes we hang out – watch DVDs, eat pizza. Classic girl stuff, like on TV. It's amazing how awesome the most normal stuff can feel when you have had a life that is the opposite of normal.

I see a counsellor twice a week too, but even that isn't so unusual for a college student.

At the university, I'm Mary-Lee Saunders. The FBI arranged it – victim protection, they call it. I don't know why the name: I guess maybe they had ID for a Mary-Lee Saunders on file. It never got out, in the media, about me being deaf either, Luke never did say anything, so no one has guessed who I am. I'm hoping no one ever does. Actually the whole thing is starting to disappear now anyway – the country has moved on to the new story; an insurance salesman in Atlanta who had three young boys imprisoned in his basement.

The apartment is a gift from my parents, which Carla advised I would not be compromising myself by accepting, so I still have most of the money in my bank account too, most of the money from Shaylene. Carla also advised that I sue the city attorney's office of Flagstaff and the FBI for, she says, detaining me after they picked me up outside the cabin. But I think: What were they supposed to do? Take me to a hotel to tell me that my mother wasn't my mother?

Anyway, I have had to make depositions and statements; I am constantly in the courthouse, even though Shaylene's case won't go to trial. I don't want to spend any more time there than I have to.

The Watsons have rented a place in Phoenix, now, to be close to me. I'm eighteen – they kind of have to do things around me, and I have made it clear that I want a relationship with them but I don't know them yet, and that's the first step.

I apologised to them, of course. For running away. For giving them something – me – and then taking it away.

I know what it feels like when someone takes a life from you.

I also told them I wasn't moving to Alaska, not even for the month till my eighteenth birthday, and they were surprisingly cool with that. I realised something, when I was in Flagstaff, or maybe when I came back from Flagstaff – I like the way it doesn't rain. I like the way it's either night or day.

I like that I might see Coyote again.

Anyway.

Anyway, today, they're coming over for lunch. For the very first time. I mean, we've had meetings. That sounds formal . . . and they kind of were, actually. Getting to know each other. Usually with an interpreter. And Jennifer wrote me a letter. It said all kinds of stuff – sad stuff, happy stuff. Love that I can't reciprocate yet, memories that I don't share.

But then, at the end, it said:

> *We only thought about ourselves. How badly we*
> *wanted you back, how much we loved you and missed you.*
> *We weren't thinking about you, about what you needed.*
> *I'm sorry.*

And I cried until I couldn't see the page.

This evening, it's the first time with Victoria and Richie. The others, the older ones, I'm not meeting till Christmas. I've said that I'll go to Alaska for the holidays. James is back in Paris. He's pissed at me, I think. It's understandable. But I've written to him. I talked about how much I love the Expressionists, which is his special field of study.

I'm hoping he'll write back.

But Victoria and Richie live with their parents – they couldn't stay with the grandparents forever. So now they're down here, in Arizona, for the week. Tomorrow we're going to the desert. Richie wants to touch a cactus and find a lizard, says Jennifer.

A red light set into the wall turns on – it's what tells me that there's someone at the door. This whole place has been set up for me.

As I pass the TV, I see that the weather is on. The announcer is pointing to a map, where something swirls greyly over the coast.

443

The closed captions say:

As the cold front sweeps up the eastern seaboard, NOAA has put out a warning to all shitting – to all shipping, that . . .

And I laugh, thinking of Shaylene, and how much she would have loved that one, it's almost like they did it for her, those unseen typists. I can almost see her in my head, saying, *it's a WEATHER FORECAST. The CONTEXT. The CONTEXT.*

I go to answer the door. As I do I pass a mirror and catch a glimpse of myself – pale, dark hair, looking nervous. But hopeful too, I think. It's strange: it's still true what I said to my (mom), that she stole my past from me, she took away my yesterdays.

But that's OK. Because now I am a person made of tomorrows.

When I open the door, Jennifer is standing there, looking beautiful as always, as if someone, some omnipresent imp, goes around backlighting her wherever she walks, dusting her with freckles; there's a cute little girl clinging to her legs, a pink clip in her hair – she looks happy, and I think, that could have been me, but then I push down the bitter thought.

Nice to see you again, says Jennifer, in sign. They've been learning, taking online classes. She leans forward, like she's about to give me a kiss, on the cheek, but then she catches herself, puts her hand out instead. I take it and shake it. Our eyes meet at the same time, and she looks embarrassed, which makes me embarrassed too. The little girl raises her hands, and Jennifer picks her up.

Michael, who seems a tiny bit less like he's going to have a coronary at every moment, though my guess is he still hits the Scotch occasionally, holds out a bunch of flowers. He points to it, then to me, and hands them to me. He has a way to go, with the signing.

I don't see Richie –

And then I do, as a boy with spiky hair comes tearing up the steps. He skids to a halt just as I sign 'thank you' to Michael. He says something but he's turned away from me so I don't see.

Michael crouches down. *You remember what we discussed?* he says. And then the next bit is just [   ] to me, because I can't see his lips.

I shake my head at him, like, don't worry about it.

The boy frowns. He turns to me properly, like Michael has evidently just told him to do. *Wow,* he says. *She really can't hear, huh?*

No, I say out loud, *but I can read lips.* I don't know if his eyebrows shoot up because I spoke, or because of the sound of my voice, the weird tone I guess it probably has, but more and more I don't care.

Cool! says Richie. *Can you teach me?*

Sure, I say.

He grins.

I want to learn too, says the girl, Victoria.

Of course, honey, I say.

She smiles, and Jennifer smiles. *After lunch you can play with my dolls,* Victoria says. She says it like she's a queen and has just given me the keys to the kingdom.

I'd like that, I say.

There's a tug on my sleeve.

Do you like baseball? asks Richie.

Michael glances at me, instantly awkward, but I smile at him to say, it's OK. I mean, he's competitive. So what? His wife and kids still love him. He doesn't lock up children in prisons of ice. He doesn't steal toddlers. Everyone has faults – get over it. I'm actually kind of looking forward to having a dad.

Instead of answering Richie, I go back into the hallway and get my bag, pull out my new DeMarini. I show it to him. His eyes go big like moons.

I point to the chalkboard that I keep by the door, and the chalk on the shelf next to it. I CAN talk, and I mind less now that people might think it sounds funny, but it still feels weird in my throat. Writing is more natural – at least till we can all sign properly, and with Jennifer, it won't be long at all. I can believe, now, that she kept up the search for me, every day, kept up the media appearances and all that stuff. I can totally picture it. The woman is fierce.

Later, I'll take you to the batting cage if you like, I write on the board. I show it to Richie, and he grins even wider.

Yes! he says. *That would OWN.*

I wipe the board and write:

:)

An image pops into my head then: the elks, all gaunt, their flanks just like this, like :)))). I hope the rain has fed the grass, in the Dreaming, and that the elks are eating and getting fat.

Something makes me erase the smiley and write, *Do you ever have ice cream for dinner?* I show it to Jennifer.

She frowns. *No, why?* she mouths exaggeratedly. *That would be super unhealthy.*

I shrug, like, no reason. And it's cool. It's totally cool. Everyone is different, you know?

There's a moment of stillness. Then, to my surprise, Victoria makes this squirming movement, and her mom knows what it means because she puts the little girl down. Victoria rushes up to me.

My new sis–

She says, and the last part is lost to me because she's hugging my legs, taking me completely by surprise, but it must be *sister* she must have said, *my new sister*. She looks up, her warm little arms still around my legs, and says,

I'm so glad you stopped being lost.

I feel tears prickling at the corners of my eyes and I smile down at her. I wonder if this is something her memory will preserve – this moment of looking up at me; me looking down at her. The small-ness, the safety. It gives me a tingly feeling, the idea that I might end up in her childhood memories – it's like a way of living forever. For a second I have a glimpse of time stretching out before me, time with this family, an endless series of moments, coming towards me one after another like waves at a beach, unstopping, unstoppable.

I crouch down and put my arms out and hug her back. And suddenly a memory comes to me – that time in the park with Shay-lene, when I saw the family all together, and felt so much on the outside, like I would never have that, like it would always just be me and her. Like looking into a brightly lit room from the cold.

Now? Now I'm on the inside. I am within that fastness, that closed-off place, that brightness, and it might not be what I imagined but it's not bad either.

I'm glad I'm not a bird, I think, floating around unanchored in the sky. I might not hear anything. But I have touch, I have feeling in my fingertips, and that means I have love. You can have almost anything taken from you, but unless you're very, very unlucky, you'll always have your sense of touch, and that means everything.

Do I smell burning? says Michael.

I stand back and let them in and Jennifer bustles past me,

laughing, to sort out the disaster in the kitchen, and I follow her, Richie holding my hand all of a sudden, like it's completely natural, the most natural thing in the world, and all the time as I go down the hall with them, I'm thinking, it's going to be OK. It's totally going to be OK.

3 . . .

I LOOK OUT OF THE taxi window when it stops, but all I see is mist.

I've been travelling for, like, six thousand hours, approximately. Two plane journeys, a fricking awful train that stopped in every godforsaken place in the middle of nowhere, and now this taxi ride. The driver is a man. I'm alone in a car with a man, and, yeah, I'm being cautious, I'm being alert, but I'm not scared. I like not being scared.

I've started carrying an iPad – it's good for writing on really quickly. *We're here?* I write. My finger traces the words on glass. It's weird, how we spend so much time touching glass these days. I don't know what it means, but I think it means something. Like, for thousands of years what people touched was fur and bone and wood. Then stone, for a long time also, flint mainly; and then metal. Plastic. And now glass. We are a people who spend much of our time looking through surfaces, into other depths and dimensions, and a lot of the things we touch are not real, but just symbols for other things, pictures.

We interact more with logos than we do with real things.

While I'm thinking this, the taxi driver is peering at the message I have written on the screen. He is a pale guy with receding hair and a beer belly. He laughs. *Here is a big place,* he says. *But aye, this is what you wanted. And your hotel's only a half-hour walk back that way.* He points back down the road, into the white mist.

How much? I write.

Two hundred pounds, he says, and I pay it, even though I'm sure he's stiffing me. It makes me feel like a badass, peeling the money off the roll in my backpack. Fat stacks.

I get out, and now I can see a wooden fence and some grass in front of me.

The taxi driver leans out of the window. *Keep going straight ahead,* he says. *About two hundred yards. Mist'll lift as the sun burns it off. It's only the dew does it.*

I walk, as the taxi turns around. I still have a slight limp – I really didn't take care of myself after leaving the hospital. Maybe I'll always have a limp.

I follow the fence, and the clumps of foliage along it. I can see the dim shapes of sheep, wreathed in mist like an aura, moving around ̶wly on the other side, chewing at the grass. After about two hundred yards, like the taxi driver said, the fence stops and I find myself walking into a field, pocked with holes, and with raised tufts of grass everywhere.

I stand, and I wait.

Sure enough, the sun slowly rises, and the mist slowly dissipates – the landscape has its eye half open, for the longest time, and then it very lazily opens it, and the valley reveals itself.

A mountain looms up in front of me, on the far side of a narrow, crystal clear lake, little grey stones on its bottom, as if the water wasn't there at all, and you only know it is because the mountain is reflected in it, pointing downwards, and usually, I mean generally, mountains point UP.

So: crystal water, shimmering stones, and two mountains, one going up and one going down; identical.

Purple heather spills down the mountainside, an improbable colour, and around me are all the greens and browns of the hills, which flow either side of the mountain, to the distance, like wrinkled sheets. Craggy rocks and slopes of scree run down the mountainside, and the odd sheep clings to the incline.

There is no stag, right now, but I fully expect one to come along at any moment. I know it will. Because, in the end, how far is a stag from an elk? I don't know if I took the elks from the stags on Shaylene's cross-stitches, or if we were both being affected by Arizona, the place's memory, like Coyote said. But now it seems to me those antlers have always been there, around me, in her pictures, in the Dreaming, in the handle of the knife Coyote gave me.

I stand there, and I wait for the elk to come.

Elk, stag, whatever.

And right now, I'm happy to wait. I have never seen anything like this place in my life. I said to the taxi driver, *Take me to the mountains, to a beautiful view. And I need a hotel.* He just nodded, like it was a perfectly normal request. We drove all the way from Aberdeen.

I take a breath, drawing the air of the Scottish Highlands into me, feeling it sucking into my bronchioles and then into my bloodstream, spinning. It's cool and fresh and it smells like bracken and peat and crystal water, teeming with salmon. It tastes like the velvet smoothness of a stag's antler, and the colours of the landscape in front of me may not be totally crazy like those cross-stitches that Shaylene used to do, but they ARE intense, as if the air is clearer, cleaner, and everything is made more vivid by it; brighter.

I was right.

It doesn't look anything like the cross-stitches.

No.

It's more beautiful.

It's MORE.

ACKNOWLEDGEMENTS

As EVER, MY THANKS GO, in no particular order, to my wife, Hannah; my editors, Rebecca McNally and Cindy Loh; the ace agenting team of Caradoc King, Mildred Yuan and Louise Lamont; and Will Hill, author and tireless Second Reader. All these people have improved the book immeasurably with their excellent and astute comments at various stages.

OK, I lied. There is a *bit* of an order. But after Hannah, there is no order of importance.

Honestly.